"You look good enough to eat."

"Thank you, Aidan." Madisyn looked down at her tank top and jeans. Since her kitchen wasn't as large as Aidan's, things might get heated. Or at least a girl could hope. "Ready for your next lesson?"

"You bet. Lead the way."

She did just that. "Today we're going to make a frittata. It's almost like a quiche without the crust."

"Cool."

After they entered the kitchen, Madisyn grabbed all the necessary items: eggs, bell peppers, breakfast sausage, cheese, green onions, and jalapeno peppers. She laughed at Aidan's surprised expression. "It's really easy, you'll see. This can be served for breakfast or brunch."

"Great. Usually, I'm a late sleeper on the weekends."

Madisyn smiled. "And here I thought you were an early riser on all occasions." She opened the cabinet in search of a mixing bowl and cutting board.

Aidan took the items out of her hand and placed them on the counter. "Only when you're in my bed."

2 GOOD

CELYA BOWERS

Genesis Press, Inc.

INDIGO LOVE STORIES

An imprint of Genesis Press, Inc.
Publishing Company

Genesis Press, Inc.
P.O. Box 101
Columbus, MS 39703

Copyright © 2009 by Celya Bowers

ISBN: 13 DIGIT : 978-1-58571-350-9
ISBN: 10 DIGIT : 1-58571-350-3
Manufactured in the United States of America

First Edition

Visit us at www.genesis-press.com
or call at 1-888-Indigo-1-4-0

DEDICATION

This book is dedicated to my mother, Celia Mae Bowers Shaw Kenney, and a very dear person I recently lost, Falice (Fay) Lee.

ACKNOWLEDGMENTS

2 Good would not have been possible if not for the incredible support of the following people:

My family: Darwyn Tilley, Jeri Murphy, William Kenney, Sheila Kenney, Kim Kenney, Shannon Murphy, Yolanda Tilley, Celya Tilley, and Rod Kenney.

I would like to thank my friends: Erica Black, Cherry Elder, Sharon Hickman-Mahones, Donna Lefear, Beverly Cofer, Lewis Stewart, Roslin Williams, Deandra Garrett, Darlene Ramzy, and Lisa-Lin Burke.

The special people in my life: Kennedy Tilley, Eddie Lee. Thank you for making this world a much nicer place.

To my fans, both new and old, thank you for giving me the chance to be a part of you. Keep those emails coming!

My military friends and fans: Bless you for defending our country.

My critique group: Diane Kelly, Angela Cavener, and Michella Chappell. Thanks for all the meetings at Starbucks, now I'm hooked on coffee!

The members of Celya's Corner: Louise Brown, Gail Surles, Paula Washington, Pamela Washington, Clara Washington, Mattie Washington, Kenneth Portley, Melody Alvarado, Ingrid Johnson, Alice Pollock, Nalen Busto, Shirley Washington, Tammy Hill, Kerry Elder, Winston Williams, Dawn Moore, Mary Tompkins, Ruthie Scroggins, Jessie Kenney, Sherry Kenney, Judy Brown, Shaunette Smith and Eulanda Bailey.

If I omitted anyone, blame my head, not my heart.

Peace,

Celya Bowers
www.celyabowers.net
celya.bowers@sbcglobal.net

CHAPTER 1

It was Monday morning and she was through being the fool.

Madisyn O'Riley had had it. Her now ex-boyfriend loved to push her to the limit, but this time it had backfired. Catching him in a compromising position wasn't anything new for Madisyn, but last weekend she had been strong and chucked his no-good behind to the curb permanently.

He was surprised, to say the least, but it made Madisyn feel as if she'd conquered Mt. Everest. Nothing could take away her feeling of jubilation, not even the thought of having to deal with a new boss.

She had been an administrative assistant at Brandt, Anderson and Mallory Advertising for over five years, but today felt like her first day. She loved her job and would miss her former boss, but time marched on and so did she. As she prepared for work that morning, she looked at her reflection in the mirror. Her honey-brown skin was clear. Her bright green eyes stared back at her. People always asked her if she wore colored contacts. She didn't. She had inherited her green eyes, honey-brown complexion and her figure from her mother. Her plump mother, Madisyn was what most people referred to as thick. But she didn't mind. She was happy with her body for the most part.

She checked out her starched white blouse, closely inspecting it for any flaws. Not seeing any, she walked back into her bedroom and picked up her jacket, then headed for her garage.

The heat greeted her as she raised her garage door by way of the remote. Why did North Texas have to be so hot during the summer? Since she lived in Dallas and it was the middle of June, she knew the day was going to be a scorcher.

Madisyn arrived at work early that morning in order to get a jump on preparing things for her new boss, who was due to arrive in a week. She needed to order his nameplate and business cards and issue a service order for the IT department to change the computer to his specifications. She was busy working her magic when her friend and co-worker, Keisha Allen, approached her desk.

Keisha was dressed in a too-short dress that hugged her slender frame. She had a knack for wearing just about anything and making it look drop-dead sexy. She'd always told Madisyn how proud she was of her body, that she wasn't ashamed to show it. Keisha sported the latest complicated and trendy hairstyle, complete with required quota of hair weave, and her makeup was always perfect, making her pecan-brown skin almost glow.

"I like that dress, girl," Madisyn said politely. Privately, she thought Keisha looked like a call girl, albeit a high-dollar one. Madisyn had been raised to say something nice no matter the circumstance, but Keisha continually pushed that envelope.

"Thanks. But not now. Your new boss is on his way up. He is hot, girl. H-O-T!" Keisha said.

"Yeah, yeah, fine words from a woman whose thermostat is stuck on purgatory anyway. Any man not wearing a wedding band would be hot to you." And even if he were wearing one, Madisyn mused.

"Don't hate because I date. You're just jealous. I told you Darnell wasn't good enough to spit on. You're pretty, Madisyn, and it's time for the world to see the real you. Some men like a healthy woman."

Typical Keisha. Just because Madisyn didn't weigh a hundred pounds and wear a size two, Keisha thought the end of world was upon her. "You know, you might be right," Madisyn lied. "But I don't want to change for a man. I want him to change for me." Not that she thought she needed much changing. She was comfortable with her size fourteen frame.

"Hey, why don't we start that new change tonight? My cousin Aisha is giving a party."

"You mean the one that's dating the Dallas Cowboy?"

"The same," Keisha said, smiling. "You know, since she moved in with him a few months ago, I hardly ever see her anymore. Aisha said something about his friends dropping by to recruit for some of the local charities."

So that was Keisha's motivation. She would be in the midst of professional athletes. Madisyn liked her friend, but Keisha only saw dollar signs when it came to dates. That could never work for Madisyn. The next man she dated would be her soul mate.

"So, Madisyn, are you game? We can have dinner and then go to the party."

"Yes, put me down for it."

Keisha nodded and headed back down the hall. "See you at dinner," she called.

———

Later that day, Madisyn could finally take a breather. Her new boss, who wasn't due to report to work for another week, had showed up earlier that day, ready to work. Nothing was ready for him, of course, making her look like an idiot.

Now she had just enough time to grab some dinner with Keisha at their favorite restaurant before they headed to the party. Murphy's was a little home-style restaurant located just a few blocks from the office. The place was always packed with people from every walk of life, and tonight was no exception. Madisyn entered the restaurant and sought out her friend.

Keisha waved at her from a table in the corner. Returning the gesture, Madisyn headed to her friend. "How did you get here so fast?"

Keisha took a sip of her caramel-apple martini. "I don't have a fine new boss watching my every move. My boss is probably in his girlfriend's office right now, doing the wild thang, and with no idea what time I left."

Madisyn settled into her chair, refusing to get involved in office chatter, and changed the subject. "What are you going to eat?"

Keisha looked over the menu and smacked her lips. "Girl, I can't eat too much before we head to the party. Maybe I'll have a salad or something light. I don't want to look fat or bloated." She cleared her throat. "Not that you don't look nice, Maddie. But you should wear more makeup to dress up your green eyes. Most women would kill for eyes like yours."

Madisyn wasn't upset at Keisha's comment. She'd known Keisha since junior high and she'd always had the same outlook. Size mattered, whether it was physical or financial. To Keisha "the bigger, the better" applied only to bank accounts. Madisyn felt sorry for her friend.

Later at the party, Madisyn realized she was quite out of her safe, straid element. The gathering was being held at Aisha's home, which she shared with her boyfriend, Kerwin Gallagher, running back for the Dallas Cowboys. Madisyn had met him a few times over the last year. He didn't act the way the media portrayed professional football players. While he wasn't a saint, he was nice enough.

Every woman at the party was dressed in a short skirt or dress and stilettos that looked much too painful to walk in. Keisha was in her element with all the football players hovering around her. She was like a kid in a candy store. She hadn't said two words to Madisyn since they hit the party.

Madisyn looked down at her frame hidden in a black suit and sighed. She looked pretty boring compared to the other women. Maybe Keisha was right about the makeover, she thought.

Aisha came over to Madisyn as she held up the wall in a corner of the large house. Aisha was dressed in the requisite short mini dress and four-inch stilettos, which made the slender woman appear to be about six feet tall.

"This is a lovely party, Aisha. I thought Keisha was kidding about the athletes being here. What on earth are these men doing here?"

"They thought it would be a great way to get volunteers for the charities they represent without it turning into a major media event. But it's not going as well as we'd hoped. Most of the women here are looking for a man, not volunteer work at a charity organization. The majority of these guys are already spoken for." Aisha snapped her perfectly manicured fingers. "Hey, you should meet Aidan Coles. He's representing Mature Alliance. It's so new they need volunteers really bad. They're still finalizing a lot of details, but I know he could use your organizational skills."

"What is the Mature Alliance?"

"It's an organization to teach adults to read and help them get their high school diploma."

Madisyn thought it sounded perfect. She'd wanted to volunteer, but had never known how or where to start. "And since I'm always going on about how I want to help in the community, I should volunteer for something, huh?"

Aisha shrugged her thin shoulders. "Well, yeah. Aidan could probably tell you something about it, or at least direct you to the right people in the organization. He's the founder, but I don't know how hands-on he is." She grabbed Madisyn's hand. "Come on, let's go meet him."

Madisyn didn't want to make a scene, so she allowed herself to be led across the living room to the handsome man holding court with at least ten women. He was gorgeous of course, with caramel-brown skin, short black hair, and a thin mustache framing a large natural smile. The man was some kind of sexy. His wide shoulders were her downfall. He towered over Madisyn's five-foot, ten-inch frame by at least five inches.

"Okay, scat, ladies," Aisha said. "We need to talk business with Aidan."

The women grumbled but left the area. Madisyn was impressed with Aisha's skills. "Girl, you are too much. Remind me to take you shopping with me when there's a big sale at the mall."

Aisha laughed. "Just a little crowd control." She pulled Madisyn closer to the smiling man. "Madisyn O'Riley, Aidan Coles. Aidan Coles, Madisyn O'Riley. You guys chat. I have to go police the area." She walked off.

<hr />

Aidan surveyed the woman standing in front of him. She was thick, as his mother would say. She had an easy smile, shoulder-length black hair, big, expressive green eyes and honey-brown skin. "Is that your real name?" He felt as stupid as his question.

"Yes, it is. I know I should be a middle-aged Irish woman with that name," Madisyn said, glancing across the room.

He wondered what had her attention. She definitely wasn't like every other woman in the room, making him the focus of her attention. "Not necessarily. It's just very different. I think I've met Eisha, Tisha, Tameka, you know those names. Madisyn is refreshing and original."

"Well, Aidan is not your everyday name either."

"True. Blame my mother. She had a flair for the dramatic. My full name is Aidan Sidney Coles."

Madisyn laughed. "Ouch. Aisha said you're heading up the literacy program."

"Yes, I am. It hasn't really gotten off the ground yet. We're short on volunteers," he lied. He'd had a lot of volunteers, just not anyone who was actually interested in helping people. "We already have over fifty people signed up to learn to read."

"Amazing," Madisyn said, totally in awe. "I'd be willing to volunteer."

Aidan smiled. "Really? You know there's no pay."

"Duh, hence the volunteering thing," Madisyn said, laughing. "I'm doing this for me, not for money or to get close to an athlete."

"You'd be the first," Aidan said honestly.

"I've been around sports nuts all my life. Why would I want to go out with one?"

He shrugged. "Same as most of the women here. Money. Status."

"Well, Aidan, I hate to be the one to inform you, but I'm not like most of the women here. I'm my own person. I love sports, don't get me wrong. I've followed your career since you graduated from the University of Oklahoma."

"No way," Aidan said.

Madisyn had his attention now. "Yep, you attended Oklahoma University on a full scholarship, then were drafted in the first round by the New England Patriots. Then you went to San Francisco and ultimately to Dallas, about three years ago. You are one of the best wide receivers in the league and are worth the change the Cowboys had to pay for you."

Aidan stood before her, clearly in awe. "I'm impressed you've followed my career so closely."

Madisyn shrugged. "I come from a family of athletes. My dad was a high school football coach before he retired and I have four brothers. My oldest brother, Mike, is also a high school football coach. Liking sports is not an option in our family; you have to love sports. All sports."

He nodded, understanding. She was definitely a breath of fresh air. He was tired of those women who only wanted to be with him because he played professional football. He wanted a woman who wanted to get to know Aidan Coles, the man. Was this the woman? Only one way he would find out. "The first meeting is Friday night at seven at the center. See you there."

CHAPTER 2

Darnell Whitfield walked into the office of his boss, James Harland, and took a seat. Seldom did the president of Harland, Collins, and Roarke Investments call him into his office. He could count the times on one hand in the six years he'd been employed there.

After the receptionist waved him inside the large office, Darnell cleared his throat to announce his presence. Harland motioned him to a chair.

"Close the door." Harland leaned back in his leather chair, watching Darnell as if he'd committed some crime too awful to repeat.

"You wanted to see me, sir?" Darnell asked as he took a seat.

"Yes, Whitfield. As you know, Kenneth Harris is going to retire in a few months, leaving open the position for senior investment banker. We value your hard work and your dedication to the firm."

Darnell smiled at the old man. "Thank you, sir."

"How's that wonderful girlfriend of yours? If I was twenty years younger, I'd give you a run for your money. Madisyn is everything we value here. We don't need anyone who's going to cause a scandal or bring disgrace to our firm. I have to say, you were on shaky ground with us until you met her."

Darnell couldn't reveal that Madisyn had caught him with his pants down again. "Yes, sir. I'm very thankful you gave me a second chance."

Harland laughed. "You should thank Madisyn. I'll make the announcement of your promotion at the annual banquet. That way I can see the look of surprise on Madisyn's face."

Darnell racked his brain for an excuse. "I think she might be out of town that night. Some kind of trip with her mother," he lied.

"Oh. Then we'll wait to make the announcement."

Oh, that was not good. "I'll see if I can get her to postpone it, so she can attend the banquet."

"Do that. I'd hate for you to miss out on such a great opportunity because you couldn't convince her how important this is to you."

Darnell saw the writing on the wall. If Madisyn wasn't at the banquet and by his side, he wouldn't have the promotion. Darnell smiled as he left his boss's office. A plan was already forming in his head. Madisyn would take him back; she always did. A few well-placed words, a little attention, and he'd have her back in his arms. Easy as pie.

∞

Two days later, Madisyn sat at her desk making sure everything for her new boss was in place. She hadn't been prepared for his arrival and it had showed. He'd already made her feel the fool once by showing up a week early. This time she was going to be ready.

What she wasn't ready for was the sight of her ex-boyfriend, Darnell, walking toward her desk with red roses in one hand and a box of candy in the other, his usual "Baby, I'm sorry" gift. He was dressed as impeccably as always. His tall, lean body was made for the dark suit.

"Hey, babe." Darnell smiled, handing her the gifts. "A little peace offering. You know that girl meant nothing to me. Now am I forgiven or what?"

Madisyn had heard this same trite apology many times over the last twenty-four months, and could recite it verbatim. Probably the old Madisyn would have told him everything was fine and pretended that it was. This time she was ahead of the game. It had taken her two years, but she was finally wising up. "You know, Darnell, it really doesn't matter."

He sat on the edge of her desk, carelessly pushing the stack of mail to the floor and making no attempt to pick it up. "Thanks, babe. You know what's good for you. I knew you'd understand, just like you always do. There's just something about beautiful women I can't resist."

As if that was a proper apology for finding him in bed with another woman. She wanted to wipe that overconfident look off his face. "You don't understand, Darnell." She placed the gifts on the desk. "I've been your fool for the last time. So take your flowers and candy and leave."

He stood abruptly, anger clouding his pecan-brown skin and marring his handsome face. "You're going to be real sorry, Madisyn. No man wants a big woman like you."

"I believe the lady asked you to leave in a nice polite manner," her new boss, Damon Bridges, said. "Would you like me to call security?"

Darnell turned and faced Madisyn's new and very uptight boss. He had at least three inches on Darnell.

"I believe I asked you a question."

"You're going to be real sorry, Maddie. Real sorry. You know what happens when things don't go my way." Darnell turned his cold eyes on her, then snatched the flowers and candy off the desk and stomped to the elevator.

Mr. Bridges looked at Madisyn. "Are you okay?"

Madisyn tried not to let her emotions take over. "Yes, I'm fine. Just some trash I put out. Thank you."

Damon sat in a chair and looked at her. "It's a good thing I decided to come in early today. I'm sorry he put you through that, Madisyn. If he bothers you again, please let me know. I'll toss him out personally. It'll be my pleasure." He rose, walked into his office and closed the door.

Madisyn sighed. She was making quite the impression on her new boss. Her life had to get better.

⊷

Friday evening, Madisyn stepped into the Mature Alliance building in downtown Dallas. She was suitably impressed, to say the least. She had expected the interior of the place to reflect the exterior of the dilapidated building, but as her mother used to say, 'Never judge a book by its cover.'

The inside had been completely redone to reflect the hope of the new organization. Several classrooms were on either side of the hallway. The rooms were furnished with new desks, chairs, and computers. The only thing missing was students. Madisyn couldn't wait to get started. She, too, was feeling hopeful.

She walked further down the hallway to the volunteers' meeting area and found none of the other volunteers had arrived yet. Being raised in a sports-inclined household, and knowing everything about sports, she recognized several of the area professional athletes standing around chatting. Where were the women from the party who were so eager to sign up?

"I'm glad you could make it," Aidan said, falling into step beside her. "Most of the other ladies who expressed an interest cancelled out."

"That's too bad. They're missing the chance of a lifetime. I have another friend who's also interested, but she had class tonight," Madisyn said, hoping to soften the blow of the other women bowing out.

Aidan smiled. "Good. We can never have too many volunteers. As it is, I had to enlist the help of some of my friends to get started." He nodded to the opposite side of the room.

Madisyn snorted. "Friends? You have members of the Dallas hockey, football and basketball teams. I'm shocked there aren't any Texas Rangers here tonight."

"I don't know any of those guys. Besides, it's the middle of summer and it's baseball season. I wouldn't dare ask those guys in mid-season."

Madisyn understood. "Makes perfect sense."

Aidan laughed. "Come on, I'll introduce you to the guys," he said casually. He put his arm around her shoulder and led her to the group of men.

Madisyn nodded. Was this man really going to introduce her to several of the top area professional athletes? Keisha would have a fit when she found out what an opportunity she'd missed. Madisyn looked at her clothing and shook her head in disgust. She should have worn something more exciting than the business suit she'd worn to work. Drab gray, her father called it. Drab gray with a plain white shirt. Boring.

As they approached the men, Aidan leaned down and whispered in her ear, "Don't worry, they don't bite."

Madisyn looked sideways at him. "Promise? I haven't had my rabies vaccination, so they'd better not."

"You got jokes." Aidan stopped in front of the guys and introduced her. "Gentleman, may I present Madisyn O'Riley, one of our volunteers. Madisyn, meet Jonathan Sizemore, Brent Taggot and Marcus Jackson of the Dallas Stars."

Madisyn shook the large hand of each man. He continued the introductions, "Bruno Taylor, Kenyon Frazier and Brad Green, also my fellow teammates."

Madisyn nodded. Like she needed to be told these men were some of the highest paid players in the National Football League. "Hello," she said dumbly.

He led her to the last group of men. "These are my friends from the Dallas Mavericks, Demonte Phillips, Dylan Hertz, and Matthew Hurley. All these men are at your disposal, Madisyn. If you need any assistance they will be happy to help you."

"I don't understand," Madisyn said.

The men smiled at her, then looked at Aidan. "Well, Madisyn, since you're the only volunteer to show up tonight, you're the volunteer liaison with the athletes."

Either she'd taken some stupid medicine without her knowledge or Aidan had forgotten to tell her something. "Aidan, what on earth are you talking about?"

"You get to coordinate the schedules between athletes and the clients. I'll give you all the necessary information and phone numbers. These guys aren't just volunteers. We're all investors in Alliance. Initially, we hadn't planned on participating, but you're our only volunteer. We all want this program to succeed and are willing to do whatever it takes."

Slowly the pieces were coming together. "And since I'm the only volunteer to show up, I get the joy of being program director on this side of things, right?"

"Yes. With us being so high profile, we can't sneeze without it being on the nightly news. So if we want to offer privacy and confidentiality at the center, we need someone who's not going to cause a media frenzy when we're trying to plan something or come to volunteer."

She knew enough about Aidan to know he was very focused on the program, and apparently so were the other players. "And I wouldn't cause a frenzy if I plan something for the Alliance."

"I hope I didn't offend you."

Madisyn laughed. "Oh, heck no. I'm used to being good old dependable Madisyn."

Aidan looked her up and down. "I would say good and dependable, but not old. Do you still want to volunteer?"

"Of course. You think a little extra duty is going to stop me from doing this? Please! You should see what I do at work."

He patted her shoulder. "Aisha said you'd give one hundred and fifty percent. She also said being around a lot professional athletes wouldn't turn your head. And she was right on both counts. Most women would have been trying to size up who was available and who wasn't."

"Yeah, who wants to be around all those muscular guys anyway?" Madisyn said sarcastically. She hoped lightning didn't strike her down for that remark.

The other men laughed at her statement. "Why don't we get started?" Aidan asked, gathering up a pad and pen. He motioned for her to take a seat in one of the plush chairs. "We want to be able to open in about six weeks. I know we're going to have to get some books and other supplies. I'm afraid that's going to be your department. My attorney set up a corporate account at the local bookstore and an office supply to get you started. Just give your name, and if there's any problem give me a call." He handed her a business card. "That's my home and cell number. The bookstore and office supply store are listed on the back."

Madisyn took the card with hesitation. It was like being handed the key to Fort Knox. She'd have to find a secret place to keep it. Keisha was forever rummaging through her purse for something or other. Apparently Aidan had the same thought.

"I don't have to tell you how important it is for our personal information not to get out. We want people at the center to feel their privacy won't be compromised. We can't do that if our own information gets out. We have to maintain close security not only for them, but ourselves as well."

"I quite understand. I'll keep the information locked up and safe," she promised. "Now what about scheduling?"

"That's where your dynamite administrative skills will come in." He handed her several pages of computer printouts. "These are copies of the registration forms, the times the clients are available, when we're available, etc."

She looked at the mound of papers. Talk about a huge undertaking . . . And this wasn't even her day job. "Let me see if I understand this correctly," she started. "I'm to buy the books, get the supplies, and make a schedule everyone will love in less than six weeks?" She couldn't keep the incredulity out of her voice.

Aidan grinned at her. "Pretty much."

She loved a challenge, and she couldn't ask for a bigger one than this. "Sign me up."

"Great. Let's celebrate with a little dinner. What do you say?" Aidan asked.

Madisyn couldn't believe it. She knew it wasn't a real date, but it could be a little practice for the next man. And what reasonably sane woman would turn Aidan Coles down?

Dinner was at Houston's, an upscale restaurant known for its international gourmet cuisine and located in north Dallas. After much debate, Madisyn followed Aidan's Cadillac Escalade. She parked her Chevy Trailblazer next to his, said a quick prayer and got out. Aidan was at her side before she could close her door. After she armed the SUV's security system, he grabbed her hand and led her inside.

As soon as they entered hand in hand, Madisyn and Aidan were whisked away to a cozy alcove not visible to the public. The secluded room came staffed with a personal waiter. Madisyn was speechless at the high level of service in one of her favorite restaurants.

"Madisyn, are you all right?" Aidan asked. "Would you like to go somewhere else?"

She shook her head, nervously picking up the menu the waiter had placed on the table. "That's not it. I've never seen this side of the restaurant. I usually come here once a month with my sister-in-law. We've never had our own personal waiter."

He nodded. "I think that's why I love this place so much. I can eat here and no one bothers me. It makes me feel normal."

Madisyn, like most ordinary people, had never thought of the downside of being a celebrity. "Normal is something I take for granted. I wouldn't have guessed something as simple as a gourmet meal eaten in peace could be the highlight of your day."

"Very much so, but tonight it's also the company. They have great food here. I usually eat here a couple times a week in the off season. I'd love to fix their kinds of meals at home, but I don't cook much. At all would be a better description. I was thinking about taking a gourmet chef class."

Madisyn knew why he didn't. He'd cause too much commotion and no one would learn a thing. Being a celebrity wasn't all it was cracked up to be. "How about I make a deal with you?"

He grinned at her question. "What do you have in mind?"

Madisyn didn't like the grin on his handsome face. His male brain probably thought she was propositioning him. "Not to toot my own horn, but I'm a pretty good gourmet chef. Amateur, you understand. I could teach you the basics."

"What's in it for you?"

He had every right to be suspicious, she realized. In Aidan's high profile world, no one did anything for free. "Nothing," Madisyn said honestly. "You're doing so much for the center, maybe this is my way of saying thank you for having so much faith in me to purchase the books and supplies."

He mulled over her answer, probably dissecting it to death. "And where would we have these so-called lessons?"

Okay, she hadn't thought out her generous gesture that far. "I really hadn't thought about it. My dad has a pretty big kitchen and could accommodate us. He usually plays golf on Saturday mornings with my mom, so we'd have it all to ourselves."

"Why can't we do it at my place? That way I'd be assured of privacy," Aidan said casually.

"But I don't know where you live."

Aidan smiled. "You will by my first cooking lesson. How about Saturday morning of next week? What will we cook for my first lesson?"

Another part of the plan she hadn't worked out when she opened her big mouth. "How about we start with something simple like scallops with cilantro sauce and Asian slaw?"

He cleared his throat. "That's simple? Sounds like a full-course meal."

Madisyn laughed. "Okay, how about a quiche?"

He shook his head. "How about some man food? All those eggs . . . girly stuff. How about steak and potatoes? Now that's something I can sink my teeth into."

"That's the second week's lesson."

"Oh, well then, you got a deal."

<hr/>

The next day, Saturday morning, Madisyn met her friends at Girlfrienz Day Spa near downtown Dallas for a day of pampering, gossiping and just having an old-fashioned good time with her best friends.

After dinner with Aidan the previous night, however, a good time with friends might be too much to hope for. Nothing was likely to compare to an evening with Aidan. He was funny, insightful, and just easy to be around. It was the best non-date she'd ever had. She still couldn't believe she'd agreed to give him cooking lessons. At his house, no less. Lord only knew where this man lived.

Shaking off thoughts of the mess she'd gotten herself into, Madisyn entered the spa's waiting room. As usual, she was early and her friends were late. She waved at the receptionist and took a seat in the waiting area. Her cell phone jangled just as she opened the latest issue of *Body and Soul*. She answered the call with a smile. "Hey, Daddy."

"Hey, baby girl," said Ben O'Riley in his boisterous morning voice. "Are you going to come for dinner tonight?"

"Of course. You know you and Mom are my standing date on Saturday nights." Even when things were semi-good with Darnell, she still had gone to dinner with her parents every Saturday night.

He laughed. "You know we like nothing better. But we do want you to find a nice man, settle down, and give us some grandbabies."

Here we go. "Daddy, I'm fine. Right now, you're my nice man." Madisyn was now on her parents' to-do list. They'd made it their job to find her a good man. She decided a subject change was in order. "You'll never guess who I met this week," she teased her father. He loved mysteries.

"Is he son-in-law material?"

"No, better. He's professional football material."

"Okay, I'll bite. Who?"

"Aidan Coles." She tried her best to keep her voice level and very matter of fact.

"You're kidding. I hear he finally got the funding for his pet project." Her father kept up with all the sports news. If a professional athlete sneezed her father knew about it.

"I met him at Mature Alliance. He heads the charity for it. I'm on the committee. He seems very nice," Madisyn said, not mentioning having had dinner with him the night before. Her father would view it as a marriage proposal.

"He's one of the few Dallas Cowboys that doesn't have some kind of mess linked to his name. He's about to retire, isn't he?"

"I don't know. I think he's over thirty. Probably time," Madisyn said, omitting the fact that she'd volunteered to give Aidan cooking lessons.

"You're right about that. How about I take you out to dinner tonight?"

She could see through her father's transparent attempts to set her up. Again. "Okay, Daddy, who is it this time?"

"You know, you sound just like your mother. It's Bob Carson's nephew. He's here on business and is flying back to New Jersey on Sunday. I thought you two might get along."

Her father and his buddies had made it their life's work to find her a good man. Each attempt was worse than the last, but still they tried. "Now, Daddy. If I did happen to hit it off with this guy, I could very well end up marrying him and moving to New Jersey." A little reverse psychology never hurt when dealing with hard-headed parents.

"You know I can't have that, baby girl. You'd be too far away. Your brothers would go nuts. Okay, so I'll tell Bob's nephew to take a hike and it'll be just us."

Madisyn smiled. "Thank you, Daddy. See you at seven."

"You got a date." He ended the call.

Madisyn sighed and folded her phone shut. Another dating disaster averted. She felt like jumping up and shouting praises for being single, but just then her friends sauntered in. "Can't you guys be on time for once?"

Keisha, dressed in some very tight shorts, a skimpy halter top, and high-heeled sandals, waved her remark away. "You know how hard it is to get here. You live just ten minutes away, Maddie. I live on the other side of town and I had to shake my sister Nosha in the process."

Madisyn nodded, used to hearing the saga of Keisha and her siblings. "I keep telling you that you need your own place."

"Then I wouldn't have money for clothes," she reasoned. "Well, the ones that I like, anyway."

Madisyn nodded. "I understand." She really didn't, but she couldn't think of anything constructive to say and left it at that. "I like those shoes."

Keisha smiled and sat beside Madisyn, crossing her slim legs. "I got these at the Galleria last night," she said proudly. "Cost almost a week's salary."

"Is she still talking about those God-awful hooker shoes?" Chayla Hughes asked, sitting on the other side of Madisyn. Chayla was dressed as casually as Madisyn in baggy shorts and loose-fitting blouse. "She called me the

24

second she bought them. She didn't call you, Maddie,' 'cause she knew you were at that charity thing. How did it go?"

"Pretty good. It looks like it's going to be challenging." Keisha joined in the conversation. "Were many football players there?"

Madisyn opened her mouth, but instantly remembered Aidan's warning. "A few, but the married ones. Sorry, Keisha."

Keisha shrugged. "I bet that fine Aidan Coles was there."

Madisyn couldn't deny that, since it was his pet project. "Yes, but he didn't stay very long. Probably about thirty or forty-five minutes." It was just a little lie, she told herself.

Chayla congratulated her. "You're going to love charity work. It always makes me feel so much better giving something back to the community, unlike Ms. Designer over there."

"Hey, just because I can buy top of line, don't hate," Keisha shot back at Chayla.

Chayla let Keisha's remark slide off and merely smiled. "Hey, I'm not hatin' on you. Everybody makes choices."

Keisha nodded. "Hey, you're the one who's been married since you graduated high school."

Chayla nodded. "We were twenty," Chayla corrected her. "I don't regret that choice at all. I've been happily married for fifteen years. My husband is my best friend and I have three wonderful children."

"Oh, Chayla, you're just a romantic. You and Jared fell in love the minute you guys laid eyes on each other in the fifth grade on the monkey bars," Keisha grumbled.

Chayla giggled. "Yeah, he's the only man for me."

Madisyn sighed. "I'd like that. For some man to sweep me off my feet. Mind you, he'd have to be a big man to pick me up."

Chayla playfully slapped Madisyn's hand. "You just stop that, Maddie. You're just right. Everyone wasn't made to be skinny. I'm not skinny, never have been. Besides, you want a man that loves you for what's inside as well as what's outside."

"True," Madisyn said. "You're right. No more playas, saying and doing all the right things, then making me the fool."

"That's my girl." Chayla rose from her chair, straightening her shorts. "Now let's go get pampered."

CHAPTER 3

Saturday afternoon Aidan walked through his home wondering what he'd just gotten himself into. Well, actually he knew what he'd done. For once, he'd followed his instincts and was glad he had. He had been instantly attracted to Madisyn and he'd acted on it.

No more dating the wrong women, women who were just looking for a meal ticket and had a brain the size of a peanut. He wanted a woman who wanted Aidan Coles the man, not the professional football player with the seven-digit income. He wanted a woman he could have a conversation with.

He stood in the center of his newly remodeled over-sized kitchen. He'd been serious about the gourmet cooking class when he had the room redesigned with all the newest gadgets, including dual wall ovens, top-of-the-line cooktop range with an indoor grill. His kitchen could rival that of any celebrity chef's. And at the moment, none of that mattered. He had to get his kitchen ready for cooking lessons, and quickly. He called his sounding board for just about everything in his life.

"Hey, Mom, I got a problem."

"What else is new?" Anna Coles said in her soft voice. "You're not trying to cook again, are you? Or does this have to do with a woman?"

"The latter."

"What's the problem?"

"I kind of told her I would like to learn to cook gourmet food. She volunteered to teach me."

"Well, a woman who can cook. I'm impressed. Usually those girls you date have no idea of what to do in a kitchen but press the start button on the microwave."

He patiently listened to his mother's usual rant about today's women. He'd heard this lecture many times in his adult life. He waited for his opening and took it. "Mom, I don't have any cookware," he admitted. "What should I do?"

She laughed. "The last time I visited you, we ate all our meals out. I told you to buy some pots and pans then. You're going to need some quality cookware, utensils, towels, and lots of groceries."

That meant he had to go shopping in a mall. With people. That was a disaster waiting to happen. "No, Mom. I hate to shop." He took a deep breath. "I was hoping maybe you could fly down for a couple of days and go shopping for me."

"I knew there was a real reason for this call," she said. "What am I supposed to do with your father?"

"He's not my father," Aidan said shortly. "He's the man you left my father for."

"Don't start."

"He's your second husband. He just adopted us."

"You don't know the whole picture and I refuse to wake up those horrible memories today. Whether you realize it or not, Lester saved us. I've been married to him for over twenty years and I had hoped one day you'd come to accept him."

"I do accept him, Mom. He makes you happy and treats you like a queen, but he's not my father." Aidan liked his stepfather, but in his little boy heart, he could never take the place of his father. Not now. Not ever.

"One day, you'll understand."

Today he didn't, so Aidan switched topics. "So can you come for a few days?"

"Let me check with Lester and I'll call you back," she said. "In the meantime, go on that fancy home computer you own to one of those gourmet web sites and take a look at what you're going to need."

"Okay, Mom. I love you."

"You'd better. Bye, baby."

Aidan placed the cordless phone on the counter and did just as his mother had suggested. He surfed the Internet to find out where to buy quality pots and pans. Never in a million years would he have imagined there would be so many choices. Seemed every chef and short-order cook with a television show had their own line of cookware. It was a little intimidating. He was going to need a miracle to get his sparsely equipped kitchen ready for his first cooking lesson in a week.

The phone rang an hour after he realized how much trouble he was actually in. He hoped it was his mother and he was right. "Hello."

"Hey, baby, it's Mommy."

"Mom, remember I'm thirty-three and I play professional football. I can't call you Mommy."

"One day," she promised, "you're going to break out of all these perfect little boxes you've placed in your life. Everything has to be so-so with you. Even those little stick figures you date have to look a certain way. You need a woman with substance."

"I think I've found her. She loves sports and not just football."

"Does this one eat?"

He thought of Madisyn's hearty appetite. Most women ate very little in his presence, always claiming they weren't hungry or they had had a large lunch. Not Madisyn. The previous evening, she'd torn into that steak as if it were her last supper. "Oh, yeah. She's the one that's going to give me gourmet-cooking lessons. There's just one thing."

"What?"

"I don't know if she thinks of me in those terms. At least not yet."

His mother laughed. "You mean this woman is not impressed with Aidan Coles, star multimillionaire football player?"

"No, she's not. In fact, that's what I like about her. She's excited about volunteering with Mature Alliance and that's what sealed the deal for me. You know how long I've been trying to get that started."

"Yes, I do, and I'm proud that you'll get to see it happen. Lester just booked my flight. I'll be in Dallas on

Monday afternoon. Don't bother picking me up. I'll rent a car and drive to that thing you call a home."

Aidan snickered. He loved his mother with all his heart, but that woman hated change like you wouldn't believe. She'd hated every house he'd lived in. She always complained they were too big. "Mom, it only has four-teen rooms," he patiently explained to his hardheaded mother. "I plan to retire here after this season. I need space for when you and Lester visit."

"And that's why you need five bedrooms, four bath-rooms, a den, a movie theatre room, an office, a game room, and I won't even talk about that kitchen."

"Okay, Mom. You got me. It's big. But I got a really good deal on it three years ago."

"What that place needs is lots of babies running through it."

Aidan rolled his eyes toward the ceiling. *Here we go.* "That's why I have nieces and nephews."

"Ha ha. You're breaking your poor mother's heart."

"Is that the grandmother's violin I hear?"

"I'm not going to dignify that with a reply. You just better be ready to spend some money when I get there."

He was ready for that. "I'll need groceries, too."

"I didn't just meet you, you know. You never have food! We had to go to the store for water. See you Monday."

〜〜〜

That evening, Madisyn peered across the table at her date. He was very distinguished with his short salt and pepper hair. He was dressed casually in a short-sleeved polo shirt and slacks. Unfortunately, he was attracting the attention of most of the women in the Olive Garden Italian restaurant. She had to protect her mother's interest.

"Daddy, what are you doing to all these women?"

Ben O'Riley laughed as he sipped his imported beer from a pilsner. "I don't know what you're talking about, baby girl. Next to your mother, I'm sitting with the prettiest woman in the whole state of Texas. Maybe that's who they're staring at." He took another sip. "That was good."

"How about another one?" Madisyn signaled the waiter for another round of drinks.

"How about you?" Ben looked at his daughter. "You haven't touched your glass of wine. You're wasting my retirement money." Her father had retired five years ago after being a head high school football coach for thirty years.

Madisyn laughed and took a sip. "Okay, I don't want your part of the teacher's retirement fund to go to waste."

He opened his menu, then glanced around the room. His gaze rested on something directly behind Madisyn. "You know, maybe we should go to another place. It's so smoky in here."

Something was up. Dallas had recently passed a no-smoking ordinance in all restaurants, causing quite a stir in the community. Smoke was not the reason her father wanted to leave his favorite restaurant. She glanced around the room and saw her father's sudden need to leave, Darnell. And he had the nerve to be on a date! The slender woman had her back to Madisyn, but Darnell lifted his wine glass to Madisyn in salute, mocking her. "It's okay, Daddy. I know he's not good enough to spit on. I'm over him, really. I ended it, remember?"

Her father's brown eyes searched hers for the truth. "It took you long enough to realize what a waste of space he was. A man should add to your self worth, not take away from it. I can still give him a piece of my mind, if you want."

"That's quite all right, Daddy." The last thing she wanted was to give Darnell any reason to approach her or her father. "I've never been so sure of anything in my life. It feels like a burden has been lifted from my shoulders."

The waiter appeared with the drink order. Madisyn and her father placed their dinner orders and the waiter departed.

Her father stared daggers at Darnell and his date. "I could go to the truck and get my gun."

"Daddy, no," Madisyn pleaded. "He's not worth a bullet and besides, it's against the law."

"I didn't say I'd do it. Bob knows a guy, who knows a guy, and he's kind of on call for that sort of thing."

Madisyn shook her head. "I can't believe you're even entertaining that idea. Darnell showed up at work a few days ago, with candy and flowers, begging forgiveness. My boss tossed him out."

"Good for him."

Madisyn didn't know how good it was for her new boss to kick her ex-lover out on his butt. Darnell didn't take humiliation well. There would be payback, she knew. And she would be the one doing the paying.

"Was it that nice Mr. Broadus? I really like him."

"No, it was my new boss. Josh got a promotion and was replaced by Damon Bridges. You should have seen him, Daddy. I've never seen a man react like that, and so quickly. You'd think Darnell was dating one of his daughters or something."

Her father chuckled, reaching for his beer. "I think it's the 'or something.'"

Madisyn gasped in disbelief. "Daddy!"

"What? I think you're beautiful."

"You have to say that because I'm your spinster daughter," she joked.

Ben shook his head. "No, I don't. You're beautiful. Not every man wants to lie in bed next to a stick."

"Daddy!"

"Why do you keep saying that?" He took a drink of his beer and set the glass down with a thud. "You're the spitting image of your mama, pretty eyes and all. So don't you worry about that piece of trash sitting over there." He nodded at Darnell. "He didn't deserve you anyway."

"Thank you, Daddy. I'm looking for the man who does deserve me." Madisyn lifted her glass to her lips. "I'm sure he's out there somewhere."

"He's probably in the last place you'll look."

By Monday morning, Madisyn was beginning to think her father didn't know beans about finding a man. The last place she'd look. What was that about?

Her new boss strolled into the office with his briefcase in his hand an hour early. It was barely eight and this man was already at work. "Good morning, Mr. Bridges." She pasted a plastic smile on her face.

He nodded as he walked by her desk and entered his office and closed the door, effectively putting up a barrier between them. Madisyn shook off the bad beginning and proceeded with assembling his daily schedule. Thank heavens he had meetings all day. She entered the information into the computer and emailed it to him.

Keisha walked to Madisyn's desk and sat on the edge of it. "Girl, when does that handsome boss of yours come in?"

"About ten minutes ago."

Keisha's perfectly made-up face wrinkled in a sexy pout. "You mean he's already here? No one in management gets here this early. Is he crazy?"

"Keep your voice down or he's going to hear you. Josh used to come in early all the time."

"That's because Josh was different. He was a dedicated and loyal employee. So many bosses just come in and go through the motions, but Josh was totally into his job."

"Well, I hope I can live up to Josh's reputation," Mr. Bridges said as he walked up to Madisyn's desk. "Is this your usual position, sitting on Ms. O'Riley's desk? I'm sure your boss would like to know he or she doesn't have to watch you every minute, Ms. . . . ?"

"Allen," Keisha supplied eagerly, mistaking annoyance for attraction.

He shrugged. "Ms. Allen, in this department we do our work, not visit with our friends hoping for some office gossip. So if you could leave Ms. O'Riley to her work, it would be greatly appreciated." He turned and returned to his office, closing the door again.

Keisha took her admonishing like a good Southern girl. She slid off the desk, straightened her too-short dress and pretended to fix her already perfect hair. "Did he say his first name was asshole? That is, if the master is going to let you off the plantation." She grimaced and walked down the hall to her department.

Madisyn chuckled to herself. Seldom did anyone get a barb in on Keisha, but Mr. Bridges had done it quite effectively. Her intercom buzzed, signaling an end to her joyful moment. Her boss wanted to see her.

She rose, walked to the door and knocked. After she heard him grumble something that sounded like "Come in," she entered. "You wanted to see me, Mr. Bridges?"

He motioned for her to take a seat. After she was comfortable, he began. "Ms. O'Riley, I believe your work hours are eight to five. Normally, I don't arrive at work until nine. In the future, I don't want a repeat of this morning. If your co-workers can't respect your work responsibilities then I suggest you change your acquaintances."

Madisyn tempered her anger until it was a slight simmer. "Yes, Mr. Bridges. It won't happen again." She rose and cleared her throat. "Will that be all?" *You pompous bastard.*

"No, that will not be all," he said. "Sit down. You make me nervous standing up like that. I have some questions about the email you sent me. Do I really have this many meetings?"

She laughed at his tone of disbelief. "Yes, actually that's a pretty light schedule. The board of directors' meeting was cancelled due to two of the members being out on vacation."

He shook his head. "How did Josh do all this and his job, too?"

Madisyn couldn't keep the pride out of her voice. "He was one in a million. I'm sure once you get your footing you'll do just fine."

He looked at the printout. "I wish I was as sure as you are." Brown eyes searched Madisyn's face. "Ms. O'Riley, I'm not the asshole you and your friend think I am. This is a place of business and I'm in a new position. With only a handful of African-Americans in executive management positions, we can't afford to be caught in a questionable situation. Your friend lounging on your desk like that looks bad for everyone."

"I appreciate your candor, Mr. Bridges, and as I said before, it will not happen again."

He nodded as if he actually believed her. "Good. And to show you there are no hard feelings, how about lunch today?"

Madisyn was sure it wasn't as innocent as he made it out to be. "It's a nice thought, Mr. Bridges, but you have a lunch meeting with Mr. Simpson, Mr. Brandt, and Mr. Danvers upstairs from eleven to two."

But he would not be outdone. "Well, we'll have to make it another day. I'm sure one of these days I won't have a day full of meetings."

"I appreciate the thought." She rose again. "If that's all, Mr. Bridges, I have some reports to assemble."

"Yes, for now."

She left the office and headed back to her desk. At lunch, she was going to give Keisha a piece of her mind. Her usual visits several times a day were definitely, off limits until Madisyn's new boss calmed down about his job. There was nothing worse than a new boss desperate to make a name for himself and failing.

Madisyn hoped he didn't take her down with him.

CHAPTER 4

Monday afternoon, Aidan opened his front door. The guard on duty had informed him his mother was on her way. He watched the woman who'd given him life as she approached on the circular driveway.

Anna parked the rental car and got out. She straightened her cotton dress and patted her hair. As if she'd let one hair get out of place. She noticed Aidan standing in the doorway. "Don't just stand there, boy. Come give your momma a hug."

Aidan shook his head. He was at least a foot taller than his mother, but even now she could put the fear of God in him at times. But being raised to be a good son, he walked to his mother and gave her a hug. "Hey, Mom. I'm glad you could make it. Ready to go spend some of my money?" He walked to the car. "Pop the trunk and I'll get your bags."

"Ha. I only brought one bag." She reached inside the car, pulled out her favorite carry-on bag and handed it to him.

"Mom, you never bring just one bag," Aidan said. He took the bag and headed inside with his mother behind him. "What gives? You know you always bring enough clothes for at least a week."

Anna laughed. "I thought I'd do a little shopping for me while I was helping you stock your kitchen. You wouldn't begrudge your mother a few outfits for dropping everything and flying down here, would you? Your brothers say I should let you fall on your face." She patted him on the cheek. "You know I couldn't do that to you."

Aidan was thankful his mother never listened to his brothers. Kyle and Scott were always trying to mess up his game. "They're just jealous because they're already married." He closed the front door and placed the bag at the bottom of the stairs. "I'll take your bag up in a little bit. Would you like something to drink or eat, or do you want to lie down and take a nap? It's a long flight from Chicago."

His mother looked at him sideways. "Aidan, I'm only fifty-five, not seventy-five. I do not need a nap. Nor do I need to eat. What I need is to call my husband and let him know I arrived safely. Then we're going to that computer and figure out which store we need to go to first." She pulled out her cell phone, punched the speed dial option and said, "Hi, baby, I just made it."

Aidan decided now would be the perfect time to take his mother's bag upstairs to her room, while she was on the phone with his stepfather. He hated the way they ended their conversations like teenagers in heat.

He placed the bag on the luggage stand in the corner of the room, then glanced around with pride. He'd spent most of the day cleaning the room and it looked better than anything on *Home and Garden TV*.

He walked downstairs just as his mother was ending her call. "Lester sends his love."

Aidan rolled his eyes at the ceiling. "Yeah." He took a seat on the sofa. "Ready to go look at what I found?"

His mother joined him on the sofa. "Actually, I want to talk to you about Lester first."

Aidan drew in a breath. "Not now, Mom. Can't we do this later?"

"No, we're going to do this now. You treat him like he's your pedophile uncle or something. Lester has done nothing to you. In fact he's been in your life most of your thirty-three years. Do you think your father would have been around this much? Let me rephrase that. Has your father been in your life at all?"

"He would if you'd let him," Aidan countered. "I know you left Dad to be with Lester."

Anna nodded. "I didn't want to tell you this, but I think it's time you know the truth."

"What is there to know?" Aidan asked impatiently. "I remember it like it was yesterday."

"No, you don't. You don't know the reason I left your father."

"We left on a Friday morning," Aidan said. "Dad left for work and Lester came over and got us. We never went back home again."

"Do you remember what happened prior to Lester coming to get us?" His mother fumbled with her hands.

"I remember hearing you moving something around in your room," Aidan said, remembering the day his life had changed completely.

"That something moving around in the room was me. Your father beat me before he went to work that morning. That was the last straw. He hit me a lot, Aidan."

"That's not true," Aidan countered. "He would never hurt you."

She grabbed his hand and forced him to look at her. Her eyes filled with tears. "Your father had been beating me since we married. I was taught a woman always stayed with her husband no matter what, so I did. Your brothers were older and could see what I was going through. But you were only eight. Lester rescued us from a horrible life. He saved you. He saved all of us."

Aidan didn't want to believe it. "Why did Dad tell me you were sleeping with Lester behind his back?"

"I'm going to let you figure that out on your own. I know you love your daddy, and you should. But you should also give your stepfather some respect. He sacrificed a lot for us, so I won't have you disrespecting him anymore."

"Mom, I don't disrespect him. I appreciate what he's done for you. And us," he added when his mother gave him the look. "I'll reserve judgment until I know the whole story."

"If you know the whole story you might not like the ending," his mother warned. She reached for a Kleenex and dabbed her tears away. "That was a very painful time for me. No one understood what I was going through. I couldn't go to my parents, my friends, no one. Except Lester."

Aidan let her words sink into his brain. Would his father have treated his mother so terribly then have lied about it? Why would he have lied to him all these years?

"Was I the reason Lester didn't come with you?"

"Yes."

How could one word make him feel like a Class A jerk? "It wasn't my intention to make him feel like he wasn't wanted. He's welcome here anytime, Mom."

"Well, he doesn't feel very welcome here. All I'm asking you to do is treat him better. You'll never understand how hard it was for me to end my marriage, and I'm not going to say I did it for you boys. I did it for me, too. I had hoped you'd come to accept it." She stood and walked to the stairs. "You know, I think I will take that nap. We can shop tomorrow."

"Okay, Mom." Aidan stood and watched his mother walk up the stairs. Once he heard her bedroom door close, he went to the couch. He had to somehow make things right between the two of them. He needed someone with a level head to help him out of this mess. Only one woman sprang to mind. Madisyn.

He reached for his cell phone and speed dialed her number. It was early evening; hopefully she was at home and alone. He listened as the phone rang and rang. Most likely she was out. Just as he was about to hit the end button, he heard her soft voice.

"Hello?"

"Hi, Madisyn. It's Aidan. You got a minute?"

"Sure. Is anything wrong? I haven't had time to pick up the books or the supplies yet. I probably can't pick them up until the weekend," she said on a rush.

43

"Whoa, Madisyn. Calm down. I called to talk, if you don't mind and aren't busy. I didn't call to talk about the program. I need some advice. Some female advice."

"Of course. I'm good at that. Advice, I mean. I have four brothers and they've all come to me at one time or another for help with a female. So, what did you do?"

"Well, the female in question is my mom. I upset her by talking about my dad. So what can I do?"

"Since I don't have the whole story, I really can't say, Aidan. I take it your parents aren't together?"

"No, they divorced when I was eight. My stepdad is cool and everything, but you know how it is."

"Yes, I'm well aware of how little boys love their father and no matter how happy your stepfather makes your mom, he's still not your dad."

Aidan was speechless. She actually understood what he felt when everyone around told him to get over it.

"Yes, that's true, but I hurt my stepdad's feelings."

"That's a toughie," she said. "Do you like your stepfather?"

"Of course. He helped me pick Oklahoma State from all the rest. He kept me on the straight and narrow path when I was away at school. I actually have a degree in business. When all my teammates were dazzled by drugs, money, and the limelight, he made sure I understood the consequences. He's very supportive, treats my mom like a queen and he adopted my brothers and me when he married Mom. He doesn't have any kids of his own."

"Hmmm," Madisyn murmured. "It sounds like you really like him and he obviously likes you. I don't really see the problem. As my father has repeatedly told me, 'Any man can plant a seed, but a real man will help it grow.'"

Aidan thought about her statement. True, his father hadn't been very communicative with Aidan or his brothers over the years, except when he needed money for his many vices. It had been Aidan and only Aidan fighting to keep the lines of communication open. Was his little boy heart ruling his adult heart? "That's true. But still . . ."

"There's no 'but still,' Aidan. You have to give your stepfather his props, as my nephews say. You're giving all the accolades to the wrong person."

It made so much sense when she said it. His mother had been telling him the same thing for years. Why was he holding onto the past and refusing to see what was right in front of him?

—◆—

Madisyn had begun to worry. Aidan was very quiet on the other end of the phone. She had probably just lost her volunteer status. Could she be fired from her volunteer job? "Look Aidan, if I overstepped my bounds, I apologize."

"No, no, Madisyn. Actually, you just told me the same thing Mom has been telling me for years. Looks like I have some crow to eat."

It sounded as if he had a truckload of crow to eat. "It's never easy to say 'I'm sorry,' especially when you don't realize you've hurt someone dear, but it'll all work out. You'll see."

He chuckled. "So have you always been this ray of sunshine?"

She thought about it. "Yes, I guess so. I get it from my mom. Being the wife of a coach, you have to always have hope even when there's no hope at all. She could find something good in just about any situation. And since I'm the only girl out of five children, I had to adopt that philosophy real quick."

He laughed harder. "I bet you could hold your own against your brothers. Are they older or younger than you?"

"Both. Michael, Marcus and Myles are older, and Monte is the youngest. He's still at home."

"I guess your folks had a thing for the letter M?"

"Yeah. My mom's name is Margaret."

Aidan mumbled something under his breath. Was he speaking to someone? Was it a female? Why was she so concerned if it was? She shook those thoughts away. She was getting in way over her head.

"So what are you going to do?" Madisyn asked, hoping for a safer topic instead of asking him if he was alone.

He sighed. "I don't really know. Probably talk to Lester, that's my stepdad, and hope it's not too late for us to mend our fences."

"I'm sure it's not too late. Parents are forgiving. I bet your stepdad loves you to pieces."

"Why do women always say that?"

Madisyn giggled. Talking to Aidan was like talking to one of her girlfriends. Talking to Aidan was like talking to one of her girlfriends. No pressure. Just talk. "I guess we're natural nurturers."

"Well, I'm glad you are. Goodnight, Madisyn. Talk to you soon." He ended the call.

Madisyn placed her phone on the counter and resumed her reading. She'd hoped for a peaceful evening, but had gotten something more. She'd gotten a new friend.

<hr />

The next morning Aidan woke up in his king-sized bed with a plan. First thing he had to do was to clear the air with his mother, then talk to Lester.

He decided to take his mom out for breakfast of her favorites. After he dressed, he headed downstairs to the kitchen to call the restaurant to reserve a table. But he was surprised. His mother was fixing breakfast. "Hey, I was going to take you out for breakfast. Where did you get food?" He greeted his mother with a kiss on the cheek.

"I remembered that store on the corner, so I bought a few things this morning. You know I don't play that fast food breakfast stuff. Thank goodness you have a griddle."

He knew he didn't have a coffee pot, since he wasn't a coffee drinker, but his mother enjoyed a fine cup of java with her breakfast. "Sorry, Mom, no coffee pot." He sat down at the table.

She sat a plate of food in front of him. "I know that, honey. I didn't just meet you. Put that on your list of things to buy today. I got a large cup of coffee at the store."

"Mom, you know I hate shopping," Aidan complained as he ate a forkful of eggs.

"Yes, but you know I won't always be here to do this for you. So this is going to be your lesson in shopping." She sat down across from him.

Aidan shrugged, knowing better than to contradict his mama when she was in this mood. Besides, after being enlightened by his conversation with Madisyn the night before, he owed his mother more than shopping.

"You're right, Mom. I have to start sometime."

Mother and son finished their breakfast in silence. Aidan formulated his thoughts, then broached the subject. "Mom, I've been thinking about what you said yesterday. You know, about Lester."

"What is it?"

"I was wrong and I know I can't make it up to you guys in a day, but I want you to know that I realize how much I have been hurting the people who have helped me the most."

"Oh, baby. I'm so proud. You took the first step. The rest will be easy."

He laughed. His mother and Madisyn must be two of a kind. "I hadn't realized you were such an optimist."

"Comes with being a parent."

∽∽∽∽

Two hours later Aidan and his mother shopped at the popular Kitchen Store located near North Park Mall. The

Kitchen Store was stocked with everything a gourmet chef could possibly want. Aidan was definitely out of his element.

His mother picked up a large blue pot and shoved it at him. "See, baby, this is what you need. Big enough to make stew, spaghetti, or pasta, and your lady friend can knock you out with it if you get out of line." She laughed as she added it to their cart.

Initially the idea of accompanying his mother to the store had been scary, but as usual she was right. No one in the store recognized him. It was kind of humbling and gave him a taste of what was to come when he retired and was no longer in the spotlight. He watched his mother add pots and pans to the basket. "Mom, do I really need this many pots?"

"Yes, you do. You can't cook everything in one pot. You need pans, real silverware, not the plastic stuff we used this morning. You just let me do my thing," she said, moving to another aisle of the large store.

Aidan knew when he was beat; he stood back and let his mother do what she did best. "I forgot I was with the master shopper."

She made a face at him. "Don't you forget it." She added more items to the basket. "We're going to need another cart," she said. "This one is almost full."

With a sigh, Aidan went to retrieve another cart. He hoped Madisyn was worth all this trouble.

CHAPTER 5

"I don't know what you get out of volunteering," Keisha said as she joined Madisyn on the elevator. They were returning to work after lunch on Monday. "I mean, that's time you could be shopping, or clubbing."

"I like helping people," Madisyn said. "You know my dad and his buddies have volunteered to be teachers. Sometimes it's just nice to help someone in need."

Keisha grunted. "That won't work for me. There're too many men out there that I haven't met yet for me to volunteer my free time."

Madisyn shrugged and pushed the button for their floor. "Well, I like it. Even though I haven't really done anything at the Alliance yet, I know it will be rewarding. I have to go look for books this weekend. Want to go?"

"Girl, please," Keisha said. "I'm getting my hair, nails and feet done. That's how I'm spending my Saturday. Then I'm going to the club. You should come out with us one time. I heard there's a new club opening in a few weeks and some of the Cowboys own it. So you know there will be a lot of available men there."

Madisyn shook her head. "Clubbing is a little out of my comfort zone, Keisha. I could never wear those slinky dresses like you do." The elevator announced their arrival on the floor.

"You should try at least once, Madisyn. It'll be fun. We could make it like a girls' night and get Chayla to come if Jared will let her out. You'd think they were joined at the hip. I'm surprised he lets her go to spa day without him," Keisha laughed as she stepped out of the elevator. "Oh, my gosh!" She stopped cold.

Madisyn slammed into her skinny friend, knocking Keisha further out of the elevator. "Sorry, Keisha. What are you going on about?"

"That." She pointed to the large floral display on Madisyn's desk.

Madisyn gasped. The massive arrangement was breathtaking. Yellow roses, baby's breath, and greenery filled the glass vase. Darnell is going to a lot of trouble trying to get me back, she mused. Usually he sent a dozen red roses every time he was in the doghouse.

Keisha rushed to Madisyn's desk and plucked the card from the bouquet. If the size of Keisha's eyes was any indication of what was on the card, Madisyn didn't want to know what Darnell had written on it. "It's not from Darnell," she accused. She thrust the card at Madisyn. "It's from Aidan Coles. Just what kind of service are you rendering him?"

Madisyn read the card. Surely, Aidan hadn't sent her flowers at work. How did he know where she worked? "It was nothing, Keisha. I just had a conversation with the man, not sex."

"You're telling me this man sent you," she paused to take inventory of the bouquet, "three dozen yellow roses just for a conversation."

"Yellow means friendship, not a hot time in bed. Friends. Get it, Keisha? You can be friends with a man without having sex with him."

Keisha shrugged. "But where's the fun in that?"

Madisyn picked up the vase, not expecting it to be so heavy. "What's this thing made of?" She asked no one in particular. "It feels heavy. This must be some really thick glass."

"That's not plain glass, Ms. O'Riley," Mr. Bridges announced as he walked toward his office. "They arrived right after you left for lunch. The vase is Waterford crystal."

She quickly set the vase back on the desk, knowing exactly how much the famous Irish crystal cost. What was Aidan thinking? The vase had cost more than the flowers.

"Sounds like he's taking that friend thing seriously," Keisha said sarcastically. "Next thing I know, you're going to be hanging at the club, acting just like me." She walked down the hall before Madisyn could respond.

"Who are the flowers from?" her boss asked. "It's not that man I threw out of the office the other day?"

Madisyn shook her head. "No, it was . . . Aidan Coles," Madisyn said. "I volunteer at his charity, Mature Alliance."

He nodded his head. "I wasn't aware you were dating a professional football player."

"I'm not dating him." Madisyn knew men like Aidan had his pick of women and they didn't include a chunky 35-year-old woman. Their taste ran more to the likes of Keisha. "I'm like an employee to him."

Her boss studied the flowers carefully. "I've never bought any employee flowers, and especially not roses."

He walked down the hall.

Madisyn was getting a little sick and tired of everyone walking away before she could answer them. She looked in her purse for Aidan's home number and dialed. After listening to the phone ring at least five times she hung up, promising herself to call him later. She put the information back in her purse and started opening her boss's afternoon mail.

"I can't believe you let me spend over three thousand bucks for kitchen junk," Aidan complained as he packed the Escalade. "And then you tell me that we're not done." He finished loading the SUV.

His mother just looked at him as if he'd grown another head. "No, we're not done. Those were high-quality pots, pans, mixers and other appliances every home needs. They'll last you a lifetime. Now we're heading for the mall." She opened the passenger door and slid into the seat.

Aidan sighed. This was why he hated shopping. His mother was the shopping champion. He hoped he would still have some money left over when they finished this marathon. He opened the driver's side door and slid behind the wheel. "Okay, North Park Mall, here we come."

Anna laughed. "You are your father's son. He hated spending money, too. How do you expect to get a woman if you're holding onto every penny you ever made?"

"I don't mind spending money. It's the shopping I hate. I do most of my shopping online." He didn't mention the amount of money he'd spent on Madisyn's flowers. He would have loved to see her face when they arrived at her office. He also hoped he hadn't spooked her by sending them to her job, since she'd never told him where she actually worked.

"So how much did those flowers cost?"

He looked sideways at his mother, not believing for one second that she knew. "I don't know what you're talking about."

"Then you shouldn't talk so loud on the phone. She's going to think you're stalking her."

"I thought women like romance."

"Romance, yes, stalking, no. I know you have contacts all over the place, but baby, let her tell you where she works, where she lives and what she likes. Half the fun is getting to know each other and you can't do that through other people doing the legwork for you."

He knew he'd acted too fast and probably spent way too much on the flowers. "I don't want to scare her off, but I want to stake my claim."

"Aidan, she's not a piece of gold. Just ask her out."

His mother made it sound so simple. Normally, he never had trouble asking someone out on a date, but this seemed different. He had to do it in such a way that Madisyn wouldn't feel threatened or think of it as a pity date. "Any suggestions?"

"Yes, since she's going to teach you to cook. You could offer to teach her something," his mother said. "Find out what she likes."

"I could ask her friends," Aidan said.

"Wrong."

"Wrong?"

"Wrong. Never ask her friends unless you know her closest friend. Just because she says someone is her friend, doesn't mean she's a good friend. There're a lot of scheming women out there."

He knew that already. He didn't think Madisyn was one of them, but you never knew. A man had to be prepared for the unexpected. "All right, Mom, I'll find out on my own. Who knows, it might be fun."

That evening, Madisyn walked inside her house and let out a sigh of relief. The flowers had caused more problems than she would have ever imagined. Her mouth was tired from explaining why Aidan Coles, wide receiver for the Dallas Cowboys, was sending her flowers. She placed the arrangement on the coffee table.

She instantly thought of calling Aidan. She fished his number out of her purse again and dialed. To her surprise, a woman answered the phone. Madisyn was just about to mumble an apology for dialing the wrong number, when the woman stopped her. "Is this Madisyn? Aidan is taking a nap, but I'll wake him."

Again, Madisyn didn't have time to ask her not to wake him, she was already gone. One day, she was going to have time to say her piece. Before she knew it, a sleepy Aidan was speaking into the phone. "Hey, Madisyn."

"I'm sorry to wake you," Madisyn said. "You're not sick, are you?"

He laughed. "No, my mom just wore me out shopping today. I think we must have gone to almost every store in the mall and she still wasn't satisfied. We ended up going to Grapevine Outlet Mall, too. I'm wiped out."

"I just wanted to thank you for the roses. They were beautiful and caused quite a stir."

"I'm sorry. I just didn't want to wait until this evening to give them to you. I really appreciate your help with my mom."

"It's okay. I'll let you get back to your nap," Madisyn said slowly.

"Hey, slow your roll, Madisyn. I wanted to talk to you."

"Oh?" That didn't sound good. He probably just wanted to make sure she understood her place on the food chain. She wasn't quite ready to hear the "just friends" speech so she switched gears. "Is it about the center? I thought we could discuss it over your cooking lesson."

"No, Madisyn, I want to talk to you about you."

"What about me?" Madisyn's heart started to race with anticipation. What could he want to know? Maybe he needed to run a background check on her before she started buying stuff for the Alliance.

"What are your plans after our cooking lesson?" Madisyn was floored. "Depending on what time we finish, I was thinking about going to the bookstore afterwards."

He cleared his throat. "How about catching a movie with me? There's a theatre near my house."

Should she bring it up or not? "And where exactly is that?"

"Oh, yeah, you don't know where I live." He named the subdivision and Madisyn recognized it immediately. It was an upscale part of Dallas, heavy on the *up* part.

"Wow, I bet living there is awesome. I hear they have their own theatre, a gourmet grocery store, and mini-mart."

"I got a good deal on the house. I think I'm the only single man in the neighborhood. It's gated, so I'll give you the access code. And I'll leave your name at the gate with Harry, just in case."

"Harry?"

"He works the gate on the weekends. So what's your answer?"

Madisyn hesitated. She didn't want to sound like a wimp who was too afraid to be left alone with a sexy foot-ball player, so she answered in the affirmative. "I can't wait."

"Good, I'll see you about ten."

"Ten?" Madisyn was hoping she would still get to hang out with the girls before giving Aidan his first cooking lesson. She really needed that bonding time with them before facing him.

"Yeah, the movie starts at two. I figure that will give us plenty of time for the lesson." He paused. "Is there something you aren't telling me?"

"Such as?"

Aidan cleared his throat. "Such as the reason that ten is too early is because your boyfriend or husband likes to have his breakfast at that time."

Was he really concerned that she might have a man in her bed? He probably just wanted to protect himself from jealous husbands and boyfriends, she reasoned. "No, none of the above. Just got rid of one."

"Husband?"

"Boyfriend," Madisyn clarified. "I guess I shouldn't say boyfriend, maybe acquaintance, because I didn't know him as well as I thought I did. And since I caught him cheating on me, he's an ex."

There was no mistaking the sound of relief in Aidan's deep voice. "Good! I'm not seeing anyone right now either. Too much going on in my life to include a female."

Madisyn wondered what man didn't have time for a little *amor*? It seemed men always had time for love or sex, no matter how tight their work schedule was. "Oh, come on, I know you have time for a woman."

"No, at this point I'm just trying to get the Mature Alliance up and running without problems. The rest will take care of itself."

Madisyn nodded. "Very true. Could you tell my dad your theory? It would really help me out."

"Don't tell me he's fixing you up on dates," Aidan chuckled.

"Yes. It would be okay if these guys were my type, but they're usually not even close to what I like," Madisyn complained.

"So what kind of men do you like?"

Madisyn thought carefully about her answer. "I want someone who isn't a player. I'm not into games and I want someone sincere, with a kind heart, and who's sensitive to what I want out of life. I want a man who knows God, likes kids, but doesn't have his own Brady Brunch and he must have a job and his own place. That goes without saying."

"Sounds like a tall order. They still make guys like that?"

Madisyn laughed. "I sure hope so."

CHAPTER 6

Madisyn awoke early Saturday morning, ready for the day to get started. First she had to tell the girls she wouldn't be able to make their traditional girly day, something she hadn't done since they started over six years ago. It was more than a day of pampering, it was a day of sisterhood.

Chayla was the most sensible choice to break the news to. Keisha would ask too many questions and somehow get more information out of Madisyn than she was ready to share.

She dialed Chayla's number and listened as the phone rang. Jared, Chayla's childhood sweetheart and husband, answered the phone. "Hello."

Madisyn could hear Chayla and Jared's three boys in the background arguing over the remnants of breakfast and who had to clean up the kitchen. It sounded like total chaos. When she heard the loud voices finally quiet down, she said, "Hi, Jared. It's Maddie. Can I speak to Chayla?"

"Sure thing, Maddie. Excuse all the noise from the boys. We're supposed to be going to the Ranger game later," he said in a loud voice, "but I don't know if we're going with the kitchen in such a mess. You know anybody that would like some seats to the Ranger game right behind first base?"

"Dad, not our tickets. We're cleaning, promise. You can't give away our seats."

She heard Jared snicker into the phone. "That's better. Now hurry up." To Madisyn he said, "Just a minute, I think she was on the computer earlier."

"I don't know how you guys do it with three boys," Madisyn said.

"Me either, but somehow we keep it together. JJ is almost thirteen. Makes me feel old sometimes," Jared said.

"Makes me feel even older," Madisyn admitted. "I'm his godmother."

"Here she is," Jared said to Madisyn. "Baby, it's Maddie."

The next voice she heard was Chayla's soft voice whispering to her husband, then coming on the line, "Hey, girl. What's up?"

Of her friends, Chayla was the one Madisyn trusted the most and whose advice she'd seek. "I can't make it to girly day."

"Is everything all right?" Chayla's voice was etched with concern. "Your parents okay? Do you need me to come with you?"

Madisyn laughed. "You know you've always had my back since we were kids. No, nothing like that, girl. Err, I have an appointment I have to keep."

"Okay, Maddie, this is me, Chay. Out with it. I'm not that gold-digging floozy who claims to be your friend. I honestly don't know why we still let Keisha hang around with us. It's just like it was in high school. She was always running behind us, like some little lost puppy. Some things never change."

"You know, I forgot about that. Yeah, that's why I didn't call her. I'm actually giving a cooking lesson today. That's why I can't make it."

"It wouldn't be with that handsome Aidan Coles, would it?"

"How on earth could you know his name?" Madisyn had hoped she could fool her best friend, but knew she didn't.

"I can guess that because Keisha blew up my phone Monday when he sent you those flowers. She was so upset. You'd think he was dating her or something. I told her if she quit looking in a man's wallet, she might get some flowers too."

"He was just saying thank you."

"Maddie, wake up and smell the roses. That man sent you three dozen roses in a very expensive vase. He ain't looking for no friend. He's putting down a claim on you."

Chayla was a hopeless romantic, Madisyn knew. So of course she'd think Aidan was interested in her, which was highly unlikely. "Chayla, I know you'd like to think all men are as romantic as Jared, but they're not. They're playas like Darnell, trying to have their cake and eat it too."

"Okay, Maddie, I'll drop it for now. What are you teaching him? Or the better question is, where are you teaching him these lessons?"

"Gourmet cooking lessons at his house."

Chayla shrieked. "Are you kidding me? Do you know how many women have tried to find out where he lives? That's like the best-kept secret in Dallas. Even my sister who works in sports doesn't know where he lives. He really values his privacy."

"Yes, he does. Do you want to know what dish we're going to start with today?"

Chayla chuckled. "I think I'd much rather know what he's going to teach you."

"That makes two of us," Madisyn said. "Talk to you later."

"You know I'm going to need a full report." Madisyn shook her head. "Some things never change."

~~~

Aidan was nervous.

He was actually nervous about a woman coming to his home. His mother had just left two days before, and she'd cleaned his house from top to bottom before she went back to Chicago.

Madisyn wasn't due for at least two hours. He had to calm down or he was going to be exhausted by the time she got there. He picked up the cordless phone and called one of his best friends, Alex Herring. After a few minutes of chitchat with Alex's wife Krista, Aidan connected with his buddy. "Hey, man."

"So what's up? Isn't this cooking lesson day?" Alex chuckled.

"Yeah," Aidan said. "I've just got some nervous energy and Madisyn's not due here for two hours."

"I still can't believe you use your actual address. Most of the time you use your condo when you have a woman over," Alex reminded his friend. "This girl must be special."

Aidan wanted to refute his friend's words. "You'd better be glad you live on the other side of Dallas and it would take me too long to come over there and kick your ass."

"Yeah, yeah, yeah," Alex said, dismissing his remarks. "You know, you've jumped some pretty high hurdles for a man who hasn't even had a kiss yet, and we won't even discuss getting any. Is she some kind of supermodel or something?"

"No. But you're right, she's special. Thanks, Alex."

"I didn't do anything."

"You got me to realize that she is special, and I'm damn proud to have her in my house. Later." He ended the call, relaxed and ready to face Madisyn.

Or at least he thought he was a few hours later, when Harry informed him Madisyn was on her way. He opened the front door and watched her drive up in her blue Chevy Trailblazer. He rushed outside to open her door for her. He wasn't expecting such a different-looking Madisyn. Her shoulder-length hair was pulled back in a ponytail. She wore a V-neck tank top, blue jean capris and low-heeled sandals. He helped her out of the SUV. "You look nice, Madisyn." Was that his voice sounding as highpitched as an adolescent?

She looked him up and down, taking in his short-sleeved shirt, Bermuda shorts and sandals. "You as well, Aidan. Are you ready for your cooking lesson?"

"Sure. Thought of nothing else," he teased. "I dreamed of scallops all night." He noticed several canvas grocery bags in the backseat of her SUV. "I hope you didn't buy all this for the lesson?"

"Actually, yes. I didn't figure you had much in the way of spices and whatnot. Anything you don't need I'll take home." She opened the back door of the SUV to retrieve the packages, but Aidan stopped her.

"I'll get them. Why don't you go into the house and take a seat? I'll drop these in the kitchen and join you in a bit." He reached inside the car and grabbed the bags, discreetly watching the sway of her hips as she walked into his house. He tried to shake the image from his brain, but it was too late. It was already burned there.

He took the bags into the kitchen and deposited the perishable items in the refrigerator, then joined Madisyn in the living room. She was flipping through his college football magazine. He wasn't surprised, knowing that she was a sports junkie. "You go to high school games?"

She placed the magazine on the table. "Sometimes. My oldest brother, Michael, is a high school coach. Last year his team went to state."

"Wait, is your brother Michael O'Riley? Coach of the Baldwin High Tigers, who won the state championship for the fifth consecutive season?"

Madisyn smiled with pride. "Yeah, he's been at that school since he graduated from North Texas State. That was the first time I'd ever seen him cry, outside the birth of my nephew."

Aidan knew the feeling, since the Cowboys had won the last Superbowl, the first in ten years. He, too, had shed a few tears in the locker room away from the news cameras. "Those are some emotional moments," he explained. "I thought women like to see men cry."

"Well, yeah," Madisyn agreed. "But we don't want a crybaby, either."

Aidan laughed. "My manhood is still intact."

"Definitely," Madisyn said. "Ready to start cooking?"

Aidan hoped so. "Yeah, I think I'm ready." He stood and reached out to help Madisyn up. "Are you ready?"

After she was upright, she nodded. "Lead me to the kitchen."

Aidan believed in taking any opportunity with Madisyn he could get. He grabbed her hand in his and led her into the kitchen.

"Oh, my God!" Madisyn walked further inside the room. Never in her limited experience had she seen such a spacious kitchen. It had every appliance she could ever wish for. They had an unused look. A large stainless steel side-by-side refrigerator sat in the corner. A six-burner convection oven, also stainless steel, waited to be used. What took her breath away was the island in the center of the room. It was the one she'd dreamed of. It even had the little sink to wash your hands! "Aidan, this is freaking great!"

"I love to hear women say that." He stood next to her. "Maybe not in the kitchen, though."

Madisyn laughed nervously. Was he really flirting with her? "Well, in this case, I'd be correct. The other I have no idea." She walked to the large refrigerator. She was surprised to see it well-stocked. She pulled out the ingredients they'd need. He'd left the non-perishable items in the bag sitting on the marble counter. She caressed the counter. It felt wonderful. "This is so smooth, Aidan."

"Again, words I hear in other rooms in the house," he said.

Madisyn knew he was teasing, trying to relax the tense atmosphere. For that she was very grateful. "Is that all you guys think about?"

"Probably." He washed his hands in the sink and dried them with a nearby paper towel. "I guess you women never talk about such things."

Madisyn's eyes were riveted on the sexy picture in front of her. "Huh?" How could something so mundane as hand washing seem so sensual? "I'm sorry. What?" She shook her head. The image of his large hands rubbing against each other covered in soap was too erotic for words. And it was doing crazy things to her body. "Why don't we start making the recipe?"

Aidan stared at her blankly. "You mean, scallops with coleslaw is a real dish?"

"Actually it's called scallops with cilantro sauce and Asian slaw. It's really easy. You'll see."

"I just bet." Aidan didn't sound like he believed her. "What's first?"

She reached for the containers of conveniently chopped carrots, radishes, apples. "First thing we need is a large bowl to mix this in." She glanced around the room, then at him, waiting for him to spring into action. But he just stood there.

He looked down at the floor, before raising his glance to meet hers. "I have a confession to make. My mom flew down and shopped for me, so I don't know where anything is because she put everything away. So feel free to search."

She gave him ten cool points for confessing. Then she began her search. Might as well locate everything first. She found a large silver bowl, a very expensive skillet, and a beautiful red colander. She also located a thick cutting board and some knives. "Okay, Aidan, first thing you should know is that I am a tactile teacher. I believe you have to touch the food before you can fix it. Now this recipe calls for most of the ingredients to be sliced julienne style. You know, cut like shoestring potatoes."

"I'm aware of what the term means," he said.

"Sorry. I'm usually teaching this to young children at my church. No offense intended."

"It's me. I'm a little touchy, I guess." He picked up the knife and looked at her. "Now what?"

Madisyn cleared her throat. "Well," she reached for the bowl, "first we add the carrots, radishes, apples, and scallions. I went to a specialty store near my house, and so everything is already cut up."

He did as she directed, then also added the vinegar, sugar and salt to the mix.

"We have to let it set for fifteen minutes," Madisyn said, removing the scallops from their container. "The muscle has already been removed from these, but I would still rinse them, then pat them dry."

As he did what she said, he studied her. "So how long have you been giving cooking lessons at the church?"

"Probably about ten years. I'm kind of a self-taught gourmet cook and I love to fix elaborate meals, so I started doing it to occupy my time at first." She tossed the mixture around in the bowl.

"Why did you need to occupy your time?" He leaned against the counter, watching her.

She could laugh about it now, but back then she'd been an emotional mess. "I found out something awful about my boyfriend."

"What?"

She dug into the other bag for the cilantro, lime juice, chiles, fish sauce and oil. She lined them up for him to use. "Oh, I found out he was playing me. He just wanted me to fund his artwork. He pretended to like me when he preferred men instead."

"Oh, Madisyn, I'm sorry." He reached out to touch her, but pulled back at the last minute. "I know how devastating something like that can be."

She shrugged, not wanting him to know how much his words affected her. "Hey, it was over ten years ago. So I got my heart broken, but it was a lesson well learned. The first of many lessons, as it turned out."

"I'm glad you had something to occupy your time. I hope you didn't blame yourself." He glanced at the recipe she'd printed out for him and carefully measured the ingredients and added them to the mixture.

She inhaled the aroma in the kitchen. Now it finally smelled like a home. "No, I didn't blame myself. It just made me more aware of how easily men can manipulate women. I mean, if I hadn't come over unannounced, I wouldn't ever have known."

"Oh, so you did a drop in?"

"Yep."

"So what after that?"

Madisyn stared at him. "What do you mean?"

Aidan stepped toward her. "I mean, what happened after that guy? You have this wall around you that I can't seem to penetrate."

"I don't know what you're talking about." And she actually didn't. All they were doing was a little harmless flirting, right?

"Well, I'll just have to show you." He closed the distance between them in two strides, took her in his strong arms and said, "As you can see, I'm a tactile kind of man." His lips moved toward hers slowly, purposefully, and landed on their target. To say he kissed her was an understatement. He devoured her lips, forcing them apart, letting his tongue do all his talking for him. And right now he was doing a whole lot of talking. When they finally separated, Madisyn couldn't breathe, let alone think of what the next step could possibly be.

Aidan held her close. "I hope my message got through the brick wall."

She could still taste him on her tongue, smell him in her nostrils, and wanted him after just one heart-stopping kiss. "Oh, yeah."

CHAPTER 7

Madisyn and Aidan stood facing each other, panting and staring into each other's eyes in the large kitchen. Madisyn was more confused than ever. "Do you want to continue the lesson, Aidan?" She leaned against the counter for support.

He nodded. "Look, Madisyn, I do want the cooking lessons."

"But?"

"If you're looking for an apology for the kiss, it's not going to happen. Madisyn, can't you tell I'm attracted to you?"

This was all happening too fast for Madisyn to keep up with. "No, actually, I can't. Why would you be, anyway? I think this is a little much if you just want to make sure I keep volunteering."

Aidan sighed. "Madisyn, stop and calm down. Yes, I'm attracted to you because you're passionate about Mature Alliance, and you know football stats like crazy and not just mine. You're a beautiful, smart and vibrant woman, Madisyn. How could I not be attracted to you?" She looked him up and down. "Because you look like that."

It was Aidan's turn to look confused. "Okay, explain. You're not attracted to me because of the way I look?"

"Well, it's kind of hard to put into words," Madisyn lied. It wasn't hard because she knew was attracted to him. She was just trying to fight it.

He moved closer to her again. "I'm listening."

Now she'd done it. Aidan stood before her with a scowl on his face. Madisyn took a deep breath and decided if he wanted to know the truth, then that was what he going to get. "Well, Aidan, you're a professional football player and I know you're used to a certain type of woman. I don't think I can be that woman."

"What kind of woman do you think I'm looking for?"

Madisyn shrugged, stepping back from his closeness. His cologne was driving her nuts. "You know, like those girls at the party. Like my friend Keisha."

He moved closer to her and put his arms around her, drawing her as close to his body as humanly possible. "Madisyn, you're the kind of woman I want. End of discussion." He tilted her chin upwards toward him and kissed her.

"But," Madisyn murmured against his lips.

"No more talk," he whispered as he kissed her again. And again.

Madisyn gave up her fight and kissed him back. This time when they finally came up from air, Aidan didn't give her time to voice her apprehensions. He took her hand and led her to the breakfast table and pulled out a chair for her. "Sit down, Madisyn."

After she obliged him, he sat next to her. "Aidan, are you sure about this?"

"Yes, Madisyn, I'm quite sure. I do want everything to remain as it is. I'm not looking for a wife. Just a good friend, and I feel we can have that."

"This is not some kind of booty call thing, is it? 'Cause I can save you a lot of time. I'm not into that."

"No, Madisyn. I'm attracted to you and want to see where our friendship will go. Are you game?"

She was more than game. "Aidan, are you game?" I'm at the charity." She didn't want to compromise the charity and all Aidan had worked so hard for.

"So you don't mind pursuing a friendship as long as you can remain private? What about when we go out on a date?"

"Aidan, let's take it one step at a time. I'm still trying to wrap my brain around the kisses. Can't we take it slow to make sure this is something we both want before we alert the public that we're dating?"

He nodded. "Okay, slow it is, but I want you to know this right now. At some point we're going to go out and people will see us together. When, I'm leaving up to you." He took a deep breath. "Are you sure about your answer?"

"Yes," she whispered. "As long as we take it slow." Aidan looked across the table at Madisyn. She was beautiful when she was flustered. Slow. Sure, he could take it slow. He'd just have to learn to like cold showers.

"Agreed. How about we finish the lesson?"

She rose from her chair and pretended to smooth the wrinkles out of her tank top. Unfortunately that little move made Aidan focus on her full breasts. Slow was going to be very difficult.

"Sure," she said. "Do you still want to go to the movies?" She gazed up at him, then walked back to the island where they were preparing the food. "You said no one would see us. How is that possible?"

Aidan knew pursuing Madisyn would be an uphill battle and she was proving him correct. "It's in this subdivision, Madisyn. We can even walk to it, if you want. Remember when Harry let you inside the gate?"

"Yes."

"To the left is a gourmet grocery store and next to it is the movie theatre. I can call ahead and book all of it, if that will make you feel better. Usually, I just sit at the back and no one bothers me."

She started preparing the scallops for the skillet. After she seared them on each side, she took them out and placed them on a plate. She motioned for him to join her at the counter. When he did, she handed him a plate.

"Put some of the Asian slaw on a plate with some scallops on top."

Aidan followed instructions and had to admit to himself that the dish looked pretty good. The taste would be the true test. He hoped the dish tasted as good as Madisyn's lips. "Do you want to go to the movies?"

She picked up a gold-tipped fork and tasted the scallops. "These are wonderful." She took a bite of the Asian slaw. "Delicious. You promise to be a gentleman?"

"Of course." Taking a cue from Madisyn, he picked up the fork and speared a scallop and some coleslaw on a fork and tasted it. It was delicious. The dish could rival food from his favorite restaurant.

"Then, no." She tasted the food again, this time taking a bigger portion in her mouth. "If I wanted to go to the movies with a gentleman, I'd ask my father."

Aidan was certainly at a loss for words and was getting ready to ask her what the heck was going on when he noticed the smile on her face. She'd baited him. "Oh. You got jokes. I'm goin' to have to stay on my toes with you. This is amazing, and to think I made it," he said proudly.

"Yes, you did. I told you this was an easy dish to make."

Aidan smiled at her. She made cooking enjoyable and she still hadn't given him an answer about the movie. "So what about later? I'll be the perfect gentleman, promise."

She studied him with those green eyes for an eternity before she said, "Of course I want to go to the movies with the perfect gentleman. I didn't think they made those anymore." She finished eating her portion of their lesson. "That was really good. I'd forgotten how good this dish is. You'd better finish yours before I forget I'm a guest in your house and eat the rest of it."

Aidan laughed. This woman was definitely different from the rest of the women he'd dated in the past. She didn't try to hide her hearty appetite. "I guess I made a really good meal, huh?"

Madisyn nodded. "I really love any seafood dish."

"Well, that's good to know."

Later Saturday afternoon, Keisha paced her tiny bedroom in her childhood home wondering where her friend was. It wasn't like Maddie to miss girly day. They both looked forward to getting pampered, and it just wasn't the same without Maddie there. She'd always been the buffer between Keisha and Chayla. Chayla was too good for Keisha's taste. She was constantly babbling about those godawful kids or her clingy husband.

Maddie usually confided to Keisha about anything going on her life, but this time Madisyn was keeping something from her. And Keisha didn't like it.

Keisha dialed a number on her cell phone. "Hey, where's Maddie?"

"I don't know. You're supposed to keep up with her and help me get back with her. My job is hanging by a thread."

"Look, Darnell, I didn't tell you to have a sleepover."

He took a deep breath. "Why did you tell her, anyway? That was our secret," Darnell said. "You cost me over fifty dollars in flowers and candy and she still kicked me to the curb."

Keisha sighed. Typical Darnell. Everything was just about him. "One, I didn't tell her, and two, you shouldn't have let that girl sleep over. I can't believe you did something so stupid with a tramp."

"I know you ain't jealous. I thought Maddie was your girl?"

"When the occasion calls for it, she is."

76

Madisyn was floating on air by the time she reached her parents' that evening. As usual her mother was out with her friends, leaving Madisyn's father on his own. He was sitting in his favorite chair reading the sports section of the newspaper when she located him.

"Hey, baby girl." He rose from his chair and gave Madisyn a hug. "You look wonderful today. Who's got you smiling like this?"

She knew she probably wore a stupid grin of happiness on her face, and not even her father's meddling could ruin her good mood. "Nobody, Daddy. I'm just happy to see my father." She sat on the sofa. "What's for dinner?"

"You know very well I grilled steaks. As I do most Saturday afternoons, weather permitting. So who's got you smiling as big as Texas?"

Madisyn was at a crossroad. If she didn't tell her father something, he would needle her until she blabbed everything, just as he had when she was a teenager. Some things never changed. She couldn't hide anything from her father. He'd give her the look and she would sing like a canary. "It's someone I met recently. We had lunch together. Don't worry, it wasn't Darnell."

Ben smiled. "Oh, I know that. He called the house earlier looking for you."

Oh, no. Was Darnell really trying to weasel his way back into her life through her father? "What did you tell him?"

"I told him to piss off," he said calmly. "And that if I knew where you were, I still wouldn't tell him. But that's not the phone call I want to talk about."

"Daddy, what exactly are you talking about?"

"I'm talking about Aidan Coles from the Dallas Cowboys calling here today."

Oh no. "What did he want?"

"To tell you that you left your cell phone at his house today and he'd drop it by your place later. Now do you care to tell me why this man is calling all over Dallas looking for you? He didn't hurt you, did he?"

"Of course not. I'm giving him cooking lessons, that's all." It was the first time in her life she hadn't told her father the entire truth.

"Baby girl, don't you lie to me. It's written all over your face that you're not being completely honest with me. I just need to know if I need to sell my season tickets or not."

"No, Daddy. Keep your tickets, everything is fine." Her father had had season tickets to the Dallas Cowboys football games since she could remember.

"All right. So what are you teaching him?"

"Gourmet cooking. He says he never cooks at home. I think it's true. All his cookware looked brand new and he didn't seem at home in his own kitchen."

"I'm sure that will change," her father assured her.

"It'll just take time. I'm sure he's used to eating out constantly. How are your friends going to handle you dating a football player, especially that little skinny one?"

"I'm not telling them. At least not yet."

"Baby, this will let you know who your real friends are. A true friend will be happy for you. An untrue friend will want to be in your shoes. You'll find out which is which."

Madisyn didn't need to find out. She already knew who were her real friends and who weren't. Unfortunately, Keisha fell into the latter category. "I know. That's why this has to stay our secret. Well, after you tell Mom, it really has to be our secret. You can't even tell the boys." Her brothers would hit the roof when they found out.

"That will be tough, but all right." He glanced at the clock on the wall. "Ready for dinner?"

"Always." Madisyn rose and headed for the kitchen with her father following behind her.

He chuckled as he took a seat at the small kitchen table and Madisyn prepared to microwave their dinner. She placed the food on the table and took a seat across from him. "I'm just too smart for my own good," he told his daughter.

Madisyn speared a steak and placed it on her plate. "What is it now?"

Ben cut his steak in half and placed the smaller portion on his plate. "Cholesterol," he explained. "Your mother would kill me if I ate a whole steak."

"Daddy?"

"Oh, I told you a man would be in the last place you looked and he was. You never thought volunteering would land you in spitting range of a Dallas Cowboy, did you? Good thing you were raised on football. You'll always have something to talk about."

Madisyn recalled all those summers when she was the water girl to the varsity football team and laughed at the memory. "Yeah, I don't know many people who lived and breathed football like the O'Riley clan. I think I was the only girl in school that knew more about football plays than about makeup. I wouldn't change a thing, Daddy."

"Me either."

They finished their meal with conversation about the upcoming football season. Most fathers and daughters would have discussed politics or the news, but Ben O'Riley talked about the Cowboys.

Aidan paced his living room, wondering about his next move. The movie had gone went better than he had hoped for. However, pretending to be a gentleman when all he wanted to do was make Madisyn his was a pretty difficult game to keep up.

Everything about her was starting to get to him. Granted, this was only the first lesson, but there would be many other times they would be alone. He had to find a way to channel that frustration somewhere else or both he and Madisyn would be done for.

He needed her administrative experience to keep the charity running smoothly. But something about her made him want to keep her close to him. Not as boss and employee, but as a man and a woman. Like right now. He wanted to see her, even though he'd just been with her most of the day. Yeah, she'd left her cell phone, and he could have just had someone drop it off on his behalf, but he had called her parents' home and talked to her father. Was he really losing it like that after one semi-date?

The phone rang, interrupting his chastising of himself. He picked it up on the second ring. Not many people had his home number, so he had a sneaking suspicion it might be Madisyn. "Hello," he said, trying to sound relax and cool.

"Hey man, what's up?" Kameron Drews asked.

"Not much," Aidan said, sorry he had picked up the phone. Kameron was a former college buddy and also one of the Cowboys' latest acquisitions. Trouble and the media had a way of following Kameron, so Aidan made sure he was always as far away from him as possible.

"Let's go out."

Aidan sighed. "Where's your wife? You know how she hates you going out to the club. The media always seems to find you and you end up on the front page of the *Dallas Morning News* claiming you've been framed or some nonsense."

"True dat. She's out of town for a long minute. We had a little disagreement yesterday. She found out about the club."

"You mean you decided to open a nightclub and didn't tell your wife of thirteen years? Man, what are you using for brains?"

Kameron was defensive. "Hey, it's my money. I can do what I want with it. I don't see her out there running down the field for a touchdown on Sundays. Anyway, she got in a huff, took the kids and headed to her mom's in Tulsa."

"Isn't the club about to open?"

"That's kind of why I was calling. I want you to be there at the grand opening, so she can get out of my ass. If you're there she'll know I'm not trying to push up on any chick."

"But that's a lie, isn't it? I don't think I can make it anyway." Aidan was used to his morally challenged teammates using him as shield. Kameron was the worst and had the most to lose. When he'd married his college sweetheart thirteen years ago, she hadn't signed a prenuptial agreement. She could end up with most of Kameron's money.

"Don't tell me you're seeing someone? What a time for you to try to get your groove on," Kameron laughed. "Bring her."

Aidan instantly thought of Madisyn and how uncomfortable she'd be at a nightclub around his rowdy teammates and the scantily clad women hoping to hook up with an athlete. "I don't think she's the club type." He knew Kameron wouldn't stop until Aidan agreed, and he wanted to call Madisyn. "Look, I'll try my best to make it."

Kameron decided not to press his luck. "So are we gonna hit the streets tonight?"

"No," Aidan said. "I've got a date." Aidan ended the call. Kameron was going to be trouble. Hopefully not the front page headlines kind.

CHAPTER 8

When Madisyn arrived home later that evening, she had a message waiting. She guessed it was her dad wanting to make sure she got home all right. Normally, he'd talk to her all the way home on her cell phone, but since she'd left it at Aidan's, the ritual had gone unfulfilled. She retrieved her message and listened in surprise. It was Aidan, and he wanted her to call him back.

She engaged the caller ID option and redialed his number. He was most likely out, since it was Saturday night, she reasoned as she listened to the phone ring.

"Hello?"

"A-Aidan, this is Madisyn. Is something wrong? I haven't had a chance to go shopping for supplies yet."

He chuckled. "Madisyn, I didn't call you about the center. I called because I wanted to talk to you. Why can't you see that?"

"Sorry," she apologized. "It's just that I think of you kind of like my boss, and my boss would call only if there was something wrong."

"Well, I'm not your boss. I'm your friend. Remember, we agreed on the friend thing and we sealed it with a kiss. Friends call each other, you know."

Not when one of them is a multimillionaire professional football player for the Dallas Cowboys. Madisyn was still trying to get used to the idea this man was attracted to her. "Yes, I remember. It's just that it's Saturday night and I thought maybe you'd be out clubbing or something."

"I'm not really the club type," he said. "I'm more the movies at home kind of guy. I treasure my private time, Madisyn. I know you have a bad image of professional athletes, mostly because of the media, but most of us are just average guys who like to do average things."

She knew that was true as well. "Yeah, the media does barbeque you guys if you sneeze. I know you're not all like that Kameron Drews. You'd think a camera crew followed him around twenty-four/seven, he's on the news so much. Do you know him?"

"We're on the same team," he said. "Of course I know him. Whether I'd call him a friend would be the bigger question."

Madisyn easily understood. "Would you?"

"Sometimes. But on the whole, no. You know, he's like the bad kid you knew in school. He's not so bad until he does something horrid, then you're like, I should cut my ties now."

"Been there, done that."

"Really? Who's your Kameron?"

"My friend Keisha. She was at the party. She's medium height, kind of slender, very pretty." Madisyn wished she could have lied about Keisha's looks, but it would have been pointless.

"Oh yeah, I remember. She's not as pretty as you. And she doesn't have your kind heart."

Madisyn laughed. "Good answer. You get ten points for compliments."

"Hey, I meant that. You do have a kind heart and you're patient."

Madisyn tried to decipher his words. Was he just trying to gauge her mush factor or was he genuine? "Well, thank you for the compliment and I accept it in the spirit it was given."

"Finally. Hey, how about we continue this conversation face-to-face?"

Surely she didn't mean that. "W-when?"

"I'd say right now, but you sound a little nervous about that. How about tomorrow for lunch?"

If she missed church tomorrow her father would never forgive her, and her church since childhood was located in South Dallas. "W-where?"

"You already have plans," he guessed.

Madisyn sighed. "It's just like a family tradition. We attend church together. I could meet you after."

"Why don't I join you?"

"W-what?"

"Do you have some kind of speech impediment?" He chuckled. "You haven't given me a straight answer yet. I'm asking if it's okay if I attend church with you tomorrow?"

He made it sound like a reasonable request. It would be if he wasn't who he was. Her church was small by today's megachurch standards, but enough people went there to cause a slight riot if Aidan made an appearance.

"Madisyn?"

"Aidan, I don't know about that. I mean, it's a small church and my mom would want you to eat dinner with us."

"Are your brothers going to give me grief or something?"

"No, they'll probably give me grief."

"Good. How about I attend church with you and drop you at your parents. What time shall I pick you up?"

It sounded simple. "Why don't you stay for dinner? I mean, you're going to drop me off anyway, you might as well stay for dinner."

"Are you sure? I don't want to impose on your family time."

"Yes, I'm quite sure." She sighed. Tomorrow was going to be a long day. When she showed up at her tiny church with Aidan Coles, it was going to be a day of explanations. "I'll see you in the morning."

∞

Aidan hung up the phone confident he was making the right move. Going to church with Madisyn's family was going to be a first for him. He hadn't attended a place of worship in fifteen years. What was it about this woman that had him jumping all kinds of hurdles?

The next morning, Aidan dressed in his best dark suit and headed to Madisyn's house. His normal off-season routine on Sunday mornings was to eat a late breakfast and read the paper. Funny how a woman can make you change your entire schedule, he told himself. But it would only be this one time.

He rang the doorbell at the small house, instantly liking the cozy neighborhood. The huge trees in her front yard gave her porch shade from the Texas sun. He heard the door open and he had to do a double take. He'd expected Madisyn to be dressed in traditional Sunday clothing. Instead, she was dressed in a suit that seemed welded to her curvy body. Not that he was complaining.

"Good morning, Aidan," Madisyn said softly as she motioned him inside. "You look very handsome."

He looked her over again as he closed the door. "And you look like a goddess." He kissed her on the cheek, inhaling her fresh scent. Giving in to the urge, he kissed her softly on the lips. "Are you ready?"

She licked her lips and nodded. "I just have to get my purse from the bedroom. Have a seat."

He walked into the living room and took a seat on her couch. The denim sofa was comfortable. Instantly he reached for the remote, but stopped mid-grab. He didn't want Madisyn to think he had to be entertained every minute. He decided to check out the photos on her fireplace mantel. Madisyn appeared before he could really inspect them.

"Okay, I'm ready," she announced, standing in the doorway.

He nodded and joined her. He took her hand, led her outside and helped her inside the Escalade. After he was seated behind the steering wheel, he looked at her. "Hey, maybe you'd like to drive since I don't know where I'm going?"

Madisyn's head snapped in his direction. "Oh no, I couldn't."

"Oh, come on. You know you want to," he teased. Never in his life had he ever let a female drive his ride. The SUV was his baby.

"I don't know, Aidan."

Her hesitation was beginning to eat at him. Why hadn't she jumped at his offer? "Why not?"

She sighed. "You forget I grew up around men. I know what you guys do. You have to be in control every second and you can't have that in the passenger seat. I know you mean well, but you'd have a heart attack by the time we got to church."

How did she know him so well? He had to prove her wrong, even if it killed him. "I promise I'll sit in the passenger seat and won't say a word."

Still she hesitated for what seemed liked forever. When finally he heard her release her seat belt, he sighed in relief.

Madisyn walked around to the driver's side and he opened the door and slid out. He waited until she was seated and showed her the controls to move the seat to her liking. She snapped her belt in place and smiled at him. "One word of dismay from you and I'm pulling over."

"You got it." He closed the door and walked to the passenger side and slid in. She started the SUV and they were off. It was different not being in the driver's seat and she was right, it was driving him nuts. But he'd promised to be good. He thought a little conversation would ease his jangled nerves, so he took a deep breath and received a hard, mind-zapping stare from Madisyn. "So how long have you attended this church?"

She eased onto the freeway, just as the navigational operator came on and announced it was time for a tune-up. Madisyn laughed. "You know, you could have just called OnStar and asked for driving directions. I didn't have to drive."

"Yeah, but where was the fun in that? How long have you been going to church?"

"All my life," she said simply. "My great-grandfather helped build this church in the '40s. My dad is on the church advisory board. Two of my brothers are on the deacon board. My family is real involved in the church."

"No kidding," Aidan said. "So what do you do at church?"

"I teach Sunday school to first and second graders. My sister-in-law Rasheeda and I share the duties. Next Sunday is my turn."

He heard the pride in her voice. It was the same as her voice when she talked about the center. She was definitely a people person. "I guess I'll have to come back next Sunday to see you in action." Had he really just said that? Where was his brain?

A smile quickly formed on her round face. "Only if you want to. I know that might be boring for you. But I appreciate the thought. You might want to see if you survive Sunday dinner at my parents' before you commit to another Sunday."

She had his curiosity piqued. Her family couldn't be that bad. After all, he was used to being chased by football groupies, so he felt certain he could handle a small family gathering. "It'll be fine, I'm sure."

She pulled into the parking lot of a small church. He guessed there were about fifty to seventy-five cars there. They ranged from the old to the very new. She parked next to a black Lincoln Navigator. He'd gotten out and gone around to help with her door when he heard a tiny voice exclaim, "Aunt Maddie!"

He closed the door as Madisyn walked up to the little girl and picked her up. The small girl had two ponytails and hugged Madisyn fiercely. "I miss you. Can we go movies?"

Madisyn looked at Aidan, smiling. "I told you." Then she turned her attention back to the little girl. "Yes, we'll go next weekend as long as your parents say it's okay."

The little girl grinned as if Madisyn had just said yes. Then she realized Aidan was standing too close to Madisyn. She pointed a tiny finger at Aidan and hugged Madisyn closer.

He smiled at the child. "Hi, I'm Aidan. I'm a friend of Aunt Maddie."

Madisyn blushed. "I'm sorry. Aidan, this is my niece Megan. Megan, this is Aidan."

Megan turned her attention to her aunt. "I sit with you," Megan announced as she shimmied down to the ground.

"Sure, baby."

"Madisyn?" A tall African-American man with Madisyn's green eyes marched toward them with a slender woman trailing behind him.

Madisyn sighed. She was hoping for a little time to get her explanation together, but already her family was descending upon her and Aidan. "Hey Marcus, Rasheeda."

Megan stood her ground, holding Madisyn's hand. Marcus stared at Aidan. "Hey, aren't you Aidan Coles of the Dallas Cowboys?"

"Yes, I am. I'm a guest of Madisyn's today." He extended his hand to Marcus. "It's very nice to meet you, Marcus."

Marcus stood rooted to the spot until his wife nudged him toward the church. "We'll see you guys inside," Rasheeda said as she winked at Madisyn.

Aidan thought he'd done very well. But that was just the first sibling he'd encountered. Megan was going to be the real test.

Madisyn picked up the little girl again and looked at Aidan. "Might as well get this over with."

Aidan nodded, holding Madisyn's free hand and they went inside the building. The minute they entered everyone turned in their direction. This was going to be tougher than training camp.

After services were over and Aidan had greeted almost everyone at church, they were finally headed to Madisyn's parents' house. This time he drove, mostly because Megan wanted to ride with them.

When they arrived at the O'Riley home and parked, Marcus ran out to greet them. "Hey, Aidan, I hope my daughter wasn't too much trouble for you," he said in a rush.

Aidan laughed as he opened the door for Madisyn and Megan. "No, Madisyn did all the work. She sat in back with Megan. I just drove here. Don't worry, I'm used to kids. I've got three nieces and two nephews."

Marcus nodded. "How did you meet Maddie?"

Aidan helped Madisyn and Megan out of the SUV and they headed into the house. Marcus followed behind them. "She volunteers for my charity and she's giving me cooking lessons."

Aidan had thought that would appease Marcus, and for a brief second it looked like it was going to work. But apparently the O'Rileys were playing tag team. Michael, Madisyn's oldest brother, was up next. He took a seat by Aidan on the sofa when Madisyn went to the kitchen to help with lunch.

"You know, we're a little protective of Maddie," he said in his concerned brother's voice. "I read how you professional athletes can get. I don't want my only sister to get hurt."

Aidan wasn't shocked by Michael's no-nonsense attitude. He was very much like Madisyn in that respect. Unlike Marcus, Michael wasn't impressed Aidan was a football player. Michael was concerned about his sister. "I quite understand. At this point we're just friends." He wanted to reassure Michael. Unlike Marcus, Michael was built like a linebacker.

"Good. The last thing she needs is some guy trying to use tired player moves on her. She's my only sister and I will do anything to keep her happy. Darnell slipped through my sensors but that won't be happening again, if you get my meaning."

Oh, Aidan got it all right. He knew a threat when he heard one. "Yeah, I read you loud and clear."

Michael leaned back, smiling. Aidan had apparently satisfied him. "Good. Hope you can see my team play one Friday night. We won state last year, making it five in a row. So the pressure is really on this year. Every high school in our district wants to take us down."

He'd switched gears seamlessly, Aidan thought. Now that the issue of dating Madisyn was settled, they chatted about football. "I'd like to attend a game or two, but I'm really strapped for time. I'm opening the Mature Alliance as well as dealing with football, but I'm really going to try."

Michael nodded. "If you're short on volunteers, let me know. I always require the team to do something in the community during the season. Last year we collected canned goods for the food banks."

"That's cool," Aidan said. "I love giving something back to the community. Dallas has been very good to me the last few years. It took me a while to get the Alliance started but now it's getting off the ground. It's one of the best ideas I've ever had. Next to getting to know Madisyn."

Michael smiled. "Yeah, she's definitely special."

CHAPTER 9

Much later after the Sunday afternoon inquisition, Madisyn and her mom went shopping for the Alliance supplies at the local office supply store. Her mother volunteered to help since she was a retired elementary school-teacher, and she knew what Madisyn needed to buy.

Yeah, right, and Madisyn was a size two. Margaret O'Riley might have her heart in the right place, but her ulterior motive was to browbeat Madisyn into a confession about Aidan.

Her mother grabbed a shopping cart as soon as they entered Office Depot. She dropped her large purse into the cart. "How old are these people? I know Ben and his buddies plan on teaching, but they have no idea of what they've gotten themselves into." Margaret aimed the cart for the paper supply section.

"According to most of the paperwork their ages range from eighteen to seventy," Madison told her mother.

"But it doesn't matter what age they are, Mom, they're all starting at the same level."

"Well, don't we sound like a representative for the Mature Alliance already?" Her mother picked up a packet of spiral notebooks and put them in the cart. "Or are you the president of the Aidan Coles Fan Club?"

Madisyn shook her head. This was going to be a battle of wills and her mother was already winning. "No, Mom. I just really believe in Mature Alliance. It can really help the community."

"I know it can," her mother agreed. "So many of the older people at church could benefit from it, but you know how old people are with their pride. We should do this at the church."

Madisyn nodded. She knew of at least five of the church's older members that had trouble reading the Bible verses. "I wonder if we could get some of the men to drive them to the center for a class."

"I don't know if that would work. And they probably wouldn't want everyone knowing they can't read. You'll have to think of something else." She spotted writing tablets and put those in the basket as well.

Madisyn picked up a large box of pencils, a box of pens and one of markers. "I'll just have to brainstorm with Chayla for an idea." She glanced around the aisle for file folders and spotted some neon-colored ones. "Do you think these would be better than the manila folders? They'd be easier for them to identify."

Her mother picked up the folders and looked at Madisyn. "I know you mean well, but you're taking away their pride by picking these. I know the colors would easier to identify, but unless there are fifty different colors this is only going to work for the first five people."

Her mother placed a hand on Madisyn's shoulder. "I know your heart's in the right place. But just imagine what it took for these people to sign up for the program in the first place."

"I can't imagine," Madisyn whispered.

"Yes, you can. You finally gave Darnell the boot. It took you two years to see what kind of person he really was, but this time you didn't forgive him and pretend it didn't happen. You took action."

Madisyn didn't view her breakup as all that. She was just tired of not being treated as if she didn't matter.

"Wow, Mom, I don't think I did all that."

"You did, but what about this new man? You just got rid of Darnell and you show up at church with Aidan Coles."

"Mom, we're just friends," Madisyn said. She'd known it was coming, but had expected more from her mother. "We met at the charity. He's very focused."

Her mother picked up another pack of spiral tablets.

"Honey, there's nothing wrong with him coming to church with you, friend or not. I just want you to know what you're up against. There're a lot of women out there who'd give their next hair weave or pair of expensive shoes to be where you are. You need to figure out what makes you happy before you even think about getting serious with him."

"Mom, it's only been a week. We're friends."

Her mother looked at her as if Madisyn had just told her she knew where the weapons of mass destruction were. "Have you kissed?"

"Kissed?"

"You know, swapped spit. Tongue action? I was young once too, you know." Her mother reached for the plastic binders. "I think you should get these one-inch binders."

Madisyn shook her head at her mother, not believing for one second the kind of questions this woman was asking about Aidan. "Mom, I don't think I understand what you're asking me."

"Yes, you do, and your non-answer tells me that you have at least kissed this man. How was he?"

Okay, surely she didn't just go there! "W-what?"

"Is he a good kisser?" Her mother asked in a slow, loud voice.

"Mom, please, not here," Madisyn pleaded.

"Oh, come on, Madisyn. You can tell me. He watched you like a hawk at church today. I don't think he has a friends kind of thing on his mind. I thought he was going to knock Brian on his butt when he hugged you."

Madisyn remembered the incident. Brian Hatfield had embraced Madisyn because she'd helped him land an internship at her company, but Aidan just stared holes through him. "Yeah, thank goodness Brian didn't notice."

Her mother continued putting more supplies into the shopping cart. "Okay, Maddie, spill it. Are you giving Aidan more than cooking lessons? Before you tell me that I'm way over the line, I have a right to know."

Madisyn stared at her mother. "Mom, have you started taking some kind of medication I should know abour?"

Margaret shook her head. "Answer my question and I'll answer yours. You know I'll just nag you until you finally snap from the pressure."

That was true. Her mother should have been in Iraq questioning the prisoners. Osama Bin Laden would have been captured and under the jail by now. No one could survive Margaret O'Riley's intense inquisitions without breaking. Madisyn picked up some index cards, deciding to use them as cue cards, and put them in the basket. "Okay, Mom, for the last time, Aidan and I are just friends. I have no intention of sleeping with him." Okay, that was just a small lie, and to her mother no less. "I volunteer at his charity and that's the only free thing he's getting from me outside of the cooking lessons." She held her hands in the air, palms up. "Is that good enough?"

"No, but it'll do for now."

"Thank goodness," Madisyn said. "Mom, if I had any news to tell you, I would."

"I know you would." Her mother waited a heartbeat and asked, "What about those flowers?"

"Who? What?"

"Keisha told me about them. She said she was concerned about you getting in over your head."

"More like she's concerned about herself," Madisyn mumbled.

"Well, at least you know what kind of friend she is. A real friend wouldn't have called and told me something like that. She was hoping I was going to stick my nose in your business. That girl has always been boy crazy."

"I know, Mom. She called Chayla wanting to know why Aidan would spend so much money on me when I wasn't a size two."

Margaret shook her head. "I don't know why that girl thinks that way. Her mother would have a fit if she heard Keisha talking like that. Now, Maddie, you know I raised you better than to run behind some man. He gives a good first impression, but I'll reserve my judgment until later. It's in his favor that he didn't run when Megan attached herself to him. I know Aidan is rich, but I hope you're looking past all that glitter and celebrity."

Either her mother now had selective hearing or she just wasn't listening to Madisyn. It wouldn't be the first time. "If it were more than friendship, yes, Mom, I would look past all those millions of dollars, his very large house, and living in the public's eye. I know he has a good heart. He and the other athletes are funding the Alliance themselves, so they can run it the way they want. There're no grants or public donations, it's the athletes."

"Well, that's refreshing. I get so sick and tired of always seeing them on the news crying about how the press is picking on them for no reason when they break the law." She put a case of folders in the cart. "You're going to need these. You should also go to the teacher supply store and get some of the alphabet tablets. You know, the ones they use in first grade when kids are first learning to write."

Madisyn glanced at the overflowing shopping cart. She had easily piled up a few hundred dollars' worth of supplies and hadn't even scratched the surface. Aidan hadn't given her a budget and her upcoming trip to the schoolbook store would probably run a few hundred as well. "Mom, I can't go to the teacher supply store. I don't have a membership card." Only teachers with identification were allowed to shop there.

"I still have my card," her mother said. "We could go tomorrow afternoon. Maybe you could take the afternoon off," her mother suggested slyly. "We could have lunch, then go the bookstore."

"That sounds nice, Mom, but I just got a new boss and he's very jumpy. I can't take off right now. I can come by right after work and we can go. We can have dinner downtown."

"Sounds good. I'm dying to eat at that new trendy Italian restaurant." Margaret loved anything Italian. "I was trying to talk your father into taking a trip to Italy for our anniversary."

"You know Daddy's idea of vacation is San Antonio."

"I want to go to Italy. I've been dreaming of it for a long time. We're both retired, and we can afford it, but you know your daddy."

"What did he say?"

"He said he was born in Texas and he's going to die in Texas and saw no reason to leave the state. He said he'd go anywhere I wanted to go as long it was within the state."

Madisyn snickered. That was typical Ben O'Riley. He loved Texas. As far as she knew, he'd never been out of the state a day in his life. "Mom, I'm sure you guys could come to some sort of compromise." She guided the cart to the checkout area.

Her mother followed quietly. "Your father? Compromise about leaving his beloved state of Texas? I don't think so."

⁂

Aidan stretched out on his sofa to take a nap. He'd initially thought Madisyn was kidding about her family, but she hadn't been. He'd met her entire family, nieces, nephews, cousins, and even friends that had known her since time began. He was wiped out.

But he had enjoyed himself. The O'Riley clan had treated him just like any other man who had an interest in Madisyn—with extreme caution. In their own way, each one had issued a veiled warning of what would happen to his body parts if he hurt Madisyn. Except for Marcus. Apparently he was the biggest football fan in the family, and it definitely showed.

It was little Megan who'd zapped all his energy. After she decided he was okay, she wouldn't let him breathe. He'd had to read to her, sit by her at dinner. He hadn't dared try to kiss Madisyn in her presence. So now he was laid out on his custom-made suede couch, ready for an afternoon nap. For some reason, as tired as his body was, sleep wouldn't come. His eyes refused to close. Frustrated, he turned on the television, hoping something on the oldies channel would lull him into a nap.

An hour later, Aidan was just about ready to throw the remote at the TV. Why couldn't he just freaking close his eyes? He had an early meeting tomorrow with his attorney about the Alliance, then he was meeting with his financial consultant. He needed to be alert, not tired from an outing. His cell phone buzzed on the table, annoying the crap out of him. He watched it dance across the coffee table and caught it just before it fell on the hardwood floor. He unfolded the phone and brought it to his ear. "Hello?"

"Aidan, this is Madisyn."

She didn't sound right, instantly alarming him. "What is it? Do you need me?" He sat up.

She chuckled. "No, no, it's not that. It's about the Alliance. I just bought some supplies and the cart ran up faster than I realized, so I was wondering, or rather Mom and I were wondering . . ."

"Madisyn, spit it out." Aidan stood looking around for his car keys. "Did they give you a hard time at the store?"

"No, they were quite accommodating once I mentioned my name. Thanks for that, by the way."

Aidan was confused. "Okay, Madisyn, you've got my blood pressure going sky high. Why don't you just tell me what you want to say and we'll go from there?"

She took a deep breath. "I guess I didn't start well. I was wondering about the budget. I spent about five hundred dollars at the office supply store. I don't want to exceed my budget on my first outing."

Aidan understood her concern. His attorney had had the same concern when Aidan suggested setting up the account for Madisyn. "As long as the Alliance needs it, it's fine. I'll let you know when you get near the cut-off mark. Did you get any books?"

"Mom wants to go tomorrow evening after I get off work. I can use her teacher's discount at the schoolbook store, but I wanted to be sure I'm not overspending."

"Tell your mom thanks, but don't use her discount. It could be viewed as fraud, since it's not for a state-supported school. We don't want this to come back and bite us later. I didn't get anything set up there and I don't know if I can get it set up by the time you go shopping tomorrow." He saw the perfect opening and was about to suggest he join them shopping, but Madisyn halted everything.

"Oh, how about I get them and you can reimburse me? I thought the store would have more elementary books than the local bookstore."

He hadn't thought about it in those terms. The students would be starting from scratch. "That's good thinking, Madisyn. By your next shopping trip everything should be in place. Remember, there are over fifty students already."

She cleared her throat. "About that," she coughed. "My dad and his retired friends want to volunteer their time as well. I told him I'd have to clear it with you before I could assign them any students."

His heart swelled with pride. At least she respected what he did at the Alliance. "Tell them we can always use volunteers. I'm sure there'll have to be some kind of orientation for all of us anyway."

"I guess I'm scheduling that, too?" Madisyn laughed.

"Yes, I'm afraid so," Aidan said ruefully. "We're going to have to end up paying you for doing so much for the Alliance."

"No, you won't. You're doing something positive for the community. So many people don't volunteer for anything and you're starting up a place where adults can learn to read and I'm a part of that. That's all the payment I need."

"It's been a dream of mine for a long time. I see too many people walking around who can't write anything but their name and barely that. Someone had to do something. That's why there's no charge if anyone wants to learn to read and write. It will always be free."

"That's great," Madisyn said. "I understand your passion about it. There are some people at the church that need the Alliance, but they're too proud to admit it. I'm trying to figure out how to get them there without taking away their pride."

"I'm sure you'll come up with something," he said, knowing this woman had taken ownership of his heart.

CHAPTER 10

Monday morning, Madisyn walked into her office building ready to face her boss and whatever he was going to throw at her. Right after she got her morning shot of caffeine. She had just given her order when someone joined her at the counter.

"It feels like a century since I've seen you," Josh told her as he gave his coffee order.

Madisyn turned around at the sound of the masculine voice. "Josh!" She hugged her former boss. "It's so nice to see you." She reached for her cup and took a sip. "How's Damon working out?" The barista handed him his order.

Madisyn thought of how to answer him. "I think he's still settling in."

"Good answer." He took a sip. "You got a minute?"

"For you, always." She nodded at a vacant table. "Why don't we sit there?"

After they were both seated, Josh spoke. "I talked to Damon over the weekend and he seems to think you guys might have gotten off on the wrong foot. Is that so?"

"Not really. I'm sure it will all even out soon," Madisyn said confidently. "He's just finding his way." She took another sip, hoping Josh wasn't in a prying mood so early in the morning.

"Now Maddie, come on, this is me. I know Damon can be a bastard at times. If you're already doing the Miss Congeniality thing, there must be some real trouble. So tell me what's going on, and maybe I can help."

She didn't think Josh could help. Only time could. "It'll be fine, Josh. Once he gets his footing, he'll loosen up and relax."

He leaned back in his seat, laughing. "Obviously you don't know the Damon I know. He never relaxes. That's part of his makeup. He's what you young people call a tight-ass."

Madisyn slapped her hand over her mouth to cover her laughter. "It's nothing, Josh."

"You and I both know each other pretty well. And you know you're not leaving this coffee shop until you tell me what's going on. How long we sit here is up to you."

"All right, Josh. He can be brusque, which is fine with me. He did toss Darnell out the other day and I'm grateful for that. He just needs to relax about his job."

Josh nodded. "He told me about his confrontation with Keisha."

"I don't have a problem with that. She totally deserved it and finally someone got a barb in on her."

Josh shrugged. "Just remember who your real friends are, Maddie. This is a workplace first."

"I know, Josh."

"Damon also told me Aidan Coles sent you flowers." This time she couldn't hide her laughter. "I wouldn't have thought one floral delivery would cause so much trouble."

"You know it's all over the building. When a woman receives three dozen roses in a crystal vase, and from the last good Dallas Cowboy, as the press calls him, news travels fast. I didn't make it to church yesterday, but my wife told me he attended church with you. So is there something you want to tell me?"

Madisyn shook her head. "Josh, I can honestly say there is nothing I want to tell you. We're just friends. I'm volunteering at his charity."

"And he had dinner with your family," Josh stated.

"Does Emily tell everything she knows?" Madisyn asked of Josh's wife.

"To me, yes." He reached across the table and touched Madisyn's hand. "You know I'm only concerned about you."

That didn't bode well. "What is it, Josh?"

"Maddie, you know how those professional athletes are. I just don't want you to get your hopes up. You deserve someone that loves you and only you."

"I want that someone too. After Darnell, I'm going to be very selective about my next man. We're going to have more in common than just skin color."

"Now that's my girl."

Aidan walked into the building that housed the law office of his old college buddy, Chase Hartman. He'd been Aidan's lawyer for the last ten years and Aidan had been Chase's only client for the last five.

Chase's building was located in a secluded part of downtown Dallas's high-rent district. The three-story building held its own against the tall, regal buildings. Chase's office was on the second floor. The third floor was a glorified gym for him.

Aidan took the elevator to the second floor and entered Chase's outer office and called out for his friend.

Chase greeted Aidan with a smile. "Hey man, you're early. My secretary isn't even here yet." Chase motioned for Aidan to enter his private office.

"Exactly." Aidan sat down in the leather club chair. "I appreciate you seeing me early like this. But your secretary goes nuts every time I call. I can just imagine what she'd do if she actually saw me. You know I really hate a fuss."

Chase laughed. "Yeah, I hate it when beautiful women just fawn over me like that."

"Hey, it could have happened if you hadn't busted your knee our sophomore year of college. You could have had women dropping at your feet all the time. You would have been a great running back."

Chase smiled back at him. His dark chocolate skin contrasted with his recently whitened teeth. "Destiny had something better in mind, apparently. If I hadn't busted my knee, I wouldn't have changed my major to pre-law and become the next Johnny Cochran, without the celebrity client list."

"What am I?" Aidan asked mockingly.

Chase grinned. "You're my only client. Don't get me wrong, Aidan, I love being your attorney. But it would be nice to get involved in a little scandal every now and then, just to keep me on my toes."

"So I'm boring?"

"No, man. You're a good man and have your head on straight. You haven't let your celebrity status go to your head, and I appreciate that."

Aidan nodded, knowing exactly what his friend wasn't saying. "It's like owning a sports car and never being able to go a hundred miles an hour. It's not that you want to drive that fast. You just want to be able to know how it feels. Sorry, man, but you're stuck with me, just as I am. Just think of all that free time you have for your golf game. You could be a slightly older Tiger Woods."

"Not funny. You know my handicap is still three digits. I need a golf doctor," Chase said. He reached for a file and placed it on his desk. "You don't happen to know anyone, do you?"

Instantly, Ben O'Riley came to mind. "I just might. Were you able to get everything in order for Alliance?" Chase leaned back in his prized leather chair. "I got most of the details ironed out, but I wanted to firm up a few details about this Madisyn O'Riley."

"Yeah?"

"Now don't get your back up," Chase warned. "I'm using my attorney cap right now. You're giving her an undisclosed amount of money to run through. The Alliance needs a checks and balance system to make sure the money is actually being spent for supplies and those supplies are being used at the center. If we're not careful

"Aidan, think about what you're doing. She's a volunteer. This is what volunteers do. They do whatever needs to be done."

"I know that, Chase. Just trust me."

"I always do. Double it is."

◈

"Maddie! I haven't talked to you all weekend," Keisha said as Madisyn stepped off the elevator. "I know you had your phone with you and called you constantly. So you can't call your girl back?"

Madisyn took a deep breath. She knew it was going to be one of those days. Yes, she had noticed Keisha blew up her phone over the weekend, but Madisyn wasn't in the mood to hear about how many men wanted to buy Keisha drinks at the club. "Sorry, had a busy weekend. You know Sunday I'm with my family most of the day." She walked to her desk, hoping Keisha wouldn't follow her.

But she did. She stood with her hands on her slender hips, waiting for a better explanation. "That doesn't explain about Saturday. Is your dad okay? You know I thought he was too young to retire. He's probably just bored, girl."

"No, Daddy is fine." Madisyn turned on her computer and avoided Keisha's penetrating gaze. "I had temporary misplaced my cell phone, so I didn't know about the messages until Sunday."

"Why did you miss girly day? Don't tell me they had you doing time at the charity already?"

"No, I spent some time with my mom," she lied. Madisyn hoped God would forgive her for the whopper she'd just told. "I probably won't be there this Saturday, either."

Keisha glanced at her watch, then at Mr. Bridges's door. "Is he in yet?"

Madisyn looked back at her boss's closed door. The blinds were closed and the room was dark. "I don't see a light, but you know bosses have been known to sit in their office in the dark and watch people around here."

Keisha nodded. "Yeah, my boss is king of that little maneuver. I can't even count how many times I've gotten in trouble for not being at my post."

Madisyn knew exactly how many times Keisha had gotten written up for not being at her workstation. Eleven. Most people would have been history by now, but Keisha had found a loophole. She knew her boss and a manager were having an affair and Keisha used that information to her advantage. "Well, I don't think Mr. Bridges is in yet, but I don't want a replay of last week. So why don't we meet for lunch?"

"Sounds good. Are we still on for dinner tonight?" Keisha stared at Madisyn, waiting her answer.

"I'm sorry, I'm meeting Mom. We're going shopping tonight." Madisyn didn't dare mention she was going to buy schoolbooks for the charity. Keisha would never let her hear the end of it.

Keisha shrugged and walked down the hall. "Call me when you're free of your mama."

Madisyn sighed and began her workday. She wanted to be more prepared for Mr. Bridges when he strode in.

Thank goodness Keisha was at her desk. Madisyn was printing her boss's daily calendar when her phone rang.

"Good morning, Madisyn O'Riley, can I help you?"

"Well, I certainly hope so, Ms. O'Riley. I was going to be downtown and wondered if you were free for lunch. I realize it's last minute and only a three-hour notice, so I understand if you can't."

Aidan had called to invite her to lunch and then was giving her an out? Had the world suddenly turned on its axis? "Well, I would love to go to lunch with you, but I've already made plans with a co-worker."

"I understand. I know you're buying books tonight," he said. "I was just taking care of some Alliance business this morning. There'll be other times."

He made turning him down sound so sensual, she thought. She racked her brain for something to keep him on the line. His voice had a calming effect on her. "Is everything okay at the Alliance? I'm not over budget, am I? Is that why you're calling? You can tell me."

Aidan laughed. "You're definitely the glass is half-empty type, aren't you? I wanted to meet you for lunch because I wanted to see you. If it's about the Alliance, I'll let you know."

Okay, so he wanted to see her. Hadn't he seen enough of her yesterday? And her family? Was he really interested in her in *that* way? *Steady, girl,* she warned herself. He was used to making a woman feel as if she really mattered, just as Darnell had. She had to remember that or she'd be the fool again.

"Madisyn?" Aidan snapped her back to reality.

"Yes, Aidan."

"I asked you to dinner Wednesday night."

She normally spent Wednesdays with her niece. "Why don't you come to my house for dinner?"

"Are you ashamed to be seen with me?"

"No, it's just that Wednesdays I usually keep my niece Megan, and that way I can do both. She usually goes to sleep about eight. So about eight-thirty?" She was already thinking of an amazing dinner of grilled salmon when Aidan intercepted her plan.

"How about I come at seven and I'll bring dinner. You shouldn't have to babysit and cook for me on the same night. How about something from Houston's? I know they make wonderful seafood dishes," he said.

"That sounds fine." It really didn't, but she didn't have a good excuse to back out of the date. Now hopefully Keisha wouldn't show up unannounced and ruin it all for her.

CHAPTER 11

"Maddie, what is going on with you?" Keisha demanded as they headed to their respective cars after work. "You're letting your needy family run your entire life. You don't have any free time anymore. Tonight it's your mama, Wednesday it's your niece. Friday night I'm sure you have something do that at that charity. You know, I bet Aidan isn't even going to be there," Keisha grumbled.

"It's only for the next few weeks. You know I don't spend that much time with Mom 'cause of all the organizations she belongs to. So I'm grateful for any time I can spend with her. I don't complain when you're in a dating frenzy and cancel out on me at the last minute."

"But this isn't about a man," Keisha complained. "If it was a man, I could relate. This being with your family and volunteering stuff is just beyond me. It's just not natural." Keisha reached her car and unlocked her door. "I know you think I'm man crazy, but I'm not. I just like having a good time and I believe a man should pay for it. You should adopt that philosophy. You're always doing stuff for everybody else, but never yourself."

Madisyn thought Keisha's idea of a good time usually involved someone else's husband or boyfriend. "I think I'm doing fine just the way I am. I like being with my family, Keisha."

She shrugged. "My way sounds like a lot more fun." She got in her car and left.

Madisyn shook her head and disarmed her alarm. One day all that fun was going to catch up to Keisha. Madisyn just hoped she was nowhere near Keisha when it did.

Darnell watched Madisyn motor out of the employee parking lot. He had planned to be back in her good graces by now.

Madisyn was proving very difficult. He'd planned on showing up at the spa she frequented on Saturday, but those plans went bust when Keisha informed him she wasn't there.

He had to figure out another way to get to her. He started his car and followed her. If he couldn't get Madisyn back and get her to accompany him to his company's annual awards banquet, he could kiss that senior investment banker gig good-bye. Yeah, he had to come up with something spectacular.

"Now what is she doing at this place?" Darnell watched Madisyn park in front of the schoolbook store in downtown Dallas. Since it was the middle of summer and most of the schools weren't in session, the store wasn't crowded. She got out of her car and walked inside the store. He could walk in and pretend he just happened by and noticed her SUV. She might believe it. Not.

He watched as her mother parked behind Madisyn's SUV. Thank goodness he hadn't followed his first thought. Madisyn's mother didn't like him and didn't pretend to like him, and that was where his trouble started and ended.

With another attempt thwarted, Darnell started his car and headed for his North Dallas condo. There's always next time, he vowed to himself.

⚬⚬⚬⚬⚬

Later that night Madisyn let herself into her house. Shopping with her mother was always like running a marathon. But for that, her mother was the perfect person to shop with. Having been an elementary school teacher for over thirty years, her mother knew exactly which books were needed.

Madisyn checked her phone for messages. Her blood curdled as she listened to the first one. It was Darnell.

"Hey baby, I saw you shopping with your mama tonight. You know we need to talk about when you're taking me back." The call ended.

Madisyn shook her head. She knew Darnell used any method necessary and he wasn't above threats to get his way. She'd been on the receiving end of his wrath once, and once was enough. "I'm not going to let him intimidate me," she told the room.

The phone rang, shattering her last nerve. Surely that idiot wouldn't call her again. She answered the phone on the next ring. "Hello?"

to make sure everything is on the up and up, we could be on the nightly news."

"I know, Chase. She called me last night wanting to know how much to spend. She was afraid she'd exceeded the budget with $500."

"So she doesn't know she has a budget of a half mil?"

"No, she doesn't, and I plan to keep it that way. I told her that I'd tell her when she was getting close to the budget cap. By the way, I need you to establish an account for her at the local schoolbook store."

Chase stared at him as if he'd grown another head. "Are you serious? You're giving her more access to the money?"

"Yes, I am. If I want Mature Alliance to be taken seriously, everything needs to be in place when it opens next month. You know the press is going to be looking for anything negative they can find, and I don't plan on them finding anything."

Chase shrugged, took out his gold pen and started scribbling notes on a legal pad. "It'll probably take a few days to get it set up. By Friday at the latest," he promised.

Aidan smiled. "Good. Madisyn is buying some books today and I told her that we'd reimburse her. I'll tell her to fax the receipt to you."

Chase nodded, still scribbling. "Sure, no problem. I'll take it out of Alliance's operating budget."

Aidan cleared his throat. "I want you to double whatever she pays."

"What?"

"She's going out of her way to purchase the books. I just want her to know she's very appreciated."

"Baby," Darnell whined. "I don't know why you're trying to act like you don't want me. I'm an investment banker, how are you going to do any better? You know that girl meant nothing to me. You should have called before coming to my place anyway. You know I hate drop-ins. I should be angry at you for barging in my place unannounced, but I'm willing to let it go this time."

Madisyn sighed. She was definitely going to get an unlisted number and change the locks tomorrow. "Darnell, that was not the first time I caught you with your pants down, so to speak. I'm tired of you taking me for granted. I need to be appreciated. You can't give me something you don't have."

"Why are you being such a bitch about this? You always take me back. What's so different this time?"

"This time I don't want you back." She pushed the end button and threw the phone on the couch. The phone rang again, rattling her. She exhaled and answered it. "Look, Darnell, I told you I don't want you. Leave me alone or I'll report you to the police."

"Madisyn, this is Aidan."

"Oh, dear. I'm sorry, Aidan. I thought you were someone else. Please forgive me."

"Nothing to forgive. Is everything all right?"

"No, but I think it will be soon," she said. She forced herself to calm down. "It's nothing for you to worry about."

"If it has you upset, it's something," Aidan said. "Either tell me what's going on or I'm coming over."

Now she really didn't need this man in her house. The last thing she needed was this man in her house. Frightened or not, having him in her house was an invitation to disaster. "That's not necessary. I just had to make Darnell understand that I don't want him. I'm going to have my locks changed tomorrow." She hoped she sounded calmer than she felt.

"I'm definitely coming over. You shouldn't be alone at a time like this. Did he threaten you?"

She let out a shaky breath. Aidan was worse than her brothers. "Not really."

"I'm on my way. I'll call you when I'm on the road."

Click. He was gone.

Madisyn stared at the phone. What had she just done? She shouldn't have answered the phone in her present state of mind. Her brain had no filter and she had blurted out details she would have normally kept to herself.

It was too late to recant anything now. Aidan had probably already gotten in his Escalade, punched in her address and was on his way. She had no choice but to wait.

<hr />

Aidan walked through his house muttering to himself. "Who made you Madisyn O'Riley's keeper? She's a grown woman and can handle her own battles," he told himself. "You can't take over her life." Even with all those inspiring phrases running through his brain, he still grabbed his keys and headed for the garage.

Once seated in the SUV, he pushed the little blue button on his navigational system and asked for the phone number for a locksmith in Dallas County. After getting the information he needed, he waited to be connected with Lucky Charms Key Service.

"Lucky Charms, home of the best key repairs in Dallas. This is Ian, how may I help you?"

Aidan took a deep breath. He knew he was overstepping his bounds terribly, but this was for Madisyn's safety and his peace of mind. "Yeah, I need a lock changed."

"Now?"

"Yes, now," Aidan said through gritted teeth. "You're a 24-hour service, correct?"

"Yeah, but you know it's gonna be time and a half," Ian said.

"So, can you do the work or not?" Aidan headed for Madisyn's house.

"Yeah. What exactly is the work?"

"Change the locks on a house," Aidan said.

"What's the address?"

Aidan rattled off the address as he sped down the freeway. Good thing Madisyn's house wasn't that far from his. He could probably beat the locksmith there.

"We'll be there in about thirty minutes. The job shouldn't take over an hour." The call ended.

Aidan laughed as he pushed the end button on his cell phone. "It should take about ten minutes," he said to the SUV's interior. "Ian thinks he's talking to an idiot." Aidan had changed many a lock in his day, but if he went to the local hardware megastore, it would be on the news.

He arrived at Madisyn's ready to run in and save the day, but he forced himself to calm down. After ten minutes, he finally rang her doorbell. He wasn't ready for the Madisyn that answered the door.

She was dressed in a too-large T-shirt and shorts. Her hair was pulled back in a ponytail. She looked vulnerable and frightened. She rushed into Aidan's arms.

"Oh, I'm so glad you're here. Thank you for coming."

He held onto her tightly, liking the feel of her lush body snug against his. "Madisyn, I'm glad you're all right. I called the locksmith and he's on the way." He waited for her outburst, but he thought he'd beat her to it. "I know I overstepped my bounds as a friend, but I knew you needed to feel safe and you shouldn't have to wait until the morning."

She stepped back from him and invited him inside. "Thank you, Aidan. That was very thoughtful." She took his hand and led him to the sofa. "I appreciate you coming, but really you didn't have to." She sat down on the couch.

He did the same, sitting close to her. "This discussion is closed, Madisyn. Quit telling me it's not necessary. I hope we're close enough friends that if I called you in the middle of the night, you'd come running."

She laughed, wrapping her arms around him. "I can't imagine you in peril, but it's a deal."

He kissed her forehead, not wanting to pressure her into anything they'd both be sorry for later. He just wanted to reassure her. Over the next few minutes he felt her heartbeat settle down to a slow, steady beat. She was finally relaxing.

About twenty minutes later the doorbell rang. Madisyn sat straight up, her brain already on red alert. The bell sounded again. She blinked at him. "The locksmith," she said.

He rose before she could manage to do so. "I'll get it," he said. Aidan went to the door and opened it.

A short pudgy man of about forty-five, with shocking red hair, stood in the doorway. "I'm Ian from Lucky Charms." He flashed a plastic identification badge at him.

Aidan nodded and let him inside. "Madisyn," he called. "The locksmith is here."

Madisyn joined him in the entryway. She was taken aback when she laid eyes on Ian's uniform. Then she set those green eyes on Aidan. "You called the most expensive locksmith in Dallas!"

"But you're good, right?" Aidan looked at Ian.

"Of course. We're worth every penny, ma'am."

Madisyn shrugged. "I could call my dad."

Ian looked from her to Aidan. "We still charge for the service call."

Aidan decided now was the time to take over. "Well, you'd better get started."

Ian nodded and set his toolbox down on the hardwood floor. "We have two kind of locks." He told them the difference between them. "Which would you like, sir?"

Aidan cleared his throat. "Ms. O'Riley is the person you need to direct your questions to."

Ian laughed. "Very smart, man." He looked at Madisyn. "Which one, miss?"

Madisyn laughed. "The second one. I have three doors."

"Okay," Ian said, opening his tool box. "I'll get to work. Shouldn't take too long and I'll be out of your hair."

Thirty minutes later, Madisyn and Aidan were seated on her couch again. Ian had changed the locks in record time and left.

She yawned, but forced herself to keep her eyes open. Aidan had been wonderful just sitting there letting her use him as a pillow.

"Madisyn, I'd better go. You need your rest."

She tried to think of a way to ask him to stay without it sounding like a come-on. Thinking about such an intimate invitation only made her sigh with want. Finally, she gave in to the inevitable and stood. "Thank you for coming, Aidan. I really appreciate it."

He stood next to her. "Madisyn, I don't think you should stay here tonight. You're a bundle of nerves, and I doubt you'd get a moment's sleep."

She didn't either, but didn't want to alert her family of her troubles with Darnell just yet. She had to work this out on her own. "You're right. I'll make a reservation at a hotel near work."

Aidan shook his head. "I think a hotel would only increase your uneasiness about the situation. I was thinking of a place secure, private, where you'd be assured a good night's rest."

"I can't go to my parents'," Madisyn reasoned. "Dad won't be satisfied until Darnell eats some lead, and I just can't let that happen. My daddy believes in Texas justice. Shoot first, ask questions later."

"I wasn't thinking of your parents," Aidan said quietly.

Madisyn didn't have any other options. Chayla was married with children and there was no way she could get a good night's sleep there. And Keisha was *so* out of the question. "I don't have any other options, Aidan."

He smiled down at her. "I was thinking you could sleep at my place."

Madisyn's mouth hung open in surprise, shock and insult at his suggestion. "Look, Aidan, I don't know what you think, but I'm not doing that."

"Madisyn," he started in a calm, sane voice. "In case you didn't realize, I have five bedrooms. You can have your choice of an upstairs or downstairs bedroom. I just want you to be able to sleep, and right now you can't do that here."

Madisyn wanted to object, she should have objected, but in the back of her mind, Aidan made sense. He hadn't done anything disrespectful to her so far. Not that her house wasn't safe. After all, she now had new locks. Still . . . "All right, Aidan. I just need to get some clothes for work tomorrow."

He nodded. "I'm right behind you, baby." And he followed her to her bedroom.

CHAPTER 12

Aidan glanced over at Madisyn as he drove to his house. She clutched her overnight bag as if she had a nine-millimeter pistol in it and was ready to use, if he so much as looked at her wrong. His idea had made a lot more sense when he suggested it an hour ago. But now he realized it for the monumental mistake it was.

He wanted Madisyn in the most elemental way possible. It was going to be difficult to fall asleep knowing she was in his house and not in his bed.

As if she could see the wheels of lust turning in his brain, she shifted in her seat and cleared her throat. "If you've changed your mind, Aidan, I quite understand. You can just drop me at a hotel," Madisyn said quietly. "Given the change in our relationship, it might not be a good idea for us to be in the same place under such trying circumstances."

It sounded practical, very adult, but he wasn't having it. Now he wanted her to stay at his house more than ever. He might have to keep a bucket of ice near his bed, but she was spending the night in his house. "Madisyn, we're adults and we can handle this. It'll show you that I'm totally serious."

"Oh, then you don't want to have sex with me?"

He chuckled. Was she doing this on purpose? He was going to have to take an ice-cold shower the minute they got to his house. "Of course I want you, but we should wait for the right time and the right place. I'm not going to take advantage of a situation. That's not my style."

"I know. I just wanted to state my little disclaimer up front so you wouldn't think I was trying to seduce you and planned all this."

"I called you, remember?" Aidan turned into his sub-division and waved at the night guard as he passed. "Madisyn, I'm just helping out a friend, nothing more." He felt like an idiot for lying, but he had to reassure her that he would be on his best behavior or she'd insist on going to a hotel.

Madisyn sighed. "Okay, Aidan. I'll relax. I'm going to say this once and we'll forget it."

It was his turn to sigh. "What?"

"Thank you for being my friend."

<hr />

Darnell followed the Escalade until he couldn't. He watched the security guard wave the SUV inside the gated subdivision. The security guard motioned him to the visitor lane. Darnell figured he could probably give the uniformed man a feeble excuse and he'd let him pass. He prepared his story for the guard.

"Sorry, sir, only residents allowed past this point," the guard said as he waved a black Lexus through the gate.

Darnell cleared his throat and put on his most sincere voice. "My girlfriend just went inside. And she was with another guy. You can't blame a brother for trying to get what's his."

"I hear you, but you still can't go through the gate. You'll have to confront her somewhere else."

Darnell was stumped. "That's my woman in there."

"Maybe so. But they pay me way too much for me to let you in. I'm not getting fired for helping a man who doesn't know when to let go. If she's riding with another man and he lives here, you ain't got a chance anyway, brother. So turn your ride around and leave or I'll be forced to call Dallas's finest. You'd be amazed at their response time for this neighborhood."

Darnell knew when he was licked. "All right, man. I'll leave." He turned around and headed back to his house. On the way, he made a call on his cell phone. "Keisha, we need to meet. Now."

The next morning, Madisyn woke up early. She hated to admit it, but Aidan was right. She'd slept like a baby in his house. She'd felt safe and secure.

Now she wanted to repay Aidan for his kindness, especially since he was going to have to drive her to work and pick her up. After she dressed for work, she went downstairs to make breakfast. She fixed omelets, bacon, hash browns and French toast. She was setting the breakfast table when Aidan entered the roomy kitchen.

From the look on his face, Aidan was both delighted and frightened to death. He stood by the counter and surveyed all the food Madisyn had fixed. "You eat like this every morning?"

She shrugged, not wanting to admit that she usually ate a big breakfast every day of her life. Maybe he didn't like women who ate a lot. Boy, was he backing the wrong horse. To Madisyn, food came before any man. "Sometimes."

"Good. I like a woman with a good appetite." He grabbed two plates, coffee mugs and handed one plate to her. "I hate it when women act like they don't eat anything and you can hear their stomach growling."

Madisyn nodded and began piling food on her plate. "I've found it's just easier to be yourself from the beginning, although some of my friends don't believe that." She sat at the table and waited for him.

After Aidan settled at the table, Madisyn poured the coffee. "You don't mind if we say grace, do you?"

"No, of course not." He reached for her hand.

Madisyn timidly took his. And they both prayed silently. After that all talking ceased and they enjoyed the breakfast.

"This is very good, Madisyn. Maybe this Saturday, you can teach me breakfast food." He smiled as he sipped orange juice, ignoring the coffee. "In another couple of weeks, breakfasts like this will be a thing of the past. At least until the season is over."

She'd thought athletes could eat what they wanted and never worry about calories. "You mean you eat healthier in season?" She finished off her omelet.

"Usually I try to eat high-carb meals to offset all those workouts. I'm fairly small for a wide receiver. I barely weigh 220. I have some friends that tip the scale at three and some change."

"Well, I'm not sharing my weight with you." Madisyn hated to admit they only had seventy pounds between them. Suddenly, her delicious breakfast seemed fattening.

"I wasn't asking. I think you look great." He flashed that sexy smile at her. "Besides, my mama would have my hide on a platter if I dared ask a lady her age or her weight. My height and weight are plastered on every program and also the official Cowboy website."

She hadn't realized that. "You guys really don't have much in the way of privacy."

"In some ways. Like sometimes we have to talk to the media, and I'd rather not. They usually misquote me or get some stats wrong, but what can you do? They don't know anything about my private life, Madisyn. I promised to keep you away from the press and I mean to keep my promise." He glanced at his gold watch. "What time do you have to be at work?"

Work. Career-focused Madisyn had totally forgotten she had to go to work that morning. Their morning had been too perfect to think about work. "Eight." It was just a little after seven. It would probably take about thirty minutes to get there from Aidan's place. "I guess we'd better get going. I'll just get my things."

"You might as well leave your clothes here," Aidan told her as he rose from the table. "I'll bring you back after work."

She nodded, not wanting to break the spell of their morning together. Her practical nature should have insisted that he take her home directly after work, but the romantic in her wasn't ready for their time together to end. "I'll just get my purse then."

Aidan breathed a sigh of relief as he watched Madisyn walk into her office building. He didn't think anyone recognized him, but that wasn't really his concern. His concern was the safety of the woman who had just left his company.

Madisyn was really getting to him. In a little over a week, she was already closer to him than he would have imagined. He didn't know what it was about her, but he had to find out. A loud, obnoxious horn from an impatient driver jolted him back to the present. He put the SUV in gear and headed back home.

Just as he entered the freeway, his cell phone rang. He answered it before it rang again. "Hello?"

"Man, what are you doing out so early?" Chase asked.

"You know you still have a few weeks left before summer training camp. I thought you'd be getting as much sleep as possible."

"I took Madisyn to work."

"Oh. Is there something you want to share?" Chase might be a man, but at times like these, he was such a woman.

"Actually, before you get all excited, she slept in a guest room. Her ex called, so she had her locks changed last night and I didn't want her to stay alone."

"And of course she agreed."

Aidan laughed. "I like your version better. It took a little talking to convince her, but she finally relented."

"Is the ex stalking her?" Chase went from concerned friend to attorney. "I mean, if he's a physical threat we could file a restraining order against him."

"The vibe I'm getting from her is that he's a threat. I don't really know to what extent yet. I'll ask her when I pick her up from work today. But I do want you to file an order. Why don't you come to the house this evening and interview her?"

"Aidan, this woman might not want you taking over her life. Sisters don't take kindly to a man thinking he's running things. Especially sisters who have been handling their own business just fine without a professional athlete thinking he has to come and save the day. And besides, you need to be focused on the Alliance. Have you given any thought yet to what kind of grand opening celebration you want?"

Aidan hated to admit it, but he'd momentarily lost his focus and had totally forgotten about his charity. "No, man, this thing with Madisyn and her ex has got me nuts right now. So can you come by tonight?"

"Like I'd tell my only client no," Chase teased. "I'll bring the necessary paperwork, too. I think I need to meet this woman anyway, if she's got you by the short hairs already."

"She doesn't. We're just friends right now. And I don't want you trying to mess up my game."

"So I guess that means I can't be charming, huh?"

Aidan laughed. "Not if you want her father to help you with your golf game."

"That's the help? Some old guy you're trying to get brownie points with because of his daughter?"

Aidan chuckled at Chase's worried voice. "Calm down, counselor. I haven't asked Ben yet, so that's our little secret."

"Oh, please tell me you haven't already met the folks. They're going to take your player's card for this. Not that it got much use anyway."

"Actually, I attended church with her last Sunday."

Chase cleared his throat. "Could you repeat that, please?"

Now it was Aidan's turn to laugh. "Yeah, man, you heard me right. I went to church with Madisyn and had Sunday dinner with her family."

Chase was silent for at least a minute. "I'm so glad I'm sitting down or right now I'd be in a wreck somewhere. Aidan, you barely know this girl, and already you're attending church with her. Wait 'til Kameron hears this. He's not going to let you hang out with him and the boys anymore."

Aidan thought that sounded great. He hated the club scene anyway. Nothing could compare to being alone with Madisyn. "Now that's something I can handle. See you tonight."

Keisha's jaw dropped as she watched Madisyn slide out of a SUV. That Cadillac Escalade Hybrid was a top-of-the-line model, with fancy rims. The ride had been tricked out to the highest degree. Who did Maddie know with a ride like that?

Her brothers were too sensible to own an SUV like that. It could be only Aidan. Could Darnell have been right? When he'd called her the previous night, she'd just assumed he'd been smoking weed again and was hallucinating when he said Aidan was at Madisyn's last night. But why would Aidan have spent so much time with Madisyn?

She'd called Madisyn earlier this morning and got her answering machine. Darnell was staked out in front of Madisyn's house and said Madisyn wasn't there. It was time for Keisha to get some solid answers. She hurried through the maze of people until she got to the coffee shop. That was usually Madisyn's first stop, and there she was. Madisyn was collecting her predictable order of hazelnut coffee.

"Girl, who was in the tricked-out Escalade? Did one of your brothers get a new car? Where's your car?"

Madisyn took a sip of coffee, stalling for time. "Keisha, I just got here. Can I have a minute to catch my breath?"

Keisha stood and waited impatiently. "Well, come on, girl. Spill it. Was it that fine Aidan Coles? Are you guys hitting it? I told you Darnell wasn't worth your time.

Don't let him talk you into taking him back. He's just trying to get a promo at his job."

"How do you know he's trying to worm his way back? And how do you know the reason for his crawling?" Madisyn walked toward the bank of elevators.

Keisha was right behind her, not wanting Madisyn to get away. "You're trying to avoid the main question. Was that Aidan?"

"Yes," Madisyn said as they entered the elevator. "He was kind enough to give me a lift this morning."

"I just bet," Keisha said. "You know, I hear his condo is the bomb."

"Oh, really?" Madisyn asked.

Keisha wondered at her friend's answer. "Where did he take you last night?"

"How do you know I was with him last night?" Madisyn stared at Keisha.

Now she'd gone and done it. Darnell had reported he'd followed Madisyn and Aidan to a swanky part of town. After her best research all she'd found out was that Aidan owned a condo. But apparently he took Madisyn to another place. Was that his real home? And why take someone who looked like Madisyn?

CHAPTER 13

That evening Aidan picked Madisyn up from work as promised, driving up just as she exited the building. She didn't even have time to wave bye to Keisha. But that didn't stop her friend from calling her by way of cell phone.

Aidan chuckled as he maneuvered through the traffic to get on the freeway. "I bet you a hundred kisses that's your friend. I saw her staring when you got in."

"Most likely," Madisyn said. She was sure Keisha just wanted to confirm it was Aidan. She opened her phone as it rang again. Might as well get this mess over with. "Hey, girl."

"Don't you 'hey girl' me. I want to know if that's the fine Aidan Coles in that ride."

Madisyn pondered how to answer her friend. There was no use trying to fabricate a story because Keisha would hound her until she knew all details. "Yes, it is."

"Is that a perk for doing volunteer work?" She laughed. "I might need to join you this Friday if I can get curb service from a professional athlete."

"You should volunteer because you want to help, not to find a man." Madisyn darted a glance in Aidan's direction and saw he was grinning. He was enjoying this.

"Says you," Keisha said. "But I'm not the one riding in an Escalade. I'll come by later for all the dirt."

"There's no dirt."

"What about poor Darnell?" Keisha asked. "You're just leaving him out in the cold. He's trying to make amends for what he did. You know you're going to take him back, why make him suffer?"

Aidan reached for her cell phone before Madisyn could answer. She handed it to him and watched in amazement. "Keisha, this is Aidan. Your conversation is upsetting Madisyn, so good bye." He closed the phone and handed it back to Madisyn. "Sorry."

Madisyn shook her head. "I'm the one who should apologize. I shouldn't have taken the call in the first place with you in the car. That was very rude of me. I'm used to being alone in the car, and Keisha can be demanding when she wants to know something."

"Why don't we just forget it? I don't want to spend time talking about someone who isn't you."

Madisyn smiled. "Did you hire a date doctor or something?"

"Why?"

"You always seem to say the things I need to hear the most," Madisyn reasoned. "I appreciate it."

"Well, I don't have a date doctor feeding me lines. I guess you can thank my mom for drilling good manners into my head. If it makes you feel better, that's all the thanks I need."

Madisyn sighed. "See what I mean? You get ten more points for being sensitive."

"You may not think I'm so sensitive when I tell you my plans for the evening," Aidan said quietly. "My college friend Chase is coming over for dinner."

"So you want me to cook you guys something? I don't mind. You went beyond the call of a friend last night, so I owe you."

He shook his head. "No. I've got dinner taken care of. I'm picking it up. Chase is also my attorney and I told him about your ex. He's filing a restraining order for you."

"Aidan, I can take care of myself. I don't need you trying to protect me from Darnell."

He reached his hand across the console and grabbed her hand. "I know you can look after yourself, Madisyn. I never said you couldn't. I'm just trying to help. Chase handles all things related to the law for me. I just don't want anything to happen to you. If I have the resources to help you, I will."

"I appreciate the thought, Aidan, and don't think I'm not grateful, because I am. It means you really care about me." Madisyn was actually glad Aidan had thought of calling his lawyer although she didn't want to admit it. Darnell had been known to throw a fit when things didn't go his way and could turn violent if the situation called for it. Luckily, in the past his fits hadn't been directed at her very often.

"I'm not taking over your life, Madisyn. I just want to make sure that you're safe. And if taking out a restraining order on your ex will make you safe, then I'm all for it."

Later that evening, Madisyn met Aidan's attorney. Chase Hartman didn't look anything like an attorney. His athletic build, charming smile, and expensive-looking suit shattered the stereotype of attorneys. The attorneys in her building reminded her of the cast of one of the *Nerd* movies. Not this man.

After dinner, they sat in Aidan's living room and discussed Madisyn's options. The more Chase explained what he did for Aidan, the more he did sound like an attorney. He opened his briefcase and took out a stack of papers that would choke a horse. Madisyn felt both dismayed and fearful.

Aidan sensed her fear. "Don't worry. Chase is one of those better safe-than-sorry kinds of attorneys. We probably won't use 90 percent of the forms."

Chase looked up from those papers and laughed. "Yeah, Aidan knows me pretty well. I do like to have all my bases covered." He cleared his throat. "Madisyn, I don't know you as well as Aidan, so I'm going to have to ask you some questions about Darnell to better gauge the situation."

Spoken like a true attorney, Madisyn mused. She looked at Aidan and he was smiling at her. "Of course, ask me anything, I have nothing to hide."

Chase nodded as he reached for his yellow legal pad, a tiny tape recorder, and a pen. He scribbled about half a page before he asked the first question. "What were Darnell's exact words when he called yesterday?"

She took a deep breath. "It wasn't so much his words, but his tone. I was involved with Darnell for over two years and this wasn't the first time we'd broken up."

Chase wrote some more. "Explain. Was it normal that he'd just think you'd take him back?" Chase looked in Aidan's direction.

She was about to venture into tricky waters. "Well, yes and no. Yes, he probably did think I'd take him back. I had in the past. But no, I wasn't taking him back this time. I'd made a decision that I deserved someone who actually wanted to be with me. Darnell wants me to take him back and thinks he can pressure me into it."

"You think he would hurt you?"

"If it came down to it, yes, he would. If it was between me and what he wanted, he would definitely hurt me. And because his promotion is contingent on whether I attend the annual party with him, I'd say he's more than a threat. His boss really likes the effect I've had on Darnell's life," she explained.

"So he has a big stake in whether you take him back. This isn't good. What does he do for a living?"

"He's an investment banker at Harland, Collins and Roarke. He's up for a senior banker position."

Chase shook his head. "I'm so not liking this. Harland, Collins and Roarke is one of the top ten investment firms in Dallas. Senior investment banker is a coveted position. The next step would be partner. Madisyn, you could be in real danger if he doesn't get what he wants."

"Yes, I know."

Chase set the legal pad down on the table. "Madisyn, you've never refused to take him back before. I'm afraid phone calls and office visits are just the beginning. You'll probably need to change your phone number, plus you should be very aware of your surroundings."

"Chase, I appreciate your concern, but I can't let Darnell dictate what I do. I'll be careful, but I won't carry a gun. If I change my phone number, my family will be instantly alarmed. The last thing I need is the O'Riley boys playing security guard twenty-four hours a day."

Chase laughed. "Sounds like that's exactly what you need. Then Aidan and I wouldn't be so worried about you."

Madisyn glanced in Aidan's direction. The look in those brown eyes told her that he, too, was very worried about her. "I admit I need help, but I don't want to alert my family unless necessary."

Chase slipped back into attorney mode. "Okay, there has to be a happy medium we can all reach without you feeling like a victim and Aidan worrying about your every move. First thing is that we need to file this order. Now it's not going to stop him from calling so I suggest using caller ID."

"Oh, I have it," Madisyn said. "I admit I usually just pick up the phone without looking, but I will start looking before I answer."

"Any strange phone numbers, please write them down," Chase said. "We can trace those. I have a friend in the FBI," he explained.

"How about a bug on her phone?" Aidan asked. "That way we'd have a copy of the conversation."

It sounded useful, but Madisyn didn't like the idea. "I'd feel like I'm in some police state, or worse yet, that I'm living at home with my parents."

Aidan sat closer to her. "You know, Madisyn, you could always stay at my place until this blows over."

"Oh no, Aidan. My dad would kill us both. I promise to be careful."

He smiled at her. "I knew you were going to say that, but I wanted you to know you had that option."

"Thank you, Aidan, but I will not let Darnell think he's getting over on me." Madisyn didn't think staying at Aidan's was much of an option since the change in their relationship. She had barely made it through the previous night without giving in to temptation and walking down the hall to Aidan's room. Thank goodness her sensible side had kicked in and saved her from doing something she'd regret later.

Aidan didn't want to let go of the discussion but the stern look on her beautiful face told him that he should. She was trying to maintain her independence and he had to let her. Or at least let her think so.

Chase looked up from his papers and glanced at both Aidan and Madisyn. He cleared his throat and began his attorney speak. "Okay guys, here's the game plan. I'm going to file this restraining order tomorrow on Madisyn's behalf. After all the paperwork is done, Darnell will be served with the papers. Now this will probably spark some kind of retaliation."

Madisyn didn't have to guess what Chase wasn't saying. "So I need to watch my back. Actually, tomorrow night I'll have the perfect bodyguard."

The men looked at her in confusion. Aidan couldn't figure out what was going on in her stubborn brain. Maybe she was going to spend time at her parents? "What do you mean, Madisyn?"

She grinned. "Don't tell me you forgot our dinner date tomorrow night? Remember, my niece is spending the night and you said you'd bring dinner," she reminded him.

With everything that had happened to Madisyn in the last twenty-four hours, Aidan couldn't remember anything. "Sorry, baby, I forgot."

Chase cleared his throat again at Aidan's slip of the tongue. Or was it? Maybe he wanted Chase to know how much Madisyn meant to him.

"So, are you still coming tomorrow night?" Madisyn looked at him with those big green eyes, daring him to say no.

"Of course. I'll bring dinner, just like I promised. I'll come over as soon as you're home from work." He kissed Madisyn on the cheek.

"See, I have the best bodyguard money can buy." She kissed him gently on the lips. "And worth every penny."

Aidan pulled Madisyn into his arms and kissed her fully. He didn't care what Chase thought. He just wanted to keep his woman safe.

CHAPTER 14

Wednesday morning, Madisyn thought she was going to lose her ever-loving mind. Besides Aidan playing babysitter to her last night, he'd blabbed to her family and now her brothers had gotten into the act.

She was still simmering with anger when her brother arrived at her house to drive her to work that morning. As good-natured as Michael was, Madisyn was giving him the blues.

"Look, Maddie," Michael said when the silence in the car became unbearable. "I know you're mad Aidan spilled the beans, but Darnell could hurt you and I'm not about to let that happen."

Madisyn stared at her brother. "You seem to forget I'm an adult, Mike, and can handle my own business. I'll take care of Aidan later."

"He's only looking out for you. How many men do you know who would go to all this trouble?"

Madisyn had to admit, if to no one but herself, that few men would indeed go to all this trouble to keep a woman safe.

"Maddie, I like Aidan. He's very straightforward and hates Darnell as much as I do. I know you think you can handle Darnell, but he's pulled the wool over your eyes before, and he could do it again." He took a deep breath.

"And before you get your back up about Darnell, listen to what I'm saying."

"And what would that be?" She really hated when Mike got this 'I'm right, so listen' voice.

"We've all been there, Maddie. Don't think you're the first person to be tricked by someone they trusted. You're not. Darnell was too slick for his own good and you finally saw through it. I just don't want you to backslide."

"I think catching him in bed with that tramp was all the proof I needed, and that wasn't even the first time. I won't be backsliding or anything else anytime soon. I think that's why I'm so cautious with Aidan."

Mike pulled up to her office building and parked. "Aidan is good people. He does what he says he going to do. He came to church with you and had dinner with our family. He even played with Megan. I don't know many men who would do that. I know in the two years you were with Darnell, he never set foot inside the church and he didn't like Megan."

Madisyn couldn't argue with her brother about that. Aidan was very different from Darnell in every sense of the word. He was kind, supportive, gentle and too easy to talk to. "He's also coming this Sunday. He wants to see me teach Sunday school."

Michael smiled broadly. "See what I mean? My money is on Aidan. See you at five o'clock. Marcus is bringing Megan over about six."

Madisyn shook her head as she released the seat belt. As much as the men in her family got on her nerves, she could never stay mad at them long. "Yeah, yeah, I guess.

We'll just have to see, won't we? Marcus isn't going to drool over Aidan again, is he?"

Mike laughed. "Of course. Why do you think he jumped at the chance to bring Meg over? Just be thankful it's date night for him and Rasheeda or there would have been four for dinner."

Madisyn slid out of the car. "Thank goodness for date night. Thanks, Mikey." She closed the door before he could tell her how much he hated that nickname.

She was still laughing as she entered the office building and headed for the coffee shop. After she got her morning fill of caffeine she headed to her office.

"Madisyn, where's your car?" Keisha asked as she walked toward her desk. Today's ensemble was a black suit with a skirt Madisyn thought was too short for the office, but right for Keisha. She glanced past Madisyn's shoulder to Mr. Bridges's darkened office. "Is the master in?"

Madisyn chuckled as she turned on her computer. "Will you let that go? He's just settling in."

Keisha shrugged. "Where's your ride? Didn't I see your brother dropping you off? I was hoping to get a glimpse of Aidan today."

"Sorry, it was Mike. He was feeling charitable so he picked me up this morning." She hoped the lie sounded a lot stronger to Keisha than to her own ears.

"Is something going on with you, Maddie? You can tell me. Has Darnell done something to you?"

"Why on earth would you assume such a thing?" Madisyn tried to focus on her work to calm her nerves.

She knew today was going to be a test of wills because today was the day Darnell would be served with the restraining order.

"No reason. I know he probably wants to get back with you in the worst way, so there's no telling what he could or would do."

She retrieved her boss's email and prepared his daily calendar. "Well, I can handle him. If he hadn't cheated so much, I wouldn't be having this problem right now."

"Maybe you drove him to it," Keisha said. "Maybe he couldn't take all that family togetherness and wanted you all to himself. Maybe he likes spontaneity."

"Maybe he forgot the meaning of monogamous too? I thought you didn't like him because he was an invest-ment banker and played the corporate game?"

"No, I didn't like him because of what he was doing to you and why he was dating you." Keisha glanced at her gold watch. "Gotta go. My boss is timing me. Somebody ratted me out and he has people watching me constantly. I think it was the master." She gave Madisyn a princess wave and scurried down the long corridor to her cubicle.

That afternoon, Darnell sat in the weekly meeting of his superiors at Harland, Collins and Roarke, hoping that Daniel Harland would just shut up and adjourn the meeting already. He yawned as he gazed out of the window on the twenty-third floor of the Danite building in downtown Dallas.

"Are we keeping you from something, Darnell?" Daniel asked impatiently.

Darnell quickly answered. "No, sir."

"According to our records, we haven't received your RSVP yet. The annual dinner is in less than a month. I can't tell you how important that evening is to the firm. And I can't wait to see the expression on Madisyn's beautiful face when we announce your promotion to senior investment banker. It would be a great to time to announce your engagement."

Darnell knew exactly how important the annual dinner was to Harland, Collins and Roarke. The firm was very big on family traditions and moral values, and Harland adored Madisyn. He was constantly asking Darnell when he was going to marry her. He decided a little misdirection was in order. "You know how women are, sir. Madisyn wants to find the perfect dress before I can respond about the annual dinner."

Bradley's tanned face beamed. "You just tell her anything she wears will look beautiful on her."

"Yes, sir." Darnell hated knowing that Madisyn held the key to his future at the firm, not graduating top in his class at Princeton or the work he'd done.

Harland adjourned the meeting but asked Darnell to stay behind. Once they were alone in the room, the charming smile was gone and a very serious look clouded the older man's tanned face. "There's someone waiting in the lobby to see you."

Darnell nodded, thinking it was Madisyn; she must have finally come to her senses. He walked to the lobby and his heart sank. It wasn't Maddie, but a young man dressed in a Dallas County Constable uniform.

"Darnell Whitfield?"

"Yes."

He handed Darnell a folded piece of paper. "Sorry, man." He left the lobby without another word.

Harland walked up behind him. "Darnell, our firm is known for our choice of employees. We try to avoid scandals at any cost. In the past, you have led quite a colorful life and your career has hung in the balance. It wasn't until you started dating Madisyn that your life settled down and you became the type of employee that we want. A constable only delivers certain types of papers. I trust there's nothing wrong between you and Madisyn or that you have not fathered a child out of wedlock. I know our values are old-fashioned but we're an old-fashioned firm. I'd hate for a moment's indiscretion to cost you your job."

"I'm sure it's an error, sir."

"I hope for your sake it is."

Darnell didn't dare open the paper in front of his boss. In addition, eyes were everywhere in the lobby. He didn't even trust his own office for something this important. Claiming he was meeting a client, Darnell left the office early.

He didn't read the paper until he was in the comfort of his condo. He read the name on the paper three times. Chase Hartman. Chase Hartman. Chase Hartman. Where had he heard that name before? He racked his brain. Then suddenly it hit him. Hard. Although Dallas was a large metropolitan city, the number of high-profile black attorneys was few. Hartman had only one client. Aidan Coles. Why was he filing a restraining order against him? Darnell might have followed Aidan and Madisyn, but that wasn't against the law. Something wasn't making sense. He quickly dialed the number listed.

The phone picked up on the first ring. "Chase Hartman," a woman said. "Can I help you?"

Darnell took a deep breath. He wasn't going to lose his temper, at least not yet. "Yes, I received an order from the courts today and it's signed by Chase Hartman."

"Yes, that's correct," the woman answered quickly. She didn't even pretend to look up the information. She just started rattling off directives. "It's effective immediately. You're not to come within five hundred feet of Ms. Madisyn O'Riley or any member of her immediate family."

"What does this have to do with Madisyn?"

"The order is on her behalf. Her name is right below Mr. Hartman's. You are also not to come to her place of employment, church or day spa. I can give you the names of those places if necessary."

"No, I really don't need you to give me the names." Darnell didn't like this woman's tone. He could easily imagine her laughing at his expense. He really hated that.

"Is there anything else I can help you with, Mr. Whitfield?"

"No, nothing else," Darnell said through gritted teeth. The fury that was slowly building inside his body was ebbing away in that same fashion as a plan of revenge formed in Darnell's mind. Madisyn was going to pay for every embarrassing moment he had endured.

———

"You know, Mike, you don't have to stay until Marcus gets here. He's just going to drop Megan off," Madisyn hinted as she unlocked her front door. He'd picked her up from work as promised, but enough was enough. She wanted a few minutes' solitude before her niece or Aidan got there.

"And I told you I'm staying until Aidan gets here. That's our deal, take it or leave it." He closed the front door and locked it. "Actually, you'd don't have an option. I'm here until Aidan gets here. Stay here. I'm going to check the back door." Madisyn knew how stubborn her brother was, especially where safety was concerned, so she just nodded and sat on the couch. She didn't have the heart to tell him that there was no way Darnell would be stupid enough to show his face after the restraining order was delivered. She turned on the television while she waited on her brother to return.

As she listened to the local news anchorman describe the devastation of the last raid in the war zone, the doorbell rang. Madisyn was about to answer it, when her brother halted her moves with only his voice.

"Don't you dare answer that door," he boomed, walking in the living room. He was carrying a large brown envelope in his hands. "This was on your back step."

He didn't hand the envelope to her, but she could see her name was scribbled on it in red. At first she assumed it was a red marker, but closer inspection made her tremble. "Is that blood?"

"No, it's paint. There's no return address, but it's got to be from Darnell." He sat the package down on the table as he walked to the front door. "Don't you dare touch it."

Madisyn huffed. "I know. Fingerprints." She wanted her life back. Curiosity started to get the better of her, and she walked to the table to closer inspect the envelope, but Mike's order stopped her.

"I told you to leave the damn thing alone. I mean that," he called from the entryway.

In all her years Mike had never used that tone with her. She now understood why her nephews were so mindful of their father. "All right. You win, big brother." She walked back to her seat on the sofa.

She heard him open the front door and welcome Marcus and Megan inside. Soon she heard the happy squeal of her niece. Meagan appeared around the corner dressed in a cute little blue jean dress with big yellow daisies on it. Megan crawled up on the couch and gave Megan a big hug.

"Miss you," she said, easing herself into Madisyn's lap. "Eat."

No matter what angst Madisyn was feeling, Megan took all that away. Her chubby little face beamed with excitement. "Sorry, baby. Food isn't here yet. I guess he's running late."

Marcus's green eyes lit up. He reminded Madisyn of a little boy at his first professional football game. "You mean Aidan is really coming over tonight? I thought Mike was just messing with me." He sat down in the chair. "I think I'll wait too."

Madisyn shook her head. "Oh, no, you don't. It's date night, so you get going. You can see Aidan this Sunday at church." She dangled the carrot in front of her brother. She had to give him an incentive not to miss date night.

"He's coming back to church this Sunday? How cool! So are you dating him? Is it serious? It must be serious if he's going to all this trouble. I can't believe Darnell is acting like this."

Madisyn laughed. "You know you're worse than Mom. You ask me a million different things at once. Now how am I supposed to answer all those questions?"

Marcus smiled. "Gotcha. Answer the most important one first. And before you ask which one is most important, it's the one about Aidan."

"Yes, he's coming to church again. He wants to see me teach Sunday school. At the moment we're friends and that's all. I think he's taking my security very personally."

Marcus nodded. "Okay, since he's coming on Sunday, I won't stay. I know Mike isn't leaving until he gets here." Marcus rose and walked to his daughter and kissed her. "I'll see you tomorrow, Megan. Be good. Mommy will come get you in the morning."

Megan nodded and hugged her father. "Bye, Daddy."

Marcus looked at Madisyn. "If it's too much, let me know and we'll come get her. I know you got a lot going on right now."

"No, I need Megan here," Madisyn said. "Tonight she's my little chaperone."

Mike walked back in the room, joining the conversation. "Maybe I should stay, too. Didn't you say he was bringing dinner?"

The last thing Madisyn needed was Mike watching Aidan's every move. "No, guys. I'm perfectly safe. What was in the envelope?"

Mike took a deep breath. "Darnell is just venting. He's just trying to scare you with all this."

Madisyn knew her brother was dancing around the pole. He was trying to spare her from bad news, but this time Madisyn wasn't having it. "Please tell me or show me what was in the envelope."

"Okay, Maddie," Michael sighed, pulling a photo out of the envelope. "It's a photo of you with gashes going through it, Maddie, I'm sorry."

Madisyn suddenly felt cold. Was it fright? Was it fury? Darnell had taken just about everything he could from her. "I'm sorry, too. At first, I thought I could handle this, but Mike, he's irrational and I don't know what to expect next. I can't believe he's acting like this." She thought for a minute. "Well, yes, I can. When he wants something bad enough, there's nothing Darnell won't do."

"So I guess you won't fight me on taking you to work?"

"At least not right now, even though I don't want Darnell thinking I'm scared of him and am running to my family to protect me. It gives him the power and I don't want that. I wish there was a way to stop him right now."

Mike nodded. "You still got your pepper spray?"

"Yes."

"Well, I'll wait until Aidan gets here, then I'll leave."

"Thank you."

———

Aidan arrived at Madisyn's house and noticed a strange car in the driveway. He knew it wasn't Darnell's car, thanks to Chase and his connections. He hoped it belonged to one of Madisyn's brothers. He parked the Escalade in front of her house, reached for the bags containing dinner, and got out of the car.

The front door opened before he could ring the doorbell. Madisyn was dressed in a cotton dress that seemed made for her body. It hugged her hips and had just enough cleavage to make him hard as concrete. It was going to be a long night.

"Aidan, how nice to see you. Megan and I were tempted to order pizza," she teased, reaching for one of the bags. "Come in, Mike is waiting to talk to you."

Oh, that didn't sit well with him. Chase had already told him about the phone call to his office. Hopefully Darnell hadn't done anything yet. Aidan wasn't prepared for a battle, but if it was for this woman, he would walk through the den of hell to keep her safe from harm. He followed Madisyn into the house. Mike greeted him as they entered the dining room. He didn't like the serious look on Mike's face. "Hey, Mike. You wanted to talk to me?"

CHAPTER 15

Mike stared at Aidan with the same intense green eyes as Madisyn. "Yeah, why don't we talk in Maddie's office, so little ears won't hear." He nodded in Megan's direction.

Aidan's heart sank as he realized this was going to be a serious conversation, not two guys discussing the latest Cowboy acquisitions. "Sure, man." He followed Mike into another section of Madisyn's house.

After they were settled in two very comfortable club chairs, Mike began. "Aidan, I'm not the type of guy to say a lot of flowery things, especially when it comes to Maddie. I'm going to cut right to the chase. Darnell means to cause Maddie real harm." He told him about the envelope with the mutilated photo. "My brothers and I are willing to do anything to make sure that this doesn't happen. Are you with us?"

Aidan wasn't shocked at Mike's attitude about Madisyn. "Yeah, man I'm with you. I've only known Madisyn a few weeks, but I know her well enough to know that she's not going to take this sitting down. I mean, yes, this is very real, and she'll cooperate to an extent, but she likes being her own person."

"True. But she's my younger sister and sometimes she doesn't know what's good for her. She's got a big heart and that gets her in trouble." Mike looked directly at Aidan.

He wanted to shrink away from that icy stare Mike was giving him, but this was for Madisyn, so the price wasn't too high. "What's your plan?"

Mike smiled. "My plan is we can take turns being her bodyguard. Yes, she's going to bitch about it, but in the end, she'll cooperate. With Darnell acting like a nut, we're going to have to up our game. With some strategic planning, we can have her covered most of the time. Since it's summer, I can take her to work and pick her up. I'm sure you'll have most of the evenings covered with the charity, right?"

Aidan nodded, knowing he was lying. The time he wanted to spend with Madisyn had nothing to do with the charity. "Yes, we need to discuss the grand opening dinner she has to plan."

"Good." Mike rose. "We'd better get back or Megan and Madisyn will wonder what happened to us." He headed for the living room.

Aidan followed Mike silently, mostly thinking about Mike's pledge to keep Madisyn safe. It made Aidan respect him all the more.

When they entered the room, Madisyn and Megan weren't there. They had set the table and were eating the meal. He'd bought steaks for him and Madisyn, and chicken for Megan.

"Sorry, we just couldn't wait any longer." Madisyn nodded at the vacant place. "Take a seat."

Mike took the cue like a man. "Well, guys, I'll see you later. Maddie, see you in the morning."

Aidan expected her to fight her brother, but Madisyn only nodded. "I need to get to work early. So could you get here about seven?"

Mike nodded and left. Aidan took a seat at the table and placed the cloth napkin in his lap. Madisyn had already prepared his food and poured him a glass of wine. He looked at the rose-colored liquid, but his mind was still on Madisyn.

"I'm sorry, I don't have any beer," Madisyn explained.

"I usually try to have some when the boys come over but I haven't had time to go shopping with all that's happened lately."

He shook his head. "It's not that, baby. What changed your mind about getting escorts?"

"The photo. I decided that if Mike thinks it's an issue, I should just go with it. Darnell is beyond rational thinking right now and I want to stay safe." She cut her steak and took a bite. "This is really good, Aidan."

She was trying to change the subject. "Thanks, babe. But I didn't cook it, I just paid for it." He glanced at Megan, who was busy eating her grilled chicken leg as if it were the finest cut of meat on the planet.

"Nothing, just as I said before," Madisyn turned her attention to her niece. "Honey, are you about finished?"

Megan nodded, but kept attacking her food. Apparently she got her healthy appetite from her aunt. She looked at Madisyn with those adorable brown eyes and lifted her small plate to Madisyn. "More?"

"Of course, baby." Madisyn rose and placed another piece of chicken on her plate. "Here you go."

Madisyn returned to eating her steak. She glanced at Aidan and his uneaten steak. "You'd better eat that or I will." She smiled at him as she cut another piece of steak.

He looked at her, knowing she was quite serious. "Okay, I'm eating." He sliced the meat, then took a bite. Delicious.

His eyes met Madisyn's. He could really get used to looking at those green eyes across the table.

———

Two hours later as Madisyn read her niece the usual bedtime story, her mind wasn't on the story of the fairy tale prince. It was on the events of the evening. She sat on the edge of her queen-sized bed, which she shared with her niece every Wednesday night. Tonight, Madisyn was glad to have someone share her bed, even if that person was a three-year-old.

She knew Darnell was capable of terrible things and she hoped it didn't come to that. All of the problems Darnell had were caused by Darnell, she reminded himself. None of it was her fault.

"Night, night, Auntie," Megan said on a yawn.

Madisyn had been so deep in thought she hadn't realized she'd stopped reading to Megan or that she was falling asleep. She kissed her niece on her forehead. "Night, baby." She stood, walked to the large bay window and made sure the locks were secured. She took one more look at her dark backyard before closing the drapes. Then she went downstairs to Aidan.

He was waiting for her on the couch when she returned to the living room. Madisyn inhaled and took a seat beside him. He wrapped her in his arms and kissed her.

Aidan's kisses blocked out all the events of the evening. They snuggled on the couch in each other's arms with barely air between them. Now this was what all those romance novels were talking about, she thought.

"I know this evening has been a lot for you to take in. How do you feel about it?" he whispered against her swollen lips.

"I don't know," Madisyn kissed his thick neck, his cheek, his ears and then finally his mouth.

Aidan put some space between them, so he could have Madisyn's total attention. "I want to make sure you're safe. Do you have any concerns?"

He pulled her back in his arms and just held her, rubbing her back. Madisyn heard the rapid beat of his heart. "I'm really concerned for Megan," she finally said.

"Did he threaten her? Baby, tell me."

"No," she said against his chest, "he didn't threaten her." It felt wonderful to be held in comfort. The sexual tension was still there, but this was good, too.

"Tell me," he pleaded. "I have to know. I won't be able to sleep tonight as it is, but I have to know what we're up against."

"You know even in this crisis you still say the right things to me, things that turn me to Jell-o."

His laugh rumbled in his chest, vibrating against her. "Well, right now you're saying all the things that turn me on. But this is neither the time nor the place. Tell me what happened."

"Darnell hasn't actually threatened Megan, but he knows how much she means to me. I think he wouldn't be above hurting her to get to me."

Aidan shook his head. "My God. I'd hope Darnell wouldn't stoop so low."

"The last year or so, most of the fights Darnell and I had were over Megan."

"Please don't tell me he was jealous of her?"

"Yes, he was. We'd argue over the time I spent with Megan. You see, we've been having Wednesday night sleep-over for the last two years so Marcus and his wife can have date night. As you know, Megan is a one-child demolition squad. Darnell thought she shouldn't spend the night with me, 'cause I wouldn't let him stay when she did."

"You mean he didn't try to convince you to let him stay anyway?"

Madisyn laughed, but it wasn't a happy laugh. It was full of misery. Two years of misery with the wrong man. "Oh, he tried, but that was the one area I wouldn't bend to his will. He started calling Megan my reason for living. And he was right."

"Madisyn, Madisyn, Madisyn, why did you let that idiot control you like that?" He kissed away her tears. "You're a beautiful woman and you deserve a man who appreciates what a great woman you are."

"Aidan, you're so good for my ego. Thank you." She snuggled closer to him. "It's a good thing Megan is here or I'd show you my appreciation."

"Time and place, baby. Let's get Darnell in jail, first. Then we can appreciate each other until we fall asleep."

"Sounds like a plan."

CHAPTER 16

"Of all the times for Mike to be on time," Madisyn grumbled the next morning as she continued getting Megan ready for daycare. Megan was much like her aunt in the fact that she didn't like getting up any earlier than she had to. She fought Madisyn at every turn, thus delaying getting dressed even further. "Come on, baby, Uncle Mike is already here and you haven't had breakfast yet."

Megan yawned. Her little eyes fluttered closed and she flopped back on the bed.

Madisyn sighed. They were so close to being ready. All she had to do was put on Meg's sandals and they'd be dressed. And now her brother was beating on the front door. She scooped up Meg and the tiny sandals and headed for the living room. She opened the door and greeted her brother. "Hey, I'm glad you're here. Unfortunately, Rasheeda hasn't showed up yet."

Mike entered the house, closed and locked the door. "Yeah, I know, she just called me and asked me to bring Meg home with me. They overslept." Mike had a sly smile on his face. "You know how it is."

Madisyn adjusted Meg in her arms. "No, how is it?" She walked to the couch and struggled with Meg to finally slide her sandals on her feet. "How about

McDonald's for breakfast? I'm sure Uncle Mike will take you when he drops me off for work."

Meg nodded. "Yeah!" She clapped her small hands together several times and ran to the front door. "Ready!"

Madisyn laughed. "Not yet. Play with Uncle Mike until I get back." She went to gather her purse and brief-case. When she returned to the living room, Meg was in Mike's lap telling him all about her time with Aidan.

"Then Uncle Aidan told me about when he was little like me. He misses his daddy."

Mike looked up at Madisyn to explain, but she only shook her head and mouthed the word "later" to him. He nodded.

"I bet you miss your daddy, too." Mike stood with Megan in his arms. "Hey, I hope you still have that spare car seat, 'cause I came in the SUV."

"Yeah, it's in the garage." Since she kept her niece often, Madisyn had had the good sense to purchase a car seat. Besides, it was the law.

Mike nodded, heading for the garage, and Madisyn gathered up her niece. When Mike returned they headed to his SUV after he made sure Madisyn's house was secured.

"So, you hear anything from Darnell?" Mike asked in a low voice, as soon as the DVD started playing a movie for Megan.

Madisyn should have known Mike's inquisition was coming. "No, not a word."

Mike navigated onto I-35, heading for downtown Dallas. "Good. So why the face?"

"Megan. I'm worried that Darnell might use Meg to get back at me. I don't know what I'd do if something happened to her and it was my fault."

Mike dared a glance in her direction. "You think he'd stoop so low as to threaten a little girl? He's going to an awful lot of trouble trying to get you back. I don't understand why this time was so different for you."

"This time is different because I'm tired, Mike. I see you and Angie, Marcus and Rasheeda, and how happy you guys are together. I want that. I don't want someone who doesn't appreciate me. I want someone to savor me. To be glad I'm in their life."

"You think you got that with Aidan?"

Madisyn laughed. "I honestly don't know. I personally think he's too good to be true and his real side will come out soon."

"You think he's hiding something?"

"Or someone," Madisyn said honestly. "You just know there's a baby momma out there waiting to make an appearance. He's got this squeaky clean image with the press but he might be just another disaster waiting to happen."

"I know this Darnell stuff has got you all turned around, but I think Aidan is for real. I know men and we don't go to this much trouble for someone we don't care about."

Madisyn wasn't ready to put her heart on the line so soon after Darnell. "We'll just have to see what destiny has in store for me. Right now I just want this Darnell mess cleared up and over. I do think we need to keep an extra eye on Meg."

"Yeah, I agree on that. You know we're going to have to let the old folks in on what's happening," Mike said, referring to their parents. "Mom will be super POed if she finds out from some other source, like Darnell calling and threatening them."

Madisyn didn't want to venture down the road of "what if." It reminded her of Chase and his "let's cover this from all angles" talk. "Well, Aidan is coming to church Sunday again. That will be the perfect time to let everyone in the family know. I don't think Darnell will go near the boys since they're just as big as he is, but you never know," Madisyn said, thinking about Mike's teenaged sons.

"No, I can't see him being stupid enough to approach MJ or Marry, but Darnell isn't thinking clearly at the moment. I'll make sure they watch their step." He parked in front of her office building. "That goes for you, too. You'd better watch out for Keisha. There's something about her I just don't like."

Madisyn unbuckled her seat belt and slid out of the passenger seat. Her brother wasn't the first person to warn her about Keisha. Maybe it was time to start listening to all those people. "I know. But we've been friends forever, and sometimes it's hard to cut the cord with old friends."

"And sometimes that cord will hang you. Just think about what I said earlier. I'll see you this evening."

Madisyn nodded. She knew her brother was right. It was time to cut her ties to Keisha. But how? It would definitely have to be done delicately. Maybe Chayla would have some answers.

Sweat dripped down Aidan's face as he tried to run all his demons away. After such a romantic evening with Madisyn he realized he'd been running from a lot of things. His relationship with her had taken a new turn, a turn he wasn't quite ready to take, but he was glad it happened. He thought he could care for her from a distance and his heart not get too involved. Last night he'd contemplated staying at Madisyn's so she could thank him the way she really wanted.

But that would have been a costly pleasure. Not only because her niece was spending the night, but because of his own celebrity. Too many people knew the black Cadillac Escalade and it would have been on the news this morning.

Right now the most important thing to Aidan was to find out where exactly Darnell was hiding and who was hiding him. He'd taken a leave of absence from work and had all but dropped off the surface of the earth. The detective he'd hired had already searched Darnell's house and had come up empty.

He stopped the treadmill as the idea popped into his head. Megan needed security. He picked up his phone and dialed Chase.

He picked up on the first ring. "Why can't I have a client who doesn't wake up until ten or eleven in the morning? You do realize it's barely eight," he groaned as he came fully awake. "Man, one of these times, I'm going to not answer the phone."

Aidan laughed, knowing his friend was always grumpy in the mornings. "Chase, I need some security for Megan."

"Who's Megan? And why the security? What happened to Madisyn?"

"Nothing happened to Madisyn. Megan is her three-year-old niece. Darnell may turn his anger toward her in order to get to Madisyn. I want a security guard for her."

"Whoa, Aidan, you're overstepping the bounds of a boyfriend, friend with benefits, or whatever you are to Madisyn. This is going to take some delicate handling. You should discuss this with Megan's parents first."

Aidan filled his friend in on the latest news and the schedule he and Madisyn's brothers had come up with to drive her to and from work. Chase shook his head with disbelief. "I'm glad you guys are together on this."

"Madisyn doesn't want anything to happen to Megan."

Chase snorted. "And that's why we're having this conversation? I think you need a ghost."

"I need a what?" Aidan sat down on his weight bench. Chase wasn't making any sense. So he knew this was going to be heavy. "What are you talking about?"

"I'm talking a form of security so secret that the protectee doesn't know he's there. If you hire a traditional security guard or bodyguard, for that matter, everyone is going to start acting differently and alerting Darnell. We know there's a leak and someone is feeding Darnell information. This way we could find out who."

"So this person wouldn't be known to anyone in Madisyn's family? How's he or she going to protect her if she's not inside the house? What happens if Darnell gets inside?"

"It won't happen," Chase said confidently.

"How can you assure me of that?"

"Have I ever led you down the wrong path?"

"No, man, you have never led me wrong. This ghost stuff is new to me. I mean, how will I know they're doing their job?"

Chase chuckled. "I guess you're just going to have to trust that I know what I'm talking about. I've used this company a few times over the years. They're always on the money and no one ever knows."

"How?"

"Remember about two years ago when that girl tried to blackmail you, saying that she was pregnant with your baby?"

Aidan had almost forgotten about Michelle, his last slip in judgment. "Vividly."

"She was trying to extort money from you, saying she needed it for an abortion," Chase supplied. "Then she suddenly stopped harassing you."

"Yeah, she said it was a mistake."

"It was a mistake, all right. I had a ghost following her and got the information I needed. She was pregnant, but it wasn't your baby."

Aidan was stunned. Chase to the rescue again. "Man. I had no idea. I don't pay you enough."

"Sure you do. This makes up for all the other times when your life is sooo boring. I'll get working on security for both Madisyn and Megan and will let you know."

Aidan knew both Madisyn and Megan would be in good hands. "I still have the detective searching for Darnell. He's taking an extended leave from his job, so he's not there or at his condo. I'm looking into some of his lady friends."

"He's slick, Aidan. You need to be careful, too. I'm surprised he hasn't outted you to the press. That would help his cause."

Aidan knew why Darnell hadn't run to the media. He couldn't take the chance of his bosses realizing that he was not with Madisyn. "It's probably just a man thang."

CHAPTER 17

Thursday evening, Madisyn just wanted some alone time. With Mike playing chauffeur she didn't have the option of solitude on the drive to and from work. Usually, she'd spend Thursday evenings reading or preparing for her Sunday school class, but instead she was waiting for the changing of the guard.

Mike sat on the couch as Madisyn prepared for Aidan's visit. Supposedly, they were going to go over the budget for Mature Alliance and discuss plans for the grand opening. She didn't even have luxury of going shopping for dinner. Aidan had promised to pick something up for them. She sighed, just wishing this whole mess with Darnell was already over. Madisyn wanted her life back.

"Maddie, I know this is getting to you, but it's all for your own good. But I do like spending this time with you."

She hated to admit it, but she liked spending time with him, too. "I only wish it wasn't a have-to situation. I just wish this was over."

"Me too, baby girl. I checked with Rasheeda and Meg is fine. She's playing in her room. And yes, the mike is on where she can hear Meg." He glanced at his watch. "What time is Aidan coming over?"

"About seven. You know you can go home if you need to," Madisyn hinted. Maybe she could have an hour of private time.

Mike laughed. "Girl, you know I'm not leaving until I see Aidan in the house."

"Yeah, I know. You want something to drink?"

"I'd love a beer, but I know you don't have any. I guess we can go to the store tomorrow after you get off work."

Madisyn laughed at her brother. "You try to make it sound like such a grand gesture. We both know I have the charity meeting tomorrow night, so I can't go shopping. Maybe we can do it Saturday after Aidan's cooking lesson?"

He knew he was backed into a corner and there was no way out. "All right. I'll pick you up about two."

"Deal."

Aidan pulled up in front of Madisyn's house with a few minutes to spare. Thank God, Chase was efficient. The ghost was already in place. Aidan had listened carefully as Chase rattled off instructions.

"Don't worry about anything. No one will ever know the ghost is in place. I've already gotten a report. The kid is fine and watching TV in her room. I can't believe they let her watch television. At least it was something educational."

"Man, let it go. This is not about what she's watching as long as she's safe. Maybe this is her unwinding time."

"She's three years old," Chase said. "I see where your loyalty is now."

Aidan laughed. "You're wrong. I just don't want to see anything happen to that little girl. How will I know the ghost is doing his job?"

"You won't," Chase sighed. "I know you're going to keep on until I tell you something about the company I'm using, so here goes. The leader of the team is a female and is the best at what she does. She has an intelligence background. I'd trust her with my life."

Aidan wanted to know more about this woman his friend trusted so much. "Who will I make the check out to?"

"Forget it. You'll never know her name. Hell, I barely know her name. You'll make the check out to cash and will be instructed where to wire the money when this is over."

Aidan knew that was about as good as he was going to get, so he dropped the subject of the ghost. "In other words, I should let you handle your business," Aidan said in his most hip-hop voice.

"Exactly." Chase ended the call.

Aidan got out of the SUV, grabbed the bags and walked the few steps to Madisyn's front door.

She greeted him before he could ring the doorbell. She was definitely dressed for the Texas heat in a tank top that hugged her chest and a pair of blue cotton capris. "Hey, Aidan." She kissed him quickly on the lips before guiding him inside. "I was just telling Mike that he didn't have to stay, but as usual he refused." She took the sack from Aidan, heading for the kitchen.

"Good man." Aidan walked into the living room and shook Mike's hand. "I'm glad she didn't talk you into leaving."

Mike grinned. "I take her safety very seriously." He looked at Madisyn as she entered the room. "Now that you're here, I'll let you guys have some private time." He kissed his sister on the cheek. "See you in the morning." He left the house without another word.

"Your brother doesn't waste words, does he?" Aidan gestured for Madisyn to take a seat. When she obliged him, he sat next to her. "But I'm glad he's so smart." He pulled Madisyn in his arms and kissed her the way he'd been wanting.

When they finally came up for air, they were both panting like marathon runners. "Well, Aidan, that was definitely worth the wait. Are you hungry?"

Now that he had her in his arms, he didn't want to let her go. "I'd rather have you."

Those pretty green eyes told him that she felt the same. But he didn't want to rush her. There was too much going on in her life to try to seduce her. Her thought processes weren't working properly. Only a heel would try to make love to her now. But he felt her curious hands traveling under his cotton shirt, and he knew he had no more control over the situation than she did.

"Are you going to kiss me or do you want to eat dinner?"

Aidan didn't answer her. He devoured her mouth. "Does that answer your question?"

Madisyn nodded. "I think you better give me your answer again."

Aidan pulled her onto his lap as close as humanly possible. "With pleasure." He kissed her soft lips, willing his body to calm down so they could both enjoy the evening.

He was lost in her kisses and her responses to his wandering hands when she suddenly stopped and eased off his lap. "Aidan, this just won't do."

He groaned in pain. She was right. This wasn't the time or the place. He closed his eyes while the lower half of his body realized there would be no sex tonight. "You're right, baby. Let's eat dinner."

"I wasn't quite thinking in those terms, Aidan," she said softly. "I was thinking more in the terms of going to my bedroom."

Aidan's eyes snapped opened at the direct proposition. Madisyn stood in front of him, smiling and extending her hand. He took it, of course. After he stood, he hugged her. "Are you sure?"

She stood on her tiptoes and kissed him. "Does it feel like I'm sure?"

Aidan gave up trying to fight the emotions surging through his body. He rubbed against her, inhaling her scent and letting it fuel his desire for her. He picked her up and carried to what he hoped was her bedroom.

"That's the guest room," she said laughing. "My room is down the hall." She unbuttoned his shirt. "You know you're the first man to pick me up like I was Scarlett O'Hara from *Gone with the Wind*."

Aidan couldn't answer her at the moment. He was too busy trying to concentrate on walking at a steady pace instead of a full-out run. He kissed her when she started chattering on about the classic movie. Their lips didn't part until they were at her bedroom door.

∞∞∞

Madisyn knew it was too late to change her mind. Not that she wanted to, but that option was gone. She and Aidan were actually going to make love. She should feel nervous, but she didn't. This was right. Aidan cared about her and she cared about him.

He put her down and she moved toward the bed with Aidan following her silently. He motioned for her to sit on the bed. Madisyn realized what a mistake that was a little too late. She was face to face with the open shirt. She stared at his chiseled stomach and sighed. She'd known he was fine, but in fact he was a work of art. His hazelnut skin was pulled tight over rock-hard muscle. "You're beautiful, Aidan," she whispered as her hands glided over his chest and stomach, remembering each hill, valley and plane of his upper body.

"Baby, you're beautiful." He pulled her to her feet and made quick work of her blouse and bra. "You're beyond beautiful." His hands gently kneaded her breasts before kissing each one.

As he began sucking on her breasts, Madisyn felt her world go fuzzy. Her legs wouldn't hold her upright anymore. She fell back on the bed, letting him do what he

Madisyn decided she liked being in the driver's seat, so to speak. Now she knew what Keisha was always talking about. She watched in amazement as Aidan unbuttoned her shorts, brazenly slipped his large hand inside and headed straight for ground zero.

There wasn't much she could do, not that she wanted to do anything but keep the party going. Her body, of its own accord, moved against Aidan's skillful fingers. She felt her body screaming for more than just a touch; she needed it all.

As if reading her lusty thoughts, Aidan eased her beside him and helped her out of her shorts and panties, throwing them on the floor. She was in her birthday suit, and she didn't feel ashamed of her body. She felt beautiful and very proud of her frame. The way Aidan's brown eyes were eating her up, Beyoncé could have walked into the room and he wouldn't have noticed.

"Okay, Aidan. Your turn," Madisyn said softly.

"With pleasure," he said, struggling out of his shorts in record time.

Madisyn watched in amazement as he stood in front of her. He was a large man. Very large. She was beginning to rethink the whole logistics of the situation. "Th-the c-c-ondoms are in the b-b-b-bathroom."

He grinned at her nervousness. "I'll be gentle, baby. Don't you worry, I wouldn't hurt you for anything. Unless you ask me to." He winked at her as he strode into the bathroom. He returned quickly with a handful of condoms and placed them on the nightstand.

Madisyn moved to the middle of her bed. "You're feeling optimistic, huh?"

He sat down on the bed and stared at her naked body.

"I won't do anything you don't want me to," he whispered, reaching for a condom.

"I know that, Aidan. I know you wouldn't disrespect me. And I love you for that, er, I mean I love that about you." She should have felt awkward with him in this situation, but she didn't. It was right. And so was he.

He leaned down and kissed her. "I know what you mean. I feel the same way." He ripped open the packet with his teeth and she watched as he slid it onto his erection.

Madisyn still had some reservations about him being able to fit, but the smile on Aidan's face made her want to try.

His mouth melted against hers as he slid next to her in bed. He pulled her on top of him and straddled her legs across his lean body. "Show me what you want," he said against her lips.

Madisyn looked at him and took the challenge. She took him deep inside her body and moved against him. His eyes fluttered closed, but his hands were planted on her waist, guiding her motions. With passion guiding her, she crushed her chest against his and kissed him with all the urgency of a horny teenager.

She couldn't believe it, but it was happening to her again, the sensation of pure pleasure coursing through her body heading straight for the border. She had no control over her body. It was hungry for Aidan and there wasn't anything she could do about it. Not that she wanted to. She just wanted more of this glorious feeling. Aidan increased the tempo as he held her closer, grinding her body to his as climax tore through them at the same exact moment and screams of delight filled the quiet room.

Grunts became moans. Moans became pants and finally settled into heaving breaths. "You were the best, baby," Aidan whispered against her neck as he eased her to his side. "Give me thirty minutes and we're going to do that again."

Madisyn chuckled as she stroked his sweaty back as their feet played a sultry game of touch. "I don't think I can. I don't think I could even manage a kiss right now."

He raised up on an elbow and looked at her. "Oh, I think we can try."

She rested her head on his chest, feeling a contentment she'd never felt with anyone. "Yes, we can. Later."

CHAPTER 18

Friday morning Aidan opened his eyes to a very strange room. Nothing looked familiar. Had he fallen asleep in the guest room again? Then he heard it. The soft sounds of Madisyn sleeping beside him.

She was lying on her side with her back facing him. Though the sheet covered most of her body, it was imprinted on his brain forever. Last night had been unscripted, but it was the greatest meal he'd ever missed. They never got around to eating dinner.

He snuggled close to her warm body and kissed her on the neck, letting his hands tease and tantalize her awake. It was barely six. They had time for a little fun before he had to leave. The last thing he needed was Mike finding them in bed together.

"Mmm, that feels wonderful." She turned over and faced him. She looked sensual and well loved. Her brown hair cascaded around her shoulders. "And if I didn't say it last night, you were spectacular."

"I feel exactly the same way, baby." He moved closer to her, pulled the sheet down to uncover her nude body. "In fact, I'm ready for an instant replay."

The look in her beautiful green eyes told him she was feeling the exact same thing. She reached for a condom packet and ripped it open with her teeth. "You don't mind if I do the honors?"

Aidan thought he'd died and gone to heaven. "Hell no. Do your thang, girl." He chuckled as he rested against the pillows. He instantly realized what a mistake he'd just made, but it was too late. Madisyn would probably torture him to no end in her quest to pleasure him. He'd just have to grin and bear it.

He watched as she leaned over him, and slid the condom on inch by excruciating inch over his shaft. He thought he'd climax before the action really got starred. "Baby, baby," he said, pulling her up for a kiss.

He rolled her over so that he was on top of her. "So wonderful," he murmured against her neck and entered her body.

"Oh," Madisyn moaned.

"Too much?" Aidan asked, ready to pull out, if necessary.

"Not enough," she sighed, tightening her feminine hold on him and wrapping her legs around him.

Aidan kissed Madisyn hungrily as he surged deep inside her. What was it about this woman that made him lose control and want to hear her scream for mercy? He didn't have time to think about that because Madisyn's hands were gliding over his chest and pinching his nipples. That was exactly when he lost it. He plunged deeper inside her until he had nowhere else to go. He increased his tempo to the sounds of her moans and touch of her hands. There was nowhere to go but to the stars. He didn't remember who climaxed first, only that it triggered an avalanche of orgasms.

When the fog finally cleared, they were both too tired to say anything. Aidan had just enough strength left in his exhausted body to kiss her on the forehead before sleep claimed them both.

※

Mike parked in front of Madisyn's house as he had done every day for the last week. But today something was different. Normally, his sister would greet him at the front door, but today, she hadn't even picked up her newspaper.

He got out of his truck and took out his set of his sister's house keys. He unlocked the front door, disabled the alarm and looked around the room. Nothing was out of place. The sack he saw Aidan bring in the house was still on the dining room table. After glancing inside the bag, he realized the food was untouched.

He heard footsteps down the hallway and went to investigate. "Maddie, what on earth?" He glanced at his sister's attire. It was almost eight in the morning, and she was still in her bathrobe, and she had the worst case of pillow hair he'd ever seen.

"Be quiet, Aidan's still asleep. I just woke up, so I'm going to take the day off. You know I don't like going into work late. So you can go back home."

"Like hell. I want to know where Aidan slept last night? Did he force himself on you?" Mike knew he was probably overstepping his bounds because his sister was an adult, capable of making her own decisions, but that was why they were in this mess right now.

Maddie grabbed his hand and dragged him to the living room. "Will you please be quiet?" She tightened the sash on her silk bathrobe. "I didn't do anything with him that I didn't want to. I can make my own decisions. Good or bad."

"I just don't want to see you get hurt. Don't get me wrong, I like Aidan. He's good people. But you're my main concern."

"I know that and I appreciate that, Mikey, but it's okay. Sometimes I can't believe how considerate Aidan is." She walked into the kitchen and opened her fridge. "I keep waiting for the other shoe to drop." She carried bacon and eggs to the counter. "Want some?"

If he was a nice brother, he would have made up some excuse and left so Maddie and Aidan could have some privacy. But he wasn't that nice a brother. "Sure, I'm starved." He sat down and watched his sister prepare breakfast.

"What do you mean, she's not at work? She's always at work," Darnell whined. "That's why she'd never go on a trip with me. She claimed she couldn't take off work or her family needed her."

"She never went anywhere with you because she knew you'd probably leave her stranded somewhere. She knew you weren't dependable," Keisha said.

"What's with the attitude? You're my only way in, so don't start. Is she sick or something?"

pleased. Aidan was relentless. He didn't let up or let go. He increased the pressure of his mouth. While his hot mouth tormented one breast, his hand massaged the other one. The intensity was too much for Madisyn. Her back arched as a feeling she hadn't felt in years made its way through her body.

"Come on, baby, I want to hear it," he whispered against her breast. "I want to hear you tell me how good it feels." He continued tormenting her.

Madisyn wanted to make the moment last longer, but her body was too greedy. She closed her eyes against the orgasm as it roared through her body. "Oh, Aidan!" She took a deep breath and smiled. "That was wonderful."

Aidan lifted his head and smiled at her. "You ain't seen nothing yet." He kissed her softly and sat up. "I hadn't planned on this happening this evening, and before we get to the point of no return, I have to know one thing. Okay maybe two."

What a time for this, Madisyn thought. He probably wanted to know if she still had any feelings for Darnell. "What?"

"Do you have any condoms? How many?"

Madisyn snorted at the serious look on his face. Then she glanced down at his erection. He was more than ready. "Yes, I have some. After I found out Darnell wasn't exactly the monogamous type, I wouldn't let him touch me without one."

Aidan nodded. "Sorry, didn't mean to bring him up. I promise I won't let you think about him again tonight." He lay beside her and took her in his arms until she was on top of him.

"I don't know. I can call and ask her, but that doesn't mean she's going to tell me. I think she's hiding something from me."

Darnell chuckled. Keisha thought she had the world by the balls just because she could work that skinny body of hers. The more he thought of Madisyn the more he regretted ever getting involved with Keisha. "Yeah, she's hiding something from you all right. Aidan Coles. He's at her place every night."

"How do you know that? What could Aidan want with her?"

"When he could have you?"

"Well, yeah," Keisha said. "I turned your head," she said smugly. "You were lying to her so you could see me. How do you know she's seeing him? Maybe it was just stuff to do with the charity."

"Are you trying to convince me or yourself?" Darnell didn't need Aidan anywhere near Madisyn. He didn't need the press getting wind of them dating or he'd definitely be in a world of trouble at work. It was hard enough getting near her with the restraining order hanging above his head. Now he had to figure out how to get around her iron curtain of a family.

Keisha sighed dramatically. "Right now, we need each other. You want to get Maddie back in your slimy clutches and I want Aidan for myself."

"You know, just 'cause this guy is loaded doesn't mean his barometer for evil is off, Keisha. As much as he's doing for Madisyn already, you have some fierce competition."

"Let the games began."

Aidan rolled over in an empty bed and his eyes snapped open. Madisyn's side of the bed was still warm. He glanced at her bedside clock. It was after eight in the morning. He was supposed to meet Chase at nine to discuss what he and Madisyn didn't go over last night about the upcoming grand opening at Mature Alliance.

He looked around for his cell phone and didn't find it. He did spot Madisyn's on the dresser. After he slipped on his boxers, he picked up the phone and immediately dialed his attorney's private line.

Chase answered on the second ring. "Chase Hartman."

"Hey, man," Aidan said.

"Aidan, I almost didn't answer the phone. Whose number is this?"

"That's why I called. I'm gonna need to postpone the meeting this morning. How about this afternoon?"

"Normally, it wouldn't be a problem, but I have a meeting, so I'll be out of the office. But just tell me what you guys discussed concerning the charity and I can handle the rest."

Aidan didn't want to be a "kiss and tell" kind of guy, but Chase was waiting for an answer and he had to think of something. "We kind of got sidetracked and the charity never came up," said Aidan.

"I bet something else did," Chase said over his laughter. "Since nothing was discussed, why did you still want to meet with me?"

"I just want to stay on top of things," Aidan said, already regretting the slip of the tongue.

"I think you already have been. If you guys happen to get anything done tonight concerning the charity, just let me know the details." Chase waited a beat before asking, "Where are you anyway?"

"I'm at Madisyn's."

"You do realize the position you've just placed her in. What if someone leaks it to the press that you spent the night at your girlfriend's house last night? Especially with Darnell wanting her back. He might up his game before we're ready."

Aidan hadn't given one thought to Darnell once he and Madisyn made love. He'd forgotten about the dangerous situation and had placed Madisyn in even more danger. "I parked in the garage, so my SUV isn't on the street announcing I spent the night."

Chase cleared his throat. "You do know you have to have breakfast with her. If you leave without having breakfast with her it will be like you were trying to hit it and leave."

"I'm here because I want to be. And I don't treat women like they're sex objects. That's not my style."

"Don't get your boxers in a knot," Chase said. "I know she's special to you and I want you to treat her well. She's not about your money. You might actually have to put your heart on the line for this one."

Aidan walked to the bedroom window and glanced out of the bay window. The neighborhood looked so peaceful. Everyone was going about his or her business with no knowledge that an NFL star was in their midst.

"Aidan?"

He snapped out of the zone he was in and remembered he had Chase on the phone. "I'm here."

"No, you're not. You're long gone, brother. Talk to you later."

Aidan chuckled as he pushed the end button on Madisyn's phone. He noticed Mike's truck out front. "Just great," he muttered. "He's going to think I took advantage of his little sister. He's probably going to kick me out of the house."

"Close, but no cigar," Madisyn said, entering the room. "He was ready to hang you from the nearest tree, but I convinced him otherwise. I just came to tell you that breakfast will be ready in about ten minutes."

Aidan looked at her. "No good-morning kiss?" He walked toward her. "I could really use one."

She held her hand out, halting him. "I have to brush my teeth first. I couldn't kiss you with morning breath."

He wanted to tell her that wasn't necessary, but he knew that was important to her. "You wouldn't happen to have an extra one, would you? I think I might cause a scene at the local 7-Eleven if I go buy one."

"I just bet you would. Give me one minute." She walked into the bathroom and soon returned with an unopened toothbrush, a towel, and a razor.

He couldn't keep the curious look off his face or the jealousy out of his tone. "Do I have to ask?"

She smiled. "It's not Darnell's. My brothers are known to stay over with a moment's notice, so I always have extra everything." She walked to the bedroom door. "I'm going to use the spare bathroom down the hall. Don't forget, ten minutes or Mike will eat all the food." She left the room.

Aidan grinned. He could really get used to looking at her beautiful face every morning. And hopefully that would be very soon. He just had to get rid of Darnell once and for all. If only he had a surefire way to make that happen. Maybe the earth would open up and swallow Darnell. With all the security measures he had in place, Darnell would need an ace up his sleeve to get to Madisyn or her niece, but as in football, it wouldn't be over until the fat lady sang.

He shook away those bad thoughts and walked to the bathroom. He hadn't paid much attention to the large room the night before but now as he glanced around, he could see this room was definitely Madisyn. Cheery bright colors greeted him, making him feel even happier. As she had directed, everything he could possibly need was sitting on the counter waiting for him.

Ten minutes later, Aidan entered the kitchen ready to face Mike. He expected the older man to hit him with a barrage of questions the minute he sat down, but Mike was too busy eating.

Madisyn had changed into a tank top and shorts. Her hair was pulled back into a ponytail and she looked very relaxed. She placed a plate filled with eggs, bacon, potatoes, and toast in front of him. "Eat up," she said, kissing

187

him quickly on the lips before taking her seat next to him.

Aidan darted a glance in Mike's direction, but he only smiled at him. Aidan instantly relaxed. He leaned and kissed Madisyn on the cheek. No use pressing his luck, he thought. "This looks great, baby." He inhaled the aroma and dug into his food.

As the three of them ate in silence Aidan marveled at how different his relationship with Madisyn had become. She was more interested in the charity than his football career.

Reluctantly, he left after Madisyn refused his help with the dishes. But she did walk him to the front door. Not wanting to upset Mike any more than necessary, Aidan left with the briefest kiss on her forehead. He shook his head in disbelief. It amazed him how fast he'd fallen in love. Aidan had known he was in trouble the moment he realized she chewed sexy.

CHAPTER 19

After Aidan left, Madisyn was faced with her stubborn brother. He had settled in on the couch and was reading the paper. She knew Mike wasn't leaving her alone, so she'd just have to deal with it. "How about we go shopping?"

He sighed and folded the paper, placing it on the coffee table. "Okay, let's get this over with. I can't believe I agreed to this. I hate shopping."

Madisyn rolled her eyes toward the ceiling. "Yes, I know. I'm really grateful," she told her brother. "However, I can always call Mom and she can take me."

Mike rose. "There's no way I'm putting the two women in my family in the path of danger. Dad would skin me alive."

"Yeah, there's that."

Although Mike complained most of the time, she still enjoyed being with him. He seemed to cheer up when they stopped for lunch at the Touchdown Zone, Mike's favorite sports bar. After they both ordered hot wings, fries and beer, Mike shocked her.

"I've had a good time today. The grocery store is next, right? I can't believe I'm having a good time. I might even hang with you tonight."

That seemingly innocent remark made her skin crawl. For him to say he was enjoying himself was one thing, but for him to forego boys' night out was quite another. She took a sip of her beer before she spoke. "Okay, Mikey, out with it." She held her hand. "And please don't tell me the Disney version."

"When we were leaving I saw Darnell parked down the street, watching your house. He didn't see me. I don't like this, Maddie. He's getting desperate and stepping up his game."

"I thought that was him, but I wasn't sure. I'd convinced myself that I was imagining it. Why would he do something so stupid? He's not supposed to be anywhere near here or he violates the restraining order."

"He doesn't care about that. He needs you and nothing is going to deter him, Maddie. I think Myles should stay with you at night."

"I can't deal with Myles O'Riley right now. You know how single-minded he gets in the summer," said Madisyn of her sibling. Myles was only a year older than she was, but when it came to his favorite team he was a kid.

"So he gets a little nuts during baseball season. He's promised to cut back when he's at your house."

Of course the men had already discussed this in detail. But Mike was with her every minute. When had he made all these arrangements? "When did you talk to Myles?"

"Didn't. Text message."

The computer age, Madisyn mused. Soon people wouldn't have to talk to one another at all. She knew when she was licked. The men in her family had discussed the problem and had come up with a solution, the end. "All right, tell Myles the first stat I hear come out of his mouth, he's out on his butt."

Mike smiled. "He knows the drill. No talk of baseball while he's there. I still don't know what you have against the Rangers. They're in the lead and headed for the pennant."

"I have nothing against the Rangers. I love them. But with Myles all I hear is stats on every freaking baseball team and how they will lose against the Rangers. Then when the Rangers lose, he walks around like he's in a deep depression." Madisyn realized how, in the scope of things going on in her life, that was pretty trivial. "You know, tell Myles if he wants to talk stats, he can. That's his thing."

"Okay," Mike said slowly. "Either way he's staying. I'm sure Aidan will understand."

Madisyn didn't doubt it for one second. "Sure he will."

"I didn't think you were really that stupid," Keisha said into her cell phone. "Did her brother see you? You know you're just digging a deeper hole for yourself?"

Darnell nodded. Tell him something he didn't already know. Right now he just needed some help fixing this mess. "Just find out if she's going anywhere tonight. I gotta talk to her." His time was running out and he didn't have many options. But for his plan to work, he needed to get her alone.

"I don't have to ask her nothing," Keisha said proudly. "Madisyn is as predictable as snow in North Texas. Friday night she has a meeting with the Mature Alliance charity. She's a volunteer."

"She was always claiming she wanted to do something, so I guess she finally did. Where is this place?"

"Forget about it," Keisha warned. "You're not going to get anywhere near her."

"Why not?" Darnell thought his plan was simple. Snatch Madisyn as she walked to her SUV. Persuade her to attend the dinner with him.

"Because, you idiot, she'll be with Aidan. It's his charity. If they're as chummy as you say, you're not going to be able to talk to her."

"Shit." Another problem he was going to have to fix. This whole mess was Madisyn's fault. If she had just taken him back as she had so many times before, none of this would be needed. He should make her pay for that alone. If he didn't get that promotion, he just might.

⁂

She watched her target. Slipping the device under his car without his knowledge had been the easy part. The hard part was listening to what had to be the stupidest man. He was talking a blue streak to someone named Keisha, who was most likely his accomplice in this mess, she guessed. If Keisha had a brain, she'd better start using it or she'd be in the jail cell next to Darnell's.

Her cell phone buzzed and she looked down at the display. Chase. She knew this case was very important to the attorney and was beginning to understand why. Aidan Coles. She answered before it buzzed again.

"Callahan."

"Hey, it's me, Chase. How's everything going?" He sounded nervous. "He was spotted parked on her street this morning. He's not supposed to come near her. You told me that you could assure her safety. I can't tell my client you've got everything under control if something happens to her."

"Chase, calm down. You're the one not in control. Yeah, I know he was parked on her street. I also know your boy spent the night. I won't go into what he was doing, but I would caution him if they're going to play house, better do it at his place. At his house there's lots of security."

He took a deep breath. Chase didn't often get rattled unless it had something to do with Aidan. She knew Aidan was his only client, thus his concern. "All right, Cadence. I know you and your team are good at what you do. Where's Darnell now?"

She hated when people used her given name. What was her African-American mother thinking? She knew exactly what she was thinking. She wanted to preserve Cadence's father's Irish heritage. "Giving some stupid girl the blues. Some women just don't deserve to live. Aidan will be with Madisyn tonight, right?"

"Yeah, what's up?"

"Nothing yet." She wanted Darnell to think no one was onto him for now. "Just tell your boy to stay on his toes. My team can only cover so much ground, so no dates."

"Gotcha." He took another deep breath. "Anything else to report?"

"Yeah. You need to relax." She ended the call.

She owned a successful security company and had jobs that took her and her elite team all over the world. She was good at what she did, but men seldom let her do her job.

Later that evening, Mike dropped Madisyn off at the Mature Alliance building for her charity meeting. He looked at her with a very serious look on his face. "Now Maddie, if things change and Aidan isn't taking you home, don't you hesitate to call me."

She appreciated his concern. "I will." She slid out of the truck and closed the door. "If anything changes I'll let you know." Aidan had promised to take her home after the meeting.

"Okay. I'll just wait until you're safely inside."

She knew that Mike wouldn't budge one inch until she entered the building. "Thanks, Mike." She walked up the walkway, knowing that she was safe for the moment. When she reached the glass doors, she turned and waved good-bye to her brother. Once inside she was greeted by one of the hockey players on the charity committee.

"Hey, Madisyn, it's nice to see you this evening." Jason Taggot extended his hand as he neared her. "Aidan is running a little late," he said on a rush. "He said he'd explain when he got here. We can wait for him in the conference room." He guided her to the large room on the left of the main offices.

Madisyn didn't really like all these men thinking she couldn't manage to stay safe for thirty seconds without someone looking after her. She took a seat at the large mahogany table and stared at him. "Aidan put you up to this, didn't he?"

Jason smiled at her. "I plead the fifth." He shifted in his seat when Madisyn narrowed her gaze at him. "It's only because he cares about you so much. He didn't give me specifics, but told me not to let you out of my sight until he got here."

What could she say? "Thanks, Jason, I appreciate your concern. You don't have to stay in here with me. I promise I won't move until Aidan gets here. I'm sure you have other things to take care of."

He shook his head. "No, I'm staying right here. I would never cross Aidan. I've only seen him really mad once in my life and I don't want to see it again."

Okay, her curiosity was piqued. "When?"

Jason shrugged. "I really shouldn't be telling you his business."

"I understand the man rules and everything. I just want some insight to Aidan."

He sighed. "It was a few years ago and his mom was trying to get him to do something for his stepfather, but Aidan flat out refused. I mean, that's so not like him."

Madisyn knew of Aidan's rocky road with his stepfather and how he wanted to patch things up now, but

195

what on earth could have caused him to act so out of character? Aidan was considerate, kind, and gentle, not this mean, unfeeling man Jason was describing. "I'm sure Aidan had his reasons."

"True, but I never pressed him for details and like I said, it's never happened again. He's usually a go-with-the-flow type of guy."

Madisyn nodded. Now that sounded like the man she'd fallen in love with. She was just about to ask Jason something when Aidan blew through the conference room door, his big strong arms carrying a fat file folder marked "Grand Opening Reception." She groaned, knowing that folder was for her. "I'm guessing that's for me."

Aidan was dressed in a loose-fitting polo and cotton shorts that stopped just above his knees. "I'm afraid so." He nodded to Jason. "Thanks, man. See you tomorrow."

"You know I got your back. Just let me know if you need anything else." To Madisyn he said, "It was nice talking to you. Hope to see you again soon." He left the room without another word.

She turned her attention to this very sexy man. "That was your doing. That poor man drove over here just to sit with me until you got here?"

"Yes, he was doing me a favor." He leaned toward her and kissed her slowly. "Is that a problem for you?"

Every time he stuck his tongue in her mouth, her brain went on vacation. "What were we talking about?"

"This." He kissed her again. The kiss started out slow and tender and quickly grew hotter than the fires of hell.

Regretfully, she ended the kiss. "You know we never discussed the charity last night."

"Do you have a problem with what we did in lieu of a discussion of the charity?" He grinned devilishly. "We discussed something much better, and our bodies did the talking. Do you regret that?"

She shook her head. That man had loved her like no other man had before or ever would again. He'd made her feel beautiful and very sexy. "No, it was wonderful."

"I'm glad. I was worried you thought I rushed you."

"No, I didn't do anything I hadn't been dreaming of the last week." She took a deep breath, forcing herself to focus on the task at hand. "If that's for the grand opening, we'd better get started or the Alliance won't get to open on time."

"You win. I wanted to make out some more, but this is more important right now." He opened the folder and quickly switched to all business. "Now, the grand opening should be the weekend before the Alliance actually opens. Chase and I thought semi-formal should work, since so many city bigwigs will be there."

Madisyn shook her head. "And you'd also be alienating the very people you want to help."

"You're right. I guess I was thinking about the wrong thing. Okay, forget about dress code then. What about food? I would like some upscale food. Not highbrow, but not sports bar, either. Is there such a thing?"

"Sure. Like the food we made last Saturday. We could have some crab dip, egg rolls, sushi, stuff like that. I'll go through my recipes and get back to you. Do you want to serve liquor?"

"I've been tossing that around in my head. Chase is totally against it because the Alliance would be liable if anyone got in a wreck or something."

"Well, we don't have to serve liquor. You could offer non-alcoholic beverages instead. You want people to focus on Mature Alliance. If you're having a lot of different people there, it would probably be a lot safer not to serve it."

"Right. You're going to need to send out invitations to the mayor, police chief, fire chief, chamber of commerce, etc., as well as take out ads in the paper. We were also thinking about maybe running some radio spots."

Madisyn nodded. "It sounds great, but I would suggest we make an announcement at the local churches. The word would get out a lot faster. There are about ten people in our church that either can't read or have difficulty constructing a simple sentence. I'd thought about doing an adult literacy class there."

"That sounds great, baby. But we can do something better."

"Like what?"

"I'll tell you Sunday, right after Sunday dinner. I have some details to work out first."

Madisyn could only imagine what was on his mind but since he wasn't ready to share, she focused on the grand opening. "Is there anything we need to discuss?"

"Yes. What do you want for breakfast?"

CHAPTER 20

After their very brief meeting, Aidan and Madisyn left Alliance headquarters and headed for dinner. "Why are we going to your place?" Madisyn asked as she realized where Aidan was going. "I thought we were going to Houston's. After such a grueling day with Mikey, I was looking forward to steak."

Aidan glanced at her as he took the exit. "I have the stuff and you can cook the steaks if you want. I'm sure we can find something else to eat, if you don't want that. Chase suggested that until this is over, we not make too many public appearances."

"So Darnell is still dictating my life?" She folded her arms across her chest. "I don't like this. I'm not having this, Aidan. You can just take me home."

"Baby, I know this isn't what you want. But right now we've got to play it this way. Darnell isn't calling the shots. I'm trying to keep you safe and if it comes down to keeping you at my house, I will do that."

"I know you guys only have my best interest at heart. I don't want to be the victim. I've been that for the last two years of my life with Darnell."

"Madisyn, calm down. I'm not asking you to give up your independence, just let me keep you safe. Do you want me to take you home? I will. It will go against everything my mother instilled in me as young man, but I will honor your wishes."

She felt like the "B word" after his little speech. "We can go to your house for dinner." She thought she'd throw the little disclaimer in, just in case. "After dinner you can take me home."

He chuckled. "I hear you, baby."

Somehow Madisyn knew she wasn't going home until the next morning.

Madisyn wasn't sure what to expect. As he promised there were steaks, potatoes, and fixings for just about anything else she could wish for.

He took steaks out of the refrigerator, smiling like a mischievous little boy. "I haven't learned how to do steaks yet, but when I do, get ready for it." He sat the meat on the counter. "Thanks for cooking, babe."

"Wait just a minute, Aidan. I love a good steak," Madisyn said, "but we're doing this together, honey." She turned on the grill accessory of his counter-top range so it would be hot and ready for the meat. "You don't mind, do you? This way you'll know how to cook steaks and next time you can return the favor."

Aidan nodded. "Sounds great, and I'm very eager to please my teacher. This will be the second-best thing you've ever put in your mouth. I would be the first."

"Modesty is not your thing, is it?" She took the steaks out of their plastic wrappers and placed them on the expensive cutting board. "The meat has to rest before we cook it. Never put cold meat on the grill, it takes longer to cook. When the meat is room temp, it will cook better."

Aidan nodded. "Noted. I'm all yours. Later, you can be all mine."

"I'd say that's a pretty tall order. But then again, I'm sure you'll rise to the occasion." Why was she flirting with Aidan like this? The woman saying such brazen things sounded more like Keisha than herself.

He laughed, pulling some dry spices out of the cabinet. "That sounds like a challenge if I ever heard one. While we're waiting for the steaks to rest, how about a glass of wine?"

She nodded. "Sounds good." She reached in the cabinet and got two wine glasses. After he poured some in each glass, they walked to the table and took a seat. Madisyn loved his kitchen. It was so peaceful. The only noise was the hum of the refrigerator. A few seconds of absolute quiet was nice, but soon the silence was deafening. "Let's talk."

"Okay, what do you want to talk about?"

She wasn't sure how to bring up the subject of his stepfather, but she had to try. "Remember when we first met and your mom had come to visit you?"

"Yeah."

"You were saying something about making up with your stepfather and I was just wondering if you'd done anything about it." She took a sip, hoping she hadn't overstepped her bounds as a new lover.

"Not yet," he said shortly. "That kind of got pushed to a back burner. I want to fly up and talk with Lester face to face. I don't feel this is something we should discuss over the phone."

She knew she was the reason Aidan hadn't made peace with Lester and she hated that. "I appreciate all that you have done and are doing for me, but you can fly up to Chicago to see him. I'll be just fine. My brothers can take over until you get back."

"You don't get it, do you?"

"Apparently not," Madisyn said. Instead of accepting her offer as the grand gesture she'd planned to make, he was making her feel as if she'd just insulted him. "Why don't you explain it to me? I feel like we're walking down two different streets at different times."

He reached for her hand and clasped it. "Baby, I know I can leave you in capable hands, but it's not like me being here making sure that you're well. If I thought I could find Darnell and beat him to a bloody pulp, I would do it and damn the consequences."

"I know that and I respect that you're willing to damage your unsullied reputation for me, but I can't have you risking all that you and the other athletes are doing with the Alliance. Darnell will get his, and he'd better hope and pray someone else gets to him before I do. I didn't deserve all the things he put me through and now it's payback time."

"Whoa, baby, I don't want you doing something stupid in the name of revenge. And before you go off on me, I'm not calling you stupid," Aidan clarified for her.

He stared at her for a long moment before saying, "I have something I need to tell you."

Oh, she really didn't like the sound of that sentence. A loaded statement like that could only mean that something really bad was going to follow. But she'd been in this place before and had always handled the news like a champ. Tonight would be no different. "Shoot."

Aidan cleared his throat, stalling for time and wondering how much he should tell Madisyn. He wished he could spill his guts and everything would be fine, but that wasn't an option. So he decided part of the truth was better than an out-and-out lie.

"Aidan?"

"Sorry, baby. Chase hired someone to watch you and your family."

She took a deep breath. "I know that. I haven't seen anyone yet, though, and neither has Marcus. You had me going for a minute there. I wasn't sure what was going to come out of your mouth."

"Actually they're already at work. It's a team of people, and no one will know the ghost is there unless Darnell makes a move. Chase set everything up."

Madisyn shook her head. "Are we talking about a glow-in-the-dark ghost or is this a code name?"

"Code name, mostly. It's like a security guard that you don't see. And yes, they're that good. I used one a while ago to do some investigating and I never saw them, never noticed them. I can tell you exactly what Megan was doing this morning. You can call Chase anytime you want to get a report. They are the ones who suggested no public dating until they have Darnell under wraps." He hoped she wouldn't be too upset.

She wrangled her hand free and sat back in the chair, letting the information sink in. "Let me get this straight," Madisyn said. "There's a group of people watching me and my family, and we'll never know that the person or persons are there."

"Basically," Aidan said, hoping that was enough to satisfy her, at least for the moment.

"What happens if they see something intimate? I don't want my family embarrassed or humiliated."

"They are discretion personified. Chase has them sign non-disclosure forms. They will not disclose anything they see in the course of the investigation."

"Why did you need a ghost?"

Aidan didn't want to relive the nightmare of bad judgment, but he'd listened to her empty her soul about Darnell and the end of their relationship. He had to reciprocate. "A few years ago, right after I came to Dallas, I started dating this young woman. About six months later, I broke it off and she told me she was carrying my baby. I'm always careful and doubted the baby was mine, so I told Chase about it and he took care of the rest."

"What happened?"

"A few months later I had the proof I needed. Once Chase confronted her with the information, she admitted I wasn't the father."

"You know, I never heard anything about that. And I pride myself on keeping up with sports gossip," Madisyn said. "This ghost person must be pretty good."

"The best."

She looked deep into his eyes, searching his soul with those green eyes. "As long as no harm comes to my family, I'm okay with the ghost watching us. Is it a man or a woman?"

"I don't know. I can tell you that it is a team of security experts."

"Aidan, this has to be costing you a fortune! I can't let you pay for this. I have some money."

He wanted to laugh at the seriousness on her face. "As every newspaper, sports magazine, and news station has reported, I have more than enough cash from my football contracts, investments and endorsements. So don't worry about the money. Let me do this for you."

She nodded. "Then let me do something for you."

"Name it."

"Let me pay for your parents to come visit. And before you get all 'he's not my father,' hear me out."

He had no choice but to comply.

She continued once she had his complete attention again. "Since you don't want to fly to Chicago right now, and I appreciate that, I was thinking next weekend would be perfect."

The idea sounded almost perfect to him, but the timing wasn't right and he wanted everything to be perfectly timed. "How about the weekend of the grand opening? I would really like for them to meet your family. And before you say anything, that's only two weeks after the date you were talking about."

She nodded. "All right. I'll look on the Net tonight when you take me home." She laughed. "We both know that's a pretty empty threat, isn't it?"

It was, but he'd never tell her that. "If you want to go home, just tell me when." He hoped she'd stay the night, but didn't want to push his luck.

"I just might do that." She kissed him gently on the lips. "I think I need some kind of antidote for your lips. My brain goes on vacation the minute my lips touch yours." She kissed him again, this time softer and longer.

He deepened the kiss by pulling her out of her chair and onto his lap. He caressed her luscious curves while her arms wrapped around neck. God, she felt wonderful. He knew he was losing his grip on sanity when she started caressing his head. She whispered something he hoped was very naughty, but he couldn't make out the words. "What?"

She moved away from him, laughing. "Time to cook the steaks."

———

"You were amazing," Madisyn breathed as she tried to catch her breath. They were in Aidan's king-sized bed and they'd just made love.

"I was just paying you back for the wonderful steaks you made for dinner. That was outstanding." He pulled her closer to him, throwing his leg over her just to make sure she couldn't take flight if she'd wanted.

She glanced around the bedroom. It was such a man's room. The large bed overpowered the room, even though it was quite a large room. The one thing she did like about the bedroom was the skylight above the bed. It was a romantic's wet dream to be in large bed with a man who could curl your toes while you looked up at the stars while he was doing just that.

She cuddled closer to Aidan's naked body. "This is so beautiful, Aidan. I could stare at the stars every night."

He kissed her on her neck. "Not tonight you won't. I've got plans for you and they don't include stargazing." He moved on top of her.

Madisyn welcomed his weight. In a strange way, it made her feel closer to him with his body crushed to hers. She wound her arms around his neck, pulling him down for a kiss. The meeting of their lips ignited an inferno. Tongues dueled, fighting for control. They couldn't get enough of each other and had no plans to stop for a silly thing like breathing.

When it became necessary, they separated so Aidan could sheath his very erect manhood. He slipped inside her and they began the journey to paradise.

CHAPTER 21

Madisyn heard the insistent ring of her cell phone in the distance. Maybe if she kept her eyes closed, the ringing would go away and let her sleep. Her body was still angry at her for making love with Aidan most of last night and this morning. She turned over on her stomach and every muscle in her upper body gave her the blues.

The phone rang again and she struggled to sit up, looking around for the annoying device. Aidan was nestled next to her with his eyes closed, a smile on his handsome face and dead to the world. Still the phone rang. She realized it was in bed under the covers. She felt around for it, but touched Aidan's leg instead. His eyes popped open.

He rolled over, tackling her gently and kissing the life out of her. "Is that your phone or mine ringing?" He plundered her mouth with hot kisses.

If she'd had a coherent thought, she would have told him yes, it was her phone ringing. But since her brain had turned to mush, she moaned. Thank goodness the phone stopped ringing.

Aidan moved to cover her body completely. "Good morning," he murmured against her lips. "You look so good lying in my bed."

The phone began ringing again, interrupting their foreplay. Aidan cursed and searched for it. "When I find it, I'm throwing it out of the window," he growled.

Madisyn wanted to laugh at his irritation, but felt exactly the same way. "It could be important," she said. Her heart wasn't really in statement.

He handed her the ringing offender. "You have exactly thirty seconds to get them off the phone or I won't be able to promise anything other than breakfast."

"You're awful, you know that? Or are you just incredibly horny?" She pulled the sheet around her body and reached for the phone.

He lay down, pulling her down with him. "A little of both. You shouldn't feel so good when I'm inside you. I can't help it."

Madisyn shook her head, wondering why she'd ever thought Darnell was the one. He had never been this tactile and talkative in the mornings. She answered the phone, hoping it wasn't anything important. "Hello?"

"Maddie, are you coming to girlie day?"

It was Keisha. Madisyn should have known she'd called. She'd been hoping to avoid this conversation for as long as possible. "No, girl, I'm not going to be able to make it today. I think Chayla is still going."

"No, you both bailed on me. One of the boys has some kind of game today. I wanted to show you the new outfit I got yesterday."

Of course it had to be about Keisha. Not once did she ask if Madisyn was sick or if someone in the family had taken ill. "You'll have to show it to me some other time."

"I bought it to wear to the club. I know I'll be able to catch a big baller's eye with this dress. It makes my ass look big."

Aidan started kissing Madisyn's ears, cheek and was heading for her lips. Madisyn had to get off the phone and quick. "I'll talk to you later." She pushed the end button on the phone and threw it across the room.

Aidan laughed. "Now that was what I call an excellent play. Touchdown."

"I don't know what is about you, Aidan, but you make me throw caution to the wind. And I like it."

━━━━◦◦◦◦◦━━━━

Keisha looked at her cell phone. No, Maddie didn't. Something was definitely going on with Maddie and Keisha had to find out what. The thing with Darnell was getting old, and fast. He was beginning to sound like a whining man with no balls. All he talked about was getting Maddie back and how much he wanted the promotion.

Keisha had to find out if her friend was actually sleeping with Aidan Coles. What a waste, she thought. Aidan was one of the most highly paid wide receivers in the league and all those millions were going to waste. Maddie would never appreciate the lifestyle that came along with a professional football player. All she was interested in was doing volunteer work and her family.

She dialed Madisyn's home number and after several rings it went to voice mail. She tried the cell again and got the same response. What was really going on with her friend? Had Darnell scared her so much that she didn't want to chance a confrontation in public and had become a hermit?

After not being able to connect with her friend, she tried Darnell. He picked up on the third ring.

"What is it?" he whispered into the phone. "Why are you calling me now? I thought this was spa day? You're supposed to be keeping tabs on Maddie."

"She bailed on me. I think you've frightened her so much that she doesn't want to go anywhere alone. You'll never get to her if she doesn't leave the house."

"You let me worry about that. Your job is to keep tabs on her and you're not doing that. I can't believe she'd rather be with some dumb jock than me. What's she got?"

Keisha laughed. "About forty million dollars, for one. I can't understand why he would be with Maddie."

"Just because she isn't as skinny as you are doesn't mean she's less of a person."

"Funny, you weren't thinking that when you were sleeping with me while you guys were still a couple. In fact, your biggest complaint was that she wasn't skinny."

He sighed. "Hindsight is always twenty-twenty. Now I realize that I had a good thing and I screwed up listening to people like you. When I get her back, she'll never leave my side again."

"So what was I?"

"Now, Keisha, we both knew the score when you batted those fake eyelashes at me last year. You always have several men on the side. So don't try to play the victim. You're not Maddie." He ended the call.

Keisha was getting a little tired of everyone hanging up on her before she could respond.

❦

Darnell rolled over in bed. The space next to him was getting cold. Then the woman from the previous night walked out of the bathroom in her birthday suit and slid back in bed beside him. Her flawless brown skin looked sensual cuddling his thousand-thread-count sheets. He instantly thought of the last time Madisyn had been in his bed. He was so stupid to have cheated on her in the first place. Now he was paying a high price for infidelity. Infidelity sex wasn't worth it.

"Who was that?"

"Nobody important."

He needed to think and he couldn't do that with his current bed partner. "Why don't you run home? I'll call you later."

She slid her slender young body out of bed and began to get dressed. "I need a ride home."

Another bad decision he'd made. What was he thinking? This girl was twenty years his junior. He couldn't talk to her, he could only have sex with her, and it wasn't that good. He reached for his wallet, took out fifty dollars and threw it on the bed. "This should do it, right?"

She frowned at him, picked up the money and stuffed in it her tight blue jeans. "No, but another fifty will do it."

He shook his head and threw another bill. "For services rendered. You're just like your sister."

"You should know." She walked out of the room.

Darnell breathed easier. When he heard the front door slam closed, he eased out of bed, slipped on his boxers and headed downstairs. He wanted to make sure she was out of the house before he started Plan B. He didn't want any witnesses as his life spiraled out of control.

The aroma of a delicious breakfast woke Madisyn up later that morning. She squinted at the bedside clock. It was after eleven, way past her normal time to get up, especially on a Saturday. It was Saturday, wasn't it?

She turned over and decided she could sleep a few more minutes. Her eyes popped open. It was Saturday! She bolted up, glanced around for her clothes, and spotted Aidan walking in the room with a breakfast tray. He was dressed in an oversized T-shirt and a pair of loose-fitting shorts and no shoes. Madisyn pulled the sheet around her body as he neared her.

"I was beginning to get worried. You've been asleep a long time. I hope you're hungry." He walked to the bed and placed the tray before her. His lips brushed hers. "Good morning. I won't ask you how you slept. You look very sensual. I could have you again in lieu of breakfast." He winked at her.

If this man only knew what was actually on her mind and tired body, he wouldn't tempt her. To take her mind off her lusty thoughts she concentrated on breakfast. Knowing that Aidan didn't cook, she was almost afraid to lift the lid.

He must have sensed her hesitation and did the honors. "I have to confess I went to the corner shop for the coffee, eggs, bacon and croissants."

The food smelled so good, Madisyn wouldn't have minded what he had to do to get it. She took a bite of the eggs. "They are wonderful, Aidan."

He chuckled. "That's supposed to be enough for two." He picked up a fork and dug in.

Madisyn thought it was very erotic for them to share breakfast from the same plate. It was almost like a kiss. But as sexy as it was, nothing was going to lessen her appetite. They ate the meal in silence.

After Aidan took the dishes downstairs, Madisyn checked in with her brother. Myles didn't seem surprised to hear her voice.

"Hey, sis," Myles said. "I'm guessing everything went well last night at your meeting and you and Aidan had to discuss something in great detail." He laughed heartily. "I told Mike you were perfectly safe in the arms of a Dallas Cowboy."

"Must you put all my business on the street?" She couldn't help it, she started laughing as well. "Anything else happen?"

"Well, yeah, Keisha called a couple of times, but I let the machine pick it up. Then I could have sworn I heard someone at your back door, but when I went to check it out, no one was there."

She nodded. "Yeah, Keisha called me on my cell. She wanted to know if I was going to the spa."

"I thought it was weird she called so many times. Most people would probably try once or twice, but five times is excessive."

For most normal people, she would agree with her brother. Unfortunately, when Keisha wanted to talk about Keisha, she didn't give up until she got you. "You don't know her. This is normal."

"Women."

<hr />

After finally convincing Aidan that she needed to go home and change, he took her home. The ride in the SUV was quiet; not tension-filled, just quiet. They were both probably thinking about the night before and how everything had changed between them.

Although she had known him only a few weeks, Madisyn felt closer to him than she ever could have to Darnell. Not only did they did have so much in common, but Aidan made her feel that she was the most beautiful woman in the world.

Madisyn unlocked her front door with Aidan close behind her. To her surprise her brother was nowhere to be seen. "I guess Myles had to go out." After locking the door, she led him to the couch.

Aidan shrugged. "Another brother, I take it. Mike told me someone would be staying here at night."

Madisyn didn't want Aidan to think that she didn't trust him, but she didn't want him to feel obligated to stay with her when he had other plans. "I just don't want to become a burden to you, Aidan. You're doing so much for me and my family, I wanted to give you space."

He took a seat on the sofa with a sigh. "For the record, Madisyn, you're not a burden. I appreciate what you're trying to do, but I'm an adult and know what I'm doing. I'm here because I want to be and no other reason. Okay?"

She sat next to him. "Thank you, Aidan. I just wanted to be sure. It's funny, we haven't known each other that long, but I feel very close to you."

He pulled her into his arms. "Glad to hear it, baby."

He kissed her. "What would you like to do today?"

"How about your lesson? We could do it here."

He smiled at the innuendo. Madisyn quickly back-tracked. "I meant the *cooking* lesson."

The grin faded away. "I was so hoping," he said. "But we can do the lesson here."

She eased out of his embrace and stood. "Great. You sit tight and I'll go change, then we'll start your lesson."

Aidan nodded and reached for the TV remote. "I'll be waiting right here."

And that's where she found him later, watching the sports channel. He stood the minute she entered the living room. "You look good enough to eat."

"Thank you, Aidan." She looked down at her tank top and jeans. She had wanted to be comfortable. Since her kitchen wasn't as large as Aidan's, things might get heated. Or at least a girl could hope. "Ready for your next lesson?"

"You bet. Lead the way."

Madisyn did just that. "Today we're going to make a frittata. It's almost like a quiche without the crust."

"Cool."

After they entered the kitchen, Madisyn grabbed all the necessary items: eggs, bell peppers, breakfast sausage, cheese, green onions and jalapeno peppers. She laughed at Aidan's surprised expression. "It's really easy, you'll see. This can be served for breakfast or brunch."

"Great. Usually I'm a late sleeper on the weekends."

Madisyn smiled. "And here I thought you were an early riser on all occasions." She opened the cabinet in search of a mixing bowl and cutting board.

Aidan took the items out of her hand and placed them on the counter. "Only when you're in my bed."

That was what she'd started the game of innuendo, what was she going to do? She was going to continue the cooking lesson. "Okay, Aidan, you can chop up the onions and bell peppers. I'll cook the breakfast sausage." She needed something to do with her hands or they'd get her in a world of trouble. She started cooking the meat, sneaking a peek at Aidan. Unfortunately, he was looking directly at her.

"After you kiss me, I'll do anything you ask." He leaned down to claim his prize.

Madisyn moved out of his reach. "Don't I get say-so in this kissing business?" She tried to look serious, but knew she was probably wearing a goofy smile just like him.

Aidan kissed her. "You can say all you want, baby, but I'm still going to kiss you." And he did. "Again and again, until we both can't breathe."

She moaned against his lips. The idea sounded wonderful but she didn't want them to be just about sex. "Cooking lesson," she reminded him. "We have to finish this."

"Which this?" He smiled down at her just before he kissed her. "This?"

"No, the frittata," Madisyn said. She wanted to say the kisses.

"All right. You win this time." He resumed his chore of chopping the peppers. "We'll have this conversation again." He winked at her.

She took a deep breath. This was going to be a lot harder than she had imagined. What was she thinking inviting him into her home, especially after they'd just had sex who knew how many times the night before and that morning?

"Honey?"

Madisyn snapped back to reality when she heard Aidan's voice finally filter through. She stared at him, noticing that he was no longer chopping vegetables. "What is it?"

He pointed at the smoke now filling the kitchen. "You're burning the meat." He took the skillet off the fire. "Are you okay?" The next sound they heard was her very efficient newly installed alarm system alerting the fire department.

"Oh, no," Madisyn groaned. "Now the police and fire department will be here. How will I explain you?"

He pulled her in his arms and comforted her. "Baby, everything will be just fine. It's just the smoke alarm. Besides, don't worry about me. Losing my privacy doesn't mean crap if I don't have you."

He dropped his arms and stood back from her. That bright smile had changed to a scowl. "You still don't get it, do you?"

Madisyn shook her head, wondering what she'd had done to make him so upset with her.

He stepped closer to her. Then in a movement too fast to be recorded in her brain, he picked her up and hugged her.

She was too dizzy. Her brain was on fast forward as he started swinging her around. "Aidan, I'm going to throw up."

Only then did he let her feet hit the floor. "I just wanted to say that I love you."

CHAPTER 22

I love you.

Madisyn had played the phrase in her head countless times since Aidan left her place, and it still made her heart beat faster. After he'd said it, she'd expected him to take it back, but he didn't. How could something that started as friendship a few weeks ago turn into love so fast?

She had no idea, and that frightened her. Being this involved with Aidan was going to cause problems for them both somewhere down the line and they'd have to be ready.

Madisyn felt confident she could handle anything life threw at her. She'd definitely had enough practice with Darnell. And this time she had Aidan's love to shield her heart.

And that was a first.

She glanced at her wall clock and realized her dad would be coming to pick her up in less than an hour. Her father, like all the overprotective men in her family, refused to let her drive to her childhood home.

"I'll pick you up. It will be just like a real date. I know I can't compare to a Dallas Cowboy, but I'm pretty darn close," he'd told her hours earlier.

So Madisyn had relented and agreed to let her dad pick her up. It felt as if it had been ages since she'd driven her car and it looked as if it would be a while longer. She almost wished Darnell would make his move and they could get the show on the road.

Her father arrived promptly at seven. He was dressed in a dark suit and looked very distinguished. "Hey, baby, you're not dressed yet." He nodded at her blue jeans and short-sleeved shirt.

"Well, yeah," Madisyn said. "I was going for totally casual."

"Not on my watch," he said. "Just because you've given your heart to Aidan, it doesn't mean you're supposed to dress like a starving college student. I don't think you dressed like that when you were in college. You never know, Plan B could be just around the corner."

She knew it was a losing battle. "I'll change clothes, Dad. Take a seat."

Her dad nodded and took a seat. "That was easy. I'll be right here, baby girl."

Having been bought up a good Christian girl, Madisyn couldn't really say what she wanted to say. She wanted to tell her father that she didn't want to change and felt she looked presentable to go out to a restaurant, but instead she was going to change her clothes.

When she returned to the living room her father was nowhere to be found. She looked in the living room, the den, and the guest bedroom. She was about to open her front door when she heard a loud clanging noise coming from the garage.

Hoping that Darnell hadn't lost what little brain he had left and tried to hurt her beloved father, Madisyn hurried to the noise. The scene almost took her breath away. Her garage door was open for starters, but the thing that made her world tilt counterclockwise was her father sprawled on the cement floor, out cold.

"Daddy!" Madisyn ran to her father, who began to slowly regain consciousness. "What happened?"

He shook off the pain and struggled to sit up, running a shaky hand over his head. "Heard a noise, thought it might have been Aidan. So I went to have a talk with him. But someone jumped me."

Madisyn wiped tears from her eyes as she helped her father to his feet. "How do you feel?"

Ben laughed. "I've got one hell of a headache. I could use some aspirin."

She looked her father over with a careful eye. Except for the large knot growing on the back of his head, he looked okay. "Daddy, are you sure we don't need to go to the hospital?"

"Yes, baby girl, I'm not hurt that bad. We'd better call the cops, though. It might not have been Darnell, but I'd bet my retirement fund that he knows who it was."

She helped her dad back to the couch. After she fetched him some aspirin and water, Madisyn made two calls. The first one was to the police. The second was to Aidan. That call took much longer to finish. Aidan wanted to talk to her father. After much debating, she let her father have the phone.

She waited patiently as her father regurgitated the events of the last hour. "I was waiting for baby girl to change so we could have our Saturday night date. I heard a noise in the garage and thought it was you, but it wasn't."

After a few nods, her father handed her the phone. "Aidan said he'll be over in about an hour. I really like him." He smiled rather smugly. "He's dependable and you can count on him in a crisis. What did the cops say?"

"The usual. They'd send someone over in a while."

Aidan set the phone on the counter carefully. In the mood he was in at the moment, he could have shattered the phone into a million tiny pieces. He cursed at the room. "Where the hell was that infernal ghost I'm paying three thousand dollars a day?"

He dialed Chase's home number. Luckily his friend picked up on the first ring. Aidan didn't get a chance to light into him. Chase beat him to the punch.

"How's Mr. O'Riley? Cadence said he received a bump on the head."

Aidan was furious and that was putting it mildly. "What the hell? What am I paying for?"

"Aidan," Chase said in his most comforting voice, "you need to let me do my thing. Cadence said it wasn't Darnell and it was two of them. They had come there to do more than just hit him on the head if he got in their way. They'd come to kidnap Madisyn. The intruders won't be bothering anyone for a while. They're in custody."

Aidan took a deep breath. "There was a kidnapping attempt in Madisyn's garage?" He rubbed his hands over his face. "Please tell me that you found Darnell at least."

"I wish I could. Wherever he's hiding, it's the last place anyone would look. The cops should be at Madisyn's in about ten minutes. The thugs have been taken into FBI custody for the time being."

Aidan forced the thought process to communicate with his brain. "FBI?"

"Yeah?"

"Why? Isn't it just breaking and entering since they didn't kidnap Madisyn?"

"Attempted kidnapping is still a crime. I wanted them out of the picture for a while. Maybe it'll bring Darnell out of hiding."

Aidan hoped this fiasco would be over soon.

"Don't worry, Aidan," Chase said. "It's all taken care of. Now you need to get Madisyn out of that house. Darnell has definitely just upped his game and is not above causing her serious harm. Somehow he's getting inside information on her. Any ideas?"

"I think I might know how," Aidan said. His thoughts immediately centered on Keisha.

"Care to enlighten your attorney?"

"I don't have enough proof, but I think I'll have all the proof I need by next weekend at the opening of Kameron's club. In fact, I know I'll have the proof I need."

Chase sighed. "Is this a subtle hint that I need to get bail money ready?"

"If it's who I think it is, then yes, you'd better start channeling Johnny Cochran's legal spirit." Aidan ended the call. Then he made another call. The caller picked up on the fourth ring.

"This is Kam. How can I rock your world?"

Aidan hoped that this wouldn't bite him in his butt.

"Hey man, it's Aidan."

"What's up, brother? You mean the little woman lets you talk to your boys?"

In a million years, Aidan would never consider Kameron one of his true friends. He used people. He'd used Aidan often enough when Kam's wife suspected him of cheating, which he did on a daily basis. Aidan had always been the shield, but this time, he was going to do the using. "She's not like that. I think I can make the club's opening next weekend, if you can do a little favor for me."

<hr />

Madisyn watched the policemen inspect the garage with narrowed eyes. As a rule she didn't have much interaction with the police.

They began their investigation by taping the entrance to her garage with crime scene tape. It looked more like a murder scene on TV than just a simple breaking and entering. Two uniformed police dusted her SUV, the garage door and the door leading into the house for prints.

A plainclothes detective drilled her like a repeat offender. "You say your father was hit with a blunt object?"

She folded her arms across her chest, since it seemed to occupy the detective's interest at the moment. "Yes, I say, the paramedics say, my father says."

He smiled. "Touché. Maybe the butt of a gun or a pipe or something?"

Madisyn grinned tightly. "I guess that qualifies as a blunt object. Now what are you going to do about it?"

He glanced around the room slowly. "I'd say it's already been done. I would caution you not to stay here. I know you have a restraining order against Darnell Whitfield."

Madisyn didn't need a ton of bricks to fall on her, at least not now. She watched as Aidan's black Escalade parked in the driveway next to the police cruiser. He was like a beacon in the storm of craziness. He was her shield from everything wrong in her life.

He walked up to her and took her in his arms. His strong embrace was exactly what she needed. The tears she'd been holding back since the police arrived broke free and she wailed like a baby.

Aidan took charge of the situation. He noticed the detective's puzzled gaze. "What did you say to her?" The tone in his voice was unmistakable. And the fact that he topped the slender man by at least five inches helped.

"Mr. Coles, it's a pleasure. I'm a big fan." He took a deep breath as if transforming himself from neurotic fan to cop. "I was telling Ms. O'Riley that she needs to find other lodging until we can get Mr. Whitfield in custody."

"My thoughts exactly. I trust this will be treated with discretion and the media won't be alerted to my presence here."

"Of course." The officer resumed his work.

Aidan ushered Madisyn inside to where her father was resting on the couch. Aidan had to see for himself that the elder O'Riley was all right. Ben lay on the couch, a large bandage around his forehead.

"I'm glad to see you here, son," Ben said, struggling to sit up. "This has been some kind of mess."

Aidan nodded, noting the purple bruise under Ben's eye. "Looks like you took the worst of it. You remember anything?" Aidan sat next to Madisyn on the love seat.

Ben sat up slowly, groaning in the process. "Yeah, bits and pieces. You know, I could have sworn I saw two people in the garage, but I guess whoever it was got scared."

Aidan didn't want to refute the man's words out of respect for Madisyn. "You probably scared them away." Aidan hated not being able to tell the truth, but he knew it was the only way to get Darnell to force his hand.

Madisyn was uncharacteristically quiet. She sat beside Aidan and held his hand in an iron grip. "I'm just glad you weren't hurt any worse than you were, Daddy. I don't know what I'd do if you were hurt."

Aidan hugged Madisyn. "Now baby, we're thankful for the blessing that it is. Ben will be just fine in a few days, and when it gets dark we're going to take you out of here."

She looked at him with teary eyes.

"Under the cover of darkness," Aidan said. "If Darnell has someone watching the house, they'll have a harder time seeing us."

"It's going to be all right, baby girl. Now usually I don't cotton to this kind of arrangement, but that Darnell is a slippery fox and we need all the help we can get. So if you have to stay at Aidan's for a while, I understand."

If he'd had on a shirt with buttons, Aidan was sure every button would have popped off in pride, knowing that Ben trusted him with his only daughter.

Something wasn't right. He could feel it in his bones. It had been three hours since Trev had checked in. All he had to do was knock the old man out and take Madisyn out of the house so he could walk to her. They were supposed to meet in the parking lot of the Dallas Mall thirty minutes ago. All he wanted was to talk some sense into her head without the pretty-boy professional football player in the picture.

He hoped nothing serious had happened to Trev or Dante. Trev was a two-time felon. If he was caught, he'd go straight to prison and he wouldn't be getting out for a long time. Texas was a three-strike state and Trev would be out of luck. Dante didn't have a prior record so, if they were caught, he would be okay.

He took out his cell phone and dialed Trev's cell number one last time. If he'd chickened out or something, Darnell was going to have to go Plan C, and that was definitely going to land him in a whole lot of trouble.

He waited patiently as the phone rang continuously. Finally Trev picked up. Darnell was so rattled he didn't realize he was yelling at his cousin. "Trev, where the hell are you? Are you trying to get me killed?"

"This ain't Trev. He won't be able to assist you, Mr. Whitfield. Why don't you save us both some time and turn yourself in?" The call disconnected.

Darnell had always prided himself on being one step ahead of Aidan Coles's high-priced attorney, but he hadn't seen this one coming. He was almost sure that was Chase's voice. Almost. He couldn't imagine an attorney getting his hands dirty. Apparently he was getting help. Now it was time for Darnell to call in reinforcements. No more Mr. Nice Guy.

CHAPTER 23

Chase shook his head. How had something so simple in the beginning gone so wrong so quickly? Cadence had done her job without a doubt, but this was more than he'd signed on for.

The phone rang, jangling Chase's already jittery nerves. Glancing at the display, he took a deep breath, answered the phone and spoke to the one person who could actually settle his nerves. "Cadence?"

"Hartman, we need to meet. Now."

"Where?" He walked to the counter, looking for his car keys. After he located them, he headed to his garage, then stopped cold. "How the hell do you do that?" He stared at Cadence Callahan's tall, sleek form. "This is supposed to be a high-security subdivision." This was also the second time she'd breached his very expensive monitoring system.

She was dressed immaculately as always in a designer black suit and had had the nerve to park her lovely behind on the hood of his Jaguar. She slid off the car gracefully and walked to where he stood. Her honey-beige skin, compliments of her Irish father and African-American mother, glowed with irritation. "It's nice seeing you, too, Hartman. I thought this would be better since your house is wired. The security guard has sold you out.

He's been listening in on your phone conversations through the intercom system inside your house and selling the information to Darnell."

If Chase had been a less-than-honest attorney, he would have been a little nervous about his business being out there. But he was a good attorney with only one superstar football player for a client. No, Chase was pissed because of a worthless man trying to get away with everything. "I'm calling the board as soon as you leave."

She shook her head. "Forget it. Already done. Darnell had refused to pay him, so he went to the police and told them everything, not realizing that he would also go to jail. The police just arrested him. That's why I got in so easily this time. A source in the PD tells me that Darnell offered the guard a grand to keep tabs on your phone conversations, but kept stalling on the payment. Luckily, we set all the major parts of our plan in your office or Darnell would be home free."

Chase leaned against the wall of the garage. "Not as long as I'm breathing. That asshole just made this very personal. He invaded my personal space." He walked to his tool chest to retrieve his nine millimeter. Just as he opened the drawer where he kept his gun, he felt the unmistakable sensation of metal against the back of his neck.

"Chase, don't make me have to use this. I don't want to hurt you, but I will if you hinder this investigation," Cadence said. "I can't have you gunning for Darnell. You're going to have to be strong enough to trust me to do my job."

She was right, of course. He also knew she meant every word. "All right, Cadence, but I need some real answers about earlier today."

She smiled at him and holstered her gun. Then she did something totally out of character for the serious Cadence Callahan. She kissed him with those soft full lips of hers. "That, counselor, is privileged information."

Chase's usually sharp mind was actually blank. Well, maybe not blank, but his brain was still on that kiss. Cadence had had her tongue down his throat. In true Cadence fashion, she had taken the situation in her hands and dealt with it.

"Hartman, are you going to say anything or what?"

"Huh?" He wanted to say something sharp and astoundingly funny, but he couldn't. He couldn't get his brain wrapped around the fact that she had kissed him.

She invaded his personal space and wrapped her arms around him. "You know, I waited three years for you to bust a move and I was tired of waiting. Your lips looked soft and now that I've solved that mystery, I'll be on my way."

"You can't leave," Chase choked out.

"I think I can."

Since this was the chance he'd been waiting on, Chase decided to state his case. "Cadence, you can't kiss me like the plane is going down and then say you're leaving. That is cruel and unusual punishment."

"Let's see what's under the hood." She kissed him with such force, he was slammed against the nearest wall and she started unbuttoning his shirt.

For the first time in a long time, Chase Hartman's well-ordered life was not his own, and he liked it.

⬥

Later that evening, Madisyn let out a tired sigh. Her life wasn't her own anymore. Not only did she not have her car, she wasn't in her home and she didn't get to have her date with her father.

Madisyn now resided in Aidan's guest room. She glanced around the room as she unpacked her clothes. As rooms went, it was quite nice. A 32-inch plasma TV screen was mounted on the wall, she had a king-sized bed, and she had ample closet space. The room had a definite woman's touch. What woman?

She sat on the bed deciding how to ask her new lover just who exactly had decorated his house. Did she even have the right? After all, he was going out of his way to help her and her family, just to keep her safe. *Just suck it up, girl. It's not your business,* she told herself.

"Madisyn, can I come in?"

She rolled her eyes toward the ceiling. They'd been at Aidan's for an hour and each time he knocked before he entered her room. "Come in, Aidan."

He entered the room, walked to the bed and sat beside her. "Are you all settled in? Are you hungry?"

With all that had happened in the last few hours, the last thing on her mind was food. "No, thanks, Aidan. I think I'll just turn in early." She wanted to feel safe and there was only one way she could. In his arms.

"My door is always open, Madisyn. I didn't want you thinking that sex was my motivation for getting you under my roof."

She shook her head. "Aidan, I know you're not like that. You have only my safety in mind, right?" She winked at him. True, he did invite her for her to be safe, but there were perks for being honorable.

He leaned over and kissed her. "If you want to sleep in my bed, you'll get no argument from me."

"I want to," she said softly. "You've done so much for me in the name of keeping me safe."

"Baby, you don't have to keep thanking me." He rose and headed for the doorway. "And don't come to my bed because you think it's for services rendered. I want you in my bed because that's where you want to be and for no other reason." He left the room without another word.

Madisyn took a deep breath. Now she'd gone and done it. Aidan thought she wanted to sleep with him out of gratitude, which couldn't have been farther from the truth. She strode down the hall to his bedroom, but he wasn't there.

Where could he have gone so quickly? Hearing a loud noise and the mutterings of an angry man, she headed downstairs to the kitchen. He was standing at the counter, drinking a beer. He stared at her as she took a seat at the table.

He finished the beer and pulled another one from the fridge. "Change your mind?"

"I want, no, I *need* to talk to you."

"Talk."

"You don't make this easy," Madisyn said. "Aidan, I don't do anything with you out of thanks. If I want to sleep with you, it's because I feel safe in your arms. I feel you shield me from harm."

"I'm not your shield, Madisyn. I'm your man. I do this because I want to keep you in my life and not for any other reason."

She heard the conviction in his voice and it thrilled her heart. Without another thought she walked to where he stood, took the beer out of his hand and kissed him as if he were getting deployed to some unknown third world country and never to be seen again. When neither could breathe anymore, their lips parted. "Does that feel like I'm pitying you?"

Aidan grinned, wrapping her in a hug. "No, that feels like my baby."

"Good. Now feed me."

<hr />

Chase woke from the best dream he'd ever had. He didn't know what he'd done, but his body was making him pay. Every muscle hurt, but it was a good hurt. As he pried his eyes open, he heard the distinct sound of voices in his house. He threw back the covers on his bed wondering what he'd done yesterday. His always tidy bedroom was a hot mess, as his younger siblings would say. Clothes were scattered all over the hardwood floor. He put on his bathrobe and went downstairs. He grabbed the nearest object for protection, which was a hockey stick, and headed to where the voices were the loudest, the kitchen. Taking a deep breath, he walked inside the kitchen, then stopped cold. Cadence was standing at the counter cooking and talking on her cell phone! She was dressed in one of his shirts and looked as sexy as hell. The minute their eyes met, she cut her call short.

"Hayden, I'll get back to you. Keep me posted." She pushed a button on her phone and smiled at him. "I didn't know how long you slept on the weekends. I'm making French toast. I hope you're hungry."

He was, but suddenly it wasn't for food. It was for this very sexy woman cooking him breakfast. "You know, suddenly I'm not that hungry."

"Too bad, because we're eating breakfast. So grab a cup of coffee and park that fine butt in a chair while I finish making you the best breakfast you've ever had."

Chase was shocked into silence. He did as he was told and poured a cup of coffee. Maybe that would wake up his brain. After his brain was alert, the events of yesterday and last night came crashing back. He and Cadence had made love. Earthshaking, toe-curling love. He felt like one of those giddy females. "Cadence, I think we should talk about last night."

She continued making breakfast. "Well, I don't. Hartman, don't make it any more than it was. We had a night of incredible sex."

"Why can't it be more? You're here fixing breakfast instead of running out of here before I woke up. They call you the ghost, for goodness sake. You can disappear at will."

"I stayed because of you. I was going to leave when you fell asleep, but I couldn't. You look so cute when you're sleeping, so I just snuggled up next to you."

"Why?" She dipped the bread into the batter and put it in the skillet. "You think you know me, but if you knew the real me, you'd be quite surprised."

"I would have never figured you for a cook."

"I'm game if you are."

She smiled. "Let's see how good you are after breakfast. Then we'll talk."

‹‹‹›››

Sunday morning Madisyn hummed some silly love song as she dressed in her room. Aidan was still asleep when she'd slipped out of bed earlier, so she'd decided to let him sleep. He probably needed his rest, she thought.

As she slipped on her stilettos, she realized that she was going to need a ride to church. Although Myles wasn't staying at her house anymore, he was the most likely person to pick her up. Her phone was in her purse, which was downstairs, and the guest room didn't have a phone, so either way she'd have to leave the room.

"Madisyn, are you ready?" Aidan called from the hallway. "How about some greasy donuts on the way to church?"

She was stumped. After the day they'd had she would have guessed that the last thing he would have wanted was to spend more time with her family. "Yes, I'm ready. Aidan, you don't have to go church with me today. I completely understand."

He opened the door looking like a model. He was dressed in a dark suit that looked expressly tailored for his athletic body. "That's mighty big of you, Madisyn, but I'm still going. Just because you think you wore me out last night doesn't mean I can't function today. Wait until I tell your dad what you did to me last night." He chuckled as he walked further into the room. "You look beautiful, baby."

Madisyn glanced down at her suit. Feeling a little adventurous, she had eschewed the blouse she normally wore under the suit. Her father would still approve of the outfit. It covered all the important areas. "Thank you, Aidan. You look handsome, as always."

"If you don't stop looking at me like that with those green eyes, we're going to be back in my bed and you won't get to teach Sunday school this morning."

That thought certainly put a hold on her lusty thoughts. The children. How could she forget about the kids? "Oh, no! Where was her brain? "I need to get some candy for the kids. With all that's been going on, I totally forgot."

"No problem. We can stop at the store or you could bring them donuts instead."

She liked the donut idea. "Okay, let's go."

He led her out of the room and they left the house. After stopping for a quick unhealthy breakfast of sausage rolls, donuts and cinnamon rolls, they headed for church.

Aidan wondered if he'd be able to spot the ghost. He would like to get a look at the woman whom Chase put so much trust in. They arrived at Madisyn's church and everything looked normal, he thought. Not that he was really the person to judge normal, since it was only his second visit to the church.

He helped her get ready for her Sunday school class. The kids were more than excited to see the food than him. Apparently being a Dallas Cowboy had nothing on chocolate donuts and milk.

He sat at the back of the room while Madisyn worked her magic on the kids. They were entranced by everything that came out of her mouth, just as he was.

When Sunday school was over and church began, Aidan looked around the church as he and Madisyn took a seat. He felt comfortable at the church. He couldn't put his finger on why, but something about the place made him feel like he was home. He noticed Megan making her way to Madisyn. She crawled up on Madisyn's lap and smiled at Aidan.

He put his arm around Madisyn, bringing her closer to him. He didn't miss the look of approval from Ben. And at that moment, he knew. She was his destiny. Now he just had to get rid of Darnell and clean up the mess in their lives.

He felt someone staring at him. Not the adoring fan stare, but a bad stare. He discreetly looked around the congregation, but no one looked suspicious. He'd make a poor detective, he thought. He couldn't even spot one person out of place in a crowd of less than a hundred people.

When church was over Megan wanted Aidan to carry her. Before Madisyn could tell him otherwise he picked up the little girl and she hugged him. Aidan smiled. When it was right, it was right. With his free hand he guided Madisyn through the crowd and outside.

"Well, Mr. Coles, it's so nice to see you here again," said the minister. "It does my heart good to see Madisyn so happy." He extended his hand to Aidan.

He took it and returned the gesture. "Me too, Reverend."

He leaned closer to Aidan and whispered. "I heard about the incident yesterday. I hope the police catch the intruder before he does any real harm."

"I'm sure they will." Aidan had every faith that the ghost would do her job and Darnell would be caught. He grabbed Madisyn's hand and they walked to his SUV.

"I love you, Madisyn."

She stopped walking and stood in front of him. "Really?" She had tears in those pretty eyes. "That's the nicest gift I've ever received. I'll have to thank you later." She nodded at Megan.

"How many times?" Aidan teased.

"More than last night."

CHAPTER 24

When Madisyn and Aidan arrived at her parents' house, everyone was already there waiting for them. She glanced at Aidan before he released Megan from the car seat. "See what happens when you take the scenic route?"

He opened the back door and helped her and Megan out. "Oh baby, you know I just wanted to spend more time with two of the prettiest females in the world."

Madisyn hoisted Megan on her hip and started walking to the house. "Flattery will get you everywhere."

"I sure hope so," Aidan said as he caught up with her and took her free hand. "I sure hope so."

Madisyn didn't have time for a saucy comeback. Marcus, her starstruck brother, met them as they approached the front door.

"Maddie, what took so long? I hope Megan didn't bother you, Aidan. She can be a chatterbox sometimes."

"Just like her daddy," Madisyn quipped. "Marcus, breathe." She led Aidan inside the house. "We're going inside now."

Marcus nodded. "Thanks for bringing me down, girl. Sorry, Aidan. I don't know what it is, but every time I come within spitting distance of you, I lose it."

Aidan took the gushing in stride. "Don't worry about it, Marcus. I'm going to be around a lot, so you'll get used to me." He kissed Madisyn on the cheek.

Marcus took his daughter out of Madisyn's arms. "I will."

Madisyn looked around for her dad and didn't see him anywhere. "I want to see how Dad is doing. I didn't get to talk to him at church."

Aidan nodded. "Want me to come along?"

She shook her head. "No, why don't you get acquainted with the boys?" She took off for the kitchen, not giving him time to answer. Since it was summer, her father was outside on the patio talking to Mike and her youngest brother, Matthew.

"Daddy, how are you feeling?" She inspected her father closely. He still had a little bruising on his face, but otherwise he looked like the man she loved.

"Fine, baby girl. They gave me some really good medicine yesterday. Your mamma won't let me do much today, but I feel fine." His brown eyes searched her green ones. "Now how are you doing? Have they caught that fool yet?"

"I'm doing okay. To answer the second part, no, they haven't found Darnell yet. I wish this mess was over. Then I could have my life back."

Ben laughed. "I know it must be awful staying in Aidan's big house and having people ferry you about."

She held up her hand. "I know. This whole scene could be so much worse than it is. I'm thankful for everything Aidan's done for me. I don't think I could have made it through this without him. I just feel that when I was finally getting on my feet, here comes someone else taking over my life."

Ben shook his head at her statement. "Honey, that man is moving heaven and earth to keep you safe. He's not trying to take over your life. If he was, he would be like that idiot and cut you off from your family and friends. Has he done that?"

Madisyn shook her head. She hated it when her dad made sense.

"I didn't think so," he said. "Now take some thoughts from an old man."

"What is it, Daddy?"

"I think he's in love with you."

"Why do you think that?"

"A man knows, baby. Trust your daddy."

Madisyn knew that was about as good as she was going to get. "You know I do." She leaned down and gave him a peck on the cheek to show her gratitude. "I'm going to help Mom in the kitchen."

She thought it was a noble gesture, but when she entered the large room, her mother and sisters-in-law had everything under control.

"Maddie, tell the men that dinner's ready," her mother called over her shoulder. "By the time they get washed up and everything, the table will be ready."

"Sure, Mom." She went on her way to do as she was told. She entered the living room and laughed. All the men were watching TV all right, but apparently Megan had ruled that afternoon. They were watching Megan's favorite movie, *The Incredibles*.

Aidan noticed Madisyn the minute she walked into the room. He winked at her and motioned for her to sit next to him. She shook her head. "Sorry to interrupt the Oscar night, but dinner is ready." She went back to the dining room and, true to he̶r̶ r̶'s words, the table was just about set.

The guys filed in slowly with Megan in her father's arms. When everyone was seated and Mike had said grace, they dug into the dinner. Aidan sat next to Madisyn, holding her hand under the table.

"You know, I could get used to this," Aidan whispered in her ear. "If we have a bad season, will I still be welcome in your parents' house for Sunday dinner?"

"Sure, Daddy will just tell you what you did wrong," she teased.

"As long as he doesn't tell me how to love you, we're good." He kissed her on the cheek.

She'd waited a year for Darnell to even mutter the words, and he'd refused to come to Sunday dinner. Madisyn thought how funny love was. Aidan was everything she didn't know she wanted. He was kind, gentle, supportive and a protector. She could really get used to that.

❦

Later that evening, Aidan smiled triumphantly. Madisyn was lying next to him, sound asleep. They had had a full day. After being with her family most of it, then coming back to his house for some intense lovemaking, they both had a right to be tired.

For some reason Aidan couldn't close his eyes. He was beat, but sleep eluded him. A day like today would have normally had him running for the hills, but he'd enjoyed it and he now realized how much Madisyn's family loved her and vice versa. He wanted that closeness with his family, but he didn't have it and that was his fault.

He had chosen to alienate the one man who loved him like a son for a man who could have cared less whether he lived or died. Now it was time to fix it, or at least put forth a good faith effort.

He slid from the bed, slipped on his boxers and slacks, and went downstairs to call his parents. His mother was happy to hear his voice as always, but couldn't hide her surprise when he asked to speak to his stepfather.

"Why?" she asked with a definite edge to her voice.

"I'll not have you upsetting Lester. It's bad enough your father tried to attack him yesterday."

"What are you talking about? Why would he do such a thing?" Aidan couldn't even bear to call him Dad.

"Who knows? Anyway, Lester was outside cleaning up my car and your father just attacked him, saying something about it being payback."

Aidan was thoroughly confused. "Payback for what? 'Cause Lester rescued you from an abusive husband?"

"I guess. I think he was drunk or something, Lester only hit him once and he was out cold. He's in jail now. That's why I figured you were calling, to bail him out."

Aidan shook his head. "No, I wanted to try to patch things up with Lester or at least start, but as usual my timing is way off. Do you need me to fly up?"

"No, son. Why do you want to make up with Lester after all this time? What's wrong? You're not sick, are you?"

He chuckled. "No, Mom, I finally understand what you've been saying all these years. Lester loved us enough to take us out of a dangerous situation and gave us his name when he didn't have to. I was worshipping a man who didn't love me, but the money I made."

"I'm glad you realize that finally. Lester will be glad to hear it. All right, you can talk to him."

Aidan wanted closure, but not like this. "No, I can wait. You guys have had a strange weekend."

"Speaking of strange, I hear you've got your hands full as well with your woman."

"Apparently Chase has been sticking his nose where it doesn't belong. When did he tell you?"

"No, don't be mad at Chase. He's just doing what you pay him to do. Protect you and your family. He just wanted to make sure that we knew what was going on so if the press descended on us, we wouldn't be caught off guard. Have they caught the guy yet?"

"No, but I'm sure it'll be soon. Hey, how about you and Lester coming down for a vacation? There're some people I want you guys to meet."

His mother gasped as her brain finally caught up with the invitation. "Aidan, don't tell me? You think she's the one? After only a few weeks?"

"I don't think, I know. And I want you guys here." He heard Madisyn walking around upstairs. "Look Mom, gotta go. We'll talk later, okay?"

"But you didn't talk to Lester."

"I will." He ended the call and went upstairs.

Madisyn watched Aidan enter the bedroom. She had just finished her shower and was getting ready to put on a pair of shorts. He wore a broad grin and marched directly toward her.

She held up a shaky hand to stop him. "Again? Come on, Aidan, how about letting a girl get some rest?" She was lying, but he didn't have to know that.

He sat on the bed next to her. "That wasn't what I was smiling about, but if you're game . . ." He let the sentence drift into a sea of innuendo. "Actually, I was talking to my mom earlier and it was like a lightbulb came on." He kissed her on the cheek. "Thank you, Madisyn. You gave me the push I needed. While you were sleeping, I went downstairs to call Lester, but I talked to Mom instead. I'll wait until I can talk to Lester face to face. I wasted a lot of time trying not to acknowledge what Lester is in my life, but that's over."

She noticed the tears sliding down his cheek, but decided not to comment on it. That alone spoke volumes about what was going on inside his head. He'd been her shield so many times, tonight she would be his. She pressed her head against his chest. He was warm and his heart was thundering. She grabbed his head and rubbed it against her cheek. "I'm glad you talked to your mom. I know Lester will understand what you did and

247

why. He still loves you, no matter what. That's what a parent does."

He inhaled deeply. "I only hope I can be half the man Lester is when it comes to our children."

CHAPTER 25

"What do you mean, she's not at home?" Darnell shouted into the cell phone. The day was not going as planned. Plus, he'd never heard back from Trev yesterday, which only meant his ne'er-do-well cousin had done a bunk once again. "She has to be at home. She's always at home!"

"Just what I said, Darnell," Keisha said. "Look, I don't know what's up, but I'm going to go by there and see for myself. Maybe she's just not answering her phone or she stayed at her parents' later than usual. Who knows what happened to your cousins. I told you they couldn't be trusted, especially Trev."

"He can be trusted. I probably shouldn't have paid him beforehand, that's all. I can't believe such a simple task has spiraled out of control. I called his phone and some guy answered the phone saying I needed to turn myself in."

Keisha gasped. "I don't like the sound of that. You sure it wasn't one of Trev's boys? Sounds like a double cross."

Darnell wished it had been that easy. "I tried his main boy and he said he hadn't talked to Trev since yesterday. I tried calling Trev again earlier and it went straight to voice mail."

"So what are you going to do? That dinner thing is in two weeks and I'm sure your bosses are getting suspicious by now. You could take me in Maddie's place," Keisha pointed out.

Darnell knew a loaded gun when he heard one. Keisha had been the greatest help in all this, but she was still his biggest mistake. "Keisha, you know exactly why I can't walk into that dinner with anyone else but Maddie. My boss loves her. Thinks she's the best thing since sliced bread. He likes the influence she has on my life. And if I plan on becoming senior investment banker, then partner, which is the goal here, I need Maddie."

"So why did you cheat on her? If she meant that much to you, why betray her in such a horrible way? Only an idiot would have messed up a good thing like that. Maddie would have done anything for you."

"What can I say? I'm a man. Too much temptation."

"And that's why you're planning on kidnapping your ex? Too much temptation? You do realize that's a federal offense and you'll go to jail?"

He actually laughed. He knew he'd lost all rational thinking when he came up with this idea. "If I do, guess who's going to be in a cell next to me?"

"You don't mean me? I don't have nothing to do with this!"

Darnell felt some of his cool coming back. "Yes, you do. You've supplied me with Maddie's whereabouts. You are what's called an accessory. And although you may not have committed the crime with me, you're helping me. That gets you a free trip to the cell next to mine."

"Bastard," Keisha spat.

"Yes, I am. But you're ten times worse. You slept with your best friend's man. So you're up to your waxed eyebrows in this mess."

Keisha sighed, realizing that she was sunk. "So what's next?"

"You've got to figure out if she's home or not. If she's not, you're going to have to get her out somewhere alone, so I can make my move."

"I can't do that. Maddie's been my friend since junior high. She was my friend when no one else would speak to me. I just can't."

"It's either you give her up or you're going to jail."

Monday morning, Aidan awoke to the sounds of the shower. It was a little past six and Madisyn was already up. He leaned against the plush pillows and grinned. He could definitely get used to sleeping with her every night. Although they hadn't made love the previous night, he felt closer to Madisyn. They'd talked into the night hours and fallen asleep in each other's arms.

He was thinking about joining Madisyn in the shower when the phone rang. He knew only one person would have the nerve to call this early in the morning. Looking at the caller ID, he saw he was correct. It was Chase. He snatched the phone up and put it to his ear.

"Hey, man."

"Where's Madisyn?"

"Right now, she's in the shower. You mean your ghost couldn't tell you that? What happened to you yesterday?"

"Huh? Oh, something came up. I had to take care of it. Nothing to do with you."

Chase was bum rushing him, giving answers before Aidan could form the question. "Chase, what's going on? Is there a problem with what happened Saturday?"

"No, man. If you must know, I had some woman problems and I had to set her straight," he said.

Aidan grinned. "Don't tell me you're actually dating someone? I thought work was your mistress?"

"I wouldn't call it dating. More like we hit it and she split," Chase admitted. "Now can we get to the matter of your lady?"

"All right, man. I get it. You don't want to talk about it. You don't have to talk about it. I can wait until you're ready. Why do you want to know where Madisyn is?"

"There's been a strange car parked in front of her house since about four this morning. I ran the plates and it's registered to Harvey Slade of Dallas, Texas. This guy's got a criminal record a mile long. I can't find a link between him and Darnell, but I'm sure there is one. If he has someone watching her house like that, he's raising the stakes. Make sure she doesn't go anywhere alone, not even for lunch. Make sure she doesn't leave her work building. I can pull a few strings with the security force, but that only covers her if she's in the building."

Aidan felt the conviction in Chase's usually upbeat voice and knew instantly something had changed. "I'll make sure she understands."

"Is her brother still driving her to work?"

"I was thinking about taking her to work," Aidan confessed. "Should we keep the old arrangement?"

"Yes, so we can keep you out of it as much as possible. You never know who is watching when you drop her off. With the center nearing its grand opening, you don't want any negative publicity."

"Right," Aidan agreed. "The press would eat this up and that would defeat the purpose of the center."

"Exactly."

Aidan ended the call and waited for Madisyn to come out of the shower. He had hoped she would come out dressed in nothing but a towel, but his morning quickie thoughts were dashed when she came out tightening the sash on her silk bathrobe.

She smiled at him. "Good morning, honey." She leaned down and kissed him.

He loved the way she smelled. He wanted to bury his face in her neck and work his way down her body. When he tried to put his plan into action, she backed away. "I don't have time for that, Aidan. Mike will be here in less than an hour."

"You don't want me to take you to work?" Although Mike was the designated driver, Aidan was still hurt.

"Mike and I thought it was best to keep to the original plan. I don't want people noticing that Aidan Coles is dropping me off at work on a regular basis."

He nodded. "You're right, baby. I wanted to take you, but Chase said exactly the same thing. He said some guy has been camped out in front of your house. Do you know a Harvey Slade?"

Madisyn shook her head. "The name doesn't ring a bell. What kind of car was it?" She sat down on the bed.

"Maybe I would recognize the car."

"Chase didn't say, but I'll check. He said that Slade was from Dallas."

Madisyn sat there, her hands clasped together in her lap. Tears filled her eyes. "This only going to get worse, isn't it?"

He moved closer to her, drawing her into his arms. "Baby, we're in this together. With all the security I have in place, I know we'll catch him before he can get anywhere near you. We just have to stay on our toes."

She wiped her eyes. "I wish I could just stay here forever and never go outside."

Aidan stroked her hair. "You'll get no argument from me."

"You know I can't do that, Aidan, don't you? I have responsibilities at work and I have to finalize things for the grand opening gala in a few weeks. In a way, I'm glad I have something else to focus on now."

"How's the gala coming?" He continued stroking her hair and shoulders. He'd never thought love would feel so comforting.

She sniffed and sat up. "Pretty good. I'm ordering the food this weekend. Mom wants to try out a few more catering places this week. And before you ask, Mike has volunteered to accompany us." She took a deep breath and gazed at him with those pretty green eyes. "Don't think I don't appreciate all that you've done, because I do. I just miss being able to be on my own some of the time."

Aidan wanted to lay her cares to rest. "I understand about being independent, baby, I really do. But we're going to have to be careful right now." He wanted to show her that he truly understood. He hoped the ghost would be able to keep up with her when she was out alone. "You can drive my SUV whenever you want. If you'd rather drive a car, I have a BMW, too." He wished he could take the words back, since he'd never mentioned it before.

She shot him a look. "I've never seen it."

"Because it's kept at my condo downtown." He had just opened a major can of worms. He was going to have to explain why he had another place to live when he had this large house. "Madisyn, I can explain."

"You don't have to, Aidan. We aren't married. If you want to tell me, that's fine, but don't feel you have to tell me something you obviously didn't mean to slip out." She walked into the bathroom and closed the door.

Aidan listened to the quiet sobs of the woman he loved. Now he was really in a kettle of hot boiling water and there was only one way out.

<hr />

Get over it, girl, she told herself. *So he's got another place, big deal. You know he hasn't been there, so what's the problem?*

Madisyn gathered her dignity and looked at her reflection in the large bathroom mirror. She was over-reacting, she knew, but what did she expect? Perfection?

Yes, she did. She wanted him to be her shield, but in reality she was her own shield. When it came down to it, it was her life hanging in the balance, not Aidan's, Chase's or those of the mysterious security team.

After she finished her morning routine, she left the security of the bathroom. Aidan wasn't in bed anymore. In fact, he wasn't anywhere to be seen. She guessed he'd gone downstairs. She went to the closet, retrieved a black suit, a cream-colored blouse and her sensible shoes. Keisha would hate the entire outfit. She chuckled.

"What's so funny?" Aidan asked, walking into the room.

"Nothing," Madisyn said. "I'm going to change." She headed for the bathroom.

"Why can't you change here? I mean, I've seen you nude before."

"You want to watch me get dressed for work?" Madisyn didn't know if it was sexy, crazy, or he just wanted to get her mind off the condo thing.

"Yes, I do. I know, it sounds a little out there, doesn't it?" Aidan shook his head. "I've never asked a woman to get dressed in front of me before. It's something about you."

Madisyn decided it was somewhere between sexy and crazy, but leaning more toward sexy. Since she already had on her bra and panties, he wouldn't get to see that much. As she started to dress for work, he started explaining about the condo.

"Chase suggested I buy a place in town to take my dates to. I didn't want people knowing my address. That seemed the best way to do it."

"You needed a place to take your dates," Madisyn said calmly. "I understand, Aidan. There are a lot of women out there who will do just about anything to get a professional athlete. You never know who's psycho and who's not. So how did I rate a trip to your house and not the condo?"

"You were different from the start. I felt it. I'm sure you did, too. I feel closer to you than most of the guys I've been playing ball with since college. For the record, I haven't been in the condo for months. I was thinking of putting it on the market."

She was completely finished dressing by the end of his story. "Thank you, Aidan. But you shouldn't sell 'cause you think it's what I want. That's part of you."

He stood and walked to her, hugging her hard against his body. "But it's not part of us."

Madisyn thought her knees wouldn't support her much longer. She held onto Aidan. "Really?"

"Yes, baby. This is about us. I'll have the car brought here so you can have something to drive, but I do have one rule."

She smiled, already knowing what he was going to say. "I know I can't go anywhere alone. One of my brothers or you must be in the car, right?" She kissed him softly.

"Right." He kissed her hard and long, easing her down on the bed and covering her with his body.

Madisyn toyed with the idea of a morning quickie, but the doorbell halted all those wicked, naughty thoughts. "Mike is early," she said against his lips.

Aidan kissed her on the forehead. "I'll go let him in." He left the room, leaving Madisyn to collect herself.

After she straightened her clothes and fixed her makeup and hair, she grabbed her purse, heading down the hall. She heard both her brother and Aidan in the kitchen laughing about something. The laughter stopped when she entered the kitchen.

"Okay, what is it?"

Mike smiled at her. "Nothing. The security guard was telling me how some guy tried to bribe his way in a few weeks ago. It sounded like Darnell. I told Aidan it was nice to know some people can't be bought."

"Oh," Madisyn said. "Yeah, that's nice to know."

CHAPTER 26

After her brother dropped her off at work that morning, Madisyn had had nothing but one surprise after another. First of all when she reached her desk, she found a dozen red roses in a crystal vase waiting for her. She knew they were from Aidan, but how could he have had them delivered so quickly?

She looked at the card and her heart started beating out of control. They weren't from Aidan, they were from Darnell. He wasn't stupid enough to sign his name, but the one sentence on the card spoke volumes. *Don't think I can't still get you.*

With shaky hands she dialed Aidan and told him. Funny how he could make her feel better over the phone. "I can be there in twenty minutes, baby. You should take the rest of the day off."

"No, that's what he wants me to do. He wants me to run scared, but it's not going to happen. That was the old Madisyn. The new Madisyn isn't having that kind of mess anymore. I just wanted to tell you. Thank you so much for listening." She noticed Keisha walking in her direction. "I love you, Aidan."

"I love you, too, baby. If you need me, call me. I'll be there quicker than lightning."

"I appreciate that, honey. Talk to you later." She ended the call just as her friend reached her.

"I heard you got some flowers." Keisha entered her cubicle and took a seat in the chair. "Who sent them?"

Madisyn didn't like the feeling she was getting from her friend. "Like you don't know," Madisyn accused.

"It could have been the football player thanking you for working on his charity board or something. Darnell, most likely. Sounds like he's ready to act right, girl."

"Too little, too late. Darnell will never change. He was cheating on me for so long, I guess I started blocking it out of my head, ignoring all the signs."

Keisha toyed with one of the roses. "Well, maybe he knows what a good woman you are. You know you guys belong together. This way he can take you to that dinner and he can get that promo and you can move forward."

"What's in this for you? You've been singing his praises since I finally broke up with him. When I was with him, you could never say anything good about him. You used to call him a sellout."

Keisha shrugged. "People change, Maddie. You should know that. You've changed a lot in the last few weeks. It's like aliens came and took over your body and put a spunkier, sexier Madisyn in your place."

Madisyn thought about the changes in her life in the last two weeks and realized that although she'd had Darnell for two years, she didn't love him. She loved Aidan. "Maybe not aliens. I just made a few changes. The first one was not to take the idiot back again. Let's talk about something else."

"How about lunch at the pub across the street? We could walk, 'cause I know you didn't bring your car."

"Where's your car?"

"My sister borrowed it."

Madisyn knew Keisha loved her car more than her sister and would never let her younger sister borrow her car. "I can't do lunch today."

"If I didn't know better, I'd think you didn't want to be seen with your friend. Is that it?"

"Keisha, you know that's not true. I have some work to do. We can do something later in the week." Madisyn hoped lightning didn't strike her for lying.

"How about going out this Saturday night? I think I talked Chayla into going. Unfortunately, I think she's bringing Jared with her."

"I think it's cute that they're still crazy about each other after being married for so long. You're just hatin' on her for no reason."

Keisha grinned at her. "I heard a lot of Dallas Cowboys are going to be there, and I want to make sure I get seen. I don't want anyone messing up my game, including you." She left the cubicle.

Madisyn thought about Keisha's departing words and wondered at them. Could Keisha really mean her harm? Did she really want to find out?

<hr />

That evening when she arrived at Aidan's house, he had a surprise for her. The car had arrived as promised, but that wasn't the dealmaker. Aidan had cooked or, more likely, he had purchased a meal from his favorite restaurant. Either way, the house smelled wonderful.

The table was already set. Wine greeted her as she took a seat at the table. She waited for Aidan. He soon arrived with a plate of chicken spaghetti and placed it in front of her. "I hope you like this. It's my mom's recipe. This is the first time I tried to make it."

It smelled good and looked even better. He also brought in a salad and garlic bread. "This looks great, Aidan." She took a bite and moaned. "This is delicious. Tell your mom I'm going to need the recipe for this."

He sat down and began eating. "You can tell her yourself in a few weeks."

"That's right. I'm going to have to have a long chat when they get here. What do they usually do when they're here?"

Aidan lowered his head. "Actually, this is the first time Lester has been to Dallas. Mom has been here loads of time."

"You made your mother choose between you and your stepfather? How could you?"

"Baby, I didn't make her choose anything. Lester knew he was welcome in my house 'cause he's so good to my mom, but something always came up."

She looked up from her plate and studied him carefully. "Couldn't you tell that he was hurting inside? You have so much to make up for, Aidan. Lester must have a heart the size of Texas."

"He does. He's a good guy and loves my mom to pieces. He treats her like a queen. Always has. I won't bore you with the horrid details but when we left my dad and we moved in with Lester, he was always telling me how much our dad still loved us."

Madisyn nodded, respecting his privacy. "I know that must have been a trying time for you, but you see now who really cares for you, don't you?"

"And how. I don't eat crow often, but I know I will be eating plenty of it when I do talk to him."

Madisyn threw her napkin on the table, stood and stomped toward him. She reached for his hand, forcing the fork to fall on the table. "Come on, we're calling your dad right now."

Aidan laughed as Madisyn pulled him down the hall to the home office and thrust the cordless phone into his hand. She looked so serious that he knew he had few options at the moment. He punched out the number to his parents' home.

He took a seat, knowing this was going to a long phone call. He hadn't expected Madisyn to sit in his lap, but he wasn't going to tell her not to. It felt too good. The phone rang twice before Lester answered the phone, which meant his mom probably was out.

"Hello, Aidan. Your mom is across the street. Want me to tell her to call you back?"

That had been their typical phone conversation for the last ten years. Neither had had much to say to the other, so the fewer words that passed between them the better. Except for now. "Actually, Lester, I wanted to talk to you. I thought Mom might have mentioned it."

"No. What's on your mind, son?"

Son, Aidan thought. "It's about this thing we got going on. I know my dad is a piece of work, but Lester, he's not my father, you are. You helped me pick a college, pick a sports agent, and taught me to how to invest my money. I'm sorry I was holding onto the dream of the perfect father. I had one all along and was too stupid to realize it."

"I've waited a long time to hear you say those words, Aidan. You know I loved all three of you boys like you were my own. I gave you all my name. Twenty-five years is a long time, and it's going to take me a while to digest this."

Aidan didn't expect a gushing thank you for his apology, but he had expected Lester to be a little more forgiving. Still, he had to keep going. "I understand, Lester. I also would like you and Mom to come visit for a week when the center opens. We can talk more indepth then."

Lester couldn't hide his surprise. "That would be fine. I've always wanted to visit Dallas, but with things between us like they were, I didn't see the point."

"The point is that you have a son here, and you're welcome here anytime. I'll let you guys know when I get the plane tickets. I'm going to show you guys the best time you've had in a long time."

Madisyn shifted in his lap and faced him. She had tears in her eyes. She kissed him gently on the forehead and whispered in his ear, "I'm very proud of you." She rose and left the room, closing the door on her way out, letting him continue the conversation in private.

Once she was gone, Aidan continued his conversation with his dad. "I want you and Mom to meet Madisyn and her family. They're very nice people. I've been attending church with her."

"You're going to church now?"

Aidan laughed. "Yeah, I know. I'm as good as hooked. And you're right. Madisyn's having some issues with her ex, but hopefully all that will be over and she'll be able to go out with us."

"I'll be looking forward to it. Goodbye, Aidan."

"Bye, Lester."

Madisyn paced the living room waiting for Aidan to finish the call with his stepfather. She'd almost lost it listening to the one-sided conversation. She didn't want to start blubbering while Aidan was on the phone. Finally, she heard the door opening and Aidan taking a deep breath.

She immediately relaxed when he called her name. "I'm in the living room." She took a seat on the couch and tried to look relaxed.

He walked into the living room. Tears still streaked his cheek. Smiling, he took a seat next to her and pulled her into his lap. He kissed her with the intensity of a burning inferno. It was so intense, all Madisyn could do was hold on for the ride.

When they came up for air, Aidan looked deep into her eyes. "Thank you, Madisyn. I don't know if I could have made that call if you weren't here. I'm so glad you were."

She caressed his face, swiping at the moisture on his cheeks. "We're a team, Aidan. I know you guys didn't get everything resolved in just one phone call, but it was a start."

"It was a very good start. I can't believe I was being such an idiot all those years. I'm probably going to go bankrupt trying to make this right."

She sat up and faced him. "Aidan, love is free. If it's real love, you don't have spend a nickel on trinkets. You can't take any of that with you when you die."

"So if I didn't spend another penny on you, you would still love me?"

"I would love you more. Sometimes money makes bigger fools out of us. The love I'm looking for has nothing do with your income, but with your spirit."

He kissed her again. "I love you, Madisyn."

"Right back at you." She leaned to kiss him, but his cell phone rang, shattering their intimate moment. Silently, she slid off his lap and sat next to him.

He looked down at the phone. "It's Chase. I'd better take this." He opened the phone and said, "Hey, Chase."

Madisyn noticed Aidan's easygoing temperament suddenly took a nosedive. He sat up, and then suddenly rose and began pacing the room.

"Chase, that's a stupid plan and I'll not let Madisyn get harmed in the process." He ended the call and threw the cell phone against the wall. It shattered into tiny pieces.

Madisyn gasped at his actions. In the short time she'd known him, she'd never seen him this angry. "Aidan, what is it?"

He shot her an angry look. "Nothing. Chase just had a nutty idea and I'm not having it."

She appreciated his concern, but Madisyn was getting a little tired of everyone making decisions for her. "Is it about me?"

He sighed and looked up at the ceiling, then back at her. "Yes, but it's a crazy scheme and I won't let you do it. It's too dangerous."

Madisyn walked to him. "Shouldn't this be my decision? Don't get me wrong, Aidan, I appreciate everything you've done, but if we can get this over with faster if I do whatever Chase wants me to do, what's wrong with that?"

"What's wrong is that there is the possibility that you could get hurt. After finding you, I'm not going to lose you." He pulled her into his embrace and kissed her.

Madisyn's brain was stuck in neutral. Aidan's kiss short-circuited her brainwaves, along with the rest of her body. When they came up from air, Madisyn wanted to know about the scheme. She led Aidan to the couch and they sat down. "Okay, what's the scheme?"

He looked at her with those beautiful brown eyes. "He wants me to take you out somewhere very public. He feels that if we can draw Darnell out of hiding, we can make our move and get him into custody."

She didn't like being the target, but the plan did have some merit. She was ready to get her life back. "You know actually Keisha asked me to go out with her and the girls Saturday. Some new club is having a grand opening. My girlfriend Chayla and her husband are going."

"Is it Club Sizzle?"

"Wow! How do you know that? Oh, yeah, Keisha did say it was owned by a Dallas Cowboy. She thinks the club is going to be overrun with celebrities at the grand opening."

"I know that because one of my teammates, Kameron Drews, is the owner. He asked me to come to the opening, but I told him no. I could call and tell him that I need a VIP table."

"Could you? That would be great. And I'll make sure to tell Keisha. I think she's up to something."

"You think she's playing you against Darnell?"

Madisyn exhaled. She thought Keisha was doing more than that. "I don't have anything concrete, but if I tell her I'm going, I'll bet you a thousand bucks Darnell will know."

"How long have you guys been friends?" Aidan rubbed her hand.

"Since junior high school," Madisyn said. "But I think it's time I cut her loose."

CHAPTER 27

The next morning Madisyn watched as Keisha performed her daily parade march across the floor. Usually it took Keisha a good hour before she could settle down to work. She was dressed in a short, light-blue suit and matching three-inch stilettos. As she approached Madisyn's work area, she glanced around, making sure Madisyn's boss was nowhere in sight.

Once she was satisfied, she sat on the edge of Madisyn's desk. "Hey, how about lunch today? Surely the master is going to let you have lunch today?"

"I can't today," Madisyn lied. "I need to make some calls for Alliance to prepare for the grand opening. But I do have good news."

Keisha eyes lit up. "What? Don't tell me you're finally taking Darnell back? It certainly took you long enough. Not that I'm surprised."

"No, I'm not taking Darnell back. I'm going to go to that club this Saturday. Are you still going?"

"That's great, Maddie. We're going to have so much fun. Even with Chayla bringing old dull Jared. I'm going to call today to see if I can reserve a table."

"No, you don't have to do that. A friend of mine is going to reserve a VIP table. So that's covered."

Keisha slid off the desk, planted her hands on her small hips. "So it is true."

"What?" Madisyn tried to play it cool, but it was useless if the smirk on Keisha's perfectly made-up face was any indication.

"Maddie, we all know how getting a VIP table goes. It costs a mint to reserve a table, unless you're high profile. Now I know you couldn't get a table on your own, but your charity man could. So that leads me to believe that you're seeing Aidan Coles on a more personal level. You could have told me that you're dating him. I would have kept it to myself. He's really holding onto that good boy image, isn't he?"

"What are you talking about?"

"Oh, come on, Maddie. You know he's one of the few players that's not surrounded by scandal. He has to be seen with a certain kind of woman. Someone like you with a squeaky clean image, just like his. So is he paying you to be his shield? He's just like Darnell, using you for your rep and having a freak somewhere else."

Madisyn looked at Keisha with new eyes. Yes, she knew this friendship had run its course. Funny how a few weeks before she didn't know how to end her relationship with Keisha. But now it would be no problem. A real friend would have been happy for her, but not Keisha.

"He merely said I could bring some friends if I wanted. If you don't want to sit at the table, no one is forcing you."

"Are you nuts? Of course I want to sit there. I'll check out Aidan for myself and you'll see how fast he's going to jump ship. He'll never care for you, Maddie. Remember how Darnell never wanted to do anything with your family? That's why he never went to church with you. Aidan never will, either."

Madisyn held back a retort that would refute all of Keisha's words. Madisyn hadn't shared the news of Aidan attending church with her friend, and now she was glad she hadn't. "Well, you can check him out and give me a full report."

Keisha laughed. "And you know I'm going to check him good, don't you? I'll find out just how good a cowboy he really is."

The minute Keisha sat down at her desk, she instantly reached for her phone. She dialed the number and waited for him to pick up. It looked like their plan could work with just a few changes. She was just about to give up when he finally answered the phone.

"What?" Darnell grumbled. "I'm really busy right now."

Keisha didn't like the sound of that. "What's more important than me? You're the one who needs this plan to work, not me. My life will go on just fine either way."

"Not if I tell Maddie that you've been feeding me information about her whereabouts. Why did you call? Are you taking her to lunch today?"

"No, she's doing some kind of work for the charity on her lunch break."

Darnell grunted. "So how's this good news? I still don't have Maddie in my possession. I'm still in a mess."

"I can't tell you over the phone," Keisha whispered. "But it's worth you bringing your tired behind to the pub across the street so I can tell you." She hated she'd ever got involved with this idiot. On paper Darnell looked like a great catch. He had the right car, the right salary, and lived in the perfect upscale condo, but, in reality, he was a loser.

"All right, I'll be there about eleven. Don't come in there late, either. You know how you're always trying to make an entrance."

"You just be there, boy." She hung up the phone. She had to figure a way out of this mess without Maddie knowing that she had sold her out.

⬩⬥⬩

Chase sat behind his desk with his eyes closed. So many things needed to go right this week. One thing out of place and it would have a domino effect on his one and only client.

If they couldn't trick Darnell into action against Madisyn and then catch him before he harmed her, then the Alliance wouldn't get to open on time. If the center wasn't open, then Aidan's mind wouldn't be on training camp next month. Rumors about Aidan's probable retirement were surfacing and Chase had to deal with those. The Cowboys wanted another couple of years out of Aidan. Dangling another thirty million dollars in front of him wasn't helping, either. Aidan was ready to settle down, not play another season.

He heard his door open and close. His secretary normally knocked, so he knew it wasn't her. "Get up, man. Is this what I'm paying you for?"

Chase opened his eyes and laughed. "Yeah, boss, you caught me. I was trying to think of a master plan."

Aidan smiled back at him. "Any luck?" He took a seat in one of the leather chairs.

Chase sat up. "Actually, no. I can't think of a plan to catch Darnell without using Madisyn as bait. That's the only thing that will bring him out in the open."

He had expected Aidan to blow his top again as he had the first time Chase had brought up the plan. Instead, Aidan sat there calm, cool and collected. He looked like a man in love.

"Actually, Madisyn is on board with the idea. Her friends want to go to Club Sizzle and since Kameron is begging me to go, I can get a VIP table."

Chase chuckled. "Yeah, rumor is that the wife is hopping mad about him buying into that club without her permission."

"Yeah, I think she's still at her mom's in Oklahoma. It's going to cost Kam some money to get her back this time. She didn't sign a prenup and he doesn't want a divorce."

Chase shook his head. "What a mess. I'm just glad he's not my client. So you guys are going to come out of the closet, so to speak?"

"Yeah, I think it should be very interesting. I'll finally get to meet her other friends. If my instincts are correct, I think Keisha is our leak. Madisyn is going to tell her today, so Darnell should have the information really soon."

"Well, that solves that part of the problem. He's not using his cell phone anymore, either. He probably got a pre-paid one so we can't monitor his calls. He's gone underground. He hasn't been at his house for the last few days, so I know he's planning something big. He took out a large amount of cash and has ceased using his credit cards. But Cadence is still on the case."

"When am I going to meet this mystery woman?"

Chase smiled, remembering his last encounter with Cadence Callahan. He hoped to have another one soon, but with this case, that would have to wait. "She's already seen you," he drawled.

"Of course."

Chase took out pad and pen, ready to take notes. "Now about Saturday. Check in before you get to the club. That way I can make sure everything will be in place."

Aidan nodded. "Why don't you just come to the club and you can check it out for yourself. That way when you spot your ghost, you can whisk her off for a night of sex."

Chase laughed. He might have wished for that scenario, but in reality, Cadence's mind was going to be on the job. She would never compromise the assignment. "I'll go, but just to make sure we catch Darnell and put his ass under the jail for what he's done to Madisyn."

"Deal."

At first Aidan had been totally against Madisyn's willingness to endanger herself, but, as he listened to teammate Kameron Drews, he began to think it just might work.

"Sure, Aidan, I'll set everything up for the table. You don't mind taking a few publicity shots, do you?"

Aidan knew these pictures would probably also give Kam an alibi of sorts. Kam's wife didn't trust him, and rightly so. He was already paying for three kids outside his marriage.

"That's cool, Kam, but I need you to do a favor for me," Aidan said.

"You? I thought you were kidding. You never need favors. What is it? I owe you big anyway for covering my ass over the years."

Yes, he did, but Aidan dismissed that from his mind. That was another time and another place. That was before Madisyn O'Riley entered his world. "Forget about it. The favor I need is right up your street. I need you to play up to a woman."

"What?"

Aidan knew he had to give Kam something. "I'm trying to get some information out of a female. You're a football player and she loves athletes. We could both get what we want."

"Aidan, what's gotten into you, man?"

"Nothing. I need some information, and some women love your lifestyle. Her name is Keisha Allen. I just need you to spend a little time with her."

"Is this your lady, and you're trying to throw her off on me?"

"No, she's not my lady. You'll meet Madisyn Saturday night, along with her other friends."

Kam couldn't hide his shock. "You're bringing her to the club? Man, you never take your woman where you hang out. Oh man, you are so messing up my game. I'd hoped you'd be alone so my friend could hang out with you in front of the cameras."

"Sorry, man. My days of covering for you are over," Aidan said proudly.

"So the rumors are true," Kam said. "You're actually retiring. Man, you still have a few more years left. You're in great shape."

"Yeah, and I plan to stay that way," Aidan commented. "That's why this is my last season. It's not like I'd ever spend all the money anyway. I play football because I love the game, not for the money. Don't get me wrong, the money helped me do a lot of things I only dreamed of, like the Alliance. I'd never have been able to offer that service for free. But someone told me money can make you act a fool, and I'm tired of watching people do exactly that."

"Was that directed at me?"

Aidan wanted to laugh. Kam was on a definite path to destruction. "No, man, it wasn't. You've made some mistakes, but you always take your punishment like a man."

"True dat. I wish I could retire. I'm tired of playing, but I'm too addicted to the perks."

Aidan didn't know how to respond to that. Once, in the beginning, he had been close to Kam, but those "perks" had driven a wedge between them and now it was time to say good-bye.

"Aidan, I'll put your name on the VIP list. Don't sweat it, man. I'll show your party a good time. I owe you."

"Thanks, Kam."

⌘

Keisha took a seat at the table. The pub was crowded since it was lunchtime. She glanced around the room searching in vain for Darnell. He was nowhere to be seen. She'd almost given up on him when she noticed him walking toward her. "What took you so long?" Keisha hissed as Darnell took a seat. As usual, he was thirty minutes late.

She could see the toll this mess was taking on him. Darnell always wore neatly tailored suits, but today he wore a dingy white shirt, dirty blue jeans, and tennis shoes. "What's the problem?"

He'd noticed her staring. "Can't stand the earthy look? Man, you're nothing like Maddie."

Keisha reached for the menu. "Well, I'm not Maddie, remember? You said I was ten times prettier, ten times smaller and ten times better in bed."

He shrugged. "I lied, but then you were pretty hot for me then, weren't you? So don't think just making a full confession to Maddie now will absolve you of all this. It won't."

She hated him. Really hated him. "I know I shouldn't have looked at your trifling ass, but it's too late now. You're paying for lunch, right?"

He snatched a menu from the plastic holder. "You're just like your sister. Yeah, I got this. What was so important I had to take city transportation to get here?"

Too many things flashed into Keisha's already overloaded brain at once. "How do you know I have a sister?"

"I'm sure Madisyn mentioned it, saying how much you guys were alike, despite the age difference,'" Darnell answered calmly. "Now what's the deal?"

"Forget that. Why are you taking the bus?" She stared at him. "Where's the Benz?"

He exhaled. "Everything is a label with you, isn't it? My car is in my garage at my upscale condo, if you must know. My place is being watched, thanks to Aidan's high-priced attorney. My car is tagged. I can't rent a car because I'm not using my credit cards. So my method of transportation has changed."

Keisha hadn't realized Darnell was being watched so closely. She fell silent as the waiter came and took their order. When he left she resumed the conversation. "So where have you been sleeping? With that girl you were cheating on me with when Maddie caught you in bed?"

He smiled. It wasn't a pleasant smile. It had a sinister look to it. "Wouldn't you like to know? Don't worry about where I've been. Just know that I'm keeping it in the family."

Keisha couldn't make sense of the cryptic remark. The waiter returned with their drinks and took their lunch order. He placed a timer on the table and set it for five minutes.

"Five minutes, or it's free." He left and Darnell picked up the timer.

"You can't be too careful," Darnell said as he inspected the device. "It could be a bug."

Keisha shook her head. "You've been watching too many cop shows."

"No, I know whoever is watching me is good. Better than good. I don't know how they're watching me, but I can feel it."

Keisha, not believing a word of his crap, waved the remark away. "You're just paranoid 'cause it's taking so long for you to get Maddie back."

Darnell took a gulp of tea. "I never heard from Trev. No one has seen him since he went to Maddie's. Has she said anything? I went by her house last night and she wasn't there. It was late so I know she should have been there. She must be living somewhere else. Maybe at her parents'?"

Keisha shook her head. "No, my aunt lives on that street. But she did see Maddie at church."

"Did she say if Aidan was with her?" Darnell finished his glass of tea. "You should have gone to church with her."

"As you recall, I was with you. I should have stayed home, for all the good it did me."

"Everyone has an off time. I can't make you come every time we're together."

"I'd have settled for once," Keisha mumbled. Talk about false advertisement. Darnell was tall, had big feet and large hands, and he was carrying a Vienna sausage. "What's the great plan?"

Keisha had almost forgotten why she wanted to meet with him. "Oh yeah, she's going to the new club on Saturday."

His eyes lit up. "Well, that's something. I can make my move. I can drug her drink, drag her out of the club and my problems will be over. Yeah, this can definitely work."

Keisha sighed, wishing she'd never gotten involved with this idiot. This stupid plan was going to land both of them in jail. She had to convince him to abandon this insanity. "That's not going to work. Jared is coming, and so is Aidan. His friend owns the club and is giving Aidan a VIP table for all of us."

Not to be outdone, Darnell laughed. "It can still work. My cousin is one of the bartenders for the new place. He can spike Maddie's drink. Aidan will get blamed for using a date rape drug, ruining his good boy image, and I'll get Maddie. We can make our appearance at the dinner and my promotion will still be intact."

Keisha gasped. "You can't keep her drugged for two weeks! Her family will go nuts!"

"Keep your voice down or we'll be in jail tonight. I'll kidnap her and you'll keep her drugged?"

"No. I don't want anything to do with this. This is more than I signed on for."

"Too late."

Keisha watched this man she'd grown to hate in just a matter of minutes. At first it had been a game, but when he started talking about kidnapping and drugging Maddie, Keisha could already guess what Maddie's end would be. She didn't want that for her friend.

Keisha was going to have to do something she'd never thought she'd do. She was going to have to roll over on Darnell. She had to save herself.

CHAPTER 28

Cadence listened to the conversation between Darnell and Keisha. What was it about criminals? There was almost always a disagreement that led to their downfall. This time she was going to help the downfall along.

Keisha was just the person for the job.

Keisha and Darnell would never have guessed Cadence was a few booths away listening to their entire conversation by way of the listening device she'd planted on the menu stand. It was the best fifty bucks she'd ever spent.

Madisyn was really a victim in this entire mess. It was always the scheming friend and no-account boyfriend that messed up a good woman's life.

Cadence made notes about a strategy for Saturday night at the club. Besides her security team of four, she was going to need some reinforcements for the night out. The first thing she had to do was run a thorough background check on the bartenders, waitresses, and the bouncers. She also needed to question Darnell's cousin, who was still in custody. Maybe he was ready to roll over on Darnell.

She thought she'd already gathered enough information to get Darnell at least twenty years in jail. She left the pub and headed back to her hotel. Just as she parked

CELYA BOWERS

in front of the downtown Radisson, her cell phone rang. Chase.

"Hey," she said softly. She'd meant for it to sound brusque and businesslike, but instead it had sounded sexy. Damn.

"Cadence," Chase said. "We need to talk."

"What is it, Harman? I don't have time to break you off a piece right now. I told you that was an isolated incident." Yeah, right.

"Although the offer is very tempting, this is business. Madisyn is on board with the idea."

She watched the valet approach her. She struggled out of the rental car and handed him the keys. "I know. I just overheard Keisha and Darnell plotting the stupidest kidnapping plan I've ever heard."

Brakes screeched and horns blew amid Chase cussing a blue streak. "What? Where are you? Is Madisyn okay? What am I supposed to tell Aidan? He's going to kill me!"

She laughed. Men! Why wouldn't they just let her do her job! "Madisyn is fine. I've never lost a client, and one idiotic investment banker and a gold digger aren't going to ruin my game. Meet me at my hotel and we'll map out a plan. I think Keisha's going to be our way in. We could have this cleared up by the weekend."

"You know I've never liked Keisha. I've never met her, but from Aidan's description, she just sounds like a scheming woman. I don't know how Madisyn could have been friends with her."

Cadence agreed with Chase. "Yeah, but you know how those grade school friendships are. But I do believe Madisyn will be cutting the cord real soon."

283

Madisyn knew something wasn't right in Keisha's materialistic world. If they didn't eat together, normally Keisha would come by her desk and brag about the expensive lunch she'd just eaten and the gullible man who'd been stupid enough to buy it for her. That day she zoomed past Madisyn's desk mumbling something about payback, completely ignoring Madisyn.

If Madisyn's own life hadn't been so out of control, she would have cared, but she had her own issues to deal with. She also had a grand opening she needed to plan. Her usually full plate was now overrun with responsibilities.

Of course there was an upside to all this. Aidan. He'd been there for her when most men would have hit the ground running.

"Madisyn?"

She blinked at the sound of her name. Her former boss, Josh, stood hovering over her. "Josh, sit down. What are you doing here?"

He sat down, but scooted his chair closer to the desk. This was going to be a serious talk he didn't want anyone to hear. "I wanted to see you. Have you seen Darnell lately?"

Madisyn felt the color drain out of her face. "No, I haven't. He's not here, is he? He's not supposed to come anywhere near me."

Josh reached for her trembling hand. "Maddie, Maddie, calm down. He's not on the property. I know about the restraining order."

Madisyn shot him a look. "How could you?"

"I know because the head of security told me. I was having lunch with my wife today across the street and he was there. He looked awful and he was with Keisha. They were having a very heated conversation. My wife, on her many trips to the bathroom, heard them discussing their times together. Maddie, did you have any idea?"

She should have been upset, shocked, and hurt, but she wasn't. "No, but that explains how he knew my whereabouts a few weeks ago, among other things."

"You're not upset?"

"No, like you told me so many times before, I deserve a good man. Darnell has been trying to get me to take him back because his promotion depends on it."

Josh was confused and didn't hide the fact. "How so?"

Madisyn laughed. "Darnell is up for a promotion at his firm. They're really into traditional families and stuff. With his checkered past, he needs me there to show that he's settling down and can accept the responsibilities of his new position. Without me there, he's out of luck."

Finally understanding, Josh cracked up. "Oh, and there'll be no promotion. I can see why he's getting desperate."

"Yeah. There's a restraining order against him, but that didn't stop him for sending me flowers with a threatening note. I think Keisha had a hand in getting them on my desk."

"Oh, Maddie, you know you can stay with us."

Josh was like a father to her. She thought it was sweet that he'd offered. "Thanks, Josh, but I'm staying with a friend and he's taking my security very seriously."

"He?"

Madisyn decided Josh deserved to hear it from her. "Yes, Aidan Coles. He's the chair on Mature Alliance. You know, that charity I started volunteering on."

"Watch yourself. Don't get blinded by all that glitter."

"Don't worry, Josh. He's nice and has been to church with me twice. He's even survived Sunday afternoon with the O'Riley clan."

Josh laughed. "He survived meeting the boys?"

"They think he rocks."

"What does Madisyn think?"

"That he's too good to be true. I keep waiting for the other shoe to drop."

Josh looked at her with those soulful eyes. "Maybe there's not another shoe to drop."

"Maybe." Madisyn so wanted to believe her former boss and friend.

"You'll see. Any man who dares the O'Riley men can't be all bad." He rose and left the cubicle.

She thought about Aidan. She'd known him a grand total of three weeks, and she was already under his roof, albeit temporarily. She was sleeping with him. It had taken Darnell a year just to get her in bed.

Her phone rang. "Damon Bridges's office, Madisyn O'Riley. How can I help you?"

"Hey, Maddie," Chayla said. "Are you okay?"

"Why is everyone asking me that? My old boss was just here asking me the same thing. What's up?"

"Nothing is up with me," Chayla drawled. "I just thought I'd check on you since you're not staying at your house and I haven't seen you in two weeks."

It was true. Madisyn really missed her friend, but that would be remedied very soon. "You'll see me Saturday at Club Sizzle," Madisyn giggled. Even with all the drama that was going to unfold at the nightclub, she was actually looking forward to it.

"You mean you're actually going to the club! Oh, it'll be fun," Chayla chimed in. "I was going to back out because you know how Keisha is when she gets around professional athletes. Her morals become looser than a politician's."

"You know it," Madisyn said, wondering why it had taken her so long to notice Keisha's shortcomings. "You also get to meet Aidan."

Chayla gasped. "Girl, don't tease a married sister like that. For real?"

"Yep. Some guy he knows owns it and we're going to have a VIP table. So just give your name at the door and everything else will be taken care of."

The more Madisyn talked about the upcoming weekend, the more she realized that not only would the world know that she was dating a professional athlete, she was also going to show the world a stronger, more confident woman.

Chase took a deep breath and knocked on Cadence's hotel door. He felt like a horny teenager in heat. *You're here on business*, he reminded himself. *You don't have time for a distraction.* The door opened and he realized how stupid life was.

Cadence stood before him dressed in a blue jean halter top and a short denim skirt. Her smooth legs seemed to go on forever. She leaned against the door, laughing.

"I know I look like I'm asking for it, but I was in costume." She nodded for him to come inside. "I was going to change, but I knew you were on your way. I won't be a sec." She hurried into the bathroom.

Once the door closed, Chase let out a nervous breath. This was going to be more difficult than taking the bar exam. Cadence looked so hot! Thank goodness, she'd gone to change or he would have forgotten all about Madisyn and Aidan, and what he was supposed to be doing.

She emerged from the bathroom in a pair of baggy sweats and University of Virginia T-shirt, as if she already knew how turned on he was and that he'd have trouble focusing on anything else. She picked up her briefcase. "Why don't we sit at the table? That way we can work on the details in peace."

Chase nodded and shrugged out of his jacket. Cadence was all business. He might as well get that way, too. "How about some lunch? My treat."

She picked up a room service menu. "Don't worry, Chase. Save your money."

Chase nodded. "You know I don't like this. I'm an old-fashioned kind of guy. But I'm on your turf, so I'll play by your rules." He walked toward her. "Let's see what room service has."

After they called in an order for sandwiches, they discussed their options. Chase looked in the honor bar and grabbed a bottle of imported beer. "Why would you think Keisha is the way in?" He raised his beer bottle, silently asking if she wanted one.

She nodded. "I think Keisha is our girl because although she started this mess with Darnell, she realizes she's in over her head. I could tell by the tone of her voice. She's scared. A little push and she'll turn over on Darnell in a heartbeat. I just need a little time."

He handed her a bottle of beer and watched her twist the cap off with her hand. "I thought you wanted to get as much prison time as possible for both of them."

She took a long drink. "I do, and I know I can get Darnell for sure. Keisha is just stupid. I want to get her back for Madisyn's sake."

He smiled and took a seat at the table. Looking across at her beautiful face was going to be his downfall. "I knew you had a soft spot in there somewhere," Chase joked. "I want this over as quickly and quietly as possible. Aidan doesn't want this all over the news. So if you can get through to Keisha, I'm all for it. But time is not on your side. We have four days." He finished his beer. "I'm going to the club, too."

"You mean I get to see you trying out your mack daddy lines on the poor unsuspecting gold diggers? That should be good. I'm going to run a check on the wait staff for the club. One of them is Darnell's cousin, and we've got to get him or her out of there. He's going to drug Madisyn's drink."

"Bastard." Chase finished his beer. He hadn't liked Darnell from the start because of the way he'd treated

Madisyn. This just added more fuel to the fire. Apparently, Cadence had heard quite a bit at the restaurant. "What else did our dumb lovers talk about?"

She was about to answer when room service arrived with their food. After they left, Cadence resumed the conversation. "Did you know he's also doing Keisha's younger sister?"

Chase choked on the last of his beer. "Are you serious? How stupid is this guy?"

Cadence lifted the silver dome on her plate. "Pretty stupid. He was stupid enough to take her to his place. She's using him for money."

"Are you going to tell Keisha?" Chase lifted his lid and inhaled the aroma of a Philly cheesesteak sandwich. "These are the best in town."

"I'll have to make you a real one before I head back home to Virginia." Cadence went to the fridge and got two more beers. She placed one in front of Chase before she sat back down.

Chase was shocked. Cadence rarely shared any personal information about herself. "I didn't know you were from Virginia. Which part?"

"The good part," she answered, taking a bite of her sandwich. "Actually it's called Turner's Point, near Langley. Now can we please get back to Dumb and Dumber?"

He chuckled. "Yes, we can."

"You just make sure you get Aidan and Madisyn to the club. Make sure they don't come alone. I want this as controlled as possible. I already know it's going to be a madhouse with all those celebrities that will be there. Make sure Madisyn doesn't go to the ladies' room alone. I'll have a plant at the VIP table who will escort her."

Chase gave a low whistle. "Girl, you're worth every penny. You have this all worked out already."

Cadence laughed. "It might look easy, but everyone is going to need to stay on their toes. One slipup and Madisyn could be in a lot of trouble."

<hr />

A few days later, Madisyn sat at Aidan's computer feeling very proud of herself. She'd just ordered plane tickets for Aidan's parents. The grand opening was less than two weeks away and everything was finalized and ready.

Aidan walked into the room smiling at her. He stood behind her looking at the computer screen. "Baby, you know you didn't really have to buy Mom's and Lester's ticket."

Madisyn turned and looked at him. "I know that, Aidan, but I wanted to. I want to be a part of you reconnecting with your stepfather. My parents want to take them out to dinner when they're in town."

He pulled her out of the chair and gave her a hug. Then, he kissed her thoroughly. "You know your folks don't have to do that."

Madisyn smiled back at him, relishing this moment. "You try telling them that."

"Oh, I forgot. No one says no to the O'Rileys."

Madisyn kissed him. "Give that man a cigar."

He leaned down and smothered her lips with his. "I'd rather have what's behind blouse number one."

<hr />

Keisha left work late that night. All the drama with Darnell was starting to get to her. So much so that she didn't get her work done and had to work late to complete it. She waved to the security guard and headed for the parking garage. Her cell phone rang just as she reached her car. Darnell.

He'd been blowing up her phone all day. She'd been ignoring his calls, because she didn't have anything new to tell him, mainly because Maddie refused to elaborate on the details about the club. "Why doesn't that fool just leave me the hell alone?" Keisha didn't expect an answer and was quite surprised when she got one.

"Because he wants to see you go to jail, Ms. Allen. Which is exactly where you'll be going if you don't help me get Darnell."

Keisha looked at the tall, slender woman walking toward her. There were no other cars on the secured level and it required a badge to park there. But Keisha didn't know this woman. A woman this pretty would get noticed. She had honey-beige skin, long black hair and green eyes. The black suit she wore was tailor-made for her body. "Do I know you?"

"You will. My name is unimportant at this stage. You should be concerned with how much trouble you're in.

Darnell is planning a kidnapping, which is a federal offense. They don't have designer outfits in prison."

Keisha had known she was in over her head, but it was too late to do anything about it. "What's that got to do with me? I have nothing to do with Darnell. You want Madisyn O'Riley's ex-boyfriend, not me." She needed to get out of there as soon as possible. This woman knew about Darnell's insane plan.

Cadence stepped toward Keisha. "I know you've been sleeping with Darnell. At first, you probably viewed it as some kind of sick joke on Madisyn, taking her man from under her nose, until you found out that he was cheating on you. Then you ran and told Madisyn he was cheating. But did you know he's also sleeping with your 19-year-old sister?"

"You're lying. He'd never do that to me." She unlocked her car. This woman was certifiable.

The woman reached inside her suit jacket and took out a stack of pictures and shoved them at her. "Take a look."

Keisha snatched the pictures from the woman's slender hand and quickly looked at them. That was when she knew. So many things about her sister hadn't made sense, but now they did. Darnell had been bankrolling her sister, probably hoping to get some dirt on Keisha. "So what's this got to do with me?"

The woman nodded, as if she knew Keisha's fate. "It has everything to do with you. You help me get Darnell and I'll try to keep you out of prison."

Prison wasn't an option Keisha had been thinking of. This little scheme had spiraled out of control. "I'm not going to prison anyway. So find your snitch somewhere else."

The woman stepped closer to Keisha. "Now you listen to me, Miss Thang. You're in this up to your cheap weave. But I'm a good sport. I'll give you some time to think about it. You help me and you can possibly stay out of prison, but if you don't, you're looking at conspiracy to commit a federal crime, obstructing justice, hindering an investigation, and if that isn't enough, I can always add attempted murder."

Keisha's heart raced at the mention of the word "murder." If she got charged, that would break her mother's heart and she couldn't have that. "So what happens if I decide to help you? Darnell might try to harm me."

"Not unless you tell him. He's not going to know what hit him until he's sentenced, and then it's going to be too late. But I can only help you if you help me."

"Does Maddie know about me and Darnell? I think it would crush her."

"To my knowledge she doesn't know you or your sister slept with Whitfield. Affairs of the heart aren't my department. If you are the friend you claim to be, I suggest you come clean about everything to Ms. O'Riley before she finds out from other sources." She glanced at her watch. "Okay, what's it going to be?"

"For what?"

"Are you in or do I need to call the police?"

"What happened to letting me think about it?"

"I did. Now I need an answer."

Keisha thought about her options. She really didn't have any. She couldn't go through with Darnell's plan, it was past insane. Sleeping with him behind Maddie's back had been like a little game, but this was very real. "I'm in."

CHAPTER 29

Saturday night Madisyn was a ball of nervous energy. It took her hours to find just the right thing to wear. She finally settled on a sleeveless off-white silk dress that fell just above her knees. After she slipped on a pair of slinky high-heeled sandals, she went downstairs, where Aidan was waiting for her.

"You look good, baby," Aidan said, walking toward her. "You look too good to go to the club. I'll have to beat all the guys off with a stick." He hugged her. "You sure about this?"

She gazed up at him. His brown eyes devoured her. "Yes, I'm ready to get my life back. I know you're not going to let anything happen to me, baby." She kissed him. "Besides, I'm going to be too busy keeping all those young girls off you." She looked him up and down. "You look good, honey. Too good."

Which was true. He looked like an ad for a fashion magazine. He wore a light-green dress shirt and black slacks. The shirt showcased his muscular upper body. "You know, we could just stay in." She was beginning to rethink the whole evening.

He smiled. "Yes, but I want Darnell out of our life as quickly as possible. Plus, I'm ready to show you off to the world."

"You always say just the right thing to me to get me over my jitters." She hugged him. "Thank you."

"I should be saying thanks to you. You've helped me a lot, too, baby. Thanks to you, Mom and Lester will be at the grand opening. You don't know how much that means to me."

She reached up and gently caressed his cheek. "Yes, I do, because you're important to me." She took a deep breath. "We'd better get out of here or we'll never get to the club."

"Actually, we have a little time," he said slowly. Madisyn was confused. Why did they need to wait if he was driving them to the club? She glanced at the grandfather clock in the corner of the room. It was after ten. Surely it was late enough to be seen at the club. She studied his face carefully. "Why can't we go now?"

He studied the floor between them. "Chase thought it would be better if he drove us there. You don't mind, do you?"

"No, but you could have said something. Aidan, I'm not a high-maintenance woman. The more the merrier. And tonight I want as many people around us as possible."

"There's more. Chase wasn't real specific, but he doesn't want you accepting drinks from anyone."

She didn't like the sound of that. Not that she was a hard drinker, but a drink would have been nice. "Nothing?"

"You can only drink something from me. I arranged for a couple of bottles of champagne for the table and I ordered a special bottle for us. They should all be unopened when they arrive at the table."

Madisyn sighed. Her first appearance at a club in years and it was under high security. "I know this is for my own good, but the whole drinks thing is over the top."

"Not when one of Darnell's cousins is a bartender at Club Sizzle," Aidan pointed out. "I know Darnell is desperate, so I'm taking no chances."

"Got it." She saw the conviction in his eyes and knew Aidan was serious about her safety. She was so touched that she had to comply. She grabbed Aidan by the hand and led him to the couch. After they were seated she snuggled up next to him. "Well, I guess we have a little time to kill before Chase gets here." She flashed a smile with what she hoped passed for a seductive look. "What can we do to pass the time?"

He finally understood and pulled her onto his lap. "I'm sure I can think of one or two things that will keep us occupied until then."

Madisyn leaned down and kissed him. "I was hoping you could."

⁓

Darnell could see his plan taking shape. Although he hadn't seen or heard from Trev in over a week, he was confident everything would work out. His cell phone rang as he entered his rent-by-the-week hotel room. It was his cousin Prentice.

"Hey man, has anyone heard from Trev?" Darnell looked around the small room for any signs of a disturbance as he talked.

"No, man. Mom's saying she thinks Trev done got himself in some major trouble. I could kick his ass for making Mom worry like this. He's probably laid up with some tramp somewhere."

"I agree with you, Prentice. I don't think he ever made it to Maddie's. Everything set up for tonight? I'm really counting on you, man." Prentice was a bartender at Club Sizzle.

Prentice cleared his throat. "About that. I just got a call from the club. They told me that I didn't have to come in tonight. They said they had enough bartenders and to report next week."

Darnell didn't like the sound of that. What club would turn down extra help at a grand opening? "Did you talk to any of the other bartenders?"

"Quit trying to sound like Perry Mason. Yeah, one of my buddies got a call like that, too. Other than that, no one else."

He hated problems, and Madisyn was now becoming a very large one. "You're still going to be there, right?"

Prentice laughed. "Are you kidding? That place is gonna be packed with way too many people. Besides, I don't want to be anywhere near that place when you try to execute this insane plan."

"You know my job is relying on this."

"Darnell, I always liked Maddie and always knew one day she'd get tired of you messing over her, and she did. She's too good for a dog like you. So I think you're getting yours. As much as I would love to see you fail, I'm staying out of this."

"You said you'd help me," Darnell reminded his cousin. "You owe me."

"True. You helped me get a job when I needed it most. But there's no way I'm going to risk jail time for this. When you first told me about it, I thought you just wanted to talk to her or something. Not kidnap her and hold her against her will, just to make an appearance at a stupid dinner. That's crossing the line, and I can't help you." Prentice ended the call.

Darnell couldn't believe how everyone was bailing on him because of a few setbacks. At least he still had Keisha to help him, even though she had been acting funny all week.

——⧉——

Keisha stared at the clock in her car. That skinny woman was late. Keisha was starting to have a bad feeling about this entire situation. Perhaps Darnell was actually testing her loyalty.

She was parked in the parking lot of the local bookstore, knowing Darnell would never think to look for her there. Keisha wouldn't normally have been caught dead near a bookstore.

Her heart skipped a beat when a car parked a few spaces down from her. It was a late-model sedan, something she'd never own. The skinny woman got out, dressed in a dark suit. She was talking on her cell phone as she neared Keisha's car.

Keisha got out of her car and leaned against the door. She took a deep breath, hoping she wasn't making a mistake that would cost her her life.

"I'm glad you showed up, Ms. Allen." Skinny girl took out a small gadget the size of a credit card. She pushed a few buttons on it and the thing went nuts. "By the way, I'm Ms. Callahan."

Normally, a person would offer up their first name, Keisha mused. But this chick was all business. "Well, you already know my name. Now that I'm up to my ass in this mess, what am I supposed to do?"

Ms. Callahan looked her up and down. As directed, Keisha wore the clothes she was wearing to the club later that night. The short black dress hugged her curves.

"Thank goodness this device is small, or you'd give the game away in that dress. I'm sure Darnell won't be able to resist you in that dress."

Keisha didn't think it was a compliment, so she chose to ignore it. "He's got his heart set on getting Maddie back, so he's not going to give me a second look."

"He thinks you're still helping, right?"

Keisha nodded. "Yeah, he's been calling all day and leaving all kinds of crazy messages."

"You kept them?"

"As you directed. Now what is that going to do to me?" Keisha nodded at the small gadget.

Ms. Callahan smiled. "It's not going to do nothing to you. This is called a digi-tracker. This is an experimental device that you will put on your body in the chest area so I can also hear Darnell's voice. It works on your blood pressure. As the danger in the situation increases, so will your blood pressure. The device will alert me and I'll be at your side in a matter of minutes."

Keisha looked surprised. "You're going to be at the club? I hope you're not going dressed like that? You're going to stick out like a librarian at a strip club!"

Ms. Callahan laughed. "Oh, don't you worry. I'll be dressed appropriately for the club tonight." She stepped closer to Keisha. "Now, place this on your body and we'll test it." She handed the card to her.

Keisha took the card and slid it down the front of her dress. "Is this okay?"

"Let's see." She took something that looked like a very thin palm data assistant out of her jacket pocket. She took a metal stylus out and began punching a series of buttons.

Keisha felt the slight electrical pulses surge through her body. "Hey, this feels like a phone vibrating against my breast."

Ms. Callahan nodded. "Good, but for this to work, you can't wiggle around like that. Whitfield is going to think you're on some kind of drug or wearing a wire, since he's feeling a little paranoid." She turned the small gadget in Keisha's direction.

Keisha was shocked to see the words on the small screen. It was actually their entire conversation. "Wow, this is cool."

She laughed. "And it only cost about a million dollars right now. So if I were you, I wouldn't lose it. The federal government wouldn't take kindly to that."

"What are you doing with this, then?" Keisha didn't want to go to prison for anyone, including this skinny woman standing in front of her.

"Can't tell you, but don't worry, everything I do is in the name of justice and is legal. My first concern is getting Darnell before he gets to Madisyn. Now are you still with me on this or not?"

Keisha sighed. Like she had a choice. "I'm with you."

"Good. Now here's what you need to do tonight."

Madisyn gasped when she noticed the crowded club. "Oh, my gosh! It looks like a thousand people are here!"

Chase chuckled as he parked the car across the street from Club Sizzle. He turned to Madisyn, who was sitting in the backseat with Aidan. "Okay, here's the plan." He shot a glance at the man in the passenger seat. "Kyle is a part of Cadence's security team, and he's going to escort you guys into the VIP section. According to Kameron's club manager, it's on the second level near the DJ booth. There are three VIP sections up there. Aidan has the one closest to the booth. So that's a little added security."

Madisyn felt Chase was leaving something out. "But what?"

Chase looked from her to Aidan, who was holding Madisyn's hand. "Along with the VIP sections, the DJ booth, the restrooms are also up there. The restrooms are in the opposite corner, but the patrons will still have to come upstairs to use them."

There wasn't much they could do at this point. Darnell would have access to her just by claiming to need the facilities. "What's the upside to this?"

Chase smiled. "You will be covered. Kyle will be with you guys at all times. Cadence will be here, as well as the rest of her team."

Madisyn wanted to believe tonight would go without a hitch, but the feeling in her gut was this night would change her life forever.

"Are you okay with all this?" Chase looked in Aidan's direction. "I've got her as much protection as possible."

Aidan looked at Madisyn with a look that was so intense, it melted any resolve she had. "I'm not okay with any of this, but we've started the ball rolling, so we gotta keep it going." He moved closer to Madisyn and said, "The only way Darnell will get to you is through me, and that's not about to happen."

Aidan held onto Madisyn's hand as they were escorted to the upstairs section. She'd held up pretty well when all the press cameras started going off. Now they were seated at the large booth. Aidan hadn't known what to expect with Kameron's flamboyant style, but Club Sizzle was very tastefully done.

The booth seated about ten people and a few extra chairs were also placed there for the security team. Madisyn's friends were already there.

"Madisyn, this is awesome, girl," a woman said as she hugged Madisyn as if she were a stuffed animal. "It feels like we haven't seen each other in months instead of a few weeks."

Madisyn returned the powerful hug. "I know. I'm glad you made it, Chay." She turned to Aidan and smiled. "Aidan, this is my best friend Chayla Hughes and her husband, Jared."

Aidan reached out to shake Chayla's hand, but she didn't take it. "Aidan, we don't do handshakes." She hugged him. "It's nice to meet you, finally. You better be good to Maddie or you'll have to answer to me."

Aidan quite understood. "Gotcha. I want only the best for Madisyn. And I just know you'll keep me in line, right?" He winked at Chayla. He looked at Chayla's husband. "Do I have to hug you, too?"

Jared looked blankly at him. "Huh, what?"

Since being around Madisyn's family members, minus Marcus, of course, Aidan was used to being treated like one of the guys. But Jared stood before him completely starstruck. "It's nice to meet you, Jared." He shook his hand, then motioned for Madisyn to sit down.

Aidan looked around the roped-off section. Downstairs was crowded and noisy, but the quiet upstairs was a deep contrast. "Where's your other friend, baby?"

"Keisha likes to make an appearance. It will probably be closer to eleven before she gets here."

Aidan felt the adrenaline pumping through his body. He was ready for action and wanted this night to be over as soon as possible. He watched as Kameron walked upstairs to greet him.

He was dressed in a dark suit and sunglasses.

"Aidan, I'm glad you could make it. This must be Madisyn," he drawled. He sat in the vacant chair next to Madisyn. "How you doing? If my boy isn't taking care of you, you just give me a holla."

"Thank you, but he's doing just fine," Madisyn said, looking directly at Aidan.

Kameron nodded. "Well, I see my boy must be doing all the right things." He looked at the other people at the table and introduced himself. "I'm sending one of the waitresses up here with your bottles of champagne."

"Just make sure she doesn't open them."

Kam looked at him. "Got a little celebration going on?"

Aidan shrugged. "Something like that."

Kam rose. "Oh, okay. I'll be back up later. Do you know the fire marshal is already here talking about how we're near our building capacity? But if I want to pay him an extra grand, he'll look the other way. Like I'm stupid enough to go out like that. Nice to meet you, ladies, Jared." He went back downstairs.

Jared finally came out of his cloud. "I just met Kameron Drews," he told everyone at the table. "Wow!"

Aidan looked at Madisyn, smiling. She was being a really good sport about everything. He'd go through hell to be with her, and he had a feeling tonight was going to be a good test.

Keisha took a deep breath and handed her keys to the valet. Once she gave her name at the front door, she was escorted upstairs. In all her clubbing experience she'd never been near the VIP area when there were football players in the midst. She took in the atmosphere of the club. She was impressed, to say the least. She'd expected to see a hole-in-the-wall place that would just take all your money. But this place had lots of seating, a large dance floor, and a good sound system. The true test was the bathroom. A place this size should have at least four stalls. The young man escorted her upstairs. "The restrooms are in the far corner to the left. Enjoy your evening," he said as he left her at the top of the stairs.

Keisha glanced at the booth and saw her friends. Maddie was sitting next to Aidan, Chayla and Jared were there, a few men she didn't know, and there was only one vacant place left. Usually she was the one with a date, not the one without. That was usually Maddie. She whispered a silent prayer and walked to her friends.

"Hey, guys," Keisha said, taking her seat, not meeting her friends' eyes. If she didn't look at Maddie, she had a chance of making it through this horrible evening. "Sorry I'm late," she said softly.

"That's okay," Madisyn said. "We haven't been here that long. Keisha, this is Aidan and this is Chase." She nodded to the handsome men at the table. "You remember Jared." She pointed unnecessarily to Chayla's husband.

Tonight Keisha didn't feel like anyone's friend. If she made it out of this mess, she was going to change everything about her life, including ... oices she had made over the years. As Madisyn had told her so many times, her life was her choice. It had taken her twenty years to realize her friend was right.

Keisha shook their hands. When her hand connected with Chase, it all clicked into place. Darnell had been complaining about Aidan's high-priced attorney, Chase Hartman. So this was the man behind the man. "It's nice to meet you men." She glanced at Aidan, but he was all up in Madisyn's grill, ignoring Keisha. She couldn't have that. "Well, Aidan, it's nice to see you out. I didn't think you clubbed."

"I don't. Madisyn wanted to come out, so here we are." He poured a glass of champagne and handed it to Keisha. "There's plenty of champagne, so feel free to drink all you want."

Keisha took the glass, trying to figure out a way to get Maddie away from Aidan. She couldn't think of a believable reason. She felt a buzzing on her body. She thought it was the tracking device, but it was her phone. Her purse was in her lap. She took a sip as she looked at the phone display. Darnell. He'd sent her a message. He was in the club.

Keisha looked around for Ms. Callahan, but didn't see the slender woman anywhere in the building. She didn't want to talk to Darnell until she knew she had backup. He sent her another message. *Meet me.*

She wasn't ready.

CHAPTER 30

After a few nervous moments, Madisyn finally starred to relax. Club Sizzle was a nice place to go if you liked that kind of thing, she thought. It would be nice to go to a club every once in a while, but not every weekend, like Keisha did. Madisyn had no idea how people put themselves through this kind of torture on a regular basis.

Aidan sat next to her and was very attentive. The media had tried to enter the VIP area several times to take more pictures, but the security guards were earning every penny of their money. The reporters never got anywhere near their table.

Aidan held Madisyn's hand and talked to Chayla and Jared as if they were old friends. He was used to everyone always placating him; it was nice to actually have a conversation. They didn't chat about Madisyn or the upcoming season. They talked about Madisyn, much to her dismay.

Aidan winked at Madisyn. "So tell me about her. What is she really like?"

Chayla laughed. "This is the real Madisyn. Trusting, dependable and a hard worker. Always ready to give 150 percent. I know she's probably a dynamo for your charity. I was thinking about joining," Chayla said.

"That would be great. Madisyn planned the grand opening that will be in a couple of weeks. She's done a wonderful job." He smiled at her. In a very short time, Madisyn had become a very integral part of his life. "You guys are more than welcome to attend. The Alliance has been a dream of mine for a long time, and I'm glad I get to see it come to fruition." Aidan leaned over and kissed Madisyn gently on the lips. "I do expect a dance tonight," he whispered.

Madisyn gasped. "I thought this evening was just about bringing Darnell out of hiding. Are you sure about being on the dance floor with me?" she whispered back. He nodded. She was always trying to give him a way out, but it wasn't necessary. He wanted to be near Madisyn, no matter how high the cost. "Yeah, just as sure as I love you." He ran his fingers through her hair. "You can dance, right?"

She was just about to answer when she saw something out of her peripheral vision. It looked like Darnell walking up the stairs, but was it possible?

"Baby? Are you okay?" Aidan looked at her with concerned eyes. "Did you spot him?"

Madisyn shrugged. "I think so, but I can't be sure. It could be just the stress of the evening. But if the knot in my stomach is any indication, I'd say yes."

Aidan moved closer to her. "I won't let him near you, but you've got to play it cool, so he'll think he has the upper hand."

She nodded. She was the one who'd wanted this to play out at the club, so it was time to step up to the plate.

"I know." She listened as the DJ started playing some old-school music. "I'm not the best dancer, but I like this kind of music. Let's dance."

"With pleasure." He stood, took her hand and glanced at Chayla and Jared. "Excuse us, my lady wants to dance." They headed downstairs to the dance floor.

Madisyn felt her self-esteem hit the floor when they joined the crowd of dancers. Scantily clad woman brazenly brushed against Aidan constantly. Madisyn knew this was just part of being a celebrity, and he seemed to be taking it in stride. He moved closer to her.

"Don't worry, baby. They're just groupies, and that's not my thing. We can go back to the table if you want," he whispered into her ear. "You'll have to get used to people looking at us."

She nodded. Those weren't the words she wanted to hear, but she knew they were true. Dating a high-profile athlete, she had to learn to live with people staring at them. "I know. Those little skinny chicks better watch out. We can stay." She smiled.

He took her in his arms. "That's my baby."

<hr />

Darnell looked down on the dance floor as he walked out of the men's room and muttered a curse. It had taken him at least an hour to work his way upstairs. When he finally got a chance to nab Madisyn, she and Aidan had the nerve to go to the dance floor. Madisyn didn't dance!

He glanced around the roped-off area, looking for a place to hide to make his move. All he needed was one dark corner and he'd be set. Keisha wasn't answering his messages. Everyone was backing out on him at the last minute. He spotted Keisha sitting at the VIP table and tried to get her attention, but failed. Instead he made eye contact with Chayla. Damn.

∽

Keisha could finally breathe easier. She'd spotted Ms. Callahan in the corner dressed in a slinky red dress that showcased her figure and her honey-beige complexion. Her previously pinned-up hair hung well below her shoulders. As she walked upstairs just about every man had been looking at her. Keisha's phone buzzed at her again. She figured it was Darnell demanding her presence, but it wasn't him. It was Ms. Callahan telling her to come to the ladies' room.

Thank goodness Maddie was on the dance floor with Aidan. Keisha still didn't understand it. Nothing was making sense. Madisyn seldom danced in front of people, but here she was dancing with Aidan like she'd been doing it for years. Aidan had barely given Keisha a second glance when Madisyn introduced them. No man could resist her unless he was truly in love. Was Aidan so in love with Maddie that he hadn't noticed her? How could he be?

Keisha rose, mumbling something to the others at the table about having to go to the ladies' room. Not that anyone was paying her any attention. She had always been closer to Maddie than Chayla, but the look Chayla was giving her now was as if she knew Keisha had betrayed Madisyn in the worst way.

She walked into the ladies' room, shocked to see that there wasn't a line of women waiting to use the toilets. Another shocker, there were at least eight stalls. Ms. Callahan was leaning against the counter talking on her cell phone. The minute she noticed Keisha, she cut her conversation short. "Has Whitfield made contact with you?"

Keisha nodded. "I haven't answered him."

"Tell him you're ready to talk. Make him go over the plan again. I've got you covered, so you don't have to worry."

"But what if he gets to Maddie?"

"He won't."

"How can you be so sure?"

"This is what I do. Let me do my job."

Keisha nodded. She barely knew this woman, and she was trusting her with her life. "Okay. Any other instructions?"

"Don't let him leave the club with you."

<hr />

After two dances and a million stares, Madisyn let Aidan lead her back upstairs to their seats. To her surprise Keisha was missing from the table.

Aidan helped her with her chair and kissed her as he sat down. "You were great, baby."

"So were you," she cooed back at him, hoping this euphoric feeling would never end. "I wonder when Darnell is going to make his move?"

"I'm sure he'll do it. Be patient." Aidan poured her a glass of champagne.

"I saw him, Maddie," Chayla said on a rush. "Darnell is here inside the club. I think Keisha went to go meet him. She went toward the ladies' room and hasn't returned."

Madisyn nodded, looking in Chase's direction. He was looking at his PDA screen, ignoring everyone at the table. When he finally looked up, his face was serious. "Madisyn, make sure you don't leave this table." He turned the small PDA in her direction.

Madisyn gasped at the slightly out of focus digital picture of Keisha and Darnell talking. "I had a feeling she was in it with him, but I didn't know how deeply until now. I'll stay here."

Chase nodded. "Good. No matter what happens, you stay here. Just in case things jump off, as the youngsters say, go to the DJ booth. It's bulletproof."

She nodded, grabbing Aidan's hand. She quickly scanned the upstairs, not seeing either Darnell or Keisha. "I'm really sorry I got you involved in all this, Aidan."

"Don't worry, baby. We're in this together. And we'll see this end together and then we can move forward." He kissed her.

"You know you guys are making me sick with all this kissy-kissy," Chayla joked. "But I love seeing this side of you, Madisyn. After that idiot, you deserve some happiness."

Madisyn looked up at Aidan. "You're right, Chayla. I do deserve some happiness, and I found it."

Aidan was about to say something, but noise from downstairs claimed his attention. Madisyn looked down at the crowd. People were running for the exit as Dallas's finest rushed through the entrance.

"Man, they really mean business about that capacity thing," Aidan said, watching the melee. "Those people are going nuts down there."

"Aidan," Chase said. He pointed to Darnell making his way upstairs to the VIP section.

Aidan grabbed Madisyn's hand. "I got you, baby. He won't hurt you."

Madisyn opened her mouth to tell him how much she loved him, but suddenly an explosion occurred on the other side of the club. There was no way she or Aidan would be able to get out of the club now. Too many people trying to get out of the club's only exit would prevent that.

The police fired warning shots into the air, but no one paid them any attention. Darnell was fast making his approach toward them when Madisyn heard Chase screaming into his phone, "Cadence, what's going on?"

Aidan didn't wait for an answer as more shots rang out. "You and Chayla go to the DJ booth. He can't get to you in there. The blast is a diversion."

Madisyn was rooted to her chair. How could one plan go so wrong? She didn't want Aidan getting hurt because of her.

"Go!" he ordered.

"No, I'm staying here with you."

"Baby, this ain't the time to be brave. Take your ass to the booth, now!"

Chayla tugged Madisyn's hand. "Come on, Maddie." Madisyn looked at Aidan again as he, Chase and Jared watched the melee downstairs. "I'll go." She and Chayla crawled to the DJ booth.

The DJ opened the door and ushered them inside. "Keep down, ladies. The walls are reinforced with bullet-proof glass."

Madisyn and Chayla sat next to each other listening to chaos in the club. Madisyn felt awful for endangering her best friend. "I'm sorry, Chay. I didn't know it was going to turn out like this."

Chayla shook her head. "Maddie, you can't control the actions of a moron." She held Maddie's hand. "I know Aidan, Jared and Chase are not going to let Darnell anywhere near us."

The next few minutes were a blur. Madisyn didn't hear bloodcurdling screams anymore, but she saw people fighting to get out of the club, then rushing upstairs for safety. "Chay, look! It's like a stampede. Somebody's going to get hurt. I don't know if security is going to be able to hold all those people back."

"You'd better hope they can, 'cause all those people are going to try to get in here," Chayla said.

The door suddenly burst open and Darnell, carrying a pistol, entered. "Well, Maddie, you put me through hell, but you'll pay for it." He pointed the pistol at her. "Get up."

Madisyn did as he said. "How did you get up here? How did you sneak a gun in here?"

"That's my secret. Now, thanks to my associates, the guards and police are busy, and we're going to get out of this damn place."

Madisyn racked her brain for some kind of plan, but came up empty. People were running everywhere trying to save themselves. No one would pay her or Darnell any attention. She was as good as dead.

⚬⚬⚬

Aidan looked around to make sure Madisyn and Chayla were safe and saw that in the chaos Darnell had made his move.

"Chase, we've been had," Aidan said. "Look." He pointed to the DJ booth.

"Shit," Chase muttered.

Aidan wanted to kill him. He grabbed Chase by the shirt. "Man, so help me if she gets hurt, I'm going to kick your ass to kingdom come." He scrambled to get up.

"You're fired."

"Aidan. Don't. Listen to me. It's being handled."

Aidan turned to Chase. "Look, man, you're not handling anything. You've got my woman in the line of fire. He's going to take off with her and do who knows what to her. Tell your chick she's not getting one thin dime out of me."

"Aidan!" Chase called after him. "Just listen to me."

There wasn't anything Chase could say at this point to make Aidan stop and listen to him. He couldn't believe he'd placed Madisyn's safety in Chase's incompetent hands. Aidan bulldozed his way through all the people that now crowded the upstairs. When he neared the booth, he paused to take in the situation inside.

For the first time in her security career, Cadence was torn. She could save Madisyn but she was going to endanger the lives of so many innocent people. If she let this play out, she could just take out Darnell. But Aidan was impatient and angry as hell, and rightly so.

Darnell had had one ace up his sleeve no one knew about. No one had figured he would be able to bring a gun inside the club, but he had with the help of a waitress. Cadence had received the information too late to do anything about it.

"Aidan, stand down," she screamed just as Darnell opened the door to the booth.

Aidan turned in the direction of her voice, and Darnell raised his pistol and fired. Aidan dropped to the floor, writhing in pain. Cadence reacted instantly. She reached under her dress, pulled out her Sig Sauer compact nine millimeter, and shot Darnell as he stood in the doorway. He fell backwards right on top of Madisyn.

Madisyn opened her eyes and stared at the ceiling. This place didn't look like the club, and it was daylight. What happened? She heard the constant beep of a machine and turned toward the noise, gasping in pain. She was in the hospital.

"Oh, Maddie, you're awake," her mother said, rising from her chair and standing by the bed.

Madisyn tried to lift her hands, but they were tethered to the bed. "Mom?" She couldn't keep the fear out of her voice.

Margaret stroked her daughter's face. "Don't worry, baby. They got that awful Darnell. He's alive, but when he fell, he took you with him. Your right wrist is broken, and the left one is sprained badly. That's why you can't move them. You also broke two ribs in your fall and you got a little bruising on your face." She wiped tears away from Madisyn's eyes. "I'm just glad this mess is over. That nice Miss Callahan filled me in on all the details. I'm sorry, baby."

Madisyn didn't like the look on her mother's face. What was she leaving out? "What happened to Aidan?"

Margaret took a deep breath. "Well, the details are a little sketchy, but he was shot in the arm. He should be out in a few days." Her mother took another deep breath. "There's more."

"What?"

"The bullet pierced a nerve in his arm and he's lost some feeling in his hand. He may not get to play this season."

"Oh, my God. It's my fault." Madisyn cried uncontrollably. "I've been nothing but trouble to this man since

319

the day we met. I've cost him a mint in security, and now I've cost him his job. He loves football."

Her mother wiped her eyes. "Now, Maddie, come on. You know that's not true. He did all that because he loves you."

She shook her head. "No, I've been nothing but trouble. I'm no better than those little groupies. Look what I've done to his life. I can't let him lose everything because of me."

"You're not making sense," her mother said.

"It's my fault we were at the club. He was against bringing Darnell out in the open, but I insisted. This is all my fault because I was tired of being chauffeured around. Now the grand opening is in two weeks and he won't be able to shake anyone's hand. That's my fault. The whole city is going to hate me 'cause I ended his career."

"Now you just stop all that silly talk right now. He's a grown man and makes his own decisions."

Madisyn didn't know which pain was worst, the one in her head and side or the one in her heart. She'd finally found a man she truly loved and now she'd have to send him away. "I can't, Mom. I have to save Aidan from me."

"Shouldn't that be my decision?" Aidan stood in the doorway. His right arm was in a white cast held up by a blue sling. He was also in blue and white striped pajamas covered by a blue silk robe.

Her mother rushed over to him. "Aidan, you shouldn't be up. Come sit down and talk some sense into her. I'm going to get something to drink." She left the room.

Aidan sat down in the chair gently. "What's all this about last night being your fault?"

"I made you go to the club," Madisyn said softly. "I'm sorry, Aidan. I just wanted this mess to be over and I've just made it worse."

He scooted closer to her bed. "Baby, you didn't make me do anything that I didn't want to do. I did everything because I love you and for no other reason. This was going to be my last season anyway, so nothing was lost."

"Aidan, I cost you a ton of money. How could you possibly want to continue seeing me?"

"Because you're worth it. Madisyn, there's nothing you can say that will make me walk out of here. Besides, this story has been on the news all morning, so you've been outed, baby. Everyone in Dallas knows we're a couple. Actually something good did come from all this."

Madisyn couldn't imagine what could have been good about the gunfight at Club Sizzle. "What?"

"Kameron closed the club after just one night. He said last night was too much for him. He got a flesh wound and that was his wake-up call. He's dropping all his extra women and is going to concentrate on his marriage. He's even retiring from football."

Madisyn knew what a major event that must have been. "Oh, my gosh. You're not upset with all the trouble I caused?"

"Honey, I keep telling you, you're my other half. Nothing you can say or do is going to make me walk away from you. I love you, Madisyn."

"I love you, too, Aidan."

"But?"

"I want you to be sure. This is a big step. Why don't you think about it while I'm in the hospital? I don't want you looking at me with hate later."

"What are you saying?"

Madisyn tried her best to look at him. "I want you to really think about this, Aidan. I want all our cards on the table. No secrets, nothing that can hurt us later."

He bowed his head. When he raised it again, he looked at her. "I don't need time, I know right now. When I was shot all I thought about was getting to you. So if you have doubts, then let me know."

She didn't have one single doubt. She loved him with all her heart and then some. "I don't have any doubts, not now, not ever."

⸎

Keisha had waited patiently for three days. Madisyn was being released today, and this would probably be her last chance. There was no way she'd have the courage to face Madisyn at her house, knowing that her family and Aidan would be there. She needed to talk to Madisyn alone to say her piece so she could get on with what was left of her life.

It was early, so no one had arrived yet. She'd seen the nurse deliver Maddie's breakfast, so Keisha knew she was awake. She muttered a silent prayer that Maddie wouldn't call security when she entered the room.

She was sitting up, but not eating. Keisha knew one of Maddie's wrists was broken, but she noticed both wrists were bandaged up.

"What are you doing in here?" Madisyn glanced at the red call button. "Aren't you supposed to be in jail?" Madisyn's tone was hard.

"I wanted to talk to you. I wanted to get things straight before you went home. No, I didn't get charged, because I helped them get Darnell. He's in jail. I have to do community service and I quit working at BAM. Fired, really, since everything has come to light. They gave me the option of being fired or resigning, which really wasn't an option. I want to start over somewhere else. Where no one knows me or anything about the stupid choices I've made."

"Good for you."

Keisha took a seat. "Maddie, we've known each other since elementary school. I know I took you for granted and I'm sorry. I'm really sorry about sleeping with Darnell, but I know that's probably too little, too late. I hope you find happiness with Aidan."

Madisyn didn't say a word.

Keisha rushed on. "I know we will never be friends again and that's my fault. But I just wanted you to know, I never thought it was going to escalate out of control like it did. Before I knew it, Darnell was talking about kidnapping you. It's not an excuse, it's just what happened. When the first shots were fired, Miss Callahan had me escorted out of the club. I spent Saturday night giving my statements to the police and the FBI."

"Okay, you've said your piece. Have a nice life."

Keisha stood, knowing she'd just been dismissed. She wiped the tears from her eyes. It felt like she'd just been dumped, but only twenty times worse, 'cause it was Maddie. "Thanks for listening."

Madisyn sighed. "I can't let you go like that. As much as I should be rude to you, I can't let you leave without saying this. No, we can't ever be friends again, but I do wish you well wherever you go. You could have been a better person all along if you had tried. I'm sure there's a good, mature person in there somewhere, you just have to find her."

Keisha took a deep breath. "Bye, Maddie."

~~~

Two weeks later, Madisyn, with the help of her entire family, made it to the grand opening of Mature Alliance. Although her sprained wrist had healed, her broken wrist was still in a cast. The healing ribs were the problem. As the bones knitted back together, walking and laughing were definitely off the list. But she wasn't missing tonight for anything. And as long as she had painkillers, she'd be fine.

She was proud of all the O'Riley boys. They were all dressed in their Sunday suits and they were all fussing over her.

"Baby, I think you should be sitting down," Ben O'Riley said. They'd just entered the building and hadn't walked ten steps.

"Daddy, I promise I'm okay. The minute I don't feel well, I'll sit down."

Madisyn glanced around the room. Everything looked wonderful. The rest of the guys had pitched in with the decorating, since both Aidan and Madisyn were recuperating. "I can't believe all the guys did this. It looks great."

"Hey, we helped, too," Ben said. "The boys and I came out here a couple of nights to decorate. But it does look nice."

"Yes, Dad, you helped," Madisyn said, walking up behind them. She knew the press would never get through the O'Rileys. "Maybe later."

Aidan smiled. "See, you thought all of Dallas was going to hate you. I announced my retirement and nobody sent the lynch mob for you."

Aidan had held a press conference just days before announcing that he had only partial feeling in his right hand, due to the injuries he'd received at the club, which softened the blow of his sudden retirement.

"I was actually more afraid of what your mama was going to say," Madisyn confessed. "But thank goodness she welcomed me with open arms." She'd met Aidan's parents right after she got out of the hospital and they'd instantly liked each other.

"Same here with your folks. I'm glad they were so forgiving." He kissed her with all the pent-up frustration of the last few weeks.

She reached up and wiped her lipstick off his handsome face. "It's time for your speech," she reminded him.

"I was supposed to write a speech? It totally slipped my mind." He winked at her.

"You did not forget, Aidan Sidney Coles," his mother said. "He dictated, I wrote." She kissed her son on the cheek. "Now go up there and wow these people. I know Madisyn isn't going to sit down until you do. No matter how much pain she's in."

Madisyn glanced at Aidan's mother. She'd only met Madisyn two weeks ago and already knew her like a book. "She's right, Aidan."

Aidan walked to the podium and began his speech. "Thank you for coming to the Mature Alliance grand opening. I'm Aidan Coles, one of the founders for the organization. I'm not here as a former Dallas Cowboy, but as a concerned citizen of Dallas. Everyone should have the opportunity to learn to read and write. This is what Mature Alliance is all about." He continued listing all the qualities of the center and how they wanted to help people. But he had one surprise left. "I'd like to present our hardest working volunteer with a token of my love." He smiled as he heard the oohs and aahs from the crowd. "As you know, I was injured at Club Sizzle a few weeks ago. So was Madisyn O'Riley. I would like to present her with this." He held up a small black velvet box. The crowd applauded.

Because he knew she was a die-hard romantic, he walked to where she stood with her family. He got down on one knee and presented her with the box. "Madisyn O'Riley, would you do me the honor of being my wife?" He gazed up at her.

She held the box and nodded quickly. "Yes, Aidan."

She motioned for him to stand. "Yes, Aidan, I'll marry you." She hugged and kissed him before either remembered her tender ribs. "Oh, oh," she winced and broke the embrace.

"Oh baby, I forgot. I got caught up."

She hugged him again, this time more gently. "That's okay. You saved me from Darnell. I can take some pain for you."

EPILOGUE

One year later

Madisyn whistled as she made French toast for breakfast. It was a celebratory meal for them all. Chase and Cadence were eloping to Vegas, and Madisyn and Aidan were going along as witnesses.

Madisyn's stomach rumbled as she inhaled the aroma of the rest of breakfast cooking. At eight weeks pregnant, Madisyn had been eating food like crazy. Instead of the smells playing havoc with her stomach, they fueled her appetite. Today was no exception. Along with French toast, she'd prepared bacon, eggs, hash browns, grits, sausage and toast.

Aidan walked into the kitchen, dressed in shorts and a T-shirt. His wedding band glistened on his hand as he walked to her. Giving her his usual morning salute, he hugged her, then rubbed her belly. He ended with a kiss to her forehead. "Are you sure about flying to Vegas today? You know the doctor said you need to take it easy." He took the spatula out of her hand and directed her to a chair. "I can finish this for you."

Since announcing her pregnancy, it was useless trying to tell him she was okay. Aidan had been insisting on hiring a maid, but luckily she'd won that argument. "All right, honey. I feel fine. The trip will be fine. Remember, we're going to see your parents from Vegas."

"I know. I just don't want you over-exerting. I still can't believe Chase is actually getting married."

"I think it's wonderful. Especially since it took him a year to decide that he couldn't live without Cadence. Talk about being stubborn," Madisyn said. "That man was fighting love from the beginning."

Aidan finished making breakfast and sat across from her. "I know. He's been a good friend and I hope he has nothing but happiness. With all that's been going on the last year, he deserves a rest. I got a little surprise for him."

"What?"

"I'm sending them to Greece for a month. I hear it's romantic. What do you think?"

"I think it's great," Madisyn said. "I almost wish we could have gone there for our honeymoon, but Hawaii was just as good for as much of the island I saw." She winked at her husband, remembering they'd seldom left their hotel room.

"How about we join them in a few weeks? Providing that you're doing all right."

Madisyn sat back in her seat and stared at her husband. He'd continued to surprise her every day since they'd said their vows. He had wanted to live closer to her parents, so they both sold their houses and had one built a few miles from her parents. "I think it sounds great."

"How about we ask Chayla and Jared?"

Madisyn's heart swelled. With all the craziness with Keisha in the past, Madisyn's friendship with Chayla was stronger than ever. "That would be nice. There are so many sites to see in Greece. Chayla will love the history of the country, and Jared will probably just love being around you," she teased her husband.

"And what will you love?" Aidan rose, walked to the counter and started fixing a plate of food.

"Being with you," she said honestly. "You're my heart. Thank you so much for coming into my life and showing me real love. After Darnell I didn't think it was possible, but you showed me it was."

"Baby, you're going to make me forget about breakfast and rush you upstairs."

Madisyn blew him a kiss. Since they'd married, Aidan had settled into their life easily. He played golf with her father, hung out with her brothers, and he'd even gotten involved with her church.

Madisyn's life, however, would never be the same. She'd finally gotten used to the news media taking her pictures whenever she and Aidan were out. After her marriage, she stopped working to concentrate more time at Alliance, but Aidan had different plans for her. They'd ended up hiring someone to run it full time. For the first time in her adult life, Madisyn didn't have a job. She'd thought they'd drive each other nuts both being at home, but it had been wonderful. Aidan had learned to cook, which he did often.

He placed a plate in front of her and they began to eat. "Should we have waited for Chase and Cadence?" Madisyn asked, scooping her eggs on top of her French toast. She really missed coffee, but there was no way Aidan was going to let her have any.

He took a sip of orange juice. "Nah, they'll probably sleep late," he said with a sly grin. "They won't come over until it's time for the flight."

Madisyn nodded as she ate another bite. "So I guess that means we've got a little free time before our flight takes off. Any ideas?" She smiled at him.

Aidan reached for her hand and caressed it gently. "Oh, I think I've got about million ideas to keep you busy. I'll start at your feet and work my way up."

Madisyn licked her lips in anticipation as delicious thoughts ran through her head. "Well then, I'll just have to pay you back the good way."

Aidan rose, took her hand and led her upstairs. "Oh, I was so hoping." He kissed her, picking her up in his arms and proceeding to show her one of the many ways he was going to love her.

THE END

ABOUT THE AUTHOR

Celya Bowers was born and raised in Marlin, Texas, a small town of about 8,000 souls. With not much to do, she turned to reading to expand her horizons and soon became an avid reader. Soon she wanted the characters in the books she read to look more like her and so became a closet writer.

After attending Sam Houston State University, she relocated to Arlington, Texas. Currently she attends college to complete her bachelor's degree. When she is not studying, writing and attending meetings, she likes hanging out with her great-niece, Kennedy, who just turned three.

Celya joined Romance Writers of America in 2001 and also the local chapter of Dallas Romance Authors, where she learned more about the business of writing. She is now on their executive board as Published Author Network liaison for the second year. She is also a member of Kiss of Death and The Sizzling Sisterhood Critique groups.

When she's between deadlines and final exams, Celya likes to keep up with friends and fans, surf the Net and daydream about finally getting to Ireland for her dream vacation.

Please visit her website at *www.celyabowers.net*.

CHAPTER 1

Whitney Underwood hated funerals. Each one was more painful than the last, and she knew attending this one would be no exception. Just as she finished refreshing her makeup, a new batch of tears started to flow. She tried to hold them back but the fullness in her chest threatened to strip away her breath. Her parents had suggested she not go, but that was never a consideration. Milton Duffy was family.

She had attended the wake, and her eyes were still swollen and red. Milt's death had reunited her with Kyle, the third corner of her friendship triangle from O. Perry Walker High. Kyle had wrapped his arms around her and held her close. Although it began as the same hug they had shared when they were younger and faced disaster, Whitney felt a new awakening in his arms. She wondered if it was the reuniting of old friends or something entirely different.

She retrieved her sunglasses from the bottom of her purse, stepped into heat that spewed from the deceptive serenity of a powder blue sky, and drove around the courtyard to pick up her best friend, Dana.

"Come on in." Dana held the door open. "I'll be ready as soon as I find my other shoe, unless Mr. Doodles has been using it as a chew toy. I don't know what I'm going to do with that dog. Oh, honey," she said, staring at Whitney's red eyes and trembling hands. "Maybe you shouldn't go. I know how upset you get at funerals. Last time you threw up all over the seat of your father's new Chrysler."

"I know, but I have to go. Milt and Dad were as close as brothers. I'll just have to be strong and keep it together." Whitney blinked back tears. "Saying goodbye is something I won't have a chance to do over."

She went to the hall mirror and used the edge of a white linen handkerchief to dab moisture from the corner of her eyes.

Whitney brought Dana up to date while dusting cinnamon blush on her cheeks and arranging dark curls around her shoulders. "I met Kyle at The Bottom last night after the wake. I hadn't seen him for almost a year, but it's plain to see that the boy has been working out. That waif we used to call Mopman is as buff as they come."

"Don't tell me you and Kyle got it going on." Dana smiled and snapped her fingers.

"Cut it out," Whitney answered. "You know how much I love Kyle as a friend. I wouldn't do anything to mess up that relationship, but I have to tell you, he sure looked delicious."

"So give it up, girl. What happened?"

"Nothing, really. He walked me to my car and we talked a long time in the parking lot—it was too noisy to hear each other at The Bottom." She trembled with vivid remembrance. "He kissed me good night."

"Like a kiss kind of kiss?" Dana stopped at the door.

Whitney nodded. "I don't think there was anything to it," she said softly. "But it sure felt great."

"It would be weird if the two of you discovered each other after all this time. Kyle did look pretty delicious the last time I saw him, but then he would look yummy to a love-starved chick like me."

"You mean sex-starved, Miss Red Hot Mama." Whitney laughingly joined Dana and headed back into the heat. "You know, there's something fishy about The Bottom. I know nightclubs change hands here quite often, but it just smells fishy, if you know what I mean."

"Didn't it change hands again?"

"Yeah." She unlocked the car door and slid onto the hot upholstery. "The last time I was there it was still Tropics. I heard it's completely changed since Powell sold it to J. R. Melancon."

"Ouch!" Dana yelped when her bare thigh made contact with the tan leather. "How do you know Melancon?"

"I don't, and I don't think I want to. I do know he's a small-time gangster who profits from the suffering of others. People call him the black Godfather. He is supposedly behind a lot of the dirt that goes on in this city." Hot air shot through the vents as she adjusted the temperature controls of her Jeep Commander. Thinking it best, she failed to mention that Kyle and Melancon had been in a hushed but heated discussion when she arrived.

"So, I take it you had a shitty time at The Bottom?" Dana asked.

"No, not really. I enjoyed being with Kyle again and that band, Dreamchild, was playing. The lead singer is something from old-school soul. He croons like Sam Cooke, has a range up to Mt. Everest, and looks like a caramel Popsicle that I would just love to lick."

"Oh no!" Dana yelled in Whitney's ear. "I know you're not thinking of dating a musician."

"Not *a* musician, or *any* musician, but Leander Perry is . . ." She shrugged. "There are no words to describe him."

"Well, there's one word that carries a big wallop. Musician." Dana spit the word through the gap in her front teeth. "That homogeneous bunch of night people who will hump anything that stands still long enough for them to mount. That chronically horny—"

"I know. I know," Whitney interrupted, flipping her wrist in Dana's direction. "I'm just telling it like I saw it. The man is fine."

Whitney's words slowed as the steeple on top of Saint Aloysius Catholic Church came into view. Cold fingers of dread ran down her spine.

Milt's death reunited Kyle and me. When Kyle's arms went around me, I felt like a kid again. I can't believe we've been out of high school almost ten years."

"I've been shaking since you told me Milt was killed." Dana dabbed her sweaty brow. "I just can't imagine something like this happening to a man like Milt. You still think he was murdered?"

Whitney used the seconds before the traffic light changed to meet Dana's inquisitive frown with a deep nod of her head.

"I don't think I could look at crime scene photos," Dana said, "but I guess you see things like that all the time."

"Yeah, but this was different." Whitney now regretted using her position as Deputy Assistant District Attorney for the city of New Orleans to worm her way into the police files. "Seeing him lying there on the pavement, his body mangled, his cold face covered with fear, a scrap of newspaper clutched in his scraped fist, made me physically ill. He didn't die instantly, Dana, and I can't get the image out of my head."

Whitney drove around the church parking lot and found a space close to the side of the building. She and Dana walked briskly down the stone path, past the office window where water dripped from a cooling unit, and up the worn steps. Whitney hesitated, blew hot air into hot air and grasped the heavy iron handle, pushing her weight against the elaborately carved wooden door. Once inside the vestibule, she stopped, took a tissue from her bag and mopped humidity from her face.

"It's too hot to wear black," she mumbled.

"It's too hot to wear clothes," Dana replied.

"The service hasn't started and I already feel faint." Whitney held the imported linen top away from her body, feeling a trickle of perspiration snake down the middle of her back.

"You went to the wake, so I don't think anyone would fault you if you skipped the funeral." Dana's eyes were filled with tears.

"I had no luck convincing myself of that." She reached for Dana's arm. "We've come this far. Let's find Kyle."

Dana peered into the half-full chapel. "He's on the left side, second row."

Using Kyle's megawatt smile as a beacon, they made their way through the crowded pews, still holding onto each other as they had done when they were children. Whitney batted away tears and looked over the sea of faces. There were many from her childhood, some almost forgotten, some greatly changed, and all filled with grief.

She and Dana walked into Kyle's outstretched arms, reuniting the popular trio in shared sorrow. Then Whitney sat and blinked rapidly, trying to halt the flow of tears. The service began and Father Doyle spoke over muffled sobs, telling everyone of his admiration for a man who had passed up a promising career in music to stay in the school system and help others attain success. Whitney swallowed hard and closed her eyes, hoping to erase the grotesque image that seemed indelibly etched in her mind. She watched her parents, and even her brother, MacArthur, sob when the final dirge began.

After the service, Whitney drove in the procession, listening to Dana's chatter as they both tried to remain calm.

"The whole gang from O. Perry Walker was there," Dana commented. "I try to keep in touch, but I hadn't seen some of them since graduation. I guess tragedy has a way of bringing people together."

"It's a shame. My first lesson in the district attorney's office was on the lawlessness that exists in our streets.

Nights of bloodshed are common, especially since Katrina. Multiple homicides. A drug deal gone bad. I see it every day, but this is personal, and too damn close to home."

They spoke of their neighborhood and the lack of strangers in the insular community of Algiers. Residents on the west bank of the Mississippi, "across the river" from New Orleans, usually remained friends for life. A scarcity of jobs held most teachers in place, sometimes through several generations, and that was the case with Milt Duffy. He had taught Whitney's older brothers, Raymond and MacArthur, and had been a friend and fellow musician with her father in a '60s jazz group called Taps. Later, Milt had helped her parents launch Underwood Music School. He became a permanent fixture in their lives.

The ache in Whitney's heart was overshadowed by anger. Another senseless loss, only this time it was someone she loved.

≈≈≈

The group of high school buddies converged with other friends and relatives at the cemetery, giving each other sad pats of condolence, and repeating words of dismay. Whitney and Dana huddled with the rest of their study hall pals, seeking shade hiding under the few trees bordering St. Augustine's Cemetery.

"I've missed you," Kyle kissed her cheek. "This is as regrettable as a situation could be, but I'm glad we're all together again, and it's especially good to see you."

She returned his hug, leaving her head on his chest and enjoying his closeness. "I feel the same way. Until last night, I hadn't seen you in almost a year."

"I don't think you really saw me then. We waved in passing."

"Well, I didn't get close enough to see how you've buffed up." She squeezed his upper arm.

He shrugged, but there was a noticeable glint of pride in his eyes. "I try. It keeps my head together."

Whitney and Dana had prepared food and beverages for their old friends and now the two of them left Kyle and made their way around the gathering, passing out invitations to many who were still in tears.

They returned to the car and Dana wiped her eyes. "It wasn't an accident. Someone killed him. That is exactly why I have a thirty-eight under my pillow. Have the police come up with any leads yet?"

"Not a single one. His death is still listed as a hit and run. I have pleaded with the police to keep looking, and with my boss to use his authority and lean on them to keep the investigation open. There has to be something that was seen or heard that would offer clues to what really happened." She backed into the street amid a billowing dust cloud and waited in the line of vehicles leaving the cemetery, lost in thought.

Dana broke the silence. "You seem far away. Are you still thinking of the photographs?"

She nodded. "But I have to put it out of my mind. People are headed to my place, expecting refreshments." She looked back and smiled as a small gray bird sang cheerfully from an overhead limb, and repeated the words from a newly carved plaque on the family tomb. "Milton Lamar Duffy, 1948-2006, Rest in Peace."

———

While Whitney and Dana passed around the food and MacArthur tended bar, they caught up on everyone's adventures, and shared stories of how Milt's gentle personality had enriched their lives. Whitney's eyes were mostly on Kyle, but she did notice sparks between Dana and MacArthur. She cornered Dana in the kitchen as MacArthur and Kyle gathered the dishes and glasses from departing guests.

"What's going on between you and Mac?"

"What's going on between you and Kyle?" Dana replied.

"Don't answer a question with a question. I know you've had a thing for Mac since we were kids, but we're not kids anymore. You've seen the way my brother processes women through his life, so unless you want to be one of the herd and make me feel infinitely guilty, I suggest you stop this right now."

"I've tried for years to get your brother to notice me." She licked her lips. "Now he has, so don't go giving me a hard time about it."

"Dana—"

"Back up off me." Dana held up her hand. "Look around you. Think of why we're all here today. A man we knew and loved is gone, and none of us know if he really lived out his dream. Well, I'm going to live out mine." She grasped Whitney's shoulder. "I want Mac, and if he's willing, I'm about to see what I've been missing, even if I have to pay for it later."

"Mac just turned thirty. That same age difference that made him dismiss you without a glance when we were kids is now making you very appealing."

Dana threw the dishtowel on the counter. "So you're saying my only attractive feature is my age?"

"Of course not." Whitney glanced at her friend's challenging eyes and olive skin dotted with tawny freckles. "You're pretty as hell, and you always were, but this is Mac we're talking about." She set the tray on the counter. "Look, I know you're feeling like crap now, having just come down off a bad breakup. Don't let my brother run his weak-ass game on you. Mac doesn't know the meaning of commitment, and probably can't even spell monogamy."

"I appreciate you trying to look out for me, but I'm a lot tougher than I look. I should be. I've been dumped more times than Madonna has wigs, and my question still stands. You also just got over a bad dump, so what's with you and Kyle?"

"I wish I knew the answer to that question." Whitney sighed. "He was, I don't know, different the other night. He walked me to my car but instead of the usual hug and peck on the cheek, he tried to put his tongue down my throat. I pulled away, of course." She hung her dish towel on a ring above the sink and turned to Dana. "If I had been asked to describe Kyle before this all happened, I

doubt that I would have remembered deep dimples or that turned-up mouth begging to be kissed."

"He's changed since high school, but most of the good changes happened recently. I was with him before his mother died, and he didn't have those bulging muscles." Dana looked down. "Of course, I didn't have a size 36 chest, either. I don't see a thing wrong with the two of you hooking up. You're both single, both attorneys, and you should already know each other's bad habits, so what's your concern?"

"I'm worried that maybe we're both feeling the sadness of the moment, not anything genuine, and I don't want to spoil a great friendship." She pursed her lips and wagged her finger in Dana's face. "I also don't want to have to help pick up the pieces after Mac dumps on you."

"You don't give me much credit, do you?" Dana's voice was edged with annoyance. "Why are you so sure he'll dump on me?"

She shook her head. "Because he's Mac."

Having gotten nowhere, she waited for Dana to go the bathroom and appealed to her brother. "I see what's been going on with you and Dana, and I'm begging you, please don't get involved. Dana will end up hurt and I'll feel like crap. Don't do this to her."

"Damn, Whitney! Don't treat me like some social pariah who can't be trusted around people." Mac finished his drink and tried to justify his actions. "Dana has been coming on to me all evening. I tried ignoring her, but she kept puttin' it all out there. What do you want me to do?"

"I want you to do the responsible thing and not get involved." She touched his sleeve. "She loves you, Mac. She always has. Please don't hurt her."

After another round of goodbyes, Whitney leaned on the counter and watched them leave together. "I'm worried about them, Kyle," she said to her only remaining guest. "They won't listen and I know someone—my bet is on Dana—will be hurt."

"They're big kids now, baby. Don't worry about it." He took her hand. "Come on. I'll help you clean up."

"Thanks, but I can't allow a big corporate hotshot attorney to do dishes." She refilled his wine glass. "I'm proud of you. And really shocked that some lucky woman hasn't snapped you up."

"Some have tried."

His smile warmed her heart.

They finished clearing the dishes and sat next to each other on the sofa. Whitney propped her slipper-clad feet on the end of the table, relaxing and allowing the burdens of the day to melt from her mind. She stretched her arms over her head and yawned.

"Is that my signal to leave?" Kyle asked. His face radiated the same warmth that had comforted her so often when they were young, but it now fueled her need to be held.

"Of course not. I'm glad you're here. We all get caught up in the business of making a living, but it's been over a year since we spent time together, and that's not the way it should be with us." She reached for his hand, held it in hers and pressed it against her face. "Life is too short to lose touch with those who mean the most to us."

"You're right, and I promise to do better. I see your parents often, especially now. I did some title searches on the property they bought, and I've reviewed all of the construction documents for the new building. They didn't want to bother you. Besides, that paper stuff is my forte. Yours is prosecuting criminals." His smile was shadowed by sadness. "You know your dad is the closest thing to a father I've ever had. Your family was my family, too. Still is."

Whitney remembered the constant turmoil of the unexplained absences and sudden reappearances of Kyle's father. She also remembered hiding him under her bed when he ran away from home, and holding him in her arms when his father made his final exit.

"Yeah, I know. My dad still thinks he has three sons. I hope he doesn't impose with his phone calls. Are there any problems I should know about?"

"Not really. I helped with the negotiations for the new place and one or two other small matters, and I certainly didn't mind doing so. I've always had tremendous respect for your father and your mother. I need their closeness now as much as I did when I was young. As a matter of fact, we started communicating more often after my mother died. Your mother was there for me. She helped me with the arrangements and generally held me together."

"I know. I tried to reach you several times after the funeral but you never returned my calls. Mom said you were having a difficult time." She hugged him and looked into his eyes. "A friend in need. Remember?"

"I was something of a wreck back then. I got your messages, but I was too messed up to speak to anyone." Sitting at Whitney's feet, he removed her slippers and began massaging her toes.

"I'm not just anyone. Don't you know how much you mean to me? I love you."

"I know. I knew you were concerned, but I didn't want to weigh you down with my problems. It took a long time for me to realize that she was really gone. I stayed with her through the battle with cancer. I watched her deteriorate, suffer, and fall into that final sleep, but it was still hard to accept that she was gone. She was the center of my life."

"I'm sure she was comforted by that knowledge." As always, Whitney felt his pain.

"Sadly, I was the only comfort she had. Her other children were too busy screwing up their lives."

His voice reeked of bitterness. Whitney wanted to comfort him now, but feared her own sorrow over Milt's death might throw her into another crying fit. She knew there had been problems with Kyle's three older siblings and that his youngest sister, Callie, had become his responsibility after their mother died.

"I heard Callie is doing well at the University of New Orleans. I'm sure you were her inspiration."

"She's a good kid. Aunt Leigh helped some, but I've had to deal with most things on my own. Callie just turned twenty, and I'm happy as hell." As he looked at her, a smile toyed with his lips. "I was sure you'd be married by now."

"I had a close call, but it didn't work out."

"Would it be evil of me to say I'm glad it didn't?" When she didn't answer or return his smile, he amended his question. "What I mean is, you deserve the best, Whitney. I couldn't stand thinking of you in an unhappy marriage."

Whitney changed the subject and they drank coffee and reminisced until Whitney really began to yawn. As she walked him to the door, he stopped and began another conversation.

"I'm on the mayor's citizens assistance committee and we need as many hands as we can get. Are you interested?"

"I've got a big case going on right now and little time for myself, but . . ." She smiled. "Anything for a friend. I see it every day, but I still can't believe the devastation. All of my life, I've heard that New Orleans is like a bowl surrounded by water and that one day it would spill over the bowl, but Katrina was unimaginable."

"And all that time we were hearing that someone should fix the damn levees, but did they do it? The mayor is a friend of mine, and I know he hasn't done as much as he could have to avoid this destruction, but neither did any of the other mayors. As you said, the problem didn't start yesterday. Do you remember Miss Georgia Evans from our street?"

"Of course." Whitney smiled at the image that popped into her head. "Miss Evans taught me in second and fourth grades. What happened to her?"

Kyle's eyes filled. "Her daughter and son-in-law moved to Denver and she went to live in their home somewhere on Harrison Avenue. She was rescued from the roof of the house after being up there for six days. She was dehydrated and had been bitten by ants so many times the doctors had to search for a spot of skin large enough to place a needle. Her son Ronnie came by a few days ago and cried like a baby when he talked about it. I don't mind telling you, I cried with him."

Whitney took his face in her hands. "It's all hard. I'm afraid to count the number of people I know who've lost everything they had, or even worse, lost their lives."

"Now that we've reconnected, I'm not letting you out of my life again. You said you have a big case, but you've got to relax sometimes, so call me any day but Thursday, and we can meet at The Bottom."

"Let's meet someplace else. I'm not crazy about hanging around a place owned by Melancon."

Kyle's eyes widened. "I didn't realize you knew Melancon."

"I know he's major sleaze, which makes me want to avoid him at all costs, and certainly not patronize his establishment."

"I didn't realize he was so well known, but then I sometimes forget your work involves the underbelly of society." Kyle playfully poked her stomach.

"There isn't much of the city left, but there are a few places we can meet that aren't controlled by thugs," Whitney said. "Call me when you're free and I'll make time for my favorite Mopman." She tiptoed, tilting her face toward his.

His lips touched her face, their eyes met in a lingering gaze and his grip tightened, pulling her body to his. "Kyle, don't you think . . ." His arms encircled her, cutting off her words and her breath. His warm, wet lips fused with hers.

"What just happened here?" She moved away, still holding onto his arm.

His mouth stretched into a warm, seductive smile. "I don't know, but I sure liked it."

He leaned down and seized her mouth again. Whitney was surprised at her immediate response. This was Kyle, her friend, her confidant and partner in crime, yet a rapid burn ignited her breasts and swept downward. Just as the last vestige of restraint evaporated, the red flag of friendship flapped in her face. She moved away, still burning inside.

"You'd better watch out. I'm one of those desperate females that make up the random statistics you keep reading about. My life has been pretty barren lately. I haven't seen any action since . . ." She laughed. "I'm ashamed to say."

"How long?" His voice was low and dreamy, his eyes half closed as he looked down on her face.

"Long enough to create mammoth needs." She smiled, holding her arms apart.

"And a friend in need—"

"In this case is someone you should run from." She laughed and pushed him back. "In addition to having pressing needs, we're both high on grief right now, so let's not get carried away." She leaned her body into his. "I've missed you. I can't tell you how many times I wanted to run to the phone and call you the way I did when we were kids, to pour out my problems and spend the night trying to solve them."

The past came rushing back, and with it, memories of Milton Duffy. "Growing up isn't always fun." She wiped her eyes. "I think of the yesterdays, the simple times of life, with increasing degrees of sadness."

"No matter how busy I am, I'll make time for you whenever you call. I've missed you, and I constantly long for the simplicity of youth." He laughed. "Dana calls often. I love her and I'm always glad to hear from her, but she's a motor mouth with a hell of a lot more time to gab than I do. I know she's a cost accountant at city hall, but does she ever work? She called me one day and talked for over two hours. I kept saying 'I have to go,' and she kept talking. Didn't miss a beat."

Whitney laughed. "She does the same thing to me, but I know how to get her off the phone." Her sigh was reflective and a little sad. "I'm happy with my life, I really am, but I miss us, those nights of studying together, school dances, yard parties."

His arms enveloped her in the brotherly comfort of the past. "I miss us, too. Most of all, I miss you. Our whole gang was supportive, but I practically lived at your house. Your mom helped me with my homework, your dad taught me to throw a ball. I remember once having Mac protect me from that big Neanderthal down the street. Clyde something or other. You were my family. I loved all of you, and I still do."

The thought of pulling him into her bedroom was very tempting. She felt so right in his arms. "I love you, too." She won a fierce struggle with her desires, said goodnight and closed the door after him.

———

Even though thoughts of Milton Duffy's twisted body and terrified stare were still very fresh in her mind, Whitney was forced to put her feelings aside and forge ahead. She was working on the biggest case of her career, which left little time to think of the embrace she had shared with Kyle. Shortage of time was one of the reasons her life was socially bare. Her mother called on Friday night to remind her of the ribbon-cutting ceremony at the newly opened Underwood Music Studio, and to ask about her brother.

"I shouldn't be attempting to keep up with MacArthur. I know he's an adult, but he's hardly been home at all in the past week and as a mother, I still worry. Do you know where he's been staying?"

Whitney wished she had not been asked. "Yes, I know where he's been, Mom. He's fine." Dana had called with daily updates on her sizzling love life. She and Mac had been inseparable since the dinner. Whitney hoped that when her mother had to be told, the news would be good. "I'll be there for the ceremony tomorrow. I wouldn't miss it."

Whitney hung up and smiled at the continued nurturing she and her brothers received. Whitney admired her mother more than anyone in her life. Tessitore Amanda Shaguois, the only daughter of wealthy Creole descendants, was headed for medical school when she fell in love with saxophone player Clark Underwood. Staunchly defying her family and deferring her dreams, she became a musician's wife, accepting without hesitation the life that came with it. Having witnessed her mother's suffering and forbearance, Whitney had sworn off ever dating a musician.

She spent the evening working on a case where objectivity was nonexistent. It was another one that hit close to home, and the revolting horror of it had penetrated her soul. Filled with intense anger and anxiety, she was determined not to lose.

A child had been murdered in the underbrush behind the park in her parents' neighborhood. It was the same park where Whitney had played when she was young. She had learned to shoot a basketball into the rim that never had a net, and had danced near the jukebox when she was older. She could still remember playing in the very spot where the child was last seen.

The next morning she knew she had spent too much time examining and analyzing, and not enough time sleeping. It was a big day for her parents and she wanted very much to look good. She tried to smooth away the puffiness around her eyes, drank two cups of coffee, and dressed in a flattering lightweight white pants suit. Parking in the next block to leave room for visitors, she paused in front of the building, filled with admiration and pride. Her mother had worked with an architect on the building design. It was red brick and glass, with large white stone pillows. The front of the circular driveway had been professionally landscaped and lighted, with the Underwood name displayed proudly on a stone sign in the center.

Whitney stood with her parents and brothers as her cousin Lindsay and two other photographers snapped photos for their respective papers. Dana and Kyle joined the rest of the family and friends who had gathered for the occasion, and for Whitney, the years seemed to fade. She felt the warmth of her surroundings and enjoyed the closeness of family and friends.

She and Kyle played host and hostess, serving hot dogs, punch and cookies to the younger students, and champagne cocktails, crab puffs, shrimp biscuits, and a host of other goodies to the adults in attendance. When they touched, she searched for the magic, the spasms of passion that had left her weak and wanting, but felt only the closeness of a very dear friend.

She walked around the building with her father, watching his face as he pointed out the recording studio, a new venture for Underwood, and an accomplishment that made Clark quite proud. After Kyle left, Whitney grilled Dana about her relationship with Mac.

"Mom called last night, asking if I knew where Mac was staying. Are you sure it's wise to get so deep into this relationship? I love my brother, but we both know how he is."

"Whitney, this past week has been like a dream come true. I've wanted to be with Mac for as long as I can remember, but I could never have imagined that it would be like this. He's wonderful, Whitney, and I think he loves me."

Whitney smiled and changed the subject to work and the rigors of her current case until Dana had to leave. Whitney stayed in the office with her father, helping organize files and records. Someone opened a door in the rehearsal hall and the deeply passionate wail of a saxophone escaped. It traveled down the stairs and straight to her heart.

"If that's a student, I suggest we get him a recording contract right now."

"That's Dreamchild," Clark answered. "Mac just joined the group, and I've agreed to let them practice here."

Leaving her father, she followed the muted sound of the wonderful voice up the steps. Pushing the door open slowly so as not to disturb anyone, she was stunned by the bass percussion and by the melodious voice that sent a ripple of pleasure over her body. She scanned the room, her eyes coming to rest on softly burnished copper skin that was gloved over a finely chiseled frame. Leander Perry had looked dazzling onstage, but up close and in person, he was a dream in motion. Whitney was mesmerized.

Not bothering to look at the others, she remained focused on the face that took her breath away and the vocal aerobics like none she had heard.

His eyes met hers and she tried to distinguish their color. Soft greenish gray, quick and bright. Catlike. She stared, first at his face, then down the length of his magnificent body. She guessed six feet, not overly muscular, but strong and sturdy. His hair was straight and glossy, like a raven's wing. His smile melted her soul. She watched his body sway as his velvet voice crooned several old standards.

The rehearsal ended and Mac introduced the group, saving Leander Perry for last. "So what did you think?" Leander asked.

He took her hand in his when they were introduced, looked at her, through her, she felt.

"You were wonderful," she heard herself say. "I love your CD, but you sound different in person, stronger, more intense." His penetrating stare brought all of her nerve endings to attention. "I hope I didn't disturb you."

She knew Mac was watching and that one of the female members of the group was giving them an evil glare, but she could not stop looking at him. She felt a connection, and though it disturbed her, she couldn't move.

"We were just warming up. It's good to have a critic around, especially if they know music, and I'm sure you do. We've had some internal problems that resulted in the loss of a member and a rehearsal facility. Your parents were kind enough to allow us to rehearse here."

"Having you here should be an inspiration to the students. I'm sure my folks are happy to provide the space." Noticing Mac's severe look in their direction, she excused herself and went back downstairs.

Later, Mac told her that Leander was very ambitious. He had organized the group, most of whom were older than he was, and had kept them together, sometimes using personal funds to tide them over between gigs.

"I got a little concerned when I saw the two of you talking for so long, but I remembered your hard rule of never dating musicians." Mac searched her face. "That hasn't changed, has it?"

If the question had been asked a month ago, she would have had a ready answer. "Don't worry about me. You're the one treading on thin ice with my best friend. I asked you before and I'll do it again; don't hurt her, Mac."

"Dana and I are fine. There's nothing to worry about."

Mac's cavalier attitude did little to relieve her worries, and now she felt even more concern about her unusually strong attraction to Leander Perry. He was good looking and talented, but it was more than that. The feeling she'd got when their eyes met, the completeness and the inner communication, were different and magnificent feelings.

She had Sunday brunch with Kyle. Sitting next to him, she felt all of the love and affection that she felt for Mac or Ray. Brotherly love, not the arousal Leander stirred within her. She admired Kyle, but there was no romance.

Her eyes watered when he kissed her goodnight, and she had to pull away. He was the last person she wanted to hurt and hoped his feelings were not as concentrated as his kiss suggested. She met him again on Wednesday night, but when he called to invite her to dinner on

Thursday, she lied and said she was going to spend the evening with her parents. If he was falling for her, she had to think of painless ways to let him down.

Having said she was going to the school, she did so right after work. Her mother and father were glad to see her, but both were busy when she arrived, so she milled around in the office and finally headed upstairs, thinking she would practice piano until she was tired, and then go home.

"Hello, Whitney."

She turned at the top of the steps and stared into Leander's delightful smile.

"Hi." Her hands began to sweat. He was intensely sexual. "Are you rehearsing today?"

"We were supposed to rehearse. We need to rehearse. I just got standing gigs that will keep us busy from Friday through Sunday nights, but Izzy was on his way over with the equipment and had a flat. I've been waiting here for over an hour. Mac and the others are inside."

She saw something inviting in his eyes. "I'm sorry your plans went sour, but I'm sure you'll sound wonderful."

Someone was playing Mozart in the background, soft strings of a lilting waltz that put her in mind of love stories. She wondered if there would be one for her and Leander.

"I was about to go for a walk." Again she had lied, but she needed to explore her feelings, and not under her brother's watchful eye. "Would you like to come with me?"

"Sure. Where're you going?"

"Just over to the levee. I love to sit there and look out at the water. The calm of the river always seems to wash away the week's tension, and I've got a pile of it right now."

She purchased two sodas from the machine, handed one to Leander and continued talking as they walked from the back door of the building, across the freshly mowed grass and up the incline that led to the top of the levee. The heady smell of river water flowed into her nostrils, bringing a wave of relaxation.

"I'm working on a ghastly murder case, and sometimes it's more than I can deal with. When that happens, I like to be with my folks, and I like to sit here by the water."

He sat on the grass next to her. "I like to come here, too," he said. "I don't have to deal with anything as intense as a murder case, but that muddy Mississippi can wash away a lot of troubles. It's also inspiring. I write most of the music for Dreamchild, and sometimes I can't find my way to the next bar. Smoking cigarettes, drinking coffee, nothing helps like sitting on the levee and watching those waves go back and forth."

"Did you always want a career in music?" she asked.

"Not really," he answered, shaking his head. "I had a hard time expressing my feelings when I was a kid. I still do. My grandmother brought home an old piano her employer had given her, and I found my outlet. I would sit for hours at a time, just thumping those keys. Soft melodic notes for peaceful, reverent moods, and shrill high ones for those other feelings." He stopped talking and stared across the narrow span of water to the heart of the Central Business District.

Whitney had hoped that familiarity would lead to disinterest, but found him more intriguing than before.

"Did you have a bad childhood?" she asked.

"I always had someone who loved me, and someone who needed me, and now I have my music, so I guess I can't complain."

His admitted inability to articulate his feelings made Whitney search his face for signs of emotion. He left a lot unsaid, but she caught a glimpse of his soul when he talked about music. He offered his hand as they rose from the levee bank. She felt magnetism that was both arousing and frightening. Her heart leaped as she heard Mac's warning, thought of her own rules, and feared the recriminations she would get from Dana. It didn't lessen the attraction. She wanted to call Dana at that moment and tell her that she now understood her willingness to gamble on Mac.

Whitney spent the weekend listening to Dana rave about the wonderful times she was having in Mac's arms, but decided not to divulge her own fall into forbidden territory. They spent Saturday evening with Kyle, a movie and dinner, and Whitney was thankful to have Dana there for distraction. She told Kyle about her case and the work she still had to do, in hope that he would find other interests.

When Leander called on Monday and extended an invitation for lunch on Tuesday, she floated for the rest of the afternoon. All efforts to concentrate were lost to the handsome image that loomed in her mind. She reminded herself that she wasn't a schoolgirl and this was no first crush, but thoughts of having his arms around her outweighed her apprehension. Hardly able to sit still Tuesday morning, she made repeated trips to the restroom, combing her hair and retouching her makeup, feeling her heart dance in anticipation. She left the office at eleven-fifteen and walked the four blocks to Alchemy's Restaurant, feeling giddy with anticipation.

The early lunch crowd was already swarming Alchemy's, but she spotted him immediately. A smile spread across his face.

"Hi. You're right on time," he said, while standing to hold her chair. "I was about to order drinks, but I don't know what you like."

He was wearing a gray suit, red tie, and a very inviting smile.

"Iced tea is fine. I hope you didn't dress just for lunch. Jackets aren't required here during the day." She wanted to say he looked ravishing but did not dare.

"I know. I had a little business to conduct this morning. Besides, I don't want to look like a bum when I'm with the most beautiful woman in the city." His eyes were filled with sincerity.

They talked more about work and a little about their childhood while she nibbled on a turkey sandwich and he devoured a foot-long oyster po-boy. When it was time to leave, he held her hand on the walk back to her office. Stopping in the shadows of the Pontalba Building, he drew her close.

"I find you incredibly attractive, but it's much more than that. I don't know how to explain it. Our worlds are so different, and I'm sure you'd feel more comfortable dating a professional man, but I . . . I like you a lot and I'd be honored if, you know, we could be together, I mean as a couple."

She found his stammering irresistible. "I have a rule, or I did have a rule, that prohibited dating musicians." She saw the look on his face and quickly added an explanation. "Don't get me wrong, I find talent quite intriguing, and you're loaded with it. It's just that most musicians, my brothers included, have horrible track records when it comes to relationships, and I've never cared for fleeting romances or one-night stands."

"It wouldn't be that way for us, but I understand what you're saying." His voice quivered slightly, but she also detected defiance.

"What I'm saying is that I enjoy being with you. I still have reservations about the kind of life you lead, but I—"

"You don't know the life I lead," he interrupted. "Don't judge me by what others have done. That's not me. Okay, I have enjoyed the company of a few ladies, but that's not who I am, especially now. That kind of life no longer works for me. I want a meaningful relationship, and I very much want that relationship with you." He pulled her closer. "I need more than one-night stands and superficial attachments, and when I think of what I want, I see your face."

Emotions soared and her body became rigid against his.

He turned away, his head bowed. "I don't mean to frighten you. I just want you in my life."

She was frightened—and not of him. "I think it's too soon to make any kind of commitment for a relationship, but I do want to see you again."

He caressed her face. Pools of emotion clouded his eyes. "Soon?"

"Yeah," she whispered and closed her eyes as his mouth covered hers and his tongue dueled sweetly with hers. Enveloped by soulful sounds of a nearby street band and the smell of a humid city breeze, she released her inhibitions. "I'd like that. I'd like that a lot."

2009 Reprint Mass Market Titles

January

I'm Gonna Make You Love Me
Gwyneth Bolton
ISBN-13: 978-1-58571-294-6
$6.99

A Love of Her Own
Cheris Hodges
ISBN-13: 978-1-58571-293-9
$6.99

Twist of Fate
Beverly Clark
ISBN-13: 978-1-58571-295-3
$6.99

Sinful Intentions
Crystal Rhodes
ISBN-13: 978-1-585712-297-7
$6.99

Paths of Fire
T.T. Henderson
ISBN-13: 978-1-58571-343-1
$6.99

Reckless Surrender
Rochelle Alers
ISBN-13: 978-1-58571-345-5
$6.99

February

Shades of Desire
Monica White
ISBN-13: 978-1-58571-292-2
$6.99

Color of Trouble
Dyanne Davis
ISBN-13: 978-1-58571-294-6
$6.99

March

Chances
Pamela Leigh Starr
ISBN-13: 978-1-58571-296-0
$6.99

April

Rock Star
Roslyn Hardy Holcomb
ISBN-13: 978-1-58571-298-4
$6.99

May

Caught Up in the Rapture
Lisa Riley
ISBN-13: 978-1-58571-344-8
$6.99

June

No Ordinary Love
Angela Weaver
ISBN-13: 978-1-58571-346-2
$6.99

2009 Reprint Mass Market Titles (continued)

July

Intentional Mistakes
Michele Sudler
ISBN-13: 978-1-58571-347-9
$6.99

It's In His Kiss
Reon Carter
ISBN-13: 978-1-58571-348-6
$6.99

August

Unfinished Love Affair
Barbara Keaton
ISBN-13: 978-1-58571-349-3
$6.99

A Perfect Place to Pray
I.L Goodwin
ISBN-13: 978-1-58571-299-1
$6.99

September

Love in High Gear
Charlotte Roy
ISBN-13: 978-1-58571-355-4
$6.99

Ebony Eyes
Kei Swanson
ISBN-13: 978-1-58571-356-1
$6.99

October

Midnight Clear, Part I
Leslie Esdale/Carmen Green
ISBN-13: 978-1-58571-357-8
$6.99

Midnight Clear, Part II
Gwynne Forster/Monica Jackson
ISBN-13: 978-1-58571-358-5
$6.99

November

Midnight Peril
Vicki Andrews
ISBN-13: 978-1-58571-359-2
$6.99

One Day At A Time
Bella McFarland
ISBN-13: 978-1-58571-360-8
$6.99

December

Just An Affair
Eugenia O'Neal
ISBN-13: 978-1-58571-361-5
$6.99

Shades of Brown
Denise Becker
ISBN-13: 978-1-58571-362-2
$6.99

2009 New Mass Market Titles

January

Singing A Song…
Crystal Rhodes
ISBN-13: 978-1-58571-283-0
$6.99

Look Both Ways
Joan Early
ISBN-13: 978-1-58571-284-7
$6.99

Six O'Clock
Katrina Spencer
ISBN-13: 978-1-58571-285-4
$6.99

February

Red Sky
Renee Alexis
ISBN-13: 978-1-58571-286-1
$6.99

Anything But Love
Celya Bowers
ISBN-13: 978-1-58571-287-8
$6.99

March

Tempting Faith
Crystal Hubbard
ISBN-13: 978-1-58571-288-5
$6.99

If I Were Your Woman
La Connie Taylor-Jones
ISBN-13: 978-1-58571-289-2
$6.99

April

Best Of Luck Elsewhere
Trisha Haddad
ISBN-13: 978-1-58571-290-8
$6.99

All I'll Ever Need
Mildred Riley
ISBN-13: 978-1-58571-335-6
$6.99

May

A Place Like Home
Alicia Wiggins
ISBN-13: 978-1-58571-336-3
$6.99

Best Foot Forward
Michele Sudler
ISBN-13: 978-1-58571-337-0
$6.99

June

It's In the Rhythm
Sammie Ward
ISBN-13: 978-1-58571-338-7
$6.99

2009 New Mass Market Titles (continued)

July

Checks and Balances
Elaine Sims
ISBN-13: 978-1-58571-339-4
$6.99

Save Me
Africa Fine
ISBN-13: 978-1-58571-340-0
$6.99

When Lightening Strikes
Michele Cameron
ISBN-13: 978-1-58571-369-1
$6.99

August

Blindsided
Tammy Williams
ISBN-13: 978-1-58571-342-4
$6.99

September

2 Good
Celya Bowers
ISBN-13: 978-1-58571-350-9
$6.99

Waiting for Mr. Darcy
Chamein Canton
ISBN-13: 978-1-58571-351-6
$6.99

Fireflies
Joan Early
ISBN-13: 978-1-58571-352-3
$6.99

October

Frost On My Window
Angela Weaver
ISBN-13: 978-1-58571-353-0
$6.99

November

Waiting in the Shadows
Michele Sudler
ISBN-13: 978-1-58571-364-6
$6.99

Fixin' Tyrone
Keith Walker
ISBN-13: 978-1-58571-365-3
$6.99

December

Dream Keeper
Gail McFarland
ISBN-13: 978-1-58571-366-0
$6.99

Another Memory
Pamela Ridley
ISBN-13: 978-1-58571-367-7
$6.99

Other Genesis Press, Inc. Titles

Other Genesis Press, Inc. Titles (continued)

Bodyguard	Andrea Jackson	$9.95
Boss of Me	Diana Nyad	$8.95
Bound by Love	Beverly Clark	$8.95
Breeze	Robin Hampton Allen	$10.95
Broken	Dar Tomlinson	$24.95
By Design	Barbara Keaton	$8.95
Cajun Heat	Charlene Berry	$8.95
Careless Whispers	Rochelle Alers	$8.95
Cats & Other Tales	Marilyn Wagner	$8.95
Caught in a Trap	Andre Michelle	$8.95
Caught Up In the Rapture	Lisa G. Riley	$9.95
Cautious Heart	Cheris F Hodges	$8.95
Chances	Pamela Leigh Starr	$8.95
Cherish the Flame	Beverly Clark	$8.95
Choices	Tammy Williams	$6.99
Class Reunion	Irma Jenkins/	$12.95
	John Brown	
Code Name: Diva	J.M. Jeffries	$9.95
Conquering Dr. Wexler's	Kimberley White	$9.95
Heart		
Corporate Seduction	A.C. Arthur	$9.95
Crossing Paths,	Dorothy Elizabeth Love	$9.95
Tempting Memories		
Crush	Crystal Hubbard	$9.95
Cypress Whisperings	Phyllis Hamilton	$8.95
Dark Embrace	Crystal Wilson Harris	$8.95
Dark Storm Rising	Chinelu Moore	$10.95
Daughter of the Wind	Joan Xian	$8.95
Dawn's Harbor	Kymberly Hunt	$6.99
Deadly Sacrifice	Jack Kean	$22.95
Designer Passion	Dar Tomlinson	$8.95
	Diana Richeaux	
Do Over	Celya Bowers	$9.95
Dream Runner	Gail McFarland	$6.99
Dreamtective	Liz Swados	$5.95

Other Genesis Press, Inc. Titles (continued)

Ebony Angel	Deatri King-Bey	$9.95
Ebony Butterfly II	Delilah Dawson	$14.95
Echoes of Yesterday	Beverly Clark	$9.95
Eden's Garden	Elizabeth Rose	$8.95
Eve's Prescription	Edwina Martin Arnold	$8.95
Everlastin' Love	Gay G. Gunn	$8.95
Everlasting Moments	Dorothy Elizabeth Love	$8.95
Everything and More	Sinclair Lebeau	$8.95
Everything but Love	Natalie Dunbar	$8.95
Falling	Natalie Dunbar	$9.95
Fate	Pamela Leigh Starr	$8.95
Finding Isabella	A.J. Garrotto	$8.95
Forbidden Quest	Dar Tomlinson	$10.95
Forever Love	Wanda Y. Thomas	$8.95
From the Ashes	Kathleen Suzanne	$8.95
	Jeanne Sumerix	
Gentle Yearning	Rochelle Alers	$10.95
Glory of Love	Sinclair LeBeau	$10.95
Go Gentle into that	Malcom Boyd	$12.95
Good Night		
Goldengroove	Mary Beth Craft	$16.95
Groove, Bang, and Jive	Steve Cannon	$8.99
Hand in Glove	Andrea Jackson	$9.95
Hard to Love	Kimberley White	$9.95
Hart & Soul	Angie Daniels	$8.95
Heart of the Phoenix	A.C. Arthur	$9.95
Heartbeat	Stephanie Bedwell-Grime	$8.95
Hearts Remember	M. Loui Quezada	$8.95
Hidden Memories	Robin Allen	$10.95
Higher Ground	Leah Latimer	$19.95
Hitler, the War, and the Pope	Ronald Rychlak	$26.95
How to Write a Romance	Kathryn Falk	$18.95
I Married a Reclining Chair	Lisa M. Fuhs	$8.95
I'll Be Your Shelter	Giselle Carmichael	$8.95
I'll Paint a Sun	A.J. Garrotto	$9.95

Other Genesis Press, Inc. Titles (continued)

Icie	Pamela Leigh Starr	$8.95
Illusions	Pamela Leigh Starr	$8.95
Indigo After Dark Vol. I	Nia Dixon/Angelique	$10.95
Indigo After Dark Vol. II	Dolores Bundy/	$10.95
	Cole Riley	
Indigo After Dark Vol. III	Montana Blue/	$10.95
	Coco Morena	
Indigo After Dark Vol. IV	Cassandra Colt/	$14.95
Indigo After Dark Vol. V	Delilah Dawson	$14.95
Indiscretions	Donna Hill	$8.95
Intentional Mistakes	Michele Sudler	$9.95
Interlude	Donna Hill	$8.95
Intimate Intentions	Angie Daniels	$8.95
It's Not Over Yet	J.J. Michael	$9.95
Jolie's Surrender	Edwina Martin-Arnold	$8.95
Kiss or Keep	Debra Phillips	$8.95
Lace	Giselle Carmichael	$9.95
Lady Preacher	K.T. Richey	$6.99
Last Train to Memphis	Elsa Cook	$12.95
Lasting Valor	Ken Olsen	$24.95
Let Us Prey	Hunter Lundy	$25.95
Lies Too Long	Pamela Ridley	$13.95
Life Is Never As It Seems	J.J. Michael	$12.95
Lighter Shade of Brown	Vicki Andrews	$8.95
Looking for Lily	Africa Fine	$6.99
Love Always	Mildred E. Riley	$10.95
Love Doesn't Come Easy	Charlyne Dickerson	$8.95
Love Unveiled	Gloria Greene	$10.95
Love's Deception	Charlene Berry	$10.95
Love's Destiny	M. Loui Quezada	$8.95
Love's Secrets	Yolanda McVey	$6.99
Mae's Promise	Melody Walcott	$8.95
Magnolia Sunset	Giselle Carmichael	$8.95
Many Shades of Gray	Dyanne Davis	$6.99
Matters of Life and Death	Lesego Malepe, Ph.D.	$15.95

Other Genesis Press, Inc. Titles (continued)

Meant to Be	Jeanne Sumerix	$8.95
Midnight Clear (Anthology)	Leslie Esdaile	$10.95
	Gwynne Forster	
	Carmen Green	
	Monica Jackson	
Midnight Magic	Gwynne Forster	$8.95
Midnight Peril	Vicki Andrews	$10.95
Misconceptions	Pamela Leigh Starr	$9.95
Moments of Clarity	Michele Cameron	$6.99
Montgomery's Children	Richard Perry	$14.95
Mr Fix-It	Crystal Hubbard	$6.99
My Buffalo Soldier	Barbara B. K. Reeves	$8.95
Naked Soul	Gwynne Forster	$8.95
Never Say Never	Michele Cameron	$6.99
Next to Last Chance	Louisa Dixon	$24.95
No Apologies	Seressia Glass	$8.95
No Commitment Required	Seressia Glass	$8.95
No Regrets	Mildred E. Riley	$8.95
Not His Type	Chamein Canton	$6.99
Nowhere to Run	Gay G. Gunn	$10.95
O Bed! O Breakfast!	Rob Kuehnle	$14.95
Object of His Desire	A. C. Arthur	$8.95
Office Policy	A. C. Arthur	$9.95
Once in a Blue Moon	Dorianne Cole	$9.95
One Day at a Time	Bella McFarland	$8.95
One in A Million	Barbara Keaton	$6.99
One of These Days	Michele Sudler	$9.95
Outside Chance	Louisa Dixon	$24.95
Passion	T.T. Henderson	$10.95
Passion's Blood	Cherif Fortin	$22.95
Passion's Furies	AlTonya Washington	$6.99
Passion's Journey	Wanda Y. Thomas	$8.95
Past Promises	Jahmel West	$8.95
Path of Fire	T.T. Henderson	$8.95
Path of Thorns	Annetta P. Lee	$9.95

Other Genesis Press, Inc. Titles (continued)

Peace Be Still	Colette Harwood	$12.95
Picture Perfect	Reon e:	$8.95
Playing for Keeps	Stephanie Salinas	$8.95
Pride & Joi	Gay G. Gunn	$8.95
Promises Made	Bernice Layton	$6.99
Promises to Keep	Alicia Wiggins	$8.95
Quiet Storm	Donna Hill	$10.95
Reckless Surrender	Rochelle Alers	$6.95
Red Polka Dot in a World of Plaid	Varian Johnson	$12.95
Reluctant Captive	Joyce Jackson	$8.95
Rendezvous with Fate	Jeanne Sumerix	$8.95
Revelations	Cheris F. Hodges	$8.95
Rivers of the Soul	Leslie Esdaile	$8.95
Rocky Mountain Romance	Kathleen Suzanne	$8.95
Rooms of the Heart	Donna Hill	$8.95
Rough on Rats and Tough on Cats	Chris Parker	$12.95
Secret Library Vol. 1	Nina Sheridan	$18.95
Secret Library Vol. 2	Cassandra Colt	$8.95
Secret Thunder	Annetta P. Lee	$9.95
Shades of Brown	Denise Becker	$8.95
Shades of Desire	Monica White	$8.95
Shadows in the Moonlight	Jeanne Sumerix	$8.95
Sin	Crystal Rhodes	$8.95
Small Whispers	Annetta P. Lee	$6.99
So Amazing	Sinclair LeBeau	$8.95
Somebody's Someone	Sinclair LeBeau	$8.95
Someone to Love	Alicia Wiggins	$8.95
Song in the Park	Martin Brant	$15.95
Soul Eyes	Wayne L. Wilson	$12.95
Soul to Soul	Donna Hill	$8.95
Southern Comfort	J.M. Jeffries	$8.95
Southern Fried Standards	S.R. Maddox	$6.99
Still the Storm	Sharon Robinson	$8.95

Other Genesis Press, Inc. Titles (continued)

Other Genesis Press, Inc. Titles (continued)

Tiger Woods	Libby Hughes	$5.95
Time is of the Essence	Angie Daniels	$9.95
Timeless Devotion	Bella McFarland	$9.95
Tomorrow's Promise	Leslie Esdaile	$8.95
Truly Inseparable	Wanda Y. Thomas	$8.95
Two Sides to Every Story	Dyanne Davis	$9.95
Unbreak My Heart	Dar Tomlinson	$8.95
Uncommon Prayer	Kenneth Swanson	$9.95
Unconditional Love	Alicia Wiggins	$8.95
Unconditional	A.C. Arthur	$9.95
Undying Love	Renee Alexis	$6.99
Until Death Do Us Part	Susan Paul	$8.95
Vows of Passion	Bella McFarland	$9.95
Wedding Gown	Dyanne Davis	$8.95
What's Under Benjamin's Bed	Sandra Schaffer	$8.95
When A Man Loves A Woman	La Connie Taylor-Jones	$6.99
When Dreams Float	Dorothy Elizabeth Love	$8.95
When I'm With You	LaConnie Taylor-Jones	$6.99
Where I Want To Be	Maryam Diaab	$6.99
Whispers in the Night	Dorothy Elizabeth Love	$8.95
Whispers in the Sand	LaFlorya Gauthier	$10.95
Who's That Lady?	Andrea Jackson	$9.95
Wild Ravens	Altonya Washington	$9.95
Yesterday Is Gone	Beverly Clark	$10.95
Yesterday's Dreams,	Reon Laudat	$8.95
Tomorrow's Promises		
Your Precious Love	Sinclair LeBeau	$8.95

Order Form

Mail to: Genesis Press, Inc.
P.O. Box 101
Columbus, MS 39703

Name _____
Address _____
City/State _____ Zip _____
Telephone _____

Ship to (if different from above)
Name _____
Address _____
City/State _____ Zip _____
Telephone _____

Credit Card Information
Credit Card # _____   ☐ Visa   ☐ Mastercard
Expiration Date (mm/yy) _____   ☐ AmEx   ☐ Discover

Qty.	Author	Title	Price	Total

Use this order form, or call
1-888-INDIGO-1

Total for books _____
Shipping and handling:
$5 first two books,
$1 each additional book _____
Total S & H _____
Total amount enclosed _____

Mississippi residents add 7% sales tax

Visit www.genesis-press.com for latest releases and excerpts.

GENESIS MOVIE NETWORK

The Indigo Collection

SEPTEMBER 2009

Starring: Robert Townsend, Marla Gibbs, Eddie Griffin
When: September 5 - September 20
Time Period: Noon to 2AM

While being chased by neighborhood thugs, weak-kneed high school teacher Jefferson Reed (Robert Townsend) is struck by a meteor and suddenly develops superhuman strength and abilities. He can fly, talk to dogs and absorb knowledge from any book in 30 seconds! His mom creates a costume, and he begins practicing his newfound skills in secret. But his nightly community improvements soon draw the wrath of the bad guys who terrorize his block.

TERRIFICALLY ENTERTAINING

Allied Media Partners
1629 K St. NW, Suite 300, Washington, DC 20006
202-349-5785